St Paul's Labyrinth

Anthropologist Jeroen Windmeijer (1969) writes thrillers in which Roman and biblical history and the history of his hometown, Leiden, are brought together. His first book was very well received by both the press and booksellers, in Leiden and beyond. With *St Paul's Labyrinth* he claims his place among the great storytellers. Jeroen's thrillers are plot driven, smart and authentic.

St Paul's Labyrinth

JEROEN WINDMEIJER

KILLER READS

A division of HarperCollins*Publishers*
www.harpercollins.co.uk

KillerReads
an imprint of HarperCollins*Publishers* Ltd
1 London Bridge Street
London SE1 9GF

www.harpercollins.co.uk

This paperback edition 2018

2

First published in Great Britain in ebook format by HarperCollins*Publishers* 2018

First published in Holland in 2017 by HarperCollins Holland, as *Het Paulus Labyrint*

Copyright © Jeroen Windmeijer 2017
Translation copyright © HarperCollins Holland 2017

Jeroen Windmeijer asserts the moral right to
be identified as the author of this work

A catalogue record for this book
is available from the British Library

ISBN: 978-0-00-831847-5

Set in Minion by
Palimpsest Book Production Limited, Falkirk, Stirlingshire

Printed and bound by CPI Group (UK) Ltd, Croydon, CR0 4YY

MIX
Paper from
responsible sources
FSC C007454
www.fsc.org

PROLOGUE

The executioner draws his sharpened dagger across the convict's belly, slicing it open with a single cut. A torrent of blood gushes out, like water breaking through the walls of a dyke. The man screams in agony as his guts spill like skinned snakes down to his knees. Then the birdmen come, their eagles balanced on their leather armguards. The birds' sharp beaks take great, greedy bites of the man's exposed liver. The three other men, lashed to wooden stakes and doomed to the same fate, struggle hopelessly to escape.

The audience is ecstatic. This amphitheatre, built during the reign of Caesar Augustus, is big enough to hold sixteen thousand. Today, every single seat of its three tiers is occupied.

After the *venatio*, the staged hunt of exotic beasts, comes the spectacle of public executions. During today's underwhelming opening act, in which a few criminals were merely beheaded, many took the opportunity to relieve themselves in the catacomb latrines.

The executions are inspired by stories from ancient Greece and the public appreciates the creativity with which they are carried out. After the eagles have eaten their fill of entrails and

1

the four men have died – as in the tale of Prometheus – four wooden ramps are wheeled into the arena. In the middle of each ramp is an enormous boulder. Convicts are brought out to recreate the Sisyphean task of rolling the rocks to the top of the ramps, a feat which they naturally all fail to accomplish. The sound of their breaking bones travels all the way up to the third tier.

Another group of men is sent into the sweltering arena. They have gone without food and drink for days and must now attempt to reach the bread and jugs of water that dangle from the stands on long poles. To the crowd's delight, just before they grasp them, the poles are raised high above their heads, making the bread and water as unreachable as they were for Tantalus. When the public's attention begins to wane, starved dogs are released to rip the men apart.

Now, eight men covered in oil and pitch are brought into the ring and tied to stakes. Roman boys, none of them a day over twelve, shoot flaming arrows at the prisoners until they eventually begin to burn. The men scream as they meet their fiery end and a murmur of approval rumbles around the amphitheatre. This may not have been inspired by a Greek story, but it is a novelty that has never been seen before.

A late arrival makes his way to the stands and looks for a seat on the end of one of the benches. He is small, and his legs are crooked, but he looks sturdy, with eyebrows that meet above a long nose. He is a charismatic man and he radiates the serenity of an angel. A brief look at the young man who is already sitting on the end of the bench is all that is needed to create space. He takes his seat and sets his small earthenware jug on the ground next to his feet.

While the dead criminals are dragged from the arena and the patches of blood are covered with fresh sand, musicians and fools do their best to entertain the public with acrobatic antics. The crowd cheers as dozens of boys and girls enter the stands carrying huge baskets of bread between them. The distribution of bread at the games began two years ago in Rome and was so popular among the commoners that the practice rapidly spread to every corner of the Empire. The boys and girls walk up the steps, throwing hunks of bread into the crowds. A forest of arms reaches up to meet them where they land. Once caught, the bread is swiftly tucked beneath cloaks, leaving hands free to snatch another piece.

'*Panem et tauros*,' the youngster says mockingly to the old man next to him. Bread and bulls. He takes the chunk of bread that has fortuitously landed in his lap and, without looking, sullenly hurls it in a huge arc behind him.

But this is what most people have come for today; for the bread, but mostly to see the bullfight.

The *editor muneris*, the sponsor of today's games, orders the release of the bull by raising his arm in an impressive *saluto romano*. A deafening cheer fills the arena. The *editor* looks around the crowd, then, gratified, returns to lie on his couch. He picks up a small bunch of grapes from the lavishly spread table next to him and watches as the gigantic, wildly bucking bull enters the amphitheatre. The animal has been force-fed salt for days and denied even a drop of water. It has spent the last twenty-four hours in a stall too small for its enormous mass while its belly was battered with sandbags to cause internal bleeding. The game has been rigged before it has even begun. He cannot win today.

Now the *ministri*, the attendants, enter the arena. They taunt the bull with huge capes, assessing its strength, intelligence and fighting spirit. They wave the brightly coloured cloths with great bravado, skilfully dodging the bull's charges. Gasps of awe pour down from the stands and into the arena, like the waters of a river tumbling down a mountainside.

The bull is judged worthy of the fight. Four *venatores*, hunters, come through the four gates of the battleground on horseback, each one clutching a *verutum*, a hunting spear, in his right hand.

They enter like gods, wearing only loincloths. Spiky leaves of laurel are woven into their hair. Their horses, protected by heavy armour, are visibly frightened, but their vocal chords have been severed and they can make no sound.

They close in on the bull from four directions and it does not know which horse to attack, but the circle closes tighter and tighter around the bull until it is forced to launch itself at the nearest rider. As soon as it approaches one of the horses, the rider stands up in the stirrups to plunge his *verutum* into the bull's neck, bearing down upon it with the weight of his entire body. The *venatores* each charge at the bull in turn, goring the bull's neck at least once before retreating to loud applause. The bull is dazed and its head lolls as blood drips onto the ground from its wounds.

Then the *mactator* arrives, the star of the show, the bull killer, the man who will finish the job. He is a mountain of a man, dressed in a simple, short tunic, arms bare and lower legs covered by protectors. In each hand, he carries a pole as long as his arm, decorated with ribbons and ending in a barb. He walks towards the bull in a straight line. The more determinedly he follows this invisible path, the more the crowd admires his courage. Most of them are sitting again now, and instead of the cheers and yells that made all conversation impossible moments ago, there is silence, as though they are collectively holding their breath. The bull responds to the new threat heading towards him by scraping the sand with its hoof. With a guttural roar, the *mactator* commands the attention of the whole arena. When he is within a few steps of the bull, it charges. The *taurarius*, the bullfighter, spins neatly to avoid the attack, and before he finishes his pirouette, he drives a barbed lance between the bull's shoulder blades. The arena explodes with joy, so graceful was the parry, so perfectly aimed the lance. Now the *mactator* runs away from the bull. Then, he circles back towards it, and with an impressive leap, lands his second spear next to the first.

Those who assume that the bull has given up are about to find that they are mistaken. The animal seems to know that this is its last chance to wound his attacker. It summons all its strength to lift up its head, while blood gushes from its wounds and long, bloody strings of mucus hang from its mouth.

The *taurarius* approaches the *editor*'s box, bends one knee on the sand and bows his head. The *editor* gives a small nod of approval, upon which the *venator* at the eastern gate comes forward to place a special headcovering on the *mactator*'s head – a soft, red conical cap with a point that falls forwards – and hand him the *linteum*, the half circle of red flannel, draped over a wooden rod.

The *taurarius* walks back to the bull. He waves the cloth tauntingly, and from somewhere, the beast finds the energy to make a few desperate lunges. The enthusiasm of the audience's reaction spurs the bullfighter on to take even greater risks. This is the most dangerous stage of the fight. One moment of distraction could be fatal. The bull, stunned by pain and fear, could still mortally wound the *mactator* in a last attempt to avoid death by goring his unprotected belly with his horns.

But the liberating blast of a trumpet is already sounding and the *venator* comes scurrying over from his post at the western gate. In one hand he carries a light, curved sword – with a hilt in the form of a snake, the *falcata* – and in the other, a flaming torch. He hands over the *falcata* and takes up position behind the bull's left flank. This is the *hora veritatis*, the hour of truth, when the *mactator* will end the beast's suffering by plunging the sword between its shoulder blades and piercing its heart.

He stands before the exhausted animal. It is too tired now to even lift its head. He places his hand on its forehead and forces it to the ground, a flourish which brings a sigh of admiration from the crowd.

A minister rushes over from the eastern side of the arena. He carries a silver chalice in one hand and, in the other, a blazing torch which he points at the ground.

The bull is lying in the sand now, and the *mactator* straddles it with his knee on its right haunch and his other leg on the ground. He pulls its head back by the horn with his left hand and raises his right arm in the air. The *falcata*'s blade flashes in the sun. And then, with a masterful stroke, he brings the sword down and expertly slits the beast's throat. Blood spurts out, soaking the sand with a powerful geyser of red until the bull finally succumbs. The curved sword is buried so deeply that the snake on the hilt appears to lick the bull's wound.

'*Sanguis eius super nos et super filios nostros.*' The old man in the stands murmurs a hopeful prayer. His blood be on us, and on our children.

The *mactator* rubs his bloodied hands across his face, as though washing himself with the blood. He is a terrifying sight now; the blood has mixed with sand and sweat, but he seems unmoved, and stares out at an imaginary point in the distance.

'*Et nos servasti eternali sanguine fuso,*' the old man whispers. And you have also saved us by shedding the eternal blood. The man pulls a hunk of bread from his sleeve and tears a piece from it as he stares intently at the spectacle in the arena.

The *taurarius* takes up the blade once more, this time to cut a chunk of flesh from the bull. He shows this to the audience then puts it in his mouth and swallows it whole.

'*Accipite et comedite, hoc est corpus meum quod pro vobis datur.*' Take this and eat; this is my body which is given for you.

The old man closes his eyes, puts the piece of bread into his mouth, and chews thoughtfully, as though he is tasting bread for the first time in his life.

The *mactator* takes the chalice from the *venator* behind him and fills it with blood from the bull's neck. This he also shows to the audience before emptying it one, long gulp.

'*Bibite, hic est sanguis meus qui pro multis effunditur.*' Drink, this is my blood poured out for many. The old man retrieves a small, earthenware jug of wine from under his seat. He twists the cork from it and takes a drink, swirls the wine around in his mouth then swallows.

The euphoric crowd chants the name of the *taurarius* and he stands up to begin his victory lap. Meanwhile, a *venator* removes the bull's testicles with a pair of scissors shaped like a scorpion. These are believed to be a powerful aphrodisiac and will be offered to the *editor* later.

'*Iste, qui nec de corpore meo ederit nec de mea sanguine biberit ut mecum misceatur et ego cum eo miscear, salutem non habebit,*' the old man ends his ritual. He who does not eat of my flesh and drink of my blood, so that he remains in me and I in him, shall not know salvation.

A dog that has escaped from the catacombs seizes its chance to get close to the bull and lick at the blood still streaming from its neck. A minister delivers a well-aimed kick to its belly and it scuttles away, its teeth and muzzle red.

The people stand on the benches, waving white cloths to show their appreciation of the *taurarius*' bravery and the elegance with which he has fought. A group of men jump into the arena to lift the bullfighter onto their shoulders. They parade him past his audience as wreaths and flowers rain down on him. Two ropes are fastened to the hind legs of the lifeless animal. A portion of the applause is surely meant for the bull as it exits the arena, leaving a bloody trail in the sand. Its meat will be served at the tables of the city's wealthy families tonight. A small fortune will be paid for its tail, a delicacy when stewed with onions and wine.

The old man gets up and takes a last look at the arena behind him where the trail of blood in the sand is the only evidence that an unfair fight has taken place here today.

'*Consummatum est,*' he says, satisfied. It is finished.

1

CORAX

RAVEN

Leiden, 20 March 2015, 1:00pm

Technically, Peter de Haan's lecture was already over. He had given a brisk overview of Leiden's most important churches in his 'Introduction to the History of Leiden' for Master's students. It was part of an elective module, but it packed the small lecture theatre every year. He had stopped being surprised by it years ago, but it always did him good to see the theatre so full.

Some of the students had started to pack away their things, but they hadn't yet dared to leave their seats. One young man watched him like a dog waiting for a command from its master.

An aerial photograph of the Hooglandse Kerk was projected onto the screen behind him. At the start of the fourteenth century, it had been no more than a small wooden chapel. By the end of the sixteenth century it had grown into a cathedral so enormous that it had become too big for its surroundings, like an oversized

9

sofa in a tiny living room. The photograph also showed the Burcht van Leiden, the city's iconic eleventh-century motte-and-bailey castle. This six-foot-tall crenelated circular stone wall was built on top of a man-made mound about twelve metres high.

Peter raised his hand, and the quiet chatter in the room immediately stopped. 'I know you all want to go to lunch,' he said, with a hint of hesitation in his voice, 'but which of you are going to watch the first underground waste container being installed at the public library this afternoon?'

Most of the students looked at him politely, but none of them responded.

'You know that there's a major project starting in town at two o'clock today, installing these containers?'

'I didn't know about it, sir,' said one young man politely, keeping his hand in the air as he spoke. 'But why would we be interested in that?'

'Well now, I'm *so* glad you asked,' Peter said.

This response drew some chuckles from his audience. The students stopped what they were doing and accepted that they weren't going to be allowed to leave just yet.

Peter grabbed his laser pointer and drew a circle around the church on the screen.

'This might come as a surprise to you, but not much is known about Leiden's origins or how it developed. There aren't many opportunities to carry out archaeological research in the centre of town. The simple reason for that is that anywhere you might want to dig has been built on, as those of you who go into urban archaeology later will no doubt discover. We might, very occasionally, be given a brief opportunity to excavate when a building is demolished, but it's extremely rare. This project means that we can go down as deep as three metres, at literally hundreds of sites across the city. Who knows what might be hidden beneath our feet?'

'Or which skeletons will come out of the closet,' said the young man.

'Exactly!' Peter replied enthusiastically. 'Now it looks like we'd rehearsed that earlier, but it was actually going to be my next point. Look . . .'

He traced a route along the Nieuwstraat with a beam of red light. 'This street used to be a canal, but like many of the other canals in Leiden, it was filled in. Some canals were covered over, overvaulted, meaning that instead of being filled with sand and debris, they were just roofed over and then the roads were built on top of them. You can still walk through some of them, like tunnels, but this one was infilled. The cemetery was here, on the other side of the church. But people were sometimes secretly buried in this area, near what used to be the canal, next to the church. Those were people who couldn't afford to be buried in the churchyard but who wanted to be laid to rest as close to the church as they could get.'

His mobile phone started to vibrate in the inside pocket of his jacket.

He looked around the lecture theatre. If he kept on talking, he'd become that uncle who endlessly droned on about the past at parties.

'You can go,' he said instead. 'I'll see you all this afternoon!'

The room sprang to life again, as though he'd pressed play on a paused video. As they made their way to the door, the students filed past his desk to hand in their work. The course required a fortnightly submission of a short essay about one of the subjects they had covered.

The room was empty. Peter turned off the projector and gathered up his things. When he picked up the sheaf of papers, a blank envelope fell out from between them. He picked it up and looked at it. It was probably a note from a student apologising for the fact that various circumstances had prevented them from doing their assignment this week.

He was about to open it when Judith appeared in the doorway. She smiled. 'You've not forgotten, have you?'

'How could I possibly forget an appointment with you?' Peter said, stuffing the envelope in his bag with the rest of the papers.

He had met Judith Cherev, a woman in her early forties, twenty years ago when he had supervised her final dissertation. They had become close friends in the years that followed. She had researched the history of Judaism in Leiden for her PhD. Now she was a lecturer in the history department, as well as freelancing as a researcher for the Jewish Historical Museum in Amsterdam.

Her dark curls, accented here and there with a charming streak of grey, were effortlessly tied back with a thick elastic band. She was still a beautiful woman, slim, and dressed, as always, in a blouse and long skirt. The Star of David necklace that hung around her neck glinted in the fluorescent lights.

'Did you just send me a text?'

Judith shook her head.

Peter took his phone from inside his jacket and opened the message.

Hora est.

He smiled.

'What is it?'

'I think one of my students wanted to let me know that it was time to stop talking.'

He walked over to the door with the bag under his arm and turned off the lights. He showed the message to Judith on the way.

The *hora est* – the hour has come – was the phrase with which the university beadle entered the room exactly three-quarters of an hour into a doctoral candidate's defence of their thesis before the Doctoral Examination Board. At this point, the candidate was no longer permitted to talk, even if the beadle had entered mid-sentence. To most candidates, the words came as a huge relief.

'That's quite witty,' Judith said, handing back the phone. 'Odd that it was sent anonymously though.'

'Probably scared that their wit will get them marked down.' He deleted the message. Just as he was about to lock up the lecture hall, he noticed that someone had left a telephone on one of the tables, an iPhone that looked brand new. He walked back into the hall, picked it up and put it in his jacket pocket. Its owner would appear at his office door soon enough. The students were practically grafted to their phones.

They walked outside and headed for the university restaurant in the Lipsius Building. It had been called the Lipsius for years, but Peter still called it the LAK, the name of the theatre and arts centre that used to be there.

'Mark is probably there already,' Judith said, tenderly. 'You know him. One o'clock means one o'clock.'

Mark was a professor in the theology department, a brilliant man with a history of mental illness. He and Judith were in a 'LAT' relationship, living together in every way except that they had each kept their own little houses in the Sionshofje. Because of the *hofje*'s rules, actually moving in together would mean moving out of the Sionshofje, and neither of them wanted to leave the picturesque little courtyard.

Inside the restaurant, students and tutors sat at long tables. A monotone din of chatter and clatter filled the room. The warmth and smells from the kitchen made the air in the room stuffy and humid.

As Judith had predicted, Mark was already sitting at a table and saving two seats for them. He waved.

They visited the buffet counter on their way over to him. Peter chose an extra-large salad and a glass of fresh orange juice and Judith picked up a bowl of soup with a slice of bread and cheese.

'Well done,' Judith complimented Peter, giving his stomach a teasing little pat.

Mark was already half way through his meal by the time they

sat down. Judith kissed him lightly on the cheek, something that still gave Peter a pang of envy, even after many years.

'What are your plans for the afternoon?' Peter asked.

'I have an appointment with someone at two, sounds like an older gentleman,' Judith said. 'He's inherited some bits and pieces from a Jewish aunt's estate. He found me via the museum. I'm going to drop by and see if any of them are suitable for our collection.'

'Sounds good,' said Peter.

'Oh, usually these things end up being a disappointment, to be honest. But every now and then something special turns up. A bit like *The Antiques Roadshow*. Diaries, letters from a concentration camp, or just interesting everyday bits and pieces like kitchen utensils, tools and so on. You never know. I usually enjoy it anyway. They often just want someone to talk to . . .'

'Never a dull moment with you, is there?'

'Never a dull moment, no,' she agreed. 'And I want to plan a lecture for Monday, nothing out of the ordinary, really. I've got the next few days to myself.' She put her hand on Mark's arm.

'Yep,' said Mark. 'I'm off to Germany again. A week with no phone, no internet, totally cut off from the rest of the world. Heaven.'

Once or twice a year, Mark retreated to the depths of the German forests, beyond the reach of cell phone towers, to 'reflect', as he called it. Judith would tease him by suggesting that he had a secret mistress, but she knew that he needed time to recharge now and then. He always came back revitalised, full of energy. The only compromise he made was that he agreed to venture back into civilisation once a week to call Judith and let her know how he was.

'And this afternoon,' Mark continued, 'I want to spend a couple of hours working on an article I'm writing with Fay Spežamor. You know her, right? The Czech classicist, curator of Roman and Etruscan Art at the Museum of Antiquities.'

14

'I've met her a few times, yes,' Peter said. 'Funnily enough, hers is the only mobile phone number I know off the top of my head. If you remember the first two numbers . . .'

'Then you just need to keep adding two,' Mark finished his sentence.

None of them spoke for a while.

'Were you planning to do anything this afternoon then?' Mark asked.

'I'm going to go into town to see them install the container in the Nieuwstraat. I've been following the project a bit. The Cultural Heritage Department invited me. Daniël Veerman, Janna Frederiks . . . They've promised to let me know if they come across anything interesting.'

'Oh yes! I wanted to show you something!' Mark said suddenly, as though he hadn't heard what Peter said at all. He pushed his tray aside. Underneath it was a large envelope, addressed in neat, unmistakably old-fashioned handwriting.

'*To the most noble and learned professor doctor M. Labuschagne,*' he read with amusement. 'I need to send the author of this letter a quick reply this afternoon.' He took a large bundle of densely typed pages out of the envelope. They had apparently been written on an old-fashioned typewriter. 'This is one of those things . . .' he said, leafing through them as though he was looking for something specific. 'Ever since I graduated, people have been sending me things. Amateurs writing to tell me that they think they've found the code that makes the Book of Revelation all make sense, or that they have definitive proof that Jesus didn't die on the cross . . .'

'Or that the Apostle Peter is buried in Leiden,' Judith joked.

They laughed.

'But this . . . Look, usually it's nonsense and probably not worth holding onto, but I keep everything. I might do something with them one day. Sometimes an idea seems crazy, or the whole world thinks an author is mad, but sometimes these people are

15

just way ahead of their time. I had another one today, a Mr . . .'
He looked at the title page. ' . . . Mr Goekoop from Zierikzee,
Zeeland. It's about the Burcht. He says that it originally had an
astrological function. Look, he's even drawn some diagrams.'

Mark held up a sheet of paper with a surprisingly good pen-
and-ink illustration of Leiden's castle. The artist had left space
between the battlements so that the whole thing strongly resembled a megalithic circle, like Stonehenge.

'He has this whole theory about how the first rays of the sun
shine through the Burcht's main gate on the equinox on March
twenty-first, taking the earth's precession into account. The
precession is the way the axis moves. The earth is like a spinning
top, its axis is never exactly vertical. It's a bit complicated . . . He
uses all these calculations to try to show that the original castle
must have been built more than two thousand years ago.
According to him, the word megalith is derived from the Greek
mega-leithos, or, Great Leiden.'

'That should be easy to check. Tomorrow is March twenty-
first.'

'Yes. But actually, it's not that easy. The earth's axis has shifted
since then. Anyway, that part about the megalith is bunk, and
the rest too, probably. Look at this; he thinks he has further proof
of his theory in the three trees in the middle of the castle. Because
they're arranged in exactly the same way as the three stars on
Orion's belt. You know, like the Pyramids in Egypt.'

'And that would make the Rhine the River Nile, I suppose?'

'He says that the Rhine is the Lethe, or the Leythe, one of the
five rivers of the underworld in Greek mythology, just like the
Styx. According to him, the name Leythe is connected to Leiden
of course.'

'And this is what you spend your time on,' said Peter.

'It amuses me. You never know what someone is going to come
up with. Sometimes the amateurs make surprising discoveries.
But what fascinates me about this story is his theory that the

Burcht was a centre for sun worship. He does have a point about the name Lugdunum . . .'

'The Roman name for Katwijk.'

'That's right. But he reckons that it was originally the name given to the hill that the Burcht stands on. Lug is the name of the Celtic sun god, and *dunum* means "hill" or "mountain". "Lug Hill", or if you want to translate it more loosely, "the hill where Lug is worshipped".'

'With that sort of reasoning,' Peter countered, 'you could prove that Mr Goekoop's hometown of Zierikzee can be traced back to the Greek goddess Circe. And that would put the city of Troy somewhere in Zeeland.'

Mark put the papers back in the envelope. 'All the same, I always send these people a polite reply. That's usually enough to satisfy them.'

Judith picked up her tray. She had already eaten her soup and bread.

'Are you leaving already?' Peter asked, a little disappointed.

'I've got that appointment at two o'clock. I'm going back to my office to get my things. We could get together for a nightcap later this evening if you like?'

Peter nodded.

Judith rested her hand briefly on Mark's shoulder. He tilted his head a little to meet it, like a cat reaching to be petted. She winked at Peter and went to tidy her tray away.

'So, Lug then,' said Peter, bringing the conversation back to where they had left it.

'Yes, Lug, but there have been lots of other sun gods over the centuries of course. Fascinating subject, actually. That's what the paper I'm working on is about. A bit of pop history about how they're always born on the third day after the winter solstice, on the evening of the twenty-fourth of December, a symbolic celebration of the arrival of light in a dark world. Born to a virgin, usually in a cave, a star appears, they're adored by shepherds, kings come bearing gifts, a wise man predicts that this is the saviour the world has been waiting for, and so on . . .'

'Yes, I know those stories. By the way, did you manage to see some of the eclipse this morning?'

'No, barely gave it a thought to be honest.'

'It was cloudy anyway. I don't suppose there would have been much to see.'

'Probably, but . . . where was I? Oh yes, the sun gods . . . They always die round about the time of the spring solstice and they're resurrected three days later. Attis, Osiris, Dionysus, take your pick. The god dies or his son dies, there's a day of mourning, and then on day three, there's unbelievable joy when the god rises from the dead. Just like the natural world around them that appeared to have died in the winter, but then comes back to life.'

Of course, Peter had also read about the early Fathers of the Church and how they had become confused when they saw the similarities between the Gospels and these other stories that were evidently much older. The only explanation they could give was that the older stories were the work of the devil. Satan would have known about the circumstances under which Jesus would be born and so he established the sun gods' rites centuries earlier in order to confuse people.

'My article will lay out the parallels between all sorts of basic Christian concepts and the religion's sacred mysteries. It's terribly interesting. Take Orpheus and Eurydice, Demeter and Persephone . . . all variations of the same theme. The cult of Dionysus slaughtered a bull every year. The followers ate the meat and drank the blood so that they could become one with Dionysus, a communion, and share the power of his resurrection.'

'It's . . . Listen,' Peter interrupted him. Mark was usually fairly introverted, but once he felt at ease with someone, it could be very difficult to get him off his soapbox. 'I still need to take my bag back to my office, and the mayor's coming for the opening at two o'clock . . .'

Mark smiled and held his hands up apologetically. 'No problem.'

Peter finished his last few forkfuls of salad and emptied his glass. He opened his mouth wide and bared his teeth like a laughing chimpanzee.

'Not got anything stuck between my teeth, have I?' he asked. Mark reassured him that he hadn't.

They said goodbye and Peter walked to his office in the archaeology faculty next to the LAK.

Peter's office hadn't changed in more than twenty years. It was almost like a living room to him. The same three pictures had always hung on the walls: *The Last Supper* by Leonardo da Vinci, a poster of a famous painting of Burgemeester Van der Werff by Gustave Wappers, and a large photograph of Pope John Paul II in his popemobile.

There were weeks when he spent more time in his office than in his flat on the Boerhavenlaan. He even kept a change of clothes in the cupboard for the odd occasion when he spent the night on the three-seater sofa.

When he pulled the stack of papers from his bag, the envelope fell out onto the floor. Intrigued, he picked it up and opened it. The note inside didn't contain excuses for an unfinished assignment. Instead, written neatly in the middle of the sheet of the paper, was:

Rom. 13:11

But it was the text below it that suddenly made his mouth feel dry. He dropped the note, repulsed, as though he was throwing a used tissue in the bin.

Hora est.

2

Peter looked at his watch. Quarter to two. He would need to hurry if he was going to make it to the Nieuwstraat on time. The anonymous note had disturbed him more than he wanted to admit. That *'hora est'*, the same message that he had received by phone, made him feel uneasy. He went to his bookcase to get a bible, but then realised that he didn't have time. He knew that Romans 13:11 referred to Paul's letters to the Romans in the New Testament, but his knowledge of the scriptures wasn't good enough to be able to recall the passage from memory.

He reluctantly left the bible on his desk, then closed the door and headed for town.

It was against his principles to look at his phone when he was walking – he resented having to give way to people who shuffled around like zombies, their eyes glued to their screens – but he opened the Biblehub.com website to look up what the scripture was about.

The connection was slow. When images of hell had come up in one of his lectures, on a whim, he'd asked his students about their own ideas of hell. Without missing a beat, one young man

20

answered: 'Hell is a place where the internet is really, really slow.'

Peter hoped he wouldn't bump into anyone he knew. The page loaded sluggishly as he walked through the Doelensteeg and along the Rapenburg to the Gerecht square. He clicked on 'Romans' and, at last, on '13'. He'd reached the Pieterskerk church by the time the text finally appeared on his screen.

It was almost two o'clock now. It wouldn't do to be late. He impatiently closed the cover on his phone. He knew that the scripture would still be there when he opened it again.

He continued his route at a brisk pace, walking through the narrow alleys that led to the Breestraat, past the town hall and then he went left. As he crossed the river via the colonnades of the Pilarenbrug, the library came into view.

The council's decision to move the city's waste containers underground had been brought about by a plague of seagulls. As the crow flew, the college town of Leiden was a mere ten kilometres from the coast. Nests full of gulls' eggs were easy prey for the foxes that had been reintroduced to the dunes, and hordes of the birds had fled to the city. They pecked open the bags of rubbish left out for collection, scavenged in bins and grew increasingly aggressive. Various measures had been taken to deter them: replacing the seagulls' eggs with plastic dummies, birds of prey, pigeon spikes on roofs, all without success. The hope was that the city would be less attractive to the birds if the city's rubbish was moved underground.

Peter stopped to catch his breath on the corner of the street. He studied himself in a shop window. A little on the portly side, it was true, a day or two's worth of stubble, and a full head of hair that was just a bit too long. The image in the window was, in fact, a bit flattering; the reflection didn't show the deep lines he knew he had on his forehead or the dark circles under his eyes.

'For now we see through a glass, darkly . . .' he said to himself quietly.

21

He tucked his shirt neatly into his trousers, and felt the student's forgotten mobile phone in his jacket pocket. He made a mental note to call one of the numbers on its contacts list when he got a chance. Whoever it was would surely be able to tell him who the phone belonged to.

A large crowd had gathered around the excavation site. The Leiden press of course, local residents, all sorts of dignitaries, and workmen, recognisable from their yellow helmets and orange vests. Part of the area around the excavated pit was fenced off with barriers and red and white tape.

'Hullo! Peter!' he heard Arnold van Tiegem shouting. Peter could tell from the exaggerated joviality of Arnold's waving that he had already made a head start on the drinks reception that would be held later.

Twenty years ago, Peter's old tutor, Pieter Hoogers, had retired and vanished off into the sunset directly after his farewell address. Everyone had expected that Peter would take his place as full professor, but after a couple of months of typical academic machinations, the university had produced a surprise candidate seemingly out of nowhere: Arnold van Tiegem, a senior official at the Ministry of Housing, Planning and the Environment who had found himself sidelined. He had studied Soil Science at the University of Wageningen in the distant past and that had been deemed sufficient qualification to lead the faculty. The fact that he would also bring with him a one-off grant of five million guilders ultimately convinced the board of his suitability for the post.

After he was appointed, it turned out that Arnold was in the habit of going missing now and then, often for days at a time. At first, his disappearances were reported to the police, but because he always reappeared a few days later, people accepted the fact that he sometimes simply checked out for a while. He liked to compare these episodes with John Lennon's 'lost weekends' and saw them as part of a grand and exciting life.

Peter made his way to the tall bar tables where his suspicions were confirmed by a number of empty beer bottles and two half-empty bottles of wine.

Daniël Veerman was standing at one of the tables. He surreptitiously rolled his eyes as he moved his gaze from Arnold to Peter. Daniël was in his early thirties and the quintessential archaeologist: he had long, dark hair that undulated down to his neck, tiny round spectacles perched on his nose with intelligent eyes behind them, a trendy beard that looked casual but was well-groomed. He had once told Peter that he had done nothing but dig for treasure when he was a child. While other children played nicely in the sandpit, heaping the sand into mountains or building sandcastles with buckets and spades, he was usually found outside it, digging holes in the dirt.

Peter shook Daniël's hand and then greeted Janna Frederiks, who was leading the project for the Cultural Heritage Department together with Daniël. Peter was less familiar with Janna, a serious, remarkably tall woman – almost two metres in height – whose head was permanently bowed at a slight angle, as though she was scouring the ground in the hope of finding something interesting.

Arnold opened another bottle of beer, and poured it down his throat in a couple of gulps. Then he smoothed his long, grey hair back with a small comb, a nervous tic that he performed countless times each day. He probably thought the little flick of a mullet that this made at the back of his neck was terribly bohemian. Combined with his enormous paunch and spindly legs, he reminded Peter of a circus ringmaster. Put a top hat on his bloated head and he'd look just the part.

'He just *lives* for these moments, doesn't he?' Peter whispered to Daniël.

'He'll post the photo of himself with the mayor on Facebook as soon as it's over,' Daniël added, laughing. He gave Peter a sideways look. 'It was good of you to come, Peter. I really appreciate it.'

23

'You don't need to thank me. I'm happy to be here. I wanted to come and wish you luck. I'm here for you and Janna, not for myself, like Van Tiegem.'

'He's a great networker though, you have to give him that. And your department needs one of those, right?'

Peter was about to say something cutting in reply, but a round of applause interrupted him. Mayor Freylink had arrived in full regalia with the chain of office around his neck.

'What's the plan, exactly?' Peter asked.

Daniël carried on looking straight ahead and clapping for the mayor who was walking past close to where they were standing. 'I've dumped a bit of sand in the hole,' he answered. 'He's going to take it out with the digger. And that will be the project's symbolic launch.'

'Not very elegant, is it?'

'Well we could have sent him down there with a bucket, but I thought this would be more refined. Freylink was enthusiastic about it anyway. And he used to be a historian, as you know, so he's glad to be closely involved. He's even been to a building site to practise.'

The applause died out.

A small excavator came towards them. Little black clouds of smoke escaped from the long, thin exhaust pipe on its roof.

'I'd better get over there,' said Daniël. Janna followed him. He turned around to look at Peter. 'We're going for dinner at El Gaucho tonight with the team. You're very welcome to join us if you'd like to come along.'

Peter gave him a thumbs-up. *Maybe I could ask Judith to go with me*, he thought.

He took the opportunity to take a quick look at his phone. He skimmed through chapter 13 of Paul's letter to the Romans and recognised the contents straight away. It was about allegiance to the authorities who had been placed above you. A text which had often been misused throughout the course of history, and for which Paul had been heavily criticised. Pay your taxes, do as you are told, don't be rebellious, 'for there is no authority that does not come from God'. Whoever opposes authority opposes one of God's agencies, and thereby opposes God.

Little wonder, then, that the people of Leiden suddenly found themselves drawn to Calvin when the Spaniards were at the city's gates. He said that you *could* rebel against your rulers. People were often inclined to choose the convictions that best suited their own interests . . .

Suddenly, the student's phone began to vibrate. Peter was surprised that it hadn't happened before now; youngsters spent more time in conversation with people they couldn't see than with the people who were right next them. But first, he wanted to read the specific verse that had been written on the note. 'Let no debt remain outstanding,' he read, 'except the continuing debt to love one another, for whoever loves others has fulfilled the law . . .' Here it was, verse 11:

And do this, understanding the present time: the hour has already come for you to wake up from your slumber, because our salvation is nearer now than when we first believed.

The hour has already come . . .

'*Hora est*,' Peter repeated, absent-mindedly making quiet, smacking sounds, as though trying to taste the words on his tongue.

He read the rest of the scripture aloud to himself in a staccato mumble, as though this would help him to decipher a message hidden in the words.

The night is nearly over; the day is almost here. So let us put aside the deeds of darkness and put on the armour of light.

Someone slapped him, a bit overenthusiastically, on the shoulder. Van Tiegem.

'Come on, put that phone down,' he said, and made a playful attempt to snatch the phone from Peter's hand.

Peter irritably fended him off. 'Okay, okay,' he said, putting the phone away.

'Don't you want a beer?'

'Thanks Arnold, but I'm officially still working.'

'Oh you're good,' Arnold said, without much conviction, 'very good. I should follow your example.'

The mayor was standing next to the digger now. Someone had put a yellow safety helmet on his head, apparently more for show than anything else. He patiently posed in it while photographs were taken.

'Shouldn't you go and stand with him?' Peter suggested.

'That's actually a very good idea,' Arnold said, sounding genuinely pleased. On his way over to the mayor, he waggishly stole a helmet from a construction worker and set it at a jaunty angle on his own head. He stood next to Freylink and held two thumbs aloft as the cameras clicked.

Peter took the other phone from his pocket. It had received a message, not via WhatsApp, but another app he'd not heard of before, Wickr. He opened the message. There were just three words:

iuxta est salus

Another message arrived as soon as he'd read it.

salvation is at hand

Only then did he see the sender's name. Paul.

This was . . .

Peter started to type in a reply, but then he saw that the

messages had already disappeared. They seemed to be available for only a few seconds, just long enough to be able to read them.

He opened the phone's address book. He had to check twice to make sure that he wasn't mistaken.

It was completely empty.

3

Friday 20 March, 2:15pm

Peter looked up from the phone and scanned his surroundings, first round to the left, and then all the way back round to the right, like a security camera watching a street. But there was nothing to see. No one shiftily ducking out of sight, no man in a fedora looking at him from behind a newspaper with two peepholes cut into it.

What he really wanted right now was to go back to his office. Maybe he'd be able to uncover the joker's identity by looking through the list of students on his course? But he also knew that he needed to be seen here. In his world, success ultimately came down to who you knew, short lines of communication, cronyism, a good network. In these times of austerity, it would do him no harm to know the right people, Daniël was right about that. You could say what you liked about Van Tiegem, but the man was a born networker who had always been very successful in raising funds for the faculty.

Peter was suddenly very thirsty. He took a bottle of beer from the table and prised off the cap. He rinsed his mouth out with the first swig before he swallowed it. The beer was warm.

Freylink was sitting in the cab of the excavator now and had closed the door. The engine purred smoothly as the mayor nervously drove it towards the hole outside the library. A group of men slowly walked alongside him on either side of the digger, like coffin bearers at a funeral. They even took a dignified step backwards when they reached the edge of the pit.

Daniël stuck both of his thumbs in the air at Freylink, who pulled a lever to move the grapple. Everything seemed to be going according to plan. It was calm and controlled, which suggested that Freylink had indeed been rehearsing for this moment.

Janna came back over to where Peter was standing.

'I was ready at half nine this morning already,' she said out of nowhere.

'Ready for what?' Peter asked, but he knew the answer before he'd finished asking the question. 'Ah, the eclipse.'

'Exactly, but there wasn't much to see, really,' Janna said, sounding disappointed. 'There was far too much cloud cover, I'm afraid. It went on until quarter to twelve, but I missed most of it.'

'That's a pity.'

By now, the excavator's arm had almost entirely disappeared into the hole. The next task was to use the large bucket to collect some sand and carefully bring it up to the surface. The task demanded great precision as there wasn't much room for manoeuvre. After a flying start, the mayor seemed to be hesitating. The thrum of the machine's motor grew a little louder and the exhaust belched out more puffs of smoke. The bucket appeared to be stuck. The machine listed forwards slightly. Someone in the crowd let out a little scream. A couple of spectators laughed nervously.

A construction worker knocked on the cab window to ask if everything was all right. Freylink smiled and gave him a thumbs-up, but then mopped his forehead with a handkerchief.

The hydraulic arm started to move again. Suddenly, there was an ear-splitting noise. Breaking rocks mixed with the revving sound of an overworked motor. The little puffs of smoke had now become huge, jet-black clouds; the smell of diesel filled the air, and the machine keeled over. Two men attempted to pull it back into its original position by hanging from it, but without success.

Peter could see that the mayor's usually placid face was contorted in terror. Freylink tried to push the door open, but the machine was already toppling forwards into the pit.

As the machine became jammed, half in and half out of the earth, the spectators shrieked and jumped back, revealing the perilous position the mayor was now in. Total chaos erupted. A few people tugged at the digger's tracks, but soon gave up. The door was jammed against the wall of the pit and there was no way to open it.

Instinctively, Peter raced over to see if he could help. He crouched down next to Daniël who was banging on the window. Freylink looked back at them with a painful grimace as blood from trickled from his eyebrow and nose and spread over his face. Nevertheless, he managed to smile.

'We'll get you out of there as soon as we can!' Daniël shouted. His face was red, perhaps from exertion, or because of his embarrassment at the mayor's predicament.

Peter looked up and saw that a group of people had gathered in a semi-circle around the hole in the ground. Many of them were taking photographs and recording videos with their phones.

'Stop that!' he yelled as he leapt to his feet.

Most of them sheepishly put their phones away again.

Peter was briefly dazed after jumping up so quickly and had to hold onto Daniël to stop himself from stumbling.

Just then, Janna Frederiks came running over. 'We've got another digger down the street,' she said to Daniël. 'They're going to get it now and see if they can pull him out with a cable.'

'But we can't just leave him in that cramped little box while they're gone.'

'Well what do you want to do?' she asked. 'Smash the window in?'

'Yes, that's exactly what we'll do. It's made of plastic, not glass, so there won't be any sharp pieces. If he takes his jacket off and puts it over his head, he can protect himself from any splinters that might come loose. Look at how uncomfortable the man is. That's the mayor in there!'

Janna thought about it for a second or two and then agreed. Winching him out would take at least half an hour, even if it all went without a hitch.

Daniël knelt down on the ground again and tapped on the window. Freylink had managed to move himself around to sit on the control panel. Although it looked like he had calmed down, his bloodied face made him look terrible.

'Take your jacket off!' Daniël shouted, cupping his hands around his mouth to amplify his voice. Then he took off his own jacket to demonstrate what he wanted Freylink to do. 'We're going to break the window!' he yelled, over-articulating each word and miming the actions exaggeratedly, 'so you can crawl out. They're going to winch the machine out shortly, but we don't want to leave you in there that long. Put your jacket over your head.'

Freylink understood. He took off his jacket and draped it over his head and shoulders.

Janna came back with large hammer, a chisel and a pair of work gloves and handed them to Daniël.

After a few well-aimed strikes of the hammer, the hard plastic began to crack. Daniël knocked the window out, leaving only a few splinters. 'Don't worry. We'll get you out in no time. I'm almost done. How are you doing?'

'More in shock than anything,' came Freylink's muted voice. 'I don't think I'm hurt.'

Daniël checked the window frame for shards of plastic. When

Freylink removed his jacket, Peter was taken aback again by his bloody face and the way his hair was pasted to his clammy forehead. As soon as the mayor poked his head outside, the crowd began to applaud with relief.

He climbed onto the steering wheel and stood up a little straighter. Peter and Daniël grabbed him by his armpits and gently pulled him upwards. His trousers snagged on a hook, ripping a long tear in them as they dragged him out.

When the mayor finally emerged from the pit, there was more applause. He smiled weakly and waved. Daniël and Peter took him to the waiting ambulance. The crew started to unload the stretcher, but the mayor motioned it away and got into the ambulance himself to allow the paramedics to see to him.

The second excavator arrived, led by a group of men carrying thick cables. Daniël stuck his head inside the ambulance door. The blood had been wiped from the mayor's face already and he sat holding a handkerchief to his nose while a paramedic wound a bandage around his head. He reminded Daniël of a footballer with a head wound, being patched up before returning to the pitch.

'I can't begin to tell you how sorry I am, sir,' Daniël began.

'It wasn't your fault . . . I don't know what went wrong. I must have pressed the wrong button . . . It felt like there was some resistance and then I broke through something.'

'We're going to investigate, Mr Mayor. And again, please accept my sincere apologies.'

The paramedic finished dressing Freylink's head wound and told him he would like to take him to the hospital for further assessment, to which the mayor agreed. Before he got into the ambulance, he gave another jovial wave to the people who stood watching from a distance. The ambulance doors were closed and it quietly drove away, without lights or sirens.

The cables had been attached to the excavator, and now the other digger reversed, growling and puffing smoke while four men stood around the pit to supervise it all. The trapped machine soon began to move and, after twenty minutes, it was back on the surface.

Daniël stood waiting impatiently with a rope ladder in his hands.

'Do you want to go down?' Peter asked.

'Yes, of course! I want to see what the hell went wrong. We didn't find anything unusual when we were digging. I inspected everything myself just an hour ago.'

They both stared down into the pit. It looked like part of the bottom of it had subsided. When the all-clear was given, Daniël carefully lowered the rope ladder. He made sure that it was securely anchored into the ground with two pegs before he put his foot on the first rung. He switched on the lamp on his helmet and began to climb down.

'And?' Peter called after him.

'It smells different . . . like the air is damper, heavier. And . . .' He had reached the bottom now. 'There's been a partial collapse at the bottom!' he shouted. 'It looks like there's a space underneath it.'

'Is there room for one more?' Peter shouted. He wanted to take a look too, hoping it would take his mind off the strange text messages.

'I knew you were going to ask that! Come on!'

Peter descended cautiously, as Janna watched, looking worried and indignantly shaking her head.

Daniël took off his hardhat and pointed the headlamp at the ground below him. 'This is really bizarre. Look.'

Now Peter could see it too. It was obvious. The walls of the pit were clearly made of bricks and mortar. What on earth was this? A stone floor? Three metres underground?

Peter knelt down and leaned forward to see how far down the hole at the bottom of the pit went. He took Peter's helmet and pointed its headlamp downwards.

Suddenly he heard a groan. A soft, but unmistakable groan.

He jerked his head backwards with a sharp cry. The helmet fell into the hole.

'Have you seen a ghost?' Daniël asked, laughing nervously.

'I . . . I think there's someone . . .' Peter stammered.

The groan came again, harder now. He hadn't imagined it. Daniël had heard it too.

Peter took a deep breath. He stuck his head back into the hole, searching for the source of the groaning. Nothing could have prepared him for what he saw.

Two bare legs poked out from underneath a pile of bricks. At the other end of the pile lay the naked torso of a young man.

The headlamp only barely lit the scene in front of him, but as soon as his eyes grew used to the darkness, he gasped as though he had been punched in the stomach. What appeared before him could have been a medieval painting of the torments of hell.

The man was covered from head to toe in blood.

4

Anja Vermeulen's shift was almost over, less than two hours to go. The kitchen staff were serving meals ahead of the start of visiting hours.

She set out the patients' medication on her trolley. The general ward at Leiden University Medical Centre was known for being fairly quiet. Most of the patients were here to recover from minor surgeries like appendectomies, or to be helped with the transition back to their homes after a longer stay.

Ordinarily, nothing particularly interesting ever happened here. But today had been extraordinary. That afternoon, a young man had been brought in, a mysterious case. He had been discovered when a digger fell into a pit during excavation works in the town centre. The man, who was in his mid-twenties, was covered in blood. He'd been found lying in a cavity below the hole that had been dug for an underground waste container. Except for a loincloth, he had been completely naked. Nobody knew how he had ended up under the ground. Anja had heard the news about the accident on the local radio. It said that Mayor Freylink had been injured, but they hadn't mentioned this nameless casualty.

After he was admitted to the hospital, unconscious but in a stable condition, the young man was washed from head to toe. Not a single wound was found on his body, and miraculously, none of his bones were broken. The blood that covered his body must have come from someone else. A sample had been collected and was being tested in the hope that it would reveal clues, a disease or some other condition. The police had said they would come the next day to take photographs of the young man and question him, if he had regained consciousness.

The anonymous patient was dressed in a clean hospital gown and taken to an empty room.

At about quarter past five, Anja looked in on 'Anonymous', as the name card next to his door said. She opened the door and saw that all was as it should be. The young man, well-built, clearly the sporty type, was breathing calmly. Everything appeared to be under control.

Clothes from the depot had been left on a chair, ready for him to wear when he was discharged from the hospital.

She stood next to his bed for a while, wondering what could have happened to him. As she turned to leave, she saw his eyelids flutter, a sign that he was regaining consciousness. She turned up the dimmed light on his bedside cabinet to make sure. Now the patient was clearly blinking his eyes. Instinctively, she blinked back.

When his eyes were completely open, he only stared at the ceiling at first, disoriented. Anja took hold of his hand. He slowly turned his head to look at her, furrowed his brow, and then closed his eyes again.

'Can you hear me?' she asked softly.

He nodded weakly.

'Do you know where you are?'

He shook his head.

'You're in hospital. The LUMC. You were brought in this afternoon.'

He frowned again.

'Do you know what happened?'

The young man pressed his lips together, as though he wanted to speak but was being silenced by something stronger than himself. He tried to lift his head.

'Don't worry,' Anja said comfortingly. 'Whatever happened to you, it's over now. You're safe. Nothing can hurt you here.'

Her words were apparently what he needed to hear. The frown vanished from his forehead, his mouth relaxed and he let his head fall back onto the pillow.

'I have to leave you for a few minutes, but I'll be back as soon as I can. I won't be long.'

Anja hurried back to the ward reception desk to report the patient's progress to the doctor on call. He put her mind at rest and said that he would look in on him later. Since there didn't appear to be anything medically wrong with him, no immediate action was necessary.

She made a note in the records, along with a short summary of their conversation.

Just as she was about to go back to the young man's room, the ward telephone rang. She answered it, but kept an eye on the corridor.

'Hi, it's Patrick.'

Anja and Patrick talked almost exclusively by phone, almost never in person. He worked in the hospital's lab and often called to pass on test results.

'Shouldn't you be at home?' she asked. 'The lab's closed, isn't it?'

'Normally I would be home by now, and we are actually closed for the day, but I'm calling about the man who came in this afternoon. You know, the one who was found after that accident with the mayor.'

'Yes, he's here. He woke up a few minutes ago, although he's not said anything yet. I've just told the doctor.'

'Good, listen . . . The bloodwork was scheduled for tomorrow but his case was so interesting that I went ahead and made a start already.'

'Right. And?'

'It's not his blood,' he said, sounding slightly hesitant.

'No,' Anja said, 'but they were fairly sure of that already anyway, weren't they? I mean, he didn't have any wounds, right?'

'No, he didn't but . . .'

'What's wrong?'

Patrick fell silent.

'What's wrong?' Anja repeated the question, with an increasing mix of worry and curiosity.

'Listen, it's—'

'Hang on a second,' Anja said.

She was sure she had just caught a glimpse of someone leaving the anonymous man's room.

'I think something's not right here,' she said to her colleague. 'I'm just going to put the phone down for a second.'

'But—'

Anja threw the receiver down on the desk and ran down the hall to Anonymous' room. The light, downy hairs on both her arms stood on end, like marram grass on a bare dune. Before she even got into the room, she could see that the pile of clothes was gone from the chair.

The bed was empty.

Anja ran back to her desk to call security.

The phone's receiver was still on the desk. When she picked it up, she heard her colleague's voice again.

'Oh, there you are. Listen—'

'Sorry, I have to hang up. That man is gone.'

'*What?* But . . . Wait, wait, this is important.'

Her finger hovered over the button to hang up, but Patrick spoke so urgently that she hesitated for a second.

'You know I said the blood wasn't his?'

'Yes. So?'

'It's not human blood.'

'*What?* What do you mean?'

'It's from an animal.'

38

5

There were no more text messages. After the bizarre events of the afternoon, Peter's unease about them faded into the background.

The moment he had realised that someone was buried under the rubble, he and Daniël had crawled through the hole in the bottom of the pit. They had found a young man whose lower body was pinned to the ground. He was unconscious, but his breathing seemed normal. Working in the scant light provided by the helmet, they'd removed the bricks to free him.

A putrid stench had emanated from the man and he was sticky with the congealed blood that covered him. Peter and Daniël had retched more than once.

Getting him out of the hole had been no easy task. Another ambulance had been called for and arrived soon afterwards. After a stretcher had been lowered into the pit, two sturdy-looking paramedics had taken over. After briefly assessing him, they had put him inside a cover that looked like a body bag, then fastened him onto the stretcher and eventually lifted him up to the surface.

Peter and Daniël had taken the opportunity to investigate

further. With everyone else gone, a great silence had fallen over the site. They appeared to be in a tunnel, around two metres high and perhaps a metre and a half wide. The floor was made of stone, the walls and the vaulted ceiling that arched over their heads were constructed from red bricks.

The tunnel ran in the direction of the Burcht one way and looked like it went towards the Hooglandse Kerk in the other.

Peter had heard about the tunnels that were rumoured to run below Leiden's streets, stories that did the rounds in many Dutch cities. Supposedly, some of them had been part of the original designs when the Pieterskerk, the Hooglandse Kerk and other churches were built. Others were thought to have been created to move supplies into the town during the Siege of Leiden, when it was twice besieged by the Spanish. It was said that secret tunnels led from the Burcht and the town hall to places that had once been outside the city walls.

'This is just bizarre,' Daniël had said.

'How was this not discovered at the planning stage, before digging started?'

'We relied on the Land Registry for information about pipes and cables. And of course, we have a good idea of where the former canals are. But maybe if you go down another layer, there are things that have never been mapped. They didn't find anything when they were drilling either.'

'That doesn't seem possible.' Peter still hadn't been able to shake off his disbelief. 'Surely this would have been discovered years ago?'

'Apparently not,' Daniël had replied testily. 'Otherwise we wouldn't be standing here.'

'We need to hire one of those gadgets, a . . .'

'A GeoSeeker? Yes, exactly, that's what I was thinking.'

Peter had worked with a GeoSeeker before, a device that detected cavities below ground. They were very expensive pieces of kit.

'We'll have to put in a request for one first. I don't think we'll be able to get it until Monday.'

Daniël and Peter had walked just a few metres into the tunnel before turning around and going back to where they started.

'It's not safe to go any further,' Daniël had said. 'We'll need to set it up properly with a team, decent lights . . .'

They had climbed back up to the street, where the noise and activity had calmed down by now. Most of the spectators had gone home after the young man had been taken to hospital. The drinks reception had been cancelled, the tables had been collected by the catering company, and the drinks and food had been cleared away. A truck full of building materials had driven off as they emerged from the pit. When they were back on the surface, the police had placed two safety barriers over the hole and cordoned it off with red and white tape.

Daniël and Janna had stayed behind, as had the unavoidable Arnold van Tiegem, who had been to fetch a Belgian beer from the De Twee Spieghels jazz bar.

Peter had promised Daniël that he would wait for him so that they could walk part of the way back together.

Now, just before six, he was sitting in a shop doorway.

He had washed his hands in the toilets of a nearby pub, but no matter how much he'd scrubbed, he hadn't been able to get rid of the blood that had found its way under his fingernails. His shirt and jacket were covered in dust.

He sat in a daze, holding the phone that had been left in the lecture theatre, half-expecting a new message to arrive. But it stayed silent.

He opened Google. He noticed that the internet connection was fast now. He typed in 'Wickr' as a search term and learned that it was a mobile phone app similar to Snapchat. Wickr encrypted text messages and then deleted them when they had been read. The sender could decide how long messages would be stored for before they disappeared. The site security.nl said:

41

Wickr is based on 256-bit symmetric AES encryption, RSA 4096 encryption, and our proprietary algorithm. 'It is the first end-to-end encryption that does not require a PGP key,' according to professor and co-founder Robert Statica. According to Statica, Wickr's servers do not see user accounts. Nothing is stored except the cryptographic version of the Wickr ID and the user's hardware ID.

Peter read the text without understanding much of it, but it told him that the person who was sending him the messages wanted to remain anonymous.

He took a silver case from his other inside pocket and flipped it open. Inside was a single cigarillo, held in place with a small clip. Every Sunday, he refilled the case with exactly five little cigars. In the old days, he'd smoked in his room at the faculty, but the university's smoking ban had put an end to that. Sometimes he wistfully remembered the days when he could just light a cigar and watch the smoke curl upwards as he collected his thoughts.

He lit his last cigarillo of the week, took his earphones from his pocket and put them in his ears. Then, on his own phone, he opened a Spotify playlist that he had filled with the works of Bach. He'd become something of an expert on Bach's cantatas over the years. They had a meditative effect on him. He had once spent some time looking into the numerological symbolism in Bach's compositions, but had soon found himself out of his depth.

'*Erfreut euch, ihr Herzen, entweichet, ihr Schmerzen,*' the singer lilted softly, '*es lebet der Heiland und herrschet in euch.*' Listening to Bach was good for his German too. Rejoice, O hearts, begone O agonies, the saviour lives and reigns in you.

After he lit his cigar, he tried to keep the spindly cedarwood spill burning for as long as he could. When the flame licked at the top of his index finger, he quickly dropped it on the ground.

From where he sat, it looked like Janna, Daniël and Arnold were having a heated discussion about something. At one point,

Arnold turned angrily away from the others and disappeared into the bar. Peter assumed he had gone to get another drink.

But he came back outside not long afterwards, clumsily fastening his belt as he headed straight for Peter, with Daniël and Janna behind him.

'Come on,' he said with surprising articulacy, 'we're all going to have a look down that hole. I just want to—'

'Absolutely not,' Janna cut him off.

Daniël wobbled his head, as Indians do when they are reluctant to say either yes or no.

'I want to be the first person to walk through part of the tunnel,' Arnold said, smiling at Janna. 'Further than you went. Come on, let this old fogey have a bit of fun.'

'It can't hurt to have a quick look, can it?' Daniël said, although he didn't sound sure.

Peter turned off his music and stood up. *Speaking of networking*, he thought, watching Daniël.

Janna's jaws were tightly clamped together. It was clear that she also understood that it would be unwise to cross the great Van Tiegem. He was known for his vindictive character.

'Okay then,' she said, like a parent giving in to a spoiled child but trying to sound strict at the same time, 'but just a few minutes, and no more than twenty or thirty metres . . . I'm not taking any responsibility for this. Daniël and I will wait for you both up here so that . . .'

Arnold was already tugging at the safety barriers that had been laid over the pit. He yanked at one of them with his full weight until it suddenly moved and he fell backwards. A monstrous screech of metal on stone echoed through the narrow street.

Janna swore under her breath.

Daniël and Peter carefully lifted the barriers up and moved them out of the way.

'Is this really a good idea?' Peter tried again.

'We can hardly let him go down there on his own,' Daniël said, with more reluctance than he had shown just moments ago. 'And you know what he can be like once he's got an idea in his head . . . I don't want to be the one to antagonise him. But I don't want to upset Janna either, so if you could go with him . . .'

'Oh, great. That's all I need,' Peter mumbled like a sulky child.

Janna, who had apparently decided to make the best of a bad situation by at least making sure everything was done correctly, fetched the rope ladder and secured the two pegs firmly in the ground. She produced two bulky hardhats with lamps on them from an enormous bag and gave them to Peter and Arnold.

'You can use the light on your phone as well if you need to,' she said.

Arnold was already crawling over to the ladder on his hands and knees.

'Those who are about to descend salute you,' he said, tapping his helmet in a jocular salute.

A fiery bolt of annoyance shot through Peter.

Daniël helped Arnold by guiding his feet onto the first rung of the ladder. The ladder wobbled as he steadied himself, but he quickly found his balance.

If this was the circus, the audience would be applauding with relief now, Peter thought.

When Arnold reached the bottom, Peter got onto his knees, with his back to the pit. He felt around with his foot for the first rung. When he was sure it was secure, he lowered his other foot and began to climb down.

'You brought me up from the grave, O Lord. You kept me from falling into the pit of death,' he murmured.

He glanced into the gaping black chasm below him now and then as he descended and saw the faint glow of light from Arnold's hardhat. When he reached the hole at the bottom of the pit, he lay on his front, dangled his legs over the edge and slowly slid down into the darkness.

'You've got to see this,' he heard Arnold say in the distance, as though he was talking to no one in particular. He said it again, and this time there was a note of bewilderment in his voice. 'You've *got* to see this!'

The lamp on Peter's helmet gave off a bright, broad beam of light, but it only made the gloom beyond it seem even blacker.

Arnold had walked in the direction of the Hooglandse Kerk and then stopped, a few metres away from Peter.

'What, exactly, have I got to see?' Peter asked. But as soon as he got closer, he saw what Arnold meant. Fixed to the wall at shoulder height was a metal ring that held a blackened torch.

Arnold touched it hesitantly, as though he expected it to burn his hand. He looked at his sooty fingers and rubbed them together.

'That's what my hands look like when I clean out the grate after we've been burning logs all evening. This torch has only just been put out.'

'What *is* this?' Peter said, astonished by how calmly Arnold was handling this absurd situation, as though he had been through much worse before.

Suddenly, they heard something fall not far from where they were standing. Arnold turned around so abruptly that his hardhat fell off. He clumsily tried to catch it, but lost his balance and banged his head hard on the rough wall. He reeled and crashed into Peter, who barely managed to catch him.

'What was that?' Arnold asked. His voice came out strangled and shrill, like a frightened child's. All the bravura he'd put on display earlier was gone in an instant. He bent down to pick up his helmet.

Peter looked behind him at the spot where the faint light from outside permeated the thick, black darkness. They heard Daniël shout something, but couldn't make out the words. It was only then that Peter noticed that Arnold was bleeding from a large scratch on his forehead.

'You're bleeding, Arnold. We should go back.'

'It's nothing,' Arnold said, wiping the blood from his brow with his sleeve. 'I feel fine. Don't worry.'

Peter walked back to the spot where they had entered the tunnel and shouted up to the surface. 'Did you say something, Daniël?'

'We've thrown a rope down!' Janna shouted back. 'Can you see it?'

Peter looked down and saw a long rope coiled near his feet.

'Like Ariadne, remember, in Knossos. In the Minotaur's labyrinth.'

'Thanks! But we're coming back up in a minute!' he shouted. His words were meant for Arnold rather than Janna, but Arnold had already moved a few paces further down from the torch.

Peter put the end of the rope under a pile of bricks that had been left when the tunnel collapsed. If they didn't pull on it too hard, it would stay where it was. He had no intention of going any further into the tunnel than the rope was long.

'I hope your initial curiosity has been satisfied,' he said as he unwound the thin, strong rope. 'Let's go a bit further. We've got about thirty metres of rope here, I think.'

But Arnold had already walked away. Peter couldn't tell if this was the overconfidence of a drunkard, or the burning desire to beat him to an archaeological scoop. Peter quickened his step so that he wouldn't fall too far behind.

All at once, the light from Arnold's headlamp vanished.

'Arnold!' Peter shouted. His voice echoed through the chamber.

'I'm here!' came the distant reply. Peter realised that the tunnel must have curved away from him so that the light from Arnold's helmet was no longer visible.

They had walked about twenty metres now; Peter had let out more than two-thirds of the rope.

He walked further down the tunnel and saw that he had been right about the bend. Arnold came into view again, standing still and staring upwards as though there was something fascinating there. Peter stood next to him and looked at the same spot, but saw nothing.

'What are you looking at?'

'I'm not looking, I'm listening.' He raised his hand and pointed a finger in the air. 'Shush.'

Peter listened intently. He could hear the faint gurgle of flowing water. It was coming from . . . below them.

Arnold stamped his foot on the ground. '*Ab urbe condita . . .*' he said solemnly. 'Are you familiar with the work of Livy?'

Arnold was fond of demonstrating the knowledge of Greek and Latin he'd gained at grammar school, although in practice this was limited to recitations of a few well-known sayings and proverbs.

From the foundation of the city . . . The opening lines of Livy's history of the city of Rome.

'I wouldn't go as far as to say I was familiar with his work,' Peter replied, 'but I know that saying, naturally.'

'Exactly, this is . . . It looks like this was planned when the city was founded. I believe what we hear below us is part of a drainage system. It must be . . . You would usually expect to see ground-water this far down. You wouldn't be able to dig this without anyone knowing about it. Not if the city had already been built above you.'

Peter was becoming increasingly excited about what they had found. They couldn't even begin to imagine what the consequences of their discovery would be. But at the same time, he felt a growing disquiet. A young man covered in blood in subterranean passage . . . Who knew what other macabre things took place here?

'Listen, Arnold, this is all fantastic, and you're . . . We're the first people to come down here, apart from the poor man who ended up under a pile of rubble this afternoon . . . But let's leave it at this for now. We've satisfied our initial curiosity. We can come back tomorrow with more people, more light, and we definitely need more rope. It'd be irresponsible of us to go further now. We don't know what's down there. You've wounded your head . . . After the weekend, we'll have the Geo—'

But Arnold was deaf to his objections and walked away from him again. 'Just a bit further. This is . . .'

The beams from their headlamps cast grotesque shadows on the walls. Their footsteps sounded hollow.

We must be under the Hooglandse Kerk by now, Peter thought. But there was no sign of a way out or up. When he looked around him, he had to admit that he was impressed by the neatly constructed walls, by the solid arch of the ceiling, by the dry, even floor, by the drainage system.

They were running out of rope. It would reach as far as where Arnold was standing now, a few metres away from Peter.

Arnold carried on walking.

'Hey, will you listen to me? We're going back. We can go further tomorrow.' Peter stood with the end of the rope in his hand, not sure what to do next. His headlamp illuminated the path ahead and shone on Arnold's back.

'We can't really get lost down here. We've not seen any side tunnels, or any stairs . . . This is sensational, Peter. I just want to walk a little further.'

Aware that he was likely to lose sight of Arnold again, Peter put the rope down. He laid it carefully on the ground, next to the wall and well in sight. By the time he looked up again, his companion's light had vanished.

The silence and darkness seemed to have intensified, as though Arnold had literally been swallowed up.

Peter took a few uncertain steps forward and saw that the tunnel formed a T-junction and split off to the left and right a few metres ahead of him.

'Arnold?' he said. He cupped his hands around his mouth and called out Arnold's name again, but there was no response.

He was suddenly aware of how cold and damp it was. What

should he do now? He called out again, but all that came back was the echo of his own voice. He began to half-heartedly go down the tunnel on the right, but after a few metres, he reached a wall. This part of the tunnel was a dead end.

He turned around, making sure that he didn't let go of the wall. Without the rope, it was his only guide. He went back to the point where the path split and then walked a couple of metres into the other tunnel. He called Arnold's name again and it came out like a hiss. 'Arnold!'

He took a few more apprehensive steps.

'Arnold!' He was screaming now. His voice died away almost instantly.

He was jarred by the sudden, chilling sensation that he was being observed by something or someone hiding just beyond the reach of his headlamp beam. He was suddenly very scared, like a small child in the night, afraid of the monsters under his bed. He wanted to get out of here, go back up into the sunlight.

'Hello,' he said haltingly. 'Hello? Is anyone there?'

He had to get out of here. Now.

But before he'd even started walking back out of the tunnel, his headlamp blinked erratically and then went out. Now he was in total darkness. An instinctive fear of the dark – a deep, primitive, irrational fear – overwhelmed him. He flailed his fists around to ward off an invisible enemy.

'Yea, though I walk through the valley of the shadow of death, I will fear no evil, for thou art with me . . .' he murmured to himself.

His breaths were quick and shallow. His hands trembled as he took his phone from his pocket. The light from the screen that usually glowed so softly blazed now with the brilliance of a lighthouse beam.

Where had that bloody Van Tiegem gone? That obstinate bastard.

This was useless.

He turned back to fetch help.

He felt something cold brush past his neck.

Peter spun round in a panic. The jerking movement made his headlamp come on again. He took the hardhat off and aimed the light at the tunnel behind him. He couldn't see anything.

He shone the light on the ground in front of him and saw the end of the rope a few metres away. Tears pricked his eyes, as much from relief as from the dust in the air. He left the rope where it was in case Arnold came back.

This had been such a stupid idea! He had let himself get carried away by that damned Van Tiegem and his insistence on being first! Never, not once, had that man shown the slightest interest in the actual work of digging. But if there was ever a nice find somewhere, he was there like a shot to make sure he was front and centre on the photos.

Above all, Peter was angry at himself. They'd have to come back of course, with more people, more light, and a longer rope.

He reached the opening where they had entered the tunnel. When he was directly under the hole, he shouted upwards. 'Daniël! Janna! Hey! Can you hear me?' His voice was hoarse and cracked.

'We can hear you Peter! We're here! Did you find—'

'I've lost Arnold! He's . . . The bastard kept going, past the end of the rope. We have to—'

'What!' Janna and Daniël exclaimed together.

'You're kidding,' Janna said. 'What happened? I told you! You should never . . . This is not my respons—'

'Yes, I know that! Wait, I'm coming up.' Peter stood on the pile of rubble so that he could reach the bottom rung of the rope ladder. Afraid that something or someone might grab his legs at any moment, he frantically writhed and squirmed his body through the hole. He looked up as he climbed, and although the light was fading as night approached, he could see the worried looks on Daniël and Janna's faces.

They both held out a hand and helped him out of the pit.

Peter took off his hardhat. His face and clothes were grey with dust, like a miner coming up from the coalface after a long day's work.

He stooped over with his hands on his knees. Then he straightened up again and told them what had happened. Daniël leaned in as he listened, but Janna drew back slightly, as though she was afraid. When Peter had finished speaking, she gripped him by the collar, pulled him emphatically towards her, and turned him round so that she could examine him. A studious frown appeared on her forehead. She looked at him questioningly, making Peter suddenly feel very small.

'What's wrong?' he asked,

'Come and look,' she said to Daniël. Daniël moved closer and his eyes widened.

Janna gripped Peter's arm and squeezed it urgently. 'What really happened down there, Peter?'

Peter followed their gaze to the spot they were both staring at.

In the middle of his chest was an enormous bloodstain.

6

The three of them stared at the bloodstain on Peter's shirt, frozen like characters in a promotional still from an action film.

'That wasn't there just now, was it?' Janna asked.

Peter tugged himself free of her grasp. 'Don't be ridiculous. What do you mean by asking me what really happened down there? I've told you, haven't I? He walked into the tunnel ahead of me and then he walked around the corner. There was no rope left, but I went in after him, shouting his name. When he didn't answer, I came back to get you so you could help me.'

'And that blood on your shirt? Is it yours?' Janna demanded.

'He fell over. We heard a loud noise . . . You threw the rope down and it gave us a fright. Arnold was stumbling around and his hardhat fell off. He grazed his head on the wall and then he fell against me . . .'

Daniël stood between Peter and Janna, like a football captain trying to prevent one of his players from attacking an opponent.

'What do *you* think happened? That I was down there in the tunnel and thought, oh, I know, I'll smash Arnold's brains in, they'll never find out that I did it?'

'Well . . . everyone knows you can't stand him . . .' Janna said.

'Hey now,' Daniël intervened, 'this won't achieve anything.'

'We have to go back down,' Peter said. 'I didn't want to go any further on my own.'

'I'm calling the police first,' Janna said, taking out her phone and dialling the emergency number.

It was quiet for a moment. They heard her say 'Police' and then 'Leiden'. Peter checked the time on his own phone. It was almost seven o'clock.

Janna explained the situation. After a brief pause, her voice rose sharply. 'Excuse me, what do you mean by that?' She listened to what the person on the other end of the line had to say, then said, 'Yes, I know he's been reported missing lots of times before, but this is a totally different situation. He was in a tunnel . . . under the city, yes . . . was only discovered today . . . no, just now . . . with a colleague . . . no, they went on their own, but . . . he's gone yes . . . l *know* this isn't the first time, you keep saying that, but this time . . . *Listen* to me! He's—' She looked at her phone as though she was wondering what it was doing there. 'She hung up on me,' she said with disbelief. 'She's not allowed to do that, she's not allowed to hang up.'

'Why did she do that?' Daniël asked.

'She didn't take it seriously,' she answered bleakly. 'The boy who cried wolf . . .'

'Then perhaps we should . . .' Peter started to suggest, but he stopped mid-sentence when something in the distance caught his eye. It was already twilight, but the streetlamps gave off enough light for Peter to see a shadowy figure standing just beyond the Hooglandse Kerk, looking at them.

He appeared to raise his hand, as if he was beckoning them over. He wasn't wearing a coat and his clothing flapped around him as though his shirt and trousers were far too big. When he noticed that Peter had seen him, he abruptly turned around.

'Hey!' Peter shouted. 'Hey! You! Wait!'

Janna and Daniël looked to see who he was shouting at, but the man had already disappeared around the corner into the cobbled alley of the Beschuitsteeg.

Peter ran after him. 'Stay here!' he heard Janna shout angrily, but he kept running. He saw the man turn left and run along the Nieuwe Rijn canal. Peter ran past the American Pilgrim Museum. He saw the man cross the canal via the narrow Boterbrug and then turn left again, running towards Van der Werfpark. There was too much distance between them now for Peter to be able to catch up with him, and to make things worse, his knees had started to hurt. He decided to gamble on the man having gone to the park; he'd be able to hide himself easily there at this time of day.

Peter wheezed as he ran along the Mosterdsteeg. Sweat dripped from his brow. *I'm going on a diet on Monday*, he promised himself.

After crossing the Breestraat, he turned right at De Kler's bookshop and ran into the Boomgaardsteeg. It brought him out onto the Steenschuur, with the park shrouded in dusky shadows on the other side of the canal. He thought he saw someone go into the park via the left entrance. They were casually sauntering, as though they were enjoying an evening stroll. Was he imagining it? Peter slowed his own pace and stayed close to the Lorentzgebouw, trying not to cause suspicion by looking behind him. He went over the Steegbrug.

The shadowy figure walked behind the statue of Burgemeester Van der Werff and sat down on a bench. He still looked relaxed, almost as though he might produce a sandwich from a bag and enjoy a leisurely lunch, as office workers often did in the park. But instead, he looked straight ahead.

Peter approached the man, being careful not to be seen. Just as he was getting ready to sprint after him again, he turned to look at him.

'Ah, there you are,' he said calmly, as though they had agreed to meet at exactly this time.

Peter stared at him in bewilderment. 'What do you mean, "there you are"?' He moved closer, so that he was just a couple of steps away from him. 'Who are you?' he asked.

It was difficult to make out the man's face in the dark, but he could see that he was young, slim, clean-shaven, with medium-length dark blond hair and a plain-looking face. His clothes were so ill-fitting that they appeared to belong to someone else.

'But you're . . .' Peter said in amazement. 'You're the one who was lying in that tunnel this afternoon.'

The young man ignored Peter's words. 'I have a message for you,' he said.

'What were you doing there? How did you get there?'

'That's not relevant right now.'

'Not relevant? My colleague disappeared in that tunnel.'

The man looked at him in surprise, but seemed to be sincere. 'Disappeared?'

Deep furrows appeared on his brow. 'Even so,' he continued, 'I have a message for you.'

Peter opened his mouth to say something, but the man cut him off before he had a chance.

'You've been chosen,' the young man said abruptly, as though he was keen to avoid any discussion.

'Chosen?'

'Yes, chosen. A great honour.'

'Now listen,' Peter said with irritation, 'I don't have time for this now. My colleague has just disappeared and I—'

'I'm sorry, I don't know anything about your colleague.'

There was a short, awkward pause.

'I've been . . . chosen?' Peter asked, confused by the direction the conversation had taken.

'Yes, that's right.' The young man sat up straight. 'Have you seen *The Matrix*?'

Peter nodded impatiently.

'With the red and blue pill . . .' the man continued. 'Neo is given a choice: if he takes the red pill, he'll wake up and experience the world as it really is. If he takes the blue pill, nothing changes and he carries on as before . . .'

'And that would make you Morpheus, I suppose?'

The man scoffed. 'Peter . . .'

Peter was unpleasantly surprised that the young man knew his name.

'Listen,' the man said, getting up from the bench. They were standing no more than a metre apart now. When he spoke again, his voice was very calm. 'Just like the prisoner who escapes Plato's cave and discovers the truth, you can . . . be set free, disconnected . . . like in *The Matrix*.'

'So I need to choose the red pill?'

'You don't need to understand everything now. You will, eventually. "The hour has come." That's the message.'

'The hour has come?'

'*Hora est.*'

'*Hora est*. This is . . .' Peter let his arms fall to his sides, nonplussed. 'How do you know who I am? And who are you? Do you have a name?'

'You can call me Raven.'

Peter had run out of patience. He was exhausted from the chase, from the adventure in the tunnel, from worrying about what might have happened to Arnold. 'You know what, I'm done here—'

'Look out! Behind you!' the man said suddenly.

Peter turned around. As soon as he did, Raven pushed him backwards and he fell to the ground, hitting his head hard on the edge of the bench. He felt his skull explode with pain.

The oldest trick in the book.

The man sprinted off but then he stopped a few metres away and shouted: 'Salvation is at hand!'

7

Peter rubbed the painful spot on his head. What sort of idiot was he to fall for *that*? 'Look out! Behind you?' That was what children shouted to distract their friends in playfights.

He walked in the same direction that Raven had run, out of the park, over the Steenschuur canal. He crossed the Breestraat and went along 't Gangetje onto the Nieuwe Rijn. The street was quiet and empty. The light from the streetlamps sparkled in the canal.

What should they do? The police had clearly given Van Tiegem's umpteenth vanishing act a low priority, but everything was different this time. Perhaps one of them should go to the main police station on the Langegracht canal to explain the situation properly. The story about him suddenly going missing while exploring a secret tunnel must have sounded quite absurd.

As soon as he got back to the pit, he would talk to Janna and Daniël about what to do next, he decided.

But when he turned into the Beschuitsteeg, he saw blue lights flashing on the walls of the Hooglandse Kerk ahead of him.

He took a few careful steps forward, staying close to the houses on the left-hand side of the alley. Now he could hear the crackle of radios too. So the police had come after all. How was he going to explain his sudden disappearance? The way he'd run off earlier would make him an obvious suspect in Arnold's case. And what could he say? That he'd had a discussion in the park with a man calling himself Raven who wanted him to choose between a red pill and a blue pill? Oh yes, and that the same man had said that the hour had come and salvation was at hand?

They'd arrest him there and then and detain him until they knew what had happened to Arnold.

Peter stopped next to the last house on the street and peered around the corner. There were two police cars, and some police officers were standing around the hole with Daniël and Janna. They appeared to be discussing something urgently while one of the officers spoke into a radio. When one of the policemen looked in his direction, Peter ducked back around the corner and decided to walk the other way. *I need to find out what's going on here first*, he thought. *I want to investigate. Need to investigate. Who knows how much precious time will be lost if they arrest me?*

He retraced the route he'd taken earlier that afternoon.

The faculty was deserted by the time he got there. He opened the door with his key card and walked down the hall to his office.

Once he was in his room, he took off his dusty clothes and put his wallet and the two mobile phones on his desk. He took a clean shirt, trousers and socks from the cupboard. As he got dressed, he wolfed down two of the cereal bars he kept in his desk drawer as afternoon snacks.

He went to the toilets and craned his head under the tap as best he could. The water that streamed into the sink was grey. He dabbed his face dry with paper towels, studying himself in the small, round mirror. He looked tired. The whites of his eyes were shot with red, and there was a scratch on his nose. He ran his hands roughly through his hair, releasing a dusty shower of grit that made him look like he had a severe case of dandruff.

And there was a clearly visible piece of lettuce stuck between his teeth. He dug it out and rinsed out his mouth.

Now that he had calmed down, he could see that walking away had been a bad idea. He'd been so taken aback by the strange encounter with Raven, the messages, and Arnold's disappearance that he'd wanted to go off and investigate on his own. But where would he start?

He went back to his office and took the folder from that afternoon's lecture out of his bag. The students were required to turn up for least eighty percent of their lectures and he was required to keep accurate records of their attendance. Reading out a roll and ticking off every name individually took much too long, so he usually passed the register around the class. Of course, this sometimes meant that there were more people present on paper than were actually in the lecture hall. He usually brushed it off with a joke. ('Once again, it appears that, just like a Russian election, we have more votes than voters.')

He ran his finger down the list of names, trying to remember their faces. He only succeeded in one or two cases. He soon realised that this was utterly useless. What had he hoped to find? A student called Raven Ravensbergen? Or a red arrow pointing to a name and the words '*hora est*'?

He grumpily folded the list up again. As he slotted it back into the folder, his eye fell on the little book that he had been using on the course. More of a thick pamphlet than a book, its cover was printed on the same paper as the contents. Written on the front were the words: GEDEMPTE GRACHTENWANDELING or A WALKING TOUR OF INVISIBLE CANALS, published by the Leiden Canal Society and the Old Leiden Historical Society. It was a route around all the canals in Leiden that had been covered over or filled in.

He picked it up distractedly. How was it possible that the tunnel had never been discovered before?

He spread it open and began to read random pages, looking for answers.

59

Leiden has always been a city rich with water. Around the middle of the sixteenth century, the Italian-Flemish merchant Guicciardini described the city as a true archipelago. He counted thirty-one islands, connected by a hundred and forty-five bridges. At that time, the city was still medieval in scale.

He read on.

And even now, one is struck by the abundance of water in Leiden. Over the years, however, many of the canals have been infilled or overvaulted. This walking tour hopes to give an impression of these changes. The route covers more than thirty sites where the city's canals have been removed over the centuries, showing how the water gradually disappeared from Leiden.

How the water gradually disappeared from Leiden . . .

In the medieval city, the streets of Leiden became densely populated and, over the course of the seventeenth century, the city was expanded three times. The increased density of the buildings resulted in an increase in traffic on the streets. This was not only accommodated by the infilling of some canals, but primarily by means of moving them underground to large brickwork drainage channels, or by roofing the canals over.

The tunnel they had discovered that afternoon was so far underground that it even ran below the canals that had existed in the Middle Ages. Peter leafed through the pamphlet looking for the illustration that showed all the city's former canals.

A few years ago, the invisible canals tour had been complemented by the addition of an urban legends walking tour that

Peter and Judith had once taken. The tour guide had told them a story about each location they'd stopped at and asked the participants to guess whether or not it was true. There was a tale about the well in the Burcht that the guide had told them was false. In the seventieth century, it was believed that a tunnel started at the bottom of this well and led all the way to the 'Roman arcenal near Cat-wijck', as the contemporary sources put it. The tunnel was thought to have been built during the Spanish siege of the city in 1573–1574. According to the legend, a live herring was found in the well which was supposed to prove that it was connected to the coast. That fishy tale could obviously be disregarded as belonging to the realm of fables, but persistent rumours about the tunnels were widely accepted to be true.

Then there was Annie's Verjaardag, the café in the old city vaults which everyone 'knew' were part of an underground network of tunnels that led to the Burcht. The city had developed so densely around these areas that there had never been a serious attempt to find out how much truth there really was in the old stories.

Although Peter knew a great deal about the history of Leiden, he hadn't managed to make a correct guess about even half of the stories on the tour. The lesson he had taken away from the experience was: if a story sounded too unlikely to be true, then it probably *was* true.

He ran his finger over the Nieuwstraat, another 'invisible' canal. He squinted at the page until the fine outlines of the buildings faded away and all he could see were the red and blue delineations that formed an alternative map of the city.

He tapped his finger on the picture.

If there had been a tunnel present ab urbe condita, he thought, *then perhaps there wouldn't have been much digging needed to connect it to the roofed-over canals . . . What if it wasn't just one tunnel, but a whole labyrinth of tunnels beneath the city? My god, this could be one of the greatest archaeological discoveries of the century . . .*

He put the book down and picked up the new mobile phone again. The only apps on it were the pre-installed programs it would have been sold with, and Wickr. Tomorrow he would go to a phone store and ask if they could find out who it was registered to.

Peter jumped when his own phone rang. He involuntarily synchronised his breathing with the ringtone, breathing in when the tune played, and out when it paused.

An 0900 number. That could be the police.

Just as he was about to answer it, the ringing stopped.

Then it immediately rang again. He answered it this time.

'Is this Mr De Haan?' The voice sounded formal but friendly.

'Yes.'

'This is the Leiden constabulary of the Hollands Midden regional police. We've been looking for you, Mr De Haan.'

'So I, er . . . so I understand. I . . .' Peter felt his face redden. He would make a useless criminal, he thought. He would fall to pieces the minute he was interrogated.

'Where are you at the moment? We can come and pick you up, if that's easier for you.'

'This is about Arnold van Tiegem, isn't it? Is there any news?'

'This will be easier if we discuss it face to face. I can send a car for you. That would be the quickest way, I think. Where are you now?'

'I'm . . . I'll come myself. I can walk.'

'Sir, will you please—'

Peter hung up. He put the telephones inside his jacket and stuffed his wallet into his trouser pocket.

On his way outside he realised that his phone made him easy to trace. If he changed his mind and didn't go to the police station after all, they would have no trouble finding him. He stopped at the faculty's pigeonholes and slipped his own phone into the box that had his name above it. It was an intuitive decision that instantly felt right.

He decided to visit Judith first. She was the only person he could talk to in confidence about this absurd situation, and her house was close to his route to the police station on the Langegracht.

Less than ten minutes later, he arrived at the Sionshofje on a side street off the Haarlemmerstraat. He pushed open the heavy, green outer door and walked into the large inner courtyard, which was bordered by a brick pathway. There were no lights on in Mark's house. He was away travelling of course, but Judith's house was dark too. Surely it was too early for her to go to bed? Had she gone out?

He looked through the window, but the living room looked deserted. He knew that Judith kept a key under a flower pot near the front door. He removed it, carefully opened the door and turned on the light.

As he stepped through the door, a new message arrived.

He opened it nervously.

'Prophet!' said I, 'thing of evil! – prophet still, if bird or devil!
By that heaven that bends above us – by that God we both adore –
Tell this soul with sorrow laden if, within the distant Aidenn,
It shall clasp a sainted maiden whom the angels name Lenore –
Clasp a rare and radiant maiden, whom the angels name Lenore?'
Quoth the Raven, 'Nevermore.'

He wasn't much of a poetry connoisseur, but even he immediately recognised it as a verse from Edgar Allen Poe's famous poem *The*

Raven, about a mysterious raven's midnight visit to a man mourning the death of his lover.

Nevermore . . . The poem's distraught protagonist is denied the hope of ever being reunited with his deceased love. Peter had barely finished reading the poem when the message disappeared. Nevermore . . .

Peter called out Judith's name, but no answer broke the silence. He climbed the narrow staircase to the first floor, but it was dark there too. He hurried back downstairs.

Now he regretted leaving his own phone behind. Like many other people, he hardly knew any phone numbers by heart now that he had a smartphone.

However, just then another message arrived. He struggled to hold in an expletive.

Do not seek help. Only you can find her.

It was immediately followed by another.

Follow the black raven.

A few seconds later, the messages were gone.

Follow the black raven . . . What? Do not seek help? Find her? Judith? What did she have to do with it?

The phone vibrated again. It was a link this time. He clicked on it. A digital clock appeared on his screen. The time on it was counting down.

17:08:22 – 17:08:21 – 17:08:20 . . .

He stared at the screen, transfixed.

The starting time was displayed in the top left-hand corner of the screen. Two o'clock in the afternoon.

Almost seven hours had gone already.

THE FIRST VISION

And behold, I saw a young man standing on the bow, with his arms wide like a bird. He gazes up to the heavens but his eyes are closed. He is short, his nose is long, and despite his youth, his head is already bald. He has a friendly appearance. The play of shadows and light on his face changes his countenance from man to angel and back again.

And the prow cuts through the clear blue water, rising out of the sea on the crest of a wave and coming back down with a crash, splashing wild, white foam. But the young man does not lose his balance. He stands there as steady as a statue, like a man with a mission. He pays no attention to his surroundings. Neither to the green coast that they steadily sail past, away in the distance on the portside, nor to the dolphins who swim alongside the ship. They arc gracefully out of the water, pausing for a moment as though hanging between heaven and earth before diving back down.

And then suddenly he opens his eyes and it is as though he sees me, looks right through me. As though he wants to tell me: I know you, I know who you are. His intense, fiery gaze burns right through my soul, disregarding all barriers, all appearances, all ostentation. My mask falls away and there I stand – naked. You know who I am, he says wordlessly. I will show you the way. Follow me. Salvation is at hand.

And behold, evening comes and the young man takes a hunk of bread and a small, earthenware amphora from his knapsack. He goes over to the ship's starboard side. He raises the bread up to the setting sun with both hands and murmurs a prayer. Then he does the same with the amphora. He breaks the bread and eats it thoughtfully. He takes a drink from the jug and the wine trickles out of the corner of his mouth and into his beard. Then he seeks out a quiet place on the deck to which he can retreat. He lays his head on his knapsack, and before long, he is fast asleep.

And behold, the ship docks at a port. The marble on the temples glitters in the sun, and he can already see the great theatre and the hippodrome from the quayside. The young man picks up his travelling bag. It does not appear to contain many possessions. Without looking around or greeting anyone, he walks down the gangplank and into the town to find a bed for the night.

And the next day, he rises before the light of dawn and goes on his way. He has joined a group of travellers and pays the leader to protect him. They will travel only by daylight and stay on the great road that leads to Jerusalem, sixty miles away. He speaks to no one on the way, and when the group rests, he does not join them, but sits alone to eat his bread and drink his water.

And after three days, they enter the eternal city. They see the temple in the distance, shimmering in the sun. Many of the travellers fall to their knees, some raise their hands to the heavens and weep. But not he. He walks on, leaving the group behind him.

And he walks through the narrow streets of the city. He does not know them, but he knows they will be his home from now on. He knows where he must go, he has memorised the way. People try to stop him. Traders hold up bolts of cloth to him, invite him to taste the fruit from their stalls, extol the qualities of their pottery. Women with heavily made-up faces tug at his sleeve and ask him to join them . . . The city air is thick with the odour of charred flesh from the ceaseless burning of offerings in the temple. Beggars cling to him, faces disfigured, hands missing, legs deformed, dragging themselves over the ground. But he does not allow any of it to distract him. His eyes are fixed on a point in the distance.

And behold, he arrives in the tanners' district. Their bloody hides stink as they hang drying in the sun. Defiled by so much blood, this is the neighbourhood that is shunned by the Jews. But this is where the young man will stay, where he will practise his craft. His sewing tools, a gift from his father, are in his knapsack. He will live here for two years, far from home. He must spread his wings and go out into the world. That is his task.

He stops at a large, green door. The heavy iron knocker is shaped like a bull. He holds it in his hand and waits, as though he is unsure what to do, but then he knocks three times. The sound echoes in the hallway. He hears footsteps approaching. The door opens and an old man appears, tall, with a full grey beard and hair clipped short. The young man falls to his knees. The old man puts his right hand on his head as a blessing.

'*Pater*,' the young man says. Father.

'My son, welcome,' the old man answers. The young man stands up and they embrace each other like brothers.

And behold, just before he enters, the young man turns around unexpectedly and looks at me for the last time. He moves his lips, but no sound leaves them. I hear his words in my heart:

I am a Raven.

8

NYMPHUS

BRIDEGROOM

Friday 20 March, 8:00pm

'Father.'

The young man knelt with one knee on the rough stone floor and bowed his head.

The old man put his hand on the young man's hair and let it rest there.

'Get up now,' he said.

The young man stood up, but kept his head bowed, his eyes fixed on the floor.

'May I ask you something?'

'You may.'

The young man paused. 'Are we doing the right thing?'

'Look at me.' The man looked at him earnestly, like a parent trying to discern whether their child is challenging him or sincerely wants an honest answer. He sighed. 'Listen . . .' he said, considering his words carefully. 'I cannot expect any of you to have the insight that I have, but the hour has come, the time is now. We discussed it in our meeting this morning . . . I explained it to all of you.'

'But . . .'

'Enough!' he shouted.

This show of temper was so startling that the young man's face and neck burned with shame.

'I'm sorry, Father. I don't doubt you . . . You know I've always been faithful to you.'

'There now, all is well,' the man said unctuously, as though he was calming a frightened dog. 'This day was always going to come, sooner or later,' he explained serenely. 'It's up to us now. We decide what will be revealed and when. I have chosen someone. You know that. I'm certain that if he shows himself to be worthy . . .'

'I am sorry, Father, for doubting you.'

'Doubt is not such a terrible thing. Even Thomas doubted . . . But blessed are those who have not seen and yet have come to believe. Have faith. You are forgiven.'

'Thank you.' The young man seemed to be reassured.

'You know our history,' the man said in a lecturing tone. 'We've endured much worse than this in the past and we're still here. We've survived because we live in truth. We serve something greater than ourselves, greater than we can comprehend. And our reward will also be great, an eternal reward . . . We are storing up treasures in heaven. Where they cannot be damaged by moths or rust, nor be stolen by thieves. And where your treasure is, there will your heart be also. I'm not telling you anything you don't already know. Our Lord, who sees what is done in secret, will reward us. Remember that well.'

He ended his sermon with a smile and a fatherly pat on the young man's arm.

The young man bowed his head again, as a sign of respect. 'It's not that I doubted you, but—'

'All is well, my son, all is well,' the man reassured him again. 'Have faith in me, as I have faith in him. We must be steadfast if we are to do his will and receive what he has promised. So, let us do this well, let us not give up, and soon, when the time comes we will reap the rewards.'

'The hour has come.'

'Indeed, the hour has come.'

The old man stood up. They left the small room and went into the sparsely furnished kitchen, where a door led directly to a garden.

The young man picked up a coat from a kitchen chair and put it on. 'I'm going home. You know where I am if you need me,' he said as he left.

The old man locked the door behind him, then poured himself a glass of water and drank it slowly. Afterwards, he went upstairs to a spartan study. It contained only a rough wooden table, a chair, a single bed and a shelf filled with books.

He sat at the table and let his mind drift back to a time twenty years ago, when he was forty years old. Forty was a good, symbolic age. Forty was a number for tests and trials: the forty years that the Israelites wandered in the desert; the forty days that Moses spent on Mount Sinai before he received the tablets with the Ten Commandments; the forty days and nights that Jesus fasted before he was visited by the devil.

Not long after he had arrived in Leiden as a priest, he had become the head of a group of young, Catholic men who made it their purpose to fight against superstition and idolatry in all their forms. Their enemies were not the Christians who had left the warm bosom of the mother church – to a certain extent, that battle had already been fought – but the psychics, the mediums, the diviners, the tarot readers. They saw it as their duty to fight against these false prophets who led people away from the only path to salvation: Christ. Only he was the Way the Truth and the Life. They used their chicanery to steer their

70

customers, those poor sheep, straight onto the road that eventually led to hell.

The man and his group infiltrated all the paranormal and spiritual fairs that took place in and around Leiden. They went to every big event where the likes of Rasti Rostelli, charlatans in their eyes, came to demonstrate their skills. They sometimes even went to lectures where practices like meditation and yoga were shown in a positive light. They adhered to the Christian laws much more closely than their peers, and they were committed followers of the traditions of their ancestors.

They stood outside venues and handed out leaflets, trying to convince people not to go in. Occasionally there would be a confrontation with the organisers, or with one of the mediums who was performing. Even within his own church, there were many who did not understand why they had taken on this battle and believed that people should be left in peace to make their own choices. He preached sermons that warned that their struggle was not against flesh and blood, but against the rulers, against the authorities, against the powers of this dark world and against the spiritual forces of evil in the heavenly realms. That they must therefore put on the armour of God so that they could resist and be prepared to stand firm.

They targeted the Theosophical Society too, the International Study Centre for Independent Search for Truth or ISIS – an acronym that spelled the name of an Egyptian fertility goddess – who held monthly lectures on subjects like reincarnation, homeopathy, and the cosmos. Soon, the 'Knights of Christ', as the group had been christened, were guaranteed to turn up at every lecture. Most people tolerated the young men's presence but chose to ignore them. However, some attendees would engage them in discussion. The priest would clash violently with Ane, the ISIS chairman, who had once had the entire group removed by the police when these discussions became too heated. Two police vans had been needed to transport them to the police station on a charge of disorderly conduct. They had felt like modern-day martyrs in the back of the vans; they were suffering in Jesus' name, after all. Eventually, the threat of a restraining order convinced them to set their fight against ISIS aside.

He welcomed the opportunity to take a break from their activities. He had been plagued by epileptic fits since his early youth and they could be especially intense whenever he allowed himself to become too agitated. His fellow knights had had to prevent him from swallowing his tongue on numerous occasions when he had fallen to the ground with his mouth foaming and his whole body shaking with violent convulsions. They had panicked at first but after a few episodes they knew what they had to do. His epilepsy had even become a way of measuring the importance of each event: if its theme stirred up so much anger and frustration in the priest that it brought on a fit, then it must be of great consequence.

But now he had found a new target.

9

Friday 20 March, 8:30pm

'This is very strange,' Janna said, her austere face looking sterner than ever. She also seemed to be even more stooped than usual, as though she was standing in a room with a low ceiling and was afraid to bump her head. 'Very strange,' she said again, more to herself than to Peter.

Twenty minutes had passed since the police had called Peter. The officer who had made the call had contacted the main police station several times, but when it had become clear that Peter hadn't presented himself there, a warrant had been issued for his arrest.

After the emergency services operator had hung up on Janna the first time, she had called again and been able to convince them of the gravity of the situation. This wasn't just another Arnold Van Tiegem vanishing act that would resolve itself in a day or two. Eventually Janna and Daniël had been persuaded not to take action themselves, but to wait for the imminent arrival of a police car.

When the police had arrived, Daniël and Janna had given them a brief report of everything that had happened since Peter and

73

Arnold had gone into the tunnel. It would have been impossible to accuse the police of acting in haste; when Janna and Daniël had finished speaking, the officers had tucked away their notebooks and then stood shuffling their feet.

'What now?' Daniël had eventually asked.

'Let's . . .' one of the officers had said uncertainly. 'Let's call for backup.'

Not long after he'd made the call, two more officers, an older man and a younger woman, had arrived in another police car. They had taken two lighting units from the back seat, small silver-coloured cases that were protected with an armour of metalwork. They had switched on the lamps and shone two powerful beams into the tunnel.

The two officers who had arrived first had decided to stay above ground. The two new arrivals had gone into the tunnel with Daniël and Janna.

Once they were underground, the improved lighting allowed them to really see how impressive the tunnel's construction was.

Even the two police officers were impressed. The female officer whistled in amazement. 'This is quite bizarre, isn't it, right under the city?' she asked. Her radio crackled slightly and then grew silent about ten metres into the tunnel.

'Nothing can happen to us here, right?' her colleague asked nobody in particular. It wasn't clear if it was a casual observation or an attempt to quell his own fear.

When they reached the point where the tunnel split, they turned right then quickly hit the dead end and went back the other way.

The officers held the lamps in front of them and swept them from left to right over the ground and above their heads. The tunnel appeared to be solidly built, like a well-maintained wine cellar in a big castle.

'By the way,' the older officer said, standing still, 'the young man who was found in the tunnel this afternoon . . . he's escaped.'

'*What?*' Janna exclaimed.

Daniël clenched his fist, like a sports fan watching his team miss a huge opportunity.

'Yes, escaped,' the officer said again, as though it was nothing out of the ordinary. 'He just got up and walked away. The stupid thing is he was so covered in blood that we didn't get a chance to take any photos of him. His interview was planned for tomorrow, assuming he'd come round by then. But, there you go. Things don't always go the way you plan them.'

'The mystery deepens . . .' Janna whispered to Daniël.

'Whereabouts do you reckon we are now?' the female officer asked. She took out her mobile phone, then immediately put it away again. 'I thought as much. No coverage down here. I thought we might be able to look at a map . . .'

'I think,' her colleague said, 'I think that we're somewhere past the Hooglandse Kerk, under the Hooglandsekerkgracht, but . . .' He stood still. 'That's odd.'

Daniël and Janna stood next to the officers so that they could see what he was looking at.

He took a few steps forward and swung the lamp back and forth. Now they could all see that the tunnel didn't go any further.

'But how is that possible?' Janna said, raising her hands in disbelief like a bad amateur actress.

The younger police officer crouched down to examine the wall more closely. Then she pointed the lamp at the wall as she slowly stood up.

'I don't know what you're searching for, Indiana Jones,' her colleague said, 'but I think moving walls and secret passages are more of a Hollywood thing.'

'This whole tunnel is a Hollywood thing,' his colleague replied curtly, not taking her eyes off the wall. She studied the point where the wall and the ceiling met, then crouched down to look at the other corner.

'Nothing unusual here,' she said, finally.

The older officer turned to Janna and Daniël. 'Ladies and gentleman, whichever way you look at it, what we have here is a mystery.'

They nodded in agreement.

'We need more equipment.'

'A GeoSeeker,' Daniël said.

The man grunted in a way that was entirely open to interpretation.

'We're definitely under the Lutheran church,' said Daniël.

'Could I have that lamp for a second?' Janna asked the female officer, who passed it straight over to her.

Janna moved the lamp back and forth over the ground with a broad, systematic sweeping motion, as though she was clipping a lawn with a strimmer.

'What are you looking for, Janna?' Daniël asked.

'Didn't Peter say Arnold had wounded his head? So that means there must be blood somewhere, right?'

'I don't think it was a gaping wound. He just bumped his head. Most of the blood ended up on Peter's shirt.'

Janna ignored him and started slowly walking backwards.

The others followed along behind her, scanning the ground inch by inch.

'Here!' Janna shouted triumphantly, after she had shuffled another ten or so metres. She put down the lamp with a thud, then got down on her knees and held her nose to the ground.

The others squatted near the area where Janna thought she had seen something.

She circled a spot in the sand with the index finger of her right hand. It was slightly darker than the area around it, like something damp and red had mixed with the sand.

The younger police officer wiped her little finger over the stain and sniffed her fingertip. 'Hmm,' she said, 'that's blood, without a doubt. That metallic smell . . .'

'But it doesn't look like it's dripped here,' her colleague said, 'otherwise it would look like more like a splashed raindrop. It looks like someone fell here.'

'Arnold,' Janna concluded.

'We can't say that for certain, although I can see why you think that . . .' the older officer said, a little too gravely. 'But all we can say is that someone was here recently, that they were wounded and very probably fell, but other than that—'

'We need to go back,' the other officer said urgently. 'We can leave one of the lamps here. We need to close this place off for forensics and we need a kit to collect the blood . . .'

Daniël didn't move.

'Are you okay?' Janna asked him.

'Not really . . .' he replied. 'This wasn't what we . . .'

Janna put a hand on his shoulder. 'No, this isn't what we were expecting this afternoon. It was supposed to be a celebration.'

Daniël nodded.

'Come on, let's go.' She gave him a gentle push.

The four of them walked back, leaving a lamp behind them in the middle of the tunnel, like a beacon out at sea.

When they reached the tunnel entrance, the younger officer walked a few metres ahead of them.

'Does it continue along here?' she asked, shining the lamp down the passage. But the light fell on a wall about ten metres away. 'Looks like another dead end.'

'Peter and I walked a little way down there earlier today,' Daniël confirmed.

'Go and have a look,' the older officer grunted, with a note of cynicism in his voice. 'Maybe you'll find another secret passage.'

They helped each other climb back up to the surface. Stones came loose as they went and tumbled to the ground in a scud of gravel.

'We'll bring a ladder next time,' the older officer wheezed.

Only one police officer was waiting for them on the street.

The other sat in the front of the police car with his feet hanging out of the door and a radio in his hands.

'A report's just come in,' the officer said, holding out a hand to help them up.

The man in the car barked short sentences into the microphone, but from this distance, all they could hear was beeping and static.

He eventually put the radio back in the cradle and sat for a while, with his hands on his knees and palms facing upwards. Then he stood up and walked towards them. 'It looks like there won't be any need to continue the search down there,' he said hesitantly.

'Whatdoyoumean?' Daniël asked, the four words coming out as one.

'I've just been told that they've found a body floating in the Nieuw Rijn, under the bridge next to Annie's Verjaardag.'

Daniël covered his face with his hands.

The officer continued in an official tone: 'There's every indication that it's Mr Van Tiegem.'

10

Peter rushed outside, slamming Judith's front door behind him. He bounded across the courtyard to Mark's house and pounded on the windows, shouting his name. He realised immediately that it was useless.

Feeling helpless, he stretched out his hands, then curled his tensed fingers as though he was kneading a stress ball. His lips were tightly pressed together.

He had to go to the police of course, as he had originally intended. He would be able to explain the whole Arnold business, including why he'd foolishly run away earlier in the evening. He would be completely open and honest . . . up to the point where he'd met Raven in the park.

He pivoted around on one leg, like a soldier at the changing of the guard. At that exact moment, another message arrived.

Do not seek help. The same message as before. But now it was followed by something more sinister. If you ever want to see her alive again.

He looked up in panic. The timing of the messages was worryingly precise, as though someone was aware of every step he took.

He searched the sky. Was there a drone up there, with a camera watching him?

Do not seek help . . .

He opened Google and typed in 'black raven Leiden', but it didn't bring up anything useful. The first hit was a barber in Groningen of all things. So he tried 'raven Leiden'. A student dorm, entries in a telephone book for people called Raven, a seaside holiday park, the puppet from a children's TV show . . . they all led nowhere.

Peter was desperate to *do* something, but he didn't know where to focus his energy. He felt like the substitute in a football match who has just spent half an hour warming up on the sidelines before being told he won't be sent on.

Of course! The phone's location services. He slapped his forehead, almost as though it would wake up the grey matter inside.

He opened the settings and deactivated them. It was the obvious thing to do, but it still felt devious.

'Raven, raven . . .' he mumbled. Follow the black raven. It had to be symbolic. They couldn't possibly have meant a real raven. Could they?

He opened Google again and typed in 'raven symbol'. Less than half a second later the search term had produced tens of thousands of hits. On the first page, there was a reference to the raven that Noah had released, but Peter's eye was drawn to the words below the blue, underlined title of one of the links. 'The raven is featured as a messenger in mythological tales from all over the world . . .'

Peter had a feeling this would lead him to something useful, so he clicked on the link. It was part of a website about mythology through the ages, a subpage with an almost endless list of animals in mythological stories. He clicked on the word 'raven' and skimmed through the text.

The story about Noah again, Greek mythology, Egypt, Chinese literature . . . the raven as harbinger of death . . . Edgar Allan Poe

. . . And closer to home, the Norse myths and sagas. 'The god Odin had two ravens,' he read. 'Munin and Hugin, who flew around the world during the day, and returned to Odin at night to tell him everything they had seen the people do.'

Just like Raven in the park, Peter thought.

He impatiently clicked everything away, and shoved the phone in his pocket. Then he left the courtyard via the large door. He had no idea where he was going to go; he simply wanted to keep moving so that he would feel like he was doing *something*. He walked past the Kijkhuis cinema, and the gothic remains of the Vrouwenkerk.

The shops on the Harlemmerstaat had closed an hour ago, but the street still sounded busy. Friday nights in Leiden were as in many Dutch towns for going out.

A group of people walked by, two female students in identical red student association jackets together with two men and two women, all having an animated conversation.

'After hearing all those stories,' Peter heard one of the women say, 'it's so nice to be able to finally see where you've been spending all this time.'

Many student associations held an annual 'parents' evening' and invited parents to come and look around. It went without saying that everything was much quieter than normal on those evenings. There was no rowdiness, no beer was thrown around, and the music was kept at a volume that allowed proper conversation.

When the group passed him, Peter noticed the word DIONYSUS on the backs of their jackets. It was the god of wine, but also a fraternity of the Quintus student association. One of his colleagues had been a member and had told him about it. Peter himself had never joined a fraternity.

A thought began to take shape somewhere in the back of his mind. He stood still, closed his eyes and concentrated. He couldn't quite put his finger on what it was. Something he had seen.

Peter walked aimlessly on, but he was careful to avoid the

81

Haarlemmerstraat. He crossed the Lange Mare, a street that had been a canal until the early 1950s when it had been filled in. So they were true after all, the stories about the tunnels that ran beneath the city's many former canals. It was almost impossible to imagine.

He thought back to 1978, the first time he'd gone abroad without his parents. With the ink barely dry on his exam certificates, he'd travelled through Italy, ready to conquer the world.

He'd spent a long time in Rome, staying in a seedy youth hostel where men slept twenty to a room on bunk beds with filthy mattresses. He did everything he could to make his money last as long as possible, not even travelling low budget but no budget.

He had visited the catacombs, the city's complex system of tunnels and underground burial chambers, some of which had only been discovered in the second half of the twentieth century. Many of the tunnels had been built in secret by the persecuted early Christians. It was easy to carve out tunnels and chambers in the soft, volcanic *tufo* that formed the bedrock of Rome. After it had been exposed to the air, the rock would eventually harden, and the result was a sturdy structure, a city beneath the city, up to four layers deep. They placed their dead in elongated niches that had been carved into the walls. The graves were sealed with slabs of terracotta or marble, although these were unlikely to have prevented the smell of death and decay from permeating this underworld.

He'd taken hundreds of photographs, carrying the rolls of film around in their little canisters for weeks so that he could have them developed in the Netherlands. When he got home, he had been disappointed to discover that the many photographs he'd taken of the frescoes were washed out because he'd had to use the flash.

But who on earth had built this tunnel in Leiden? And how had it remained undiscovered for centuries? The depth of the tunnel had probably played a role, deep below the canals that had once run above it, or ran above it still.

Could there really be an entire system of tunnels under the city? It was difficult to believe. Rome had *tufo*, but here in Leiden, there was soft earth, groundwater and subsidence. How had they done it?

Peter slowed his pace. He walked a few metres into the broad alley of the Mirakelsteeg and leaned against a wall.

There was something ... something he couldn't quite remember. What was it?

He pictured in his mind's eye the one photograph he'd taken of a fresco that had come out well. It had hung on the cork board in his dorm room for years. The flash hadn't gone off, so the only illumination had come from the faint light of the catacomb's lamps. Despite being almost two thousand years old, the fresco was amazingly clear and bright. It depicted ravens flying above lily-like flowers, and a reference to the Gospel of Luke. In this well-known scripture, Jesus encourages his followers not to worry about their lives, about what they should eat, about their bodies or what they should wear. 'Consider the ravens,' he told them, 'they do not sow or reap, they have no storeroom or barn, yet God feeds them. And how much more valuable you are than birds! Consider the lilies. They neither toil nor spin. Yet I tell you, not even Solomon in all his splendour was dressed like one of these flowers ... But seek his kingdom, and these things will be given to you also.'

Follow the black raven.

All of a sudden, it came to him. He knew where he had to go.

The students he had seen earlier with their parents. That was it. At the time, he hadn't been able to make the connection. Like when you *know* you know the name of an actor in a film, but just can't quite recall it.

And then, just like that, you remember it again.

Peter retraced his steps.

He needed to go to the student association.

He needed to go to Quintus.

11

Two police officers stood on the quayside, trying to pull the floating body towards them with a hook on the end of a long pole. It was harder than it looked. The body seemed to be stuck, caught, perhaps on one of the hundreds of bicycles that were dumped in the canals each year.

An ambulance waited behind them, with two police cars parked diagonally across the street behind it. Two paramedics leaned against their vehicle and watched.

When the body didn't budge, the policemen abandoned their attempt.

'What do we do now?' one of them asked as he took photographs of the body's position in the water.

They looked around them. Small groups of people stood watching from behind the red and white tape that the police had used to cordon off the scene. A few of them held their phones in the air to take photos or record videos. The dots of light on their telephones looked like a constellation of bright little stars.

Curtains twitched behind windows here and there and people peered outside.

A rowing boat in the distance paddled towards them. Two policemen had had the presence of mind to unhitch a boat that was moored further up the canal. When they reached the body, they manoeuvred the boat alongside it. One of them took off his coat and rolled up his shirt sleeve so that he could stick his arm in the water and free the body from whatever it had snagged on.

It proved to be the handlebars of a bike.

The men in the boat took the pole from their colleagues and hooked it onto the victim's collar. They rowed the boat further down the canal, to the pier opposite the town hall that was normally used as a dock for canal tour boats. They towed the body behind them, like fishermen with a catch too big to bring on board.

They moored at the stone steps and managed between them to haul the body onto the pavement. The paramedics brought out a stretcher.

'That's the missing professor all right,' a policeman said. 'This is Van Tiegem.'

He took out his radio to report the news to the control room.

'What a sad way to go,' someone said.

Van Tiegem lay on his back, with his head rolled to the side and his eyes wide open, like someone in fright.

An officer knelt down and closed Van Tiegem's eyes, mumbling something the others couldn't hear while his colleague took photographs to document the scene.

Van Tiegem's socks had slipped down his ankles, revealing white legs with blond hairs. He had lost a shoe.

'By the look of his skin, he's not been in the water very long,' one of the officers said. 'Two hours, at most, definitely not longer.'

Two policemen rowed the little boat back to its mooring. When they came back, the four officers carried the surprisingly heavy corpse away from the water and heaved it onto the stretcher. Water streamed from the body onto the ground until the ambulance crew had wrapped it in a sheet of plastic and secured it with two straps.

The heaving and shoving had twisted Van Tiegem's jacket upwards. To their bewilderment, it revealed an empty wine bottle sticking out of the waistband of his trousers.

'Have you got some gloves for me?' one of the officers asked a paramedic.

He walked back to the ambulance and returned with a pair of latex gloves. The officer struggled them over his wet hands.

He used his thumb and forefinger like a small pair of tongs to carefully remove the bottle. The label was hanging off, but it was still legible: a Beaujolais Nouveau from the Dionysuswine estate.

'Mitra,' his colleague said. 'This bottle comes from the Mitra off-licence. There's one in the town centre, isn't there?'

'If you say so . . .' he replied, smoothly sliding the bottle into a clear plastic bag that the other paramedic had had the foresight to go and find in the meantime.

'Then we should drop by there later today. Maybe they know who bought this bottle. They might have CCTV footage.'

They rolled the stretcher awkwardly over the uneven cobbles and lifted it into the ambulance.

'Let's start by doing a house-to-house in this area, from the Koornbrug to Annie's,' one of the police team said. 'Someone might have seen something.'

He took out his notebook. They watched the paramedics put Van Tiegem's body into the ambulance.

One of them climbed into the back of the ambulance and the other shut the doors behind him, gently, as though he didn't want to wake Van Tiegem. He walked round to the front and got into the driver's seat, but before he'd even put the key in the ignition, the doors at the back flew open, and his colleague, who had been sitting almost in vigil next to Van Tiegem, leapt out. He banged loudly on the side of the ambulance and gestured wildly to the police officers.

'What the . . .' said the officer who was holding the notebook.

The two of them ran over to the paramedic who had been joined by his colleague. 'What's wrong?' the officer asked when they reached them.

'There's something . . .' the man said. 'I think you'd better come and see it yourself.'

He got back into the ambulance, closely followed by the police officer.

Van Tiegem's body was wrapped in plastic up to his neck. His exposed head was turned to the side and a puddle of water had formed underneath it.

When the two police officers had squeezed themselves into the cramped space next to the stretcher, they no longer needed the paramedic to explain why he had been so alarmed.

They could see it clearly.

There was something in Van Tiegem's mouth.

12

Peter crossed the Harlemmerstraat, then went down narrow alley of the Vrouwensteeg which took him directly onto the Kipppenbrug. When he reached the middle of the bridge, he stopped; on his left, he could see the blue lights of an ambulance or police car bouncing off the houses on the Nieuw Rijn.

A few seconds later, he set off again, turning right onto the Boommarkt.

There were still lots of students making their way to the Quintus Student Association with their parents. *That* had been the almost unconscious connection he had made earlier that had put him on the right track.

His ex-Quintus colleague had once told him about the two ravens on the society's crest. They were even called Hugin and Munin, after Odin's ravens. The members of Quintus often compared themselves to these two birds: during the day, they went their separate ways, and in the evening, they returned to the nest of the society to share their experiences and the wisdom they had gained. Many things at Quintus were named in reference to the ravens, like the Raevenzaal function room, the meeting room which was called the Raevenest, and their annual gala, the Raevenuesse . . .

Quintus was relatively new compared to the other student associations in Leiden. It had been established in 1978. The oldest association was Minerva, founded in 1814, whose membership had included members of the royal family, politicians, directors and captains of industry. After that came the SSR, created in 1886 for members of the Dutch Protestant Reformed Church. These days however, its fundamental principles were based on the Universal Declaration of Human Rights. Augustinus was originally established as a Roman Catholic Association, in 1893. For more than fifty years, until 1952, to be precise, these were the only student associations in town until they were joined by a fourth, Catena, an idealistic society that sought to move away from the traditional divisions of gender and religion. In 1978, the Fifth, or *Quintus* in Latin, was founded. They chose *'Numquam Desperate'* as their motto. 'Ne'er Despair' or – in simpler language – 'Never give up'.

Peter felt foolish for not having made the connection sooner. He was amazed that even Google had completely failed to see the link.

He recalled something else his colleague had told him: there were two stuffed ravens in the boardroom, just standing in the bookcases, not even next to each other. That was enough to convince Peter that he was on the right track. He was certain that this was what had been meant by the instruction to 'follow the black raven'.

Peter decided to introduce himself as the father of one of the members. *And just hope that none of the people on the door are studying history or archaeology*, he thought.

Which name should he use? For a son . . . Egbert? Or Diederik? Laurens? Johan? He couldn't decide between Fleur, Frederique and Johanna for a daughter.

A surname, a surname . . . Lammers was the first one that

came to mind. Johan Lammers, somehow the name sounded familiar.

He merged into the dozens of people who were heading towards the Quintus building.

The door was manned by what appeared to be association members, judging from the 'Parents' Day Committee' T-shirts they were wearing. They seemed very preoccupied with welcoming the guests.

When one of the students looked at him curiously, he waved enthusiastically to an invisible person in the distance. 'Hey, Fleur!' he shouted, just a little too loud. 'Here I am! Mummy's on her way!'

The boy glanced behind him and gave Peter a friendly nod.

'Just hanging my coat up!' he called, determined to play his role convincingly. But he kept hold of his coat. He didn't want to waste time in the long queue for the cloakroom.

He followed the lead of some of the other parents and slung the coat over his arm so that he wouldn't stand out.

He went up the ten or so steps of the wide staircase that led to a spacious hall. A staircase on the left led to large upper room. A steady stream of people passed each other as they made their way up and down the stairs.

Peter carried on walking until he arrived in another room, a hall with a bar on the right-hand side. Beyond the bar was a corridor leading to the Breestraat side of the building.

'Hi,' he said to a random student. 'I'd like to see the boardroom. Is it open this evening?'

'It certainly is, sir,' the boy replied, folding his hands at chest height as though he was enormously pleased to be able to give the right answer. 'But there are guided tours, actually. You can just join one of those.'

'Ah, excellent,' Peter said, mirroring the way the boy was holding his hands, 'but I'd like to take a quick look myself. Is it here on the ground floor, or should I . . .'

'Yes, it's here on the ground floor. You walk along the bar, down the corridor, and the boardroom is on your left.'

'Thanks awfully. I'm much obliged.'

'Not at all, sir.'

It took Peter a great deal of effort to squeeze his way through the mass of people in the room, but when he eventually reached the corridor, it was much calmer. The boardroom was open. A student in a smart suit and association tie was explaining something to a handful of parents.

The boy glanced at Peter, briefly distracted, but continued his story. 'So, as I said earlier, this is Hugin and this is Munin.' With the flourish of a consummate tour guide, he stretched out his arm to indicate the two stuffed animals. 'But which of them is Hugin and which Munin, I honestly couldn't say.'

Everyone laughed politely.

'And over there . . .' the boy turned around and his audience followed. He walked over to a case in the corner of the room. A red velvet cloth, embroidered with the Quintus crest, was draped over the case, obscuring something from view. It looked like a chest or box, about half a metre wide and half a metre tall.

'This is . . . This is the Quintus secret, and we're forbidden to reveal what lies beneath this cover.' He positioned himself between the object and the parents, to show how very serious he was. 'And this is what we drum into the new members when they've survived their initiation period . . . In the old days, we still had hazing and the potential members were really put through the mill . . . It was only after they'd proved their worth in a series of test that they were considered worthy of joining our society. That practice was abolished, but we still haze our new members. It's more playful these days, though.'

He pointed to the cloth that hid the case. 'When new students become official members, the chairman of the association pulls back the cloth to reveal what non-members will never see. And they must never breathe a word of it to anyone.'

'Could you lift the veil just a little?' asked a father. 'Literally.' The woman standing next to him jabbed him in the ribs.

'No, that's only for the initiated,' the boy said solemnly, taking pleasure in the words. 'Besides, not even I can say with certainty that the secret is actually under the cover. It may have been removed to prevent the uninitiated taking a peek when no one is looking.' He gave the father who had asked the question a stern look. 'There may be something under the cloth, or there may not be. A bit like Schrödinger's cat . . . Anyway, if you'd like to follow me.'

The group left the room. Peter made sure to let them all go ahead of him. When they were gone, he went over to examine one of the ravens more closely. He saw nothing in its beak. He ran his fingers along the feathers, gently lifting some of the looser ones up. Then he picked it up to study it from all angles, but found nothing out of the ordinary. Nor was there anything on the plinth.

What did you expect, he thought dejectedly. *A letter in its beak? A little canister on its leg?*

He examined the other raven, but there was nothing to see on it either. 'Follow the black raven,' he muttered. 'This *must* be it. There's nothing else in Leiden that it could be.'

He walked over to the case that held the secret object the boy had been talking about earlier.

Just as he was about to lift up a corner of the cover to take a look, a girl came into the room, with a group of parents trailing behind her.

She looked at Peter in surprise. 'Hey, Mr De Haan,' she said. 'What brings you here?'

'I, er . . . Yes . . . I wanted . . .'

'You were my lecturer in my first year, Introduction to Archaeology.'

The parents looked on in amusement.

'Fleur,' she reminded him.

Peter smiled, but with the best will in the world, he was unable to remember her. Blonde hair, shoulder-length, a pretty, open face . . . not particularly distinctive. But he said, 'Yes, of course I remember. How lovely to see you here, Fleur. I had no idea you were a member of Quintus.'

'I joined straight away, in freshers' week – and never regretted it.'

'Very good, very good.'

'But you . . . Is one of your children a member? I might know them.' She turned to look at her group, aware that she was supposed to be giving them a tour.

'Me? No, I . . .' he stammered. 'I was walking past and saw all those people coming in. I'm working on a book. A, um . . . There's a chapter about student societies and I'd never been to this one before. A colleague told me about the ravens, so I thought . . . Maybe it would be better if I made an appointment and came back when it was quieter.'

'Oh it's no problem. You can stay if you like.' She faced her group again. 'Sorry folks, I do apologise . . . Is everyone inside? This here . . . This is the boardroom.'

Peter decided to stay, hoping that he might get a chance to take another look under the velvet cover. He tried to look interested in what Fleur was saying, nodding every few seconds as though he was enthralled by what he was hearing.

She was telling them about the configuration of the Quintus board, the structure of the association, and eventually, about the two stuffed ravens. She took the little group over to the corner where Peter was standing and told them the same story Peter had heard from the boy earlier.

At last, the group left again. The last parent to leave, a mother, bumped into a boy as he rushed into the room. When she didn't move aside for him he was forced to take a few steps back.

Peter swiftly took advantage of their awkward moment to lift up the velvet cover. He caught a glimpse of the object which had been hidden from outsiders.

But then his attention was distracted by something falling onto the floor. At his feet lay a paperback copy of *The Hitchhiker's Guide to the Galaxy* by Douglas Adams. He stared at it in confusion but, aware that he didn't have time to stop and ponder what it might mean, he bent down to pick it up. He was just quick enough to put the book inside his jacket before the boy saw him.

'Sir,' he asked, his voice trembling slightly, 'shouldn't you be with the group that just left?'

Peter walked towards him. 'I wasn't with a group. I've already explained to Fleur, one of my students. I'm working on a book . . . I mean, a chapter about student societies . . . I thought I might have a quick look at your famous ravens . . . I happened to be in the neighbourhood and you were open, so . . .'

'Why didn't you make an appointment?'

'Of course. You're absolutely right. You know what, I'll arrange an appointment tomorrow instead . . .'

Another boy came into the room. He had a familiar face.

'Is he still here?' he asked, but then he noticed Peter. 'Ah, good. Hello Mr De Haan, Fleur told me you were here . . . You remember me, don't you? I'm on your course.'

'Ah, Egbert, yes. How nice to see so many students from my course here,' Peter said as he headed for the door. 'How are you doing, old chum?' He started to feel warm. *Old chum? What sort of nonsense is that*, he thought. *I'm not usually so jolly with my students.*

'Well I'm just fine, but the thing is, Mr De Haan . . .' He took his phone from his pocket, tapped on the screen a few times, and then showed it to Peter. It was a short article with Peter's photograph next to it on a local news website. Above it was the headline: POLICE SEARCH FOR LEIDEN UNIVERSITY LECTURER.

'I'm sorry,' he said, 'I don't know what's going on, but one of our members is calling the police now. I would like to suggest that—'

'It's just a misunderstanding, Egbert, you know who I am, don't you? It's—'

'I'm sure that's true, sir, but then surely it won't be a problem if the police come, will it? Then the misunderstanding can be cleared up.'

'This really isn't necessary, Egbert.'

Egbert straightened his back, and made himself look broader, like a man readying himself for a fight. A group of people had gathered in the hallway.

Peter realised that pushing them out of the way and escaping down the hall wasn't an option.

'Would you please come with us?'

'Yes of course, not a problem,' Peter said, trying to sound as casual as he could. He could see that he had no choice but to follow the two boys. 'There's really nothing wrong.'

He was surprised by how calm he was. Maybe he had it in him after all . . . Straight opposite the boardroom was another door. Egbert unlocked it with a key and showed Peter into a large room full of desks, computers, and bookcases overflowing with binders. Empty bottles of wine littered the floor, and beer crates were stacked against a wall. It smelled of stale booze.

Once Peter was inside the room, Egbert started to close the door.

'You really don't need to do this, Egbert,' he protested weakly. But Egbert closed the door without a word and turned the key in the lock.

I can't deal with this on top of everything else, Peter thought. *If the police come and take me to the station, I'll be there for hours.*

Now that he was alone, he took the paperback out of his pocket.

Peter had read *The Hitchhiker's Guide to the Galaxy* in the eighties. He had been carried away by the adventures of Arthur Dent, who travelled the universe with his alien friend, Ford

Prefect, after escaping the destruction of earth when it made way for an intergalactic highway.

The book must have been left there for him, he decided, otherwise it didn't make any sense for it to be there. He couldn't imagine that this old paperback had anything to do with the Quintus initiation rituals.

But why this particular novel?

Peter held it in his right hand and riffled all the pages with the thumb on his left hand.

'Ah!' he said aloud, as though he wanted someone else in the room to know that he had found something.

Tucked between pages 42 and 43 was a piece of paper, folded in half.

He opened the book properly and took it out.

Its posts are silver, its canopy gold; its cushions are purple.
It was decorated with love by the young women of Jerusalem.

The young women of Jerusalem . . .

The Song of Songs, Peter recognised it at once. You didn't need to be a biblical scholar to see it. It was unmistakable. The love poem attributed to King Solomon, the Song of Songs, was one of the shorter books of the Old Testament. People who were unfamiliar with the bible were often shocked by the overt eroticism of the verses. The breasts like fawns, the lips dripping with honey, the tongues as sweet as wine . . .

A canopy, or a chuppah . . . the tent-like covering that a Jewish bride and groom stood under during their marriage ceremony.

But now he had to find a way out of here. When the police arrived, he couldn't just nonchalantly say: *It's not what it looks like, believe me, but I'll pop by some time to explain everything.*

He put his ear against the door to listen for noise in the corridor, but could hear nothing. It sounded completely empty. He could hear music and chatter from the bar room in the distance.

The only way out was through the window. The window frame went all the way up to the ceiling and was divided into six equal panes with narrow wooden rods.

He had to act fast.

He took a half-empty bottle from a beer crate and shook the contents out onto the bottom right-hand corner of the window, just above the frame. It was dark outside, but the window gave a good view of the Breestraat. The street was quiet, except for the odd bus going by.

He took a newspaper from a desk, took out the middle page, unfolded it and pasted it against the wet window. It was an old trick that would prevent the shattered glass from flying into his face.

Leaning against one of the bookcases was a ridiculously large hammer. Its shaft was at least a metre long. Peter could only guess at what it might have been used for.

He picked it up, gripping it close to the head, and took it over to the window. He looked outside to make sure nobody was walking by, and then smashed the hammer into the glass. It broke immediately. The wet paper tore.

After two more blows, the corner of the window smashed and a large crack spread across the glass. Peter aimed two more precise taps at the damaged window, sending the cracks across the whole pane like fissures in ice. He put down the hammer then grabbed a tea towel from a desk, wrapped it around his hand and jiggled the large pieces of glass back and forth to remove them. He quickly managed to knock out most of the pane this way, creating an opening that he hoped would be just big enough for him to fit through.

He dug a few more pieces of glass out of the frame and threw his coat outside. He turned his face towards the outside of the frame, and then with his cheek pressed against the glass, stuck his leg through the empty pane. He carefully lowered his foot until it touched the pavement. The street was still quiet.

But the hole wasn't quite big enough after all: pieces of glass pricked his back. He briefly wondered if he should abandon the attempt and stay in the office.

But the choice was made for him; at that moment, the office door swung open. He craned his neck around to look – as far as that was possible – and then kept going. His jacket snagged on the broken glass.

A policeman entered the room, followed by Egbert. They both froze, with stunned looks on their faces.

Peter took advantage of their confusion to squeeze all the way through the window.

As soon as he was outside, he grabbed his coat from the ground.

The policeman was a large fellow who clearly wouldn't fit through the hole in the window. He said something into his radio, but Peter had already run across the street and onto the Papengracht.

The canopy of gold, a Jewish wedding . . . the thoughts screamed inside his head.

There was only one place in Leiden where he would find one.

13

Judith groaned softly and rolled her head from side to side on the mattress to loosen the muscles in her neck. The collar and armpits of her blouse were soaked with sweat.

She opened her eyes wide and yawned. She no longer felt sleepy but she did feel groggy and now she had a headache.

She looked around, disoriented. There was a large candle standing in the middle of the room. The room looked like a cell. She shot upright, like someone waking from a nightmare.

She swung her legs over the edge of the bed. She sat like that for a while, racking her brains to try to remember why she was here, *where* here was . . .

She appeared to be in a perfectly square room with a floor made of small terracotta tiles. There was something that looked like a drain in the middle of the floor, but it was tightly sealed shut with an iron cover. The walls and ceilings were roughly plastered with loamy clay. She estimated that the room was about two metres by two metres, and about three metres high.

Standing in the middle of the room was a fat candle, about fifty centimetres tall, the sort that would usually stand on the

99

altar in a Catholic church. A translucent gold-coloured orb seemed to float around the softly glowing flame.

Against one wall was a simple wooden plank bed with a mattress so thin that it barely deserved the name. The heavy, musty blanket offered little protection from the damp cold. Her mouth was dry.

No sounds penetrated the mouldy walls of the room. She walked over to the heavy-looking door and slammed her fists into it, but it didn't move at all.

She began to shiver uncontrollably.

'Hey!' she screamed, her voice catching in her throat. 'Hey!'

The sound echoed off the walls and then instantly died away. She banged half-heartedly on the door again.

'Hey!' she shouted once more, but the shout came out as a sob. 'What am I doing here?' she whispered. She swallowed a few times, trying to resist the urge to vomit. The tightness in her chest was so great that she could barely breathe. She stumbled over to the bed, and carefully lowered herself onto it. She lay on her back with her hands folded across her stomach and focused on her breathing.

'Where am I?' she whispered to herself. 'How did I get here?'

Slowly but surely, the memories began to resurface, in fragments, and the realisation of what had happened began to dawn on her like a meadow mist clearing in the morning sun.

14

Peter sprinted to the end of the Papengracht and turned left onto the Gerecht, the square named for Justice where criminals were once executed. He ducked into the narrow Muskadelsteeg and then turned right to go around Pieterskerk, passing the plaque that memorialised the time the Pilgrim Fathers spent in Leiden before setting sail for the New World.

The scripture in the Song of Songs described a baldaquin, a regal canopy made of beautiful cloth supported on four poles. Jewish couples always married beneath a baldaquin or chuppah. It symbolised the home that the happy couple would soon share. Whenever possible, they got married in the open air, as evening fell. If it was dark, the stars reminded them of God's promise to Abraham that he would have as many descendants as there were stars in heaven.

The only place in Leiden that would have a chuppah, or at least, the only place he could think of, was the synagogue next to the Jewish student dorm on the Levendaal. He assumed that most synagogues would have one. However, getting inside might be 'a bit of a mare', as his students would say.

He turned into the Herensteeg and passed La Bota, the little bistro where he ate so often that the staff almost treated him like family.

At the end of the alley, he went left onto the Rapenburg, the wide canal that ran through the centre of the city and was flanked by tall, stately mansions that were among some of the most expensive in Leiden.

For the second time that evening, he went over the Nieuwsteegbrug and into the Van der Werfpark where he'd met Raven earlier. He walked along the path laid with crushed shells that ran parallel to the water. He checked over his shoulder a few times, but it didn't look like he was being followed.

A short while later, he reached the Garenmarkt and saw the synagogue on the corner. The square was full of parked cars, but it was otherwise deserted.

He couldn't just ring the bell, especially now that the police were looking for him.

Peter walked past the Jewish student dorm and noticed lights on behind some of the windows. When he reached the synagogue's large door, he tried to push it open, but without much conviction. What were the chances of it being unlocked?

Then he took a few steps back and peered upwards. A light burned on the first floor, but he couldn't see any movement. He stood with his hands on his hips, unsure what he should do next.

'Maybe this isn't the place they meant?' he muttered quietly to himself. There was a bandstand in the Leidse Hout city park where open air concerts were held in the summer. It was tent-like, almost a sort of baldaquin . . . But there was no connection between the bandstand and the Song of Songs. This *had* to be the place. There was nowhere else it could be.

If there was someone inside, they might know Judith, he realised. Judith had been studying her Jewish background for as long as he had known her. She had taken courses at the Centre for Jewish Studies which was in the same building as the synagogue.

Leiden was a small city. He had never met anyone with whom he didn't have an acquaintance in common.

Resolutely, he took a step forwards and pressed the doorbell. A loud buzz penetrated the silence and echoed in the hall.

This episode might end here if the person who opened the door handed him over to the police. But it would end here anyway if he didn't get inside and find out what was waiting for him.

After a few moments, he heard a muffled voice from the other side of the door. 'Hello?'

'Yes, um . . . I'm sorry for disturbing you so late,' Peter said, raising his voice slightly. 'I'm . . . Peter de Haan, a lecturer at the university. I'm a friend of Judith's, Judith Cherev.'

He heard the door being unlocked.

'Ah, Judith, of course,' the man said as he opened the door. He was heavy-set, in his fifties, with a bushy grey beard and laughter lines around his twinkling eyes. A pair of reading glasses hung from a cord around his neck. 'You're out rather late, aren't you?' He stood in the doorway, but he kept his hand on the door.

'May I come in?' Peter asked, putting his foot on the doorstep. The man was forced to move backwards slightly. 'It's a bit of an odd story,' Peter began.

'Is it about Judith?' the man asked, sounding concerned.

'Can I come in? Then I'll tell you.'

'Can't you tell me here, at the door?'

'I'm looking for her. She's . . . gone.'

The man recoiled slightly, moving backwards so that he was now a metre or so away from the doorstep where Peter was still standing. He gave Peter a puzzled look, as though he was trying to process what he had just been told.

Peter took out the copy of *The Hitchhiker's Guide to the Galaxy* and removed the note, keeping a finger between the book's pages. He gave the note to the man, who put on his glasses and read the text aloud.

Its posts are silver, its canopy gold; its cushions are purple.
It was decorated with love by the young women of Jerusalem.

'The Song of Songs,' he said wistfully. 'The wedding day of King Solomon . . . I've devoted a great deal of study to the Song of Solomon. But what's this all about?'

Barely twenty metres away, a police car approached along the Korevaarstraat. Suddenly its siren started to blare.

Peter jumped and took a step forward so that he ended up standing in the hall. 'King Solomon's wedding day, you said?'

The man sighed irritably and motioned Peter to come further. 'Daughters of Tziyon, come out, and gaze upon King Shlomo, wearing the crown with which his mother crowned him on his wedding day.'

Now it was Peter's turn to look puzzled.

'That's the next verse,' the man said, amused. He walked ahead of Peter, up the stairs. 'I know the whole thing off by heart. It's not really that much of an accomplishment, mind you. There are plenty of people who can recite the whole Koran.'

They came to a small landing with two doors. One of them was open.

'Come in,' he said. 'I don't live here, by the way. This is our reading room. I like to sit in here and study in the evenings. It's quiet here.'

An overflowing bookcase covered an entire wall of the large room. A long table stood in the middle, with six chairs arranged around it. In front of the window was a computer on a desk. The screen was filled with Greek text, and a weighty-looking book lay open next to the keyboard.

'Take a seat,' he said.

They sat, Peter on one side of the table and the man on the other.

'My name is Awram. You can just call me Abraham, or Ap, as they called me at high school.' He smiled. 'Judith is gone, you say? What's happened?'

Peter wasn't sure which version of the story to tell him or how much of the details he should reveal. He decided that if Awram knew Judith well enough to be worried about her, it was safe to trust him.

'Yes, Judith is gone. That's it in a nutshell anyway. I don't know where she is, but I think that whoever took her set up a route for me to follow, as mad as that sounds. My hope is that I'll find her if I follow all their clues. It started with a text message they sent me: "Follow the black raven."'

'Not, "follow the white rabbit"? Like in *Alice in Wonderland*?'

'No, the black raven . . . That took me to Quintus. They have ravens on their crest. And two stuffed ravens in their boardroom. That's where I found the clue that led me here, the one you just read. There was a clock counting down on the screen too. From twenty-four hours to zero. What time is it now?'

Awram glanced at the clock that hung on the wall behind Peter. 'Just gone eleven thirty. So . . .'

'So I have just over fourteen hours.'

'And what is the reason for this . . .' Awram hunted for the right word. ' . . . for this challenge? It's a little strange to give it to you out of the blue just to . . . Just to what, actually? What's at stake here?'

'I don't know,' Peter said.

'Does Mark know about this yet?' Awram asked. 'Don't look so surprised. Of course I know Mark too. Brilliant man.'

'No, no . . . Mark is in Germany, off the grid.'

Awram cocked his head to the side slightly, waiting for Peter to tell him more.

'Listen,' Peter began. 'A tunnel was discovered this afternoon, in town. Maybe you've heard about it. There was a ceremony to mark the installation of the first underground waste container. The ground subsided and a digger fell into the hole they had dug for the container. It turned out that there was a hollow space under it. I went down there with my boss, Arnold van Tiegem,

105

and then he just mysteriously disappeared.' He hesitated. 'And now . . . Now the situation is even more complicated because they think I had something to do with his disappearance. The police are looking for me.'

Awram stared at his hands on the tabletop in silence. Then he spoke. 'Tunnels under the city . . . I thought they were just rumours, stories you get in every town. There's supposed to be a tunnel right here under the synagogue, did you know? So that the Jews could escape if there was ever a pogrom. I've heard about tunnels leading from the Pieterskerk, the Hooglandse Kerk, the Burcht . . . According to those stories there's a whole labyrinth of tunnels beneath our feet, an underground city. Do you think it's true?'

'Haven't you ever—'

'Gone looking for them? No . . . I'm a man of books, not action. Words, rather than deeds, you might say.'

'So now I was wondering,' Peter said, thinking it was now high time for deeds rather than words, 'if I might take a look in the synagogue, because the quote from the Song of Songs refers to a baldaquin.'

'Oh you can take a look, certainly,' Awram said, 'but I shouldn't think you'll find anything. Our synagogue doesn't have a chuppah, or rather I should say, it doesn't have a permanent one. We don't have many Jewish weddings in Leiden, so it's not a huge problem. We do have a chuppah that we set up whenever there's a wedding, but that's neatly packed away elsewhere in the building. So there's not much for you to see in the synagogue itself, I'm afraid.'

'Can we go and have a look anyway?' Peter insisted. 'Even if it's just to rule this place out as a possibility. Then I know I need to look elsewhere.'

Awram pushed his chair back and went over to his desk. He pulled a drawer open and took out a bunch of keys. 'Then we'll go and look. Come on.'

Downstairs in the hall, they turned left and then went down a wide passage that led to a large, brown door.

'There were a couple of workmen from the council here this afternoon,' Awram said, putting the key in the lock. 'They hit a water main when they were working on the Korevaarstraat and they wanted to make sure that it hadn't caused any damage inside this building. I let them in, but I didn't hear them leave again, so I assumed that everything . . .' He turned around. 'Actually, now that I'm telling you about it, it does sound rather suspicious. They said they were working on those underground containers, but it's just occurred to me that they aren't installing them on this side of the street. Could it have . . .' he turned the key, pushed open the door, and then he froze in the doorway. 'What's this?' he whispered.

Peter stood on his tiptoes to look inside over Awram's shoulder.

The synagogue was shrouded in darkness but the chuppah had been set up in the middle of it, lit by a single spotlight like an exhibit in a museum.

Peter put his hand on Awram's shoulder and gently pushed him inside. The poor man stood gaping at the display as though he had never seen a chuppah in his life. Peter pushed past him to take a closer look at the canopy.

A sheet hung from the middle of the chuppah, gathered and knotted to the peak of the canopy. A photograph was pinned to the cloth.

Peter carefully lifted the photo away from the cloth, but it was too dark to see what was on it.

'Can you turn the lights on?' he asked.

Awram came out of his daze and flicked a switch, flooding the whole room in bright light.

'I could have sworn that they really were from the council,' Awram said apologetically. 'The boiler suits, the logo, the casual way they went about it . . .'

Peter unfastened the photograph and came out from under the chuppah to take a better look at it.

It was a picture of the side of a mountain. In the middle was a rocky outcrop that rose up into a form that looked like a face.

Once again, he had the vague feeling that he knew what he was looking at but couldn't identify it. Then he had a flash of recognition. He knew where the photo had been taken. In fact, there was a photograph in his own album that could have been a copy of this one.

While he felt relieved that he knew what he was looking at now, a sense of unease was rising inside him. How well did they know him, he wondered. How long had they been watching him?

A few summers ago, he'd taken a solo trip – he always travelled alone – along the west coast of Turkey. Naturally he had visited Ephesus, the archaeological remains of the temple to the ancient Greek fertility goddess, Artemis of Ephesus.

Did they know he had also visited the town of Manisa then, near Izmir?

Peter squinted, partly from irritation, partly to be able to see the photo better.

He had gone there to see the House of the Virgin Mary. According to legend, Jesus' mother had lived there after the death of her son.

The trip to the Weeping Rock had been an unexpected extra. He hadn't heard of it before, but the old man who had given him a little guided tour in exchange for *baksheesh* had told him about it. Although the sun's heat had been exhausting, the trek through the barren, rocky landscape, fragrant with the scent of herbs, had been breathtaking.

What had that been about, he asked himself, feverishly. It was Niobe, a character from Greek mythology. That much he could remember, but what was the story? It was a tragedy, obviously, she was Greek after all.

'Sorry, I . . . Have you ever heard of Niobe?' Peter asked, walking over to Awram to show him the photograph.

'Niobe . . .' Awram repeated uncertainly. 'I've heard the name, but I can't remember where from.'

Peter took out the phone to google it.

As usual, the first hit was a Wikipedia page. He read the text aloud, hoping that Awram would be able to help him in some way. As he read, he recalled snippets of information from the travel guide he'd read in Turkey.

'Niobe . . . the daughter of Tantalus. Zeus invited Tantalus to eat with the gods, but he brought about his own ruin by stealing their nectar and ambrosia so that his friends could eat like gods too. He was given an eternal punishment, made to stand in a pool of water forever, with a thirst he could never quench because the water receded each time he bent to take a drink. Boughs laden with fruit dangled above him, but he could never still his hunger because each time he reached up to pluck the fruit, the branches were raised above his grasp. And to make matters worse, a rock hung over his head that could fall and crush him at any moment . . . the Torment of Tantalus.'

'They had wonderful imaginations, the Greeks,' Awram said.

'It's about the universal human experience . . . It puts it into words quite well, actually. The feeling of not quite being able to have what you want, that it's always just out of reach.'

He read on. 'Niobe married Amphion, a Phrygian king and son of Zeus, with whom she had fourteen children, seven sons and seven daughters. She told the people of Thebes, where she lived, that she was more worthy of their adoration than the mother goddess Leto. Leto was invisible, while everyone could see Niobe. Moreover, Leto had only two children, while she had fourteen. A typical case of *hubris*, overconfidence, something for which the gods always meted out severe punishment. Leto's children, Apollo and Artemis, murdered Niobe's children, whereupon Amphion, her husband, committed suicide. Niobe fled to Mount Sipylus, the mountain on the photo, and turned to stone. The locals say that it's her face you can see in the rock, but it's more likely to be Cybele, another mother goddess . . .'

He scrolled down to the bottom of the page. 'There's even a chemical element named after her, Niobium. Nb, atomic number 41—' he muttered.

'Give that to me for a moment,' Awram interrupted him, taking the photograph from Peter's hand to bring it close to his eyes. 'It's definitely a face,' he said.

'She's cried since that day,' Peter explained, drawing on his own knowledge now. 'The rock is made of limestone. When the rainwater seeps through it, it really does look as though she's crying. A river starts where her tears fall.'

'But what does this have to do with Judith?'

'Everything, or so it seems . . . it's all to do with loss, grief, death . . .' Peter thought aloud.

The poem *The Raven* was about the loss of a loved one too, without the hope of seeing each other in the afterlife.

Did this mean that Judith was in grave danger, he thought, and a jolt of fear went through him. Was there much more at stake than he had realised?

'This really is extraordinary,' Awram said as he walked over to the chuppah. He gave the photograph back to Peter, who followed him in the hope that he would find something there that would clearly show him what the next step was supposed to be. Did they want him to go to Turkey? Is that what they were trying to tell him?

Awram stood under the sheet that hung from the chuppah. He took hold of one of its corners and spread it out. There was a hole in the middle, more of a slit, in fact, embroidered all around with grey flowers. He dropped the cloth again and let out a heavy sigh.

Now Peter picked up the corner of the sheet and spread it out, just as Awram had done. 'What sort of sheet is this?' he asked.

'This is . . .' Awram laughed dolefully. 'This is one of those things . . . Look.' He took the sheet from Peter's hand and angrily yanked it loose. It drifted onto the floor. He picked up one side of the cloth. 'Take hold of those two corners,' he ordered.

They spread it out, making it easier to see that there was an opening in the middle of it, a slit.

'This is one of those persistent stereotypes,' Awram said bitterly, 'that just won't go away. In some very orthodox groups, a couple lays this sheet over the woman when they're having sex. The man puts . . . well, I'm sure you understand what I mean. The idea is that while sex is a duty within marriage, particularly the sex that leads to procreation, one must be careful not to derive too much pleasure from it. It could lead you to fall away from God. Before you know it, you're addicted to sex to the exclusion of all other pursuits. It's never been an established part of Jewish culture, it was never a widespread practice. But you'll still find this story everywhere, even in serious journalism. It speaks to the imagination . . . It's rather sensational stuff, of course.'

Peter helped Awram to fold the sheet up again.

'What now?'

'Maybe the sheet is the clue?' Awram suggested. 'This sheet is so out of the ordinary . . . If it was just about the photo, they would have used a length of string, wouldn't they?'

Peter nodded. A thought slowly began to form in his head. 'I need to think about this properly. The sheet . . . It's something you just said . . .'

Awram looked at him sympathetically, wanting to help him, but not knowing how. 'The sheet . . . sex as a duty . . .' he offered, but Peter shook his head.

'Being careful not to derive too much pleasure from it,' Awram went on. 'Addiction . . .'

Peter buried his face in his hands. 'It's about self-control,' he said at last, rubbing his hands over his face.

'That's what Judaism strives to achieve, yes. Although I think that's true of all religions, isn't it? Curbing the impulses so as not to be constantly carried away by one's passions. It leaves you free to focus on what is actually good, on God . . .'

'It's a battle . . .'

'A little like Plato . . .'

In *Phaedrus*, one of his classic dialogues, Plato compared the soul to a charioteer who must control a pair of horses. The good horse represented the human will and determination, and the bad horse represented lusts and passions.

'Yes, exactly. But it's a common trope, overcoming appetites and desires. In Buddhism, they're thought to be the cause of human suffering. In Hinduism, if you focus on the transient, things that are temporary, you get stuck in an endless cycle of reincarnation. Your soul is trapped in the material, in the physical. It's an ancient theme that crops up in many stories. All those knights fighting dragons, the famous Saint George slaying his dragon, it's all about triumphing over our animalistic nature.'

Peter had the feeling that he was getting closer, but couldn't quite put his finger on exactly what it was that he was closer to. 'In Christianity there's the Apostle Paul, of course. He was concerned with . . .' he said tentatively. The more he thought about it, the more he felt it was something to do with Paul. The messages in Wickr, the references in the note, the scripture from Romans . . .

'Paul . . .' Awram repeated, thinking out loud with Peter. 'Paul said it was better for man not to touch a woman. There was nothing wrong with marriage, but it was better to remain single.'

'And that if you couldn't control yourself, then you ought to get married. Because it would be better to be married than to burn with passion,' Peter added. 'It's about the battle . . . Paul used the language of war in a lot of his writings.'

They were silent for a few moments.

'So then, let us cast off the deeds of darkness,' Peter said, quoting Paul's words, 'and put on the armour of light.'

'That's if it is about a battle . . . and if it's about Paul the Apostle . . .'

'I don't know, it's intuition. I feel like I'm getting closer.'

'I'm sure you're familiar with the scripture in Ephesians? Paul tells the people to put on the full armour of God so that they can defend themselves against the devil. The war isn't being fought against man.'

'Yes,' Peter said enthusiastically, 'and it's followed by that text describing a Roman soldier's uniform . . .'

'Exactly.'

'It might be what I'm looking for, but . . .' Peter said, sounding uncertain. 'To go from a sheet to a Roman's soldier's armour . . . I don't know.'

'It's not a direct link, but if you think that you need to be looking at Paul, then it's really not that far-fetched,' Awram reassured him.

Peter had an idea. 'Could I borrow your phone?' he asked. 'I want to call someone.'

He didn't want to use the phone that he'd found. Someone might be listening in on it somehow.

They went back downstairs to the study, and Peter sat at the table.

Awram handed over his mobile phone. 'The battery is almost dead. Sorry. My charger is at home. But I think it will last long enough for a quick call.' Then he opened a cupboard and placed the folded cloth inside. He shook his head. Peter couldn't tell if it was from vexation or disbelief.

Peter hardly knew any phone numbers by heart these days, but he could remember Fay Spežamor's. She was a professor *and* the curator of Roman and Etruscan Art at the National Museum of Antiquities. If anyone could tell him about the uniforms of Roman soldiers, it was her.

It was late, quarter past twelve. But he decided to take the chance.

He tapped in her number. Fay answered before the second ring.

'A very good morning to you,' she said cheerfully.

'Hello, Fay,' he said. 'It's Peter, Peter de Haan. Sorry . . .'

'Peter!' she said, sounding surprised. 'Gosh, that's weird. I was just thinking about you. What's going on? I heard they were looking for you!'

'Listen,' Peter cut her off, 'this is very important. It's true, they are looking for me, but it's not . . . It's complicated.'

'I'm listening.'

Peter hesitated. He didn't know where to begin, or which details were most important.

'I'll give you the short version. My good friend Judith Cherev, you know her, she's missing. I have to find her.'

'But the police . . .'

'I'm not allowed to ask for help.'

'So what are you doing right now?'

'I think they just mean the police. But listen . . . They told me I had to follow the black raven. Quintus has a pair of stuffed ravens, so I went there . . . I found a book with a note inside that led me to the synagogue on the Levendaal. That's where I am now. They had set up a chuppah, you know, what the bride and groom stand under.'

There was silence on the other end of the line, as though there was nobody there.

'Are you still there?' Peter asked, sounding desperate.

'Yes, yes I'm here, I'm just processing it all.'

'I'm sorry for calling you so late,' he went on, 'but right now I can't think of anyone else who might be able to help me.'

Another silence.

'They left another clue here in the synagogue. It looks like following the clues will lead me to Judith. Someone is playing a very strange game with me. The problem is, I don't know how to explain it. Just now, Awram and I, we—'

'A raven,' Fay interjected, 'a bridegroom . . .'

'Yes, what about them?'

'I think I can help you.'

'Really?' Peter asked hopefully.

'I know what you're looking for,' Fay said with certainty.

'What? What do I need to find?'

'You're looking for a soldier.'

THE SECOND VISION

And behold, I saw the young man again, a few years older now, standing on the square in front of the great temple, haggling with the high priest, a pile of hides already on his cart. He buys wholesale with his fellow craftsmen, the tent-makers like himself, the sandal-makers, and anyone else who makes things from leather. The hides are costly, an important source of income for the priests. The tent-maker is the spokesman for his group, silver-tongued, despite his limited command of the language of the Jews. He speaks Greek, and Latin also, and in a strange hotchpotch of these, peppered with Aramaic and a word of Hebrew here and there, he gets a good deal, time and time again.

And behold, she walks out from the atrium, the daughter of the high priest, how beautiful she is! Her eyes are like doves behind her veil. Her hair flows in waves like a herd of goats coming down the hills of Gilead. Her teeth are as white as ewes: like a flock of sheep coming up from washing, ready to be shorn, each one bearing twins and not one of them missing. Her lips are like a scarlet ribbon, her mouth is inviting. Her smile sparkles, her cheeks are like halves of a pomegranate behind her veil. Her neck is like the tower of David, built with courses of stone and hung with a thousand shields, all of them shields of warriors.

Her breasts are like the twin fawns of a gazelle that browse among the lilies.

And the tent-maker thinks: show me your face, let me hear your voice;

for your voice is sweet, and your face is lovely. You have stolen my heart, my bride, with one glance of your eyes, with one jewel of your necklace.

The high priest looks upon the young man who stands there as though he has been struck by lightning. And he looks at his daughter who nods at them kindly. He sees the leather worker with the filthy cap in his hands, the dirty nails, and the hands stained with blood and lye, the muck in the creases of his face, standing there on bow legs like a lovesick calf.

And the young man decides: I will have myself circumcised, I will change my name. From now on, I will be Saul, like the great king of old. For the Jews, I will be a Jew. He leaves the house of his Father, who lets him go, but with sorrow, for he has recently reached the second rung of the ladder. He undergoes the seven ritual baths, abstains from unclean food, and studies the books of the ancients, the Septuagint, since the Hebrew is too difficult for him.

And behold, he has himself circumcised, but a clumsy hand makes a bloodbath of it, a mutilation of his manhood. Time heals all wounds, but this disfigurement will last a lifetime. Urination is painful. He joins the temple guards to indulge the high priest. He is fanatical, zealous about the law, intolerant of deviations from doctrine. He is at the forefront of the battle, to be a Pharisee is his goal. His orders come from the high priest, and how the young man looks forward to each meeting with him and the opportunity it brings to see *her*, the most lovely of all women. Like a lily among thorns, so is his love among the young women.

And hark, there is Stephen speaking: 'You stiff-necked people, uncircumcised in heart and ears, you are forever opposing the Holy Spirit, just as your ancestors used to do! Which of the prophets did your ancestors not persecute? They killed those who foretold the coming of the Righteous One, and now you have become his betrayers and murderers. You are the ones that received the law as ordained by angels, and yet you have not kept it.'

And behold, when the people hear these things they are enraged, and grind their teeth at him. They cover their ears and all rush together at him, shouting loudly. Then they drag him out of the city and begin to stone him. And the witnesses lay down their cloaks at the young man's feet and they stone Stephen, who calls out, 'Lord Jesus, receive my spirit.' Then he kneels down and begs, 'Lord, do not hold this sin against them.' And when he has said these words, he dies. And Saul approves of his execution.

And behold, the labourer is rewarded fittingly. The high priest sends him on a secret mission to Damascus with a letter. He is entrusted with this, he has been chosen. And at last upon his return, he will be found worthy. He will ask for the daughter's hand. How sweet is your love, my bride! How much better is your love than wine, and your scent sweeter than any spice! Your lips drip nectar, my bride, honey and milk are under your tongue, the fragrance of your garments is like the fragrance of Lebanon.

And he goes on his way, with his helpers, the letter in a leather bag, hanging at his breast by a leather cord around his neck. As he spurs his horse on over the rough road that leads to Damascus, he thinks:

I am a Bridegroom.

15

MILES

SOLDIER

Twenty-one years earlier, spring 1994

In 1994, the archaeological theme park Archeon opened its doors in Alphen aan den Rijn. This presented the priest and his 'Knights of Christ' with a new target. The park was a living museum of the Stone Age, the Roman era and the Middle Ages in the Netherlands. There were buildings in the style of each period, and the staff dressed in costume to perform historical re-enactments of typical activities like baking bread on open fires, pottery making and archery.

There was also a temple dedicated to Nehalia or Nehalennia, a fertility goddess from the region now known as the Belgian North Sea Coast and Dutch Zeeland. She was a Celtic or Germanic goddess, worshipped by travellers, particularly sailors and merchants. Her devotees made offerings of food to her and pledged to erect altars to her upon their safe return.

When one of the knights told him about the park, the priest was initially unsure how it might be relevant to their war on faithlessness. But when he understood that the park not only had a pagan temple, but that the public was entertained there twice a day with ritual offering ceremonies, he knew he had to act. While these rituals looked like innocent fun, they were disturbingly real. Two 'history interpreters' dressed as priestesses lit a flame in an offering bowl and invited the spectators to offer leaves, berries or ears of corn and beseech the goddess to bless all their endeavours. Though they thought it was only make-believe, it would allow Satan to gain access to the unsuspecting audience. Even worse, to the innocent souls of the little children who did not yet know that the devil prowled around like a roaring lion looking for someone to devour.

One of his fellow knights suggested that they take their own offering bowl with them, pour water over the wood inside it and then ask God to send down fire from heaven, but he would not allow it. It had worked for Elijah once, of course, but would God give such a sign these days? Their plan would literally be dead in the water if the fire from heaven did not arrive. Much simpler would be to kick over their burning offering bowl, and tell the crowd a story about Jesus as the light of the world. They would draw a parallel between the flames of the burnt offering and the fires of hell that awaited them if they did not repent and come to the true and only God.

There were thirteen of them that day. They bought tickets at the entrance, some of them grudgingly, complaining that they didn't want to give Archeon any financial support. They rode to the temple on the white bicycles that the park provided free to visitors. 'I'm a knight on a steed of steel,' one of them joked.

The twelve knights pedalled behind the priest, two-by-two.

Afterwards, some of them said that the fit had been triggered by the stroboscopic flickering of sunlight through the trees. As the temple came into view, he was suddenly surrounded by a light from heaven. He fell from his bike and heard a voice saying to him: 'Why are you persecuting me?'

The priest replied: 'Who are you?'

The answer came: 'I am who I am. I have many faces. I am the one you are persecuting. It hurts you to keep on kicking against the goads.'

The men who had travelled with him were stunned. Some said that they heard a voice but saw no one speaking. Others said later that they had seen the light but heard no voice.

But eventually they roused themselves to action, because their leader lay shaking and trembling on the ground, with white foam around his mouth. They saw how his lips moved, as though in conversation with an invisible partner. Someone put their fingers in his mouth to stop him from swallowing his tongue, and another put a wooden stick between his teeth. The priest was aware of none of this; he was being held spellbound by something else entirely.

The voice said to him: 'Now get up and stand on your feet. I have appeared to you to appoint you as my servant. Because you will be a witness of what you have seen and what I will show you. I will protect you from the world into which I am sending you so that you may open the people's eyes and turn them from darkness to light, and from the power of Satan to God. So that they may receive forgiveness for their sins and a place among those who are sanctified by faith in me.'

The priest grew calm and stood up, but although his eyes were open, he could not see.

One of the temple priestesses, who had been trained in first aid, came rushing over. When she discovered that he had lost his sight, she radioed the reception who called for an ambulance. She introduced herself as Florine, and held his hand until the paramedics arrived.

The priest sat on the ground and leaned against Florine, who had sat down behind him. He felt the warmth of her body through her clothes. It was wonderfully reassuring. For a few moments, he felt like a small boy being comforted by a teacher after falling over on the playground.

'They'll be here soon,' she said to him soothingly. 'Don't you worry. Everything will be all right.'

When he was eventually lifted onto the stretcher he was sorry to have to leave her.

He lay in the hospital for three days. He refused to eat or drink, like a saint who has undertaken to fast in order to find the answer to a troubling question. They gave him fluids through an IV drip against his will.

At the end of the third day, he felt the presence of someone next to his bed. They did not speak.

'Who's there?' he said nervously.

There was no answer.

'Who's there?' he said again.

'Ane,' said a voice. It sounded familiar. 'Florine told me what happened. She recognised you from your protests at our lectures every month.'

The priest tried to sit up, but immediately fell back onto his pillow.

'Florine is a witch . . .' The priest could hear that Ane was smiling as he spoke. ' . . . in the positive sense of the word. She's a follower, if you can call it that, of Wicca, the pagan religion. You know of it, I'm sure. The role of priestess at Archeon is more than just a role to her. The moment she puts on her costume, she *is* that priestess.' Ane grasped the priest's arm. 'She felt something,' he said, not removing his hand, 'a strong presence, an experience she's never had before. You looked like you were speaking to someone. She heard the voice too.'

The priest slowly nodded.

'I think I know what happened,' Ane said. 'I've also had visions. About you. I know that you intended to harm us, and that you would very much like to see us all locked up. But I believe that you've been chosen as an instrument to spread our message. The one who appeared to you at Archeon has sent me to you, to make you see again.'

Then it was as though scales fell away from the priest's eyes. When he opened them, he could see again. He stood up and washed his face with cold water. He ate the lunch that had been left in his room despite his refusal to eat, and he felt his strength return.

A nurse came by to check on him. When she realised that her patient had regained his sight, she promptly summoned the doctor on call. The doctor carried out a few quick tests, and decided that he would examine the priest that afternoon to check that there was no permanent damage.

'Can you remember what happened?' Ane asked.

'It was . . .' The priest tried to find words to describe what he had experienced over the last three days. 'It was indeed as though someone was speaking to me. Just as you and I are speaking to each other now. It was so real. I didn't see anyone at first, only a bright light. But then a voice came from within the light and spoke to me. That girl heard it too?'

'Not everything, but she certainly caught some of it. Some of your "knights" . . .' There was a note of mild derision in his voice as he said the word. ' . . . believe that they also heard the voice. Others said that they saw the light, but heard no voice.'

'You've spoken to them?'

'Some of your "followers" were here when I visited a day or two ago. I can't say they were very friendly. They were curious to know what I thought I was doing here. They were of the opinion that I should leave you alone.'

'And yet they still told you . . .'

'And yet they still told me that they had seen a light or heard a voice, yes. They were quite certain that it was—'

'Saint Paul!' the priest burst out.

'Yes, Saint Paul, precisely. They told me because, of course, they could also see the similarities between what happened to you, and what happened to Paul on the road to Damascus. He was on his way to fight against what he saw as heresy too. His plan was to arrest the members of the new Christian sect and take them back to Jerusalem. He also fell, and a divine voice spoke to him. The parallels are very clear of course. Your colleagues described it as sign, a sign from God. And *that* is why they told me. They wanted to show me that God is on their side. Your side, of course, not mine.'

'The words I heard were almost literally the same ones that Paul heard when he fell from his horse.'

'Almost the same?'

'Yes, almost but not exactly. There was one difference . . . It wasn't Christ who spoke to me.' He sat up. 'The voice wasn't a man's or a woman's. I couldn't tell you which, nor who it was that I saw. It was a sort of . . . light. Sometimes they disappeared into the light and sometimes it actually made them clearly visible, as clear as I see you now. I felt like I might have been able to touch them. And it was as though the presence wanted me to understand that what I was doing was not good, that I was persecuting something that has no evil in it.'

The priest stopped talking and remained silent for a long time, staring blankly in front of him. 'I'm trying to find the right words. The person didn't speak, as such. Their lips didn't move. I heard the voice in my head, so real, as though someone was saying the words out loud. As though they wanted to say . . .'

'As though they wanted to say what?'

'As though they wanted to say . . . "Why are you persecuting me?" That's what the voice said. As Jesus asked Paul, but then the other way around, as it were. Why was I persecuting others in Jesus' name? And the oddest thing is, it felt good, peaceful. It wasn't judgemental, I wasn't being admonished. It was more . . . more like they were taking an interest, a genuine interest. And I didn't know what to say in reply.'

Ane nodded understandingly and appeared to be very pleased by what he was hearing.

'I still need to process it all. It really was a very strange experience. And now this conversation with you . . . This feels strange too. I don't feel any hostility just now, not within myself and not between us either. I feel like I've been given great insight, but I don't know what it might be about. Is this making sense at all, Ane? Or am I raving?'

Ane smiled and put a reassuring hand on the priest's arm.

'Have you always had these fits, Tiny? May I call you Tiny?'

Tiny nodded.

'I remember you having a fit during one of your protests.'

The priest gave him a pained smile, as though he preferred not to be reminded of it.

'Since puberty.' Tiny explained, 'They didn't happen often . . . but enough to have an impact on my life. They were at their worst during puberty. Tests, drugs . . . it was all quite unpleasant for a boy of course. Not being allowed to cycle home from school on my own, going to bed on time, having to leave school parties early and so on. It can be kept under control if I take my medication, and even more so if I stick to a routine, don't go to bed too late and . . .'

'Don't get too wound up,' Ane said, smiling.

'Precisely, if I don't get too wound up. And that's exactly what I often did outside your meetings, let myself get wound up. I'm sure that was part of what caused the attack at Archeon. Although it's likely that the sunlight flickering between the trees played a part too.'

'Have you looked into it? Epilepsy?'

'I've not really studied it, no. It's something that I need to be aware of in my daily life, but I've never looked into it deeply. Not in the way you mean.'

'The Greeks thought it was a holy sickness. Did you know that? It's still considered to be divine in many primitive cultures.

They believe that the fit brings the sufferer in direct contact with their god or goddess, or whichever deity their culture worships. The word "epilepsia" even means something like "to take possession of".'

'That could also be the devil.'

'It's often interpreted that way, yes. You know the story of Jesus healing the boy possessed by a demon. When you read it . . .' He reached over to the nightstand next to the bed and took the small Gideon bible out of the drawer. He leafed through the Gospel of Mark and quickly found what he was looking for. He read it aloud:

And he asked them, 'What are you arguing about with them?' And someone from the crowd answered him, 'Teacher, I brought my son to you, for he has a spirit that makes him mute. And whenever it seizes him, it throws him down, and he foams and grinds his teeth and becomes rigid. So I asked your disciples to cast it out, and they were not able.' And he answered them, 'O faithless generation, how long am I to be with you? How long am I to bear with you? Bring him to me.' And they brought the boy to him. And when the spirit saw him, immediately it convulsed the boy, and he fell on the ground and rolled about, foaming at the mouth. And Jesus asked his father, 'How long has this been happening to him?' And he said, 'From childhood. And it has often cast him into fire and into water, to destroy him. But if you can do anything, have compassion on us and help us.'

Ane closed the bible and put it back in the drawer. He continued the story himself. 'Jesus prays, and after a great deal of screaming and convulsing, the evil spirit leaves the boy. And afterwards, the boy appears to be dead. But Jesus takes him by the hand to help him to his feet, and he stands up.'

'How stupid of me,' the priest responded. 'It never occurred to me that it was about an epileptic fit . . . Nor the story about the boy who is possessed by a whole legion of demons. Jesus orders the spirits in that boy to go into a group of pigs, and the pigs all rush off a cliff and drown in the sea.'

'That's right,' Ane agreed, 'and there are other examples. It was explained in terms of possession and evil spirits in those days because they had no understanding of what was really happening. And a fit can look frighteningly violent of course.' He seemed to hesitate, but then he continued. 'Nineteenth-century psychiatrists began to notice that their epilepsy patients were often very religious, particularly those patients with temporal lobe epilepsy. Some people thought that many of the saints might also have been epileptic, the most famous example, of course, being Saint Paul, who said he had spoken with Jesus during a fit. And many epilepsy sufferers have had intense religious experiences during their episodes. Take Joseph Smith, who founded the Mormons . . . Supposedly, he had a fit when he was fourteen that made him feel like he had been possessed by a strange force. Everything around him went dark, and a pillar of light appeared above his head and slowly descended towards him. Then he saw two people who told him that not a single one of the existing churches or sects was preaching the truth. Smith said that the two people were God and Christ.'

'Why are you telling me all of this?'

'Isn't it clear that you've just experienced something similar? You've had an encounter, you saw a person and light. You say that you feel you've received great insight, but that you don't know how to put it into words yet.'

'I had a strong feeling of . . . How can I describe it? As I said, the person asked me a question, quite a confrontational question in fact, but I didn't feel like I was being judged. Actually, it felt like the opposite of that, as though they understood me. There was . . . love. An enormous feeling of love. I can't describe it in any other way. And I had an intense feeling of unity, of space and timelessness. I couldn't possibly say how long the whole experience lasted. It might have been less than a second. I don't know.'

'Listen to me,' Ane said, 'you've had what we would call an encounter with the source of our existence. There are people who . . . We have a group. I can introduce you. They know I'm here with you now.'

'A group? What sort of group? I don't know if that's what I want. I'm still trying to understand all this. I'm a member of just *one* group, and that's the Roman Catholic Church . . .'

'I don't think that needs to change, even after you've processed what I believe has happened to you. You can still be a priest, the Father you are now, but with a different purpose. I suspect that your daily rituals will stay almost exactly the same. We're really not so very different from you.'

'I don't understand any of this,' the priest said, suddenly feeling exhausted. 'I think I'd like to sleep now. Let's speak again, provided I don't change my mind in the meantime.'

Ane stood up to leave.

'This group of yours,' the priest said. 'When was it formed? How long have you been meeting?'

Ane paused before he answered. The corners of his mouth rose for a fraction of a second, more of a muscle twitch than a smile. 'For more than two thousand years.'

16

'You're looking for a soldier,' Fay had said.

Had he and Awram been on the right track after all? The sheet with the hole in it to curb the lusts that accompanied reproduction . . . the eternal battle against being carried away by irrational impulses, humans as soldiers who had to arm themselves against unseen enemies from within and without . . .

Peter wasn't entirely convinced yet, but waiting for Fay seemed to be the best option right now. Because as far as he could see, this was all he had to go on. He stood up and gave the phone back to Awram, who was reading something on his computer. The phone died with a soft bleep.

'One of my friends is coming over,' Peter said. 'She thinks she can help me. It's strange, she said "soldier" straight away . . . the same conclusion we eventually came to. As soon as she gets here, we'll leave. I've imposed on you too much already.'

'No, no, it's quite all right.'

Peter sat down and they were quiet for a while.

'What are you working on, if you don't mind me asking?' Peter said, breaking the silence. He nodded at the computer.

'Well, believe it or not, I've been rather busy with Paul. Although I'm actually always busy with Paul in one way or another. I might spend my days studying the Torah, but he's always there in the background. I suppose you could say he's a recurring theme in my life.'

'What do you mean by that?'

'Paul is . . . I really do have a love/hate relationship with that man. First, he was a fanatical Jew who actively persecuted Christians. Then he suddenly became a Christian who tried to win Jewish souls for those very same Christians! I consider Paul to be the founder of Christianity. He was the one who ultimately caused the irreconcilable schism between Jesus' followers, who were all Jewish, and the other Jews.'

Awram sighed, as though he was trying to gather the strength to continue. 'At the time, the Jews had no problem with Jesus,' he told Peter. 'There was room for him alongside traditional Judaism . . . Of course, you know Jews love a good discussion. There's nothing they like doing more than *lernen*, studying and exchanging ideas, sometimes quite heatedly. What does this passage mean? Doesn't it contradict that text there? What did this scholar say about it? And what was that scholar's response? If it's forbidden to make a fire on the Sabbath, does the same go for turning on an electric light? And how do we interpret laws that were written two thousand, three thousand years ago for modern life? That's how Jews are, and how they have always been. These are the things Jesus discussed with the scholars of the Jewish law, the Pharisees. Is it permitted to heal someone on the Sabbath? If you are walking through a field on the Sabbath and pluck and eat an ear of corn, does that count as work? Should a woman literally be stoned if she has committed adultery, or is there room for clemency? As I said, Jews love discussion. Put two Jews in a room and you'll hear three opinions . . . It's an art, a way of life . . . So, contrary to what the Gospels would have us believe, Jesus wasn't really seen as a disruptive influence.'

129

'But what about all the stories in the Gospels about Jesus clashing with the Pharisees?' Peter asked. 'He called them a brood of vipers.'

Awram smiled with amusement, like a teacher enjoying being challenged by an intelligent student. 'Listen, I don't need to lecture you on the Gospels. The earliest Gospel is Mark, written somewhere around AD 70, so about forty years after Jesus' death. Paul writes his first letters in the mid-forties of that century. All of his letters and the ones that have been attributed to him, those are all older than the Gospels. It's only because they appear after the Gospels in the New Testament that people think otherwise. But Paul was the first to record his ideas about Jesus. *His own* ideas, mind you, Paul's. They conflicted with those of Jesus' first followers, and of Jesus' brother James and all the others who travelled with him who heard him speak, who saw him perform all those miracles that have been attributed to him. Just imagine being one of Jesus followers, *knowing* what he had said and done. Then along comes someone who has never met Jesus . . . trying to tell you what Jesus *really* meant, what his message *really* was, and that his message was much less stringent than the one you were used to. That you didn't need to be circumcised in order to belong, that you didn't need to adhere to all the strict religious laws, that you could eat whatever you wanted. They were furious of course, as you might imagine. They said: "What do you know about it? You never even met him. Surely, we're the ones who truly know what he meant? We're the ones who sat around the fire with him when he told his stories . . . Jesus told *us* what their deeper meanings were. We were there when he gave people hope, when he opened the eyes of the blind and made the lame walk again. We're the ones who heard him say that he hadn't come to abolish the law or the writings of the prophets, but to fulfil them." And they added that Jesus himself had assured them that until the heaven and the earth disappeared, every letter, every pen-stroke of the law would still be valid.'

'But wasn't their distrust caused more by the fact that Paul had first persecuted the Christians and then joined them?' Peter asked.

'Listen, Peter, the whole idea of Paul as a persecutor of Christians . . . there wasn't even any such thing as a Christian in those days. In the Book of Acts, Paul describes the lives of the Followers of the Way, as Jesus' disciples were called. He says that they all met in the temple together, faithfully, every day. In the temple! Just like all the other Jews. Nobody stood in their way. They followed Jesus as their teacher just like other people followed other rabbis.'

'So what about the trip to Damascus?'

'Paul's? So, he falls from his horse, sees a bright light, and hears a voice – depending on which of the three or four versions of the story you read – and thinks it must be Jesus . . . It's a clever piece of historical fabrication. Jesus' followers meet together every day in the temple in Jerusalem without being arrested. There doesn't appear to have been any conflict at all, but we're to believe that Paul went all the way to Damascus to prosecute Christians? This was in the year 32 or 33, not long after Jesus' death. There were only a handful of his followers left in Jerusalem. How many do you think there would have been in Damascus by then? And anyway, it really wasn't up to Paul. He had no authority to arrest anyone there. And then? So let's say he arrested "all those Christians", Awram drew quotation marks in the air with his middle and index fingers. 'What then? Would he have dragged them all the way back to Jerusalem to hand them over to the Romans? Those Romans would have seen him coming! As far as they were concerned, the problem had already been dealt with when they crucified Jesus. Were Jesus' followers harassed by the Romans after his death? Were they made to leave Jerusalem and spend their lives on the run? No, they all carried on living in Jerusalem and came together . . .' And now Awram slammed his hand flat on the table with every word. ' . . . every single day in the temple.'

'So what's—'

'The whole story is nonsense. The Romans left them alone, the other Jews, the ones who didn't follow Jesus, they left them alone too. But Paul went to Damascus . . . He probably did make that journey, but for another reason. Maybe he was a messenger, delivering a letter. Who knows?'

Peter opened his mouth to say something, but then thought better of it.

'And what many people don't realise,' Awram continued, 'is that Paul waited three full years after his so-called "conversion" to Christianity before he went back to Jerusalem. Three years! Surely, after such a life-changing experience he would have been eager to go back to see the people who had known Jesus personally? But he waits three years, goes back and stays with James for two weeks, and meets Peter, but no one else. Wouldn't you think he'd stay as long as possible so that he could meet as many of the people who had known Jesus as he could? But no, he stays for two weeks, hardly speaks to anyone, then leaves and doesn't come back for another fourteen years.' Awram took out a handkerchief and wiped his brow.

'Where has Fay got to?' Peter thought out loud. 'She should have been here by now.'

He had called her more than twenty minutes ago. To distract himself from his growing nervousness, he decided to continue the conversation with Awram. 'But as a Pharisee, a law scholar, it would have been logical for Paul—'

'Paul a Pharisee?' he said cynically. 'No man, don't be ridiculous. That's just another myth. It doesn't stand up to scrutiny at all.'

'But what about his famous words? How do they go again? That he was circumcised on the eighth day and was one of the people of Israel, of the tribe of Benjamin, a Hebrew of Hebrews and, in regard to the law, a Pharisee? He was born a Jew.'

'Yes, yes,' Awram said, unimpressed, 'and studied under Gamaliel and thoroughly trained in the laws of the ancestors.'

'Yes! That!'

'But those are all his words, his testimony,' Awram said, sounding tired. 'Really, I've had this discussion so many times. And whenever I do, I ask the same question and no one can answer it: can you show me a single conflict between the views of the Pharisees and the so-called new ideas of Jesus? This Gamaliel, this doctor of the Pharisee law, he's the one who defends the Christians in Acts. Here . . .'

He got up and went over to the bookcase to get a bible. He flipped furiously through the pages until he found the scripture he was looking for.

'Listen, Acts, chapter 5, verse 33 to 42 . . . It's right *there*. What I find so infuriating is that it's all so clear. For goodness sake, you don't have to spend years studying to be able to see it, but everyone just parrots what everyone else has said. Here, it says that the members of the Sanhedrin, the Jewish Court, explode in anger when the Apostle Peter and the others tell them that they intend to carry on telling people about Jesus, even though they've been forbidden to do so. And then old Gamaliel gets up to defend them and says:

> So in the present case, I tell you, keep away from these men
> and let them alone; because if this plan or this undertaking
> is of human origin, it will fail; but if it is of God, you will
> not be able to overthrow them – in that case you may even
> be found fighting against God!

He slammed the book closed and put it on his desk. 'And Paul apparently studied with him?' he said fiercely. 'With this Jewish scholar who is actually the only person speaking up for Jesus' followers? And then Paul is supposed to have persecuted the very Christians that his teacher had just defended? The alleged hatred that the "Jewish" Paul had for Christians isn't explained anywhere, and it would make even less sense if he really was Gamaliel's pupil. I don't believe it at all. Paul, this fake Pharisee, only ever quotes the Old Testament from the Greek translation of the Old Testament, which is full of errors. A true Pharisee would never have done that. Because obviously they read the Tanakh in Hebrew. And Paul even quotes scriptures that no one has ever been able to find in any of the Jewish literature. In 1 Corinthians he writes: ". . . that Christ died for our sins according to the Scriptures, that he was buried, that he was raised on the third day according to the Scriptures". But twenty centuries have passed and nobody has found the passage where that's written. The Messiahs had to meet many conditions, dozens of them – and Jesus doesn't meet a single one, by the way – but the vicarious suffering and rising from the dead on the third day in order to finish the job at an undetermined time in the future? That's not one of them. Judaism doesn't have the concept of the need for a saviour, the idea is blasphemous. Like Jesus, we believe that anyone who comes to God in faith and repentance will be given absolution. Human sacrifice isn't necessary. Jesus never said that he would suffer instead of others, that he would take their sins upon himself . . .'

He wiped his brow again. 'A pupil of the great scholar Gamaliel, my eye!' He laughed bitterly. 'It would be like saying that you'd studied with Sartre, but then fought people with whom Sartre had no problem, and only quoted his work in English because you don't speak French.'

'But this all suggests that there *was* conflict, doesn't it? The disciples were *forbidden* to talk about Jesus, weren't they?'

'Yes, but every "so-called conflict" . . .' He drew quotation marks in the air again. ' . . . between Jesus and the scholars that we read about in the New Testament is actually the conflict that Paul had with the Pharisees, *after* Jesus' death. The Gospels were written *after* Paul had won the argument with the original followers about how the good news should be spread. Paul's conflict with the Jews, both the Pharisees and the first council, appears in the New Testament as a conflict between Jesus and the Pharisees. As I've already said, there was room for Jesus alongside conventional Judaism. My Father's house has many rooms.' Awram stopped, as though he wanted to tell Peter something else but wasn't sure that he should.

Peter looked at the clock.

'Fay's been on her way for almost half an hour,' he said anxiously. 'Something must have happened.'

'I want to tell you one more thing,' Awram said, 'then I'll stop talking. You should consider the possible consequences of all this: Paul wasn't a Pharisee, wasn't Gamaliel's pupil . . . And that's not all.' He paused for dramatic effect. 'I'm convinced that Paul wasn't even a Jew. He was a Greek. Epiphanius quotes the Gospel of the Ebionites . . .' He shook his finger to emphasise the importance of what he was about to say. But he didn't get the chance to say it.

The doorbell rang in the hall downstairs.

Relieved, Peter got up to put on his coat. He walked out to the landing.

Out of habit, Awram went to the window to see who was at the door. 'Wait!' Awram called out to Peter, who was hovering at the top of the stairs. Awram turned away from the window and looked at him intensely. 'The police are at the door.'

17

'How did they know I was—' Peter gasped.

The bell rang again, for longer this time.

Awram tapped on the window and waved at an officer who was standing next to the police car. He pointed to himself and then down at the street to indicate that he would come to the door.

'Hurry,' Awram said to Peter, who was still on the landing. 'There's a door downstairs that leads to the dormitory next door. Go through it, walk down the hall and leave by their front door. But wait five minutes. I'm sure they'll be gone by then.'

They went down the stairs. Awram pointed at the door that led to the student dorm. 'Because you're Mark and Judith's friend. Their friends are my friends,' he said in parting.

As Peter closed the door to the dorm behind him, he heard Awram open the front door and greet the policemen with a friendly 'shalom'.

Peter found himself in a long corridor with two doors covered in posters and postcards. There were two toilets at the end of the corridor, and since he had to wait anyway, he took the opportunity to use one of them. He sat down and took the paperback book with the note from Song of Songs out of his pocket.

'What am I supposed to do with this?' he muttered. He opened the book at the place where the note was, and began to scan page 42. Then he read page 43. Neither of them appeared to contain any hidden messages. He read the quotation on the note again.

Its posts are silver, its canopy gold; its cushions are purple.
It was decorated with love by the young women of Jerusalem.

The text about the canopy had brought him here, and that had led to the photograph of Niobe, the weeping rock. Hubris, loss, grief and death . . . Nevermore . . . battling your carnal nature, freeing yourself from your inner demons . . .

What was going on? How had he, of all people, ended up being involved in this? And Judith . . . Where was she? What if something terrible had happened to her?

He flushed.

Why was Fay taking so long to arrive? Where was she?

He went to the front door. As he reached for the handle, he heard a door open in the corridor.

A boy in old-fashioned striped pyjamas stepped into the hall. He looked half asleep; the creases from his bedsheets were still on his cheeks. At first, his sleepy gaze was fixed on the screen of his phone. The soft blue glow lit up his face. But then he saw Peter and froze. 'What are you doing here?' he asked, his voice trembling slightly. He held his phone in both hands, almost as though he thought it could steady him.

'I was just visiting Awram,' Peter replied at once. 'I work at the university . . . I needed to discuss something with him.'

The boy narrowed his eyes.

'Do you live here?' Peter asked, trying to sound genuinely interested.

137

'Why are you going out this way?' the boy asked with remarkable politeness. 'Were you really on your way out?'

'Awram couldn't find the front door key,' Peter answered. He was starting to feel anxious now. This conversation was taking too long. 'You know what he's like, absent-minded professor. He said it would be all right if I went out this way instead.' He opened the front door to show he was telling the truth, then turned around to say goodbye as calmly as he could. But before he could say anything, the boy took a photograph of him.

'I'm calling the police,' the boy said firmly. He went back to his room and locked his door behind him.

When he got outside, Peter swore under his breath. He looked nervously to his left. The police car had already gone, but who knew how soon it would be back if the boy really did call the police.

Before he'd even reached the corner of the street, something caught his eye. Someone was standing under the trees by the entrance to the Van der Werfpark.

Peter stopped cold. He began to raise his fists, ready to fight.

'Here,' the person whispered, waving their right arm wildly like someone greeting a long-lost relative at Schiphol airport.

Peter took a few halting steps towards the figure under the trees. They stepped out from the shadows and stood in the pool of light cast by the streetlamp. Now Peter could see who it was.

Fay.

Peter ran over to her. 'What are you doing here?' he said urgently. 'Why didn't you come to the synagogue like we'd agreed?'

'I got held up, sorry. I couldn't find the key . . . I wanted to show you something. I tried the number you called me on but it went straight to voicemail. Then when I got to the synagogue, there was a police car outside . . .'

'The phone's battery died. Sorry.'

Peter looked into Fay's face. She was about the same age as him and had an unmistakably Slavic appearance. Her parents were Czech and had fled to the Netherlands during the Prague Spring, bringing the teenaged Fay with them. Her husband had died from cancer shortly after the birth of their daughter Agapè. Although her tremendous grief was etched on her face, she was still a beautiful woman.

Peter had only met her a handful of times, but they had clicked straight away. He had once joined one of the guided tours she gave of her department. Fay turned out to have a gift for taking a seemingly insignificant artefact and telling her audience a long, fascinating story about it from memory. She could draw so many lines of history together around one little vase or tiny pin, that her audience would wonder why it hadn't been given a more prominent place in the collection.

'Is something wrong, Peter?'

He was still on his guard, but he knew he had no other option than to let Fay in. She was the only person who might be able to help him now.

'Which key were you looking for?' he asked. 'And what did you mean when you said I was looking for a soldier?'

'Slow down, Peter. You seem very jittery.'

'A lot has happened. Sorry. But—'

'I was looking for the key to get into the museum. We can go via the Papengracht entrance,' she said as she walked into the park. 'What's happened to Judith?' she asked.

'I don't know. She's gone. I have to find her. There are clues that I . . . What are we going to do in the museum?'

'Does the name Mithras mean anything to you?'

'Erm . . . no, not much I'm afraid. I know it's the name of a god from one of the mystery religions. One where you had to be initiated before you could join . . . is that the soldier you meant?'

'Yes, it was a soldiers' religion. Or at least one that was very appealing to soldiers. Mithraism was a huge rival to Christianity until the Roman Empire made Christianity its official religion at the end of the fourth century. Today's Christians could just have easily been Mithraists. There was very little difference between them. But Christianity won, and history is always written by the winners, so now we're Christians.'

Peter felt a chill go through his body. It was like listening to his old tutor, Pieter Hoogers, again.

'Mithraism has been declared historical myth and Christianity has become historical fact.'

'The difference being,' Peter said, 'that Jesus really existed and Mithras didn't.'

'We don't know that for certain, but my point is that we've decided that exactly the same rituals and stories are myth in the case of one religion and fact in the other. It's like telling children that *Sinterklaas* is real, but Father Christmas isn't.'

'But . . . the soldier?'

They walked briskly out of the park and then along the Rapenburg canal. It was completely deserted at this time of night.

'Oh yes, right! So, when you told me about following the black raven and the Quintus ravens and the bridegroom under the chuppah, the penny dropped. Raven, bridegroom . . . soldier.'

Peter looked at her, perplexed.

'Mithras had seven stages of initiation, because in those days they only knew about five planets – Saturn, Jupiter, Mars, Venus and Mercury – plus the sun and the moon, making seven. At each stage, there was a different ritual. After you'd completed it, you achieved a new grade within the order, with new rights, but also new responsibilities. That's how you progressed.'

Is all this a sort of initiation ritual, Peter asked himself. *Is that why I'm doing this? Am I supposed to prove my worth?* 'You've been chosen,' Raven had told him.

They went over the Doelenbrug and onto Houtstraat which led to the Papengracht. Before long, they were standing outside the museum's staff entrance. Fay opened the door and disarmed the security system. There was a short beep, and then they closed the door behind them.

'The first grade is the raven, or *corax* in Latin,' Fay said, continuing her explanation. 'The raven is connected to the air element, and to the planet Saturn. You would have been a raven for quite a long time because you had to learn to completely identify with the raven, as it were. You were expected to leave your home and family during this stage, travel, go out into the world. After you were initiated, you became a sort of courier, you'd go back and forth as a messenger between the different Mithras temples, and stay with the other followers of Mithras.'

'And the second?'

'And the second grade is the bridegroom.'

Peter and Fay walked through a chamber with a very high ceiling. A door brought them into the museum bookshop. They walked past the Temple of Taffeh which had been rescued from Egypt in the 1960s when large areas of the country were flooded during construction of the Aswan High Dam.

The museum's entrance barriers were closed, but Fay opened them with a magnetic swipe card.

'Are there any cameras here?'

'Yes,' Fay answered. To emphasise her words, she gave one of the security cameras a thumbs-up. Peter put his head down and looked at the floor.

'They know me,' Fay told him reassuringly. 'They're probably not even watching . . .'

'So, the bridegroom.'

'Oh yes, the bridegroom. During the initiation rituals for the second grade, you sort of get married to Mithras, to the sun. A mystical marriage. They sometimes called Mithras *sol invictus*, the invincible sun. Not entirely uncoincidentally, there was a holiday on December twenty-fifth, three days after the winter solstice. To celebrate light's triumph over darkness.'

'Oh yes, I know that story. The pagan festival was so popular that they couldn't eradicate it, so the Catholic church thought: fine, then we'll celebrate the birth of Jesus on that date too. After all, he's also the light that's come to illuminate a dark world.'

'Spot on!'

They took the stairs to the first floor where the Roman artefacts were displayed.

'You can find the remains of the Mithraea, the temples to Mithras, all over Europe. There are more than a hundred of them in Rome alone. They're in London, in Tienen in Belgium . . . And here in Holland too, under the Reformed Church in Elst, and there's one in Helden in Limburgh. There are tonnes of them in Germany, France, Spain, and in Eastern Europe as well, Egypt, Syria, just about anywhere you can think of. It really was a widespread cult. But back to the bridegroom. So, in this phase, you cut yourself off from the rest of the world, and you aren't allowed to speak.'

As they entered the first hall, Peter's attention was immediately drawn to the bronze helmet mask that had been found on the site of the Roman fort of Matilo in the Roomburg area of Leiden.

'So the third grade is the soldier . . .' Peter said, looking at a mannequin dressed in Roman military gear.

'Yep,' Fay replied, 'and where else in Leiden would you find a Roman soldier?'

They stood in front of the model. Its copper-coloured armour glinted gently under the faint night light in the room.

There was nothing to see.

18

Peter intuitively took a step back from Fay. He leaned away from her to create even more distance between them.

Had he been set up? There was nothing to see here. Had she led him to a dead end on purpose?

Either she was a damn good actress with a perfect poker face, or she had genuinely wanted to help him.

Fay took a pen out of her pocket and used it to carefully lift up the long, horizontal, copper-coloured plates on the soldier's armour. 'What is it we're looking for exactly, Peter?'

'I wish I knew. At Quintus, I found a quote from the Song of Songs, hidden inside a book. That led me to the synagogue where I found a photo. I don't know what we're looking for now. This is a shot in the dark.'

'I wouldn't say that,' Fay said, without looking up from her examination of the ancient armour. Eventually she gave the mannequin a gentle shake, hoping it would give up its secret, but nothing happened.

'The raven, the bridegroom and *miles*, the soldier . . . The initiate's duty is a soldier's duty. Your life on earth is a military campaign in the service of the conquering god. But it's not about fighting with physical weapons. You're fighting your own nature, your own carnal lusts and desires that are constantly dragging you down, nailing your soul to your body.'

'That's what I was talking to Awram about.'

'When they began the third stage, the fighter, the soldier, was given a sword and a crown. He had to accept the sword, as a symbol of his mental struggle. But he had to refuse the crown, with the words: "No, Mithras is my crown."'

'No wonder the soldiers of the Roman legions were attracted to Mithras. All that military symbolism.'

'Soldiers were the ones who spread Mithraism across the whole empire. And merchants too, actually . . . But if we just knew what we were looking for.'

Peter thoroughly examined every inch of every display cases, but he couldn't find any evidence that their contents had been disturbed. He looked into the dark holes on the helmet mask, but it stared blankly back at him with the same expression that had been cast in bronze by its maker two thousand years ago.

He crouched down and twisted his upper body, trying to see the back of the mask, but it looked exactly as it had done twenty years ago, when he'd picked it up from the wooden floor of the finds tent on the Matilo dig.

'This is all there is here, right?' Peter asked. 'There's nothing else?'

'Yes, this is all there is,' Fay said, sounding disappointed. 'I really thought this would be it, Peter, that you'd find your next clue here.'

They stood next to each other.

'So what's the next grade?'

'The fourth grade is the lion. That one might be tricky. Leiden is full of lions. The entrance to the Burcht, gable stones on houses, the Doelengracht gates, ornamentation on bridges. It would be like finding a needle in a haystack. You really need something more concrete. Then after that, there's the Persian.'

'The Persian? As in, from Persia, what used to be Iran?'

'Exactly. Mithraism came from Persia originally. Look, Peter, you need to understand this. Because if you do, you'll stand more chance of making sense of whatever you're about come up against. In Mithraic doctrine, there are two great powers in opposition. There's Ahura Mazda, the good god who reigns over the kingdom of light, and Ahriman, the bad god who reigns over the kingdom of darkness. A sort of devil. Mithras is a mediator. He takes the middle position between the two worlds, good and evil. A bit like what the role of the Holy Spirit was thought to be in some of the early Christian sects. He's a warrior for good who helps to fight the battle against evil, but until evil is defeated, he's the link between the pure light and the human who is trapped in matter.'

'An intermediary between God and man.'

'Right, a sort of middleman. And the god Mithras that the Roman soldiers worshipped comes from Persia, but he's probably not the ancient Persian god Mithra.'

'There was something to do with a bull too. Didn't it play an important role?'

'Yes, that's right, the bull slaughter. See,' she said, as though she was giving an encouraging compliment to an unconfident student, 'you always know more than you think you do. Every temple to Mithras has an image of a man slaying a bull.' She got down on one knee. 'It shows Mithras forcing the bull to the ground, holding its head up by the horns or the nostrils, and . . .' She pulled back her right arm then brought it down violently with her hand balled in a tight fist. ' . . . stabbing the bull in the heart with a dagger. And as the bull lies dying on the ground, the blood pouring from its wound turns into ears of corn. A dog and a snake try to lick the blood up, and scorpion grabs the bull's genitals in its claws.' She stood up again.

'And what does all of this mean?' Peter asked.

'Well . . . we don't know exactly. Some people think that Mithras is the bull as well as the bull slayer. The bull is God's alter ego, as it were. He makes a ransom sacrifice that redeems everyone who believes in him. But the blood is the source of new life. In fact, that's at the heart of all the ancient mystery religions. They all attach great importance to the cycles that go on repeating in nature. Taking part in these mysteries assured you of eternal life, because you died *with* the deity and it was *with* the deity that you rose again. Another interesting thing is that their rituals took place in underground spaces, and at the door, you dipped the index and middle finger of your right hand into a bowl of water and made the sign of a cross on your forehead.'

'Seriously?' Peter exclaimed.

'Listen,' Fay said, smiling now. 'I know this all sounds incredible when you hear it for the first time, but it's really true. The cross symbol is very old, an archetype. The followers of Mithras believed that your animalistic nature, your bull nature, needed to be crucified. Man's soul is trapped in the physical world. It's held captive, it doesn't belong here at all. It belongs with God, but it's become separated from God because it's ensnared in matter. Man's spirit is trapped like a prisoner in the cage of his body. Our life's purpose is to return to God. And God's death, whether it's on a cross or not, symbolises the death of our animalistic nature, our carnality, and it frees our soul. It triumphs over the sin that caused the separation from God, so that the spirit can be reunited with God.'

'There are far more elements of Christianity in this than I thought.'

'Oh yes, and there are a lot more. They had a ritual with bread and wine, where the bread represented the bull's body, and the wine represented its blood.'

Peter was speechless.

'And what about this: "He who does not eat of my flesh and drink of my blood, so that he remains in me and I in him, shall not know salvation."'

'Did Mithras say something similar?'

'Similar? That's taken directly from the Mithraic service! All the mystery religions, including Mithraism, were about gaining eternal life, the hope of a hereafter, being reunited with loved ones. It's—'

'You know what, Fay?' Peter stopped her, overcome by a sense of pessimism and defeat. 'I don't think we're going to find anything here. Do you?'

Fay didn't reply.

Suddenly, like a signal from a satellite reaching earth after a long delay, Awram's words came back to Peter. 'Maybe the sheet is the clue,' he'd said.

'I have to go, Fay, sorry.'

'You're going? Where? Can't I help you?'

'You've already helped me enormously, truly, probably more than you realise. Coming here was a good idea though. It was the obvious place to look, but I think I have a better idea.'

'What's that?'

Peter hesitated. 'You know what, I'll let you know, okay? I'll call you tomorrow.'

'But—'

'Bye!' Peter ran to the stairs without looking back and bounded down them, three at a time. He'd been abrupt, he realised, and possibly even ungrateful, but he had to move on.

His next target was the Lakenhal, the municipal fine art museum. It was housed in a former guild hall for the cloth merchants in the textile trade, Leiden's main form of industry until well into the twentieth century. They were currently showing an exhibition of work by Leiden's most famous son, Rembrandt, and the famous triptych altarpiece *The Last Judgement* by Lucas van Leyden. The Lakenhal also held a large collection of *schutterstukken*: military portraits and war paintings, the subjects of which were usually soldiers.

The Lakenhal. The Cloth Hall. Or the Sheet Hall.

The sheet itself had been the clue.

The mobile phone buzzed as he reached the exit door. He had almost forgotten about it.

He took it out as he walked along the Papengracht.

A photo message appeared, but it took a while for the whole image to load. Peter hovered his finger above the screen, impatient to see what it would show.

It was a blurred photo of a woman lying on a makeshift bed in a dimly lit room. Her eyes were closed as though she was sleeping.

He brought the phone closer to his eyes. Just before the image disappeared in an explosion of pixels, he saw who the woman was. He recognised the skirt she had been wearing on Friday when they'd had lunch together in the LAK.

19

Quarter past two. Only twelve hours left. Less than that, eleven and three-quarter hours. And he had only found two clues.

Why had they sent him a photo of Judith, he wondered. Her eyes had been closed and she looked as though she was sleeping, but who knew if that was true? She could be dead already . . . No, no, no! He tried desperately to banish the thought from his mind. He had to find her, that was the task he had been set. By whoever was behind all this . . . Murdering Judith made no sense. But it was clear that they wanted to put pressure on him. If only he could be with her now . . . Dear, dear Judith . . .

He walked briskly along the Papengracht, making sure to stay close to the buildings.

Calling Fay had been a knee-jerk reaction. Not an entirely rash one, she was an expert . . . And then there were the associations that Awram had made which had also led to 'the soldier'. The antiquities museum had been the obvious place to look next, but there was nothing there.

You'll only see it when you understand it, as Johan Cruyff would say.

He hurried over the empty Breestraat and went into the little Kabeljauwsteeg. The next part of his route was dangerous, past the Boommarkt. He looked to the right and saw students leaving Quintus, without their parents now.

Eventually, he took his chances and ran onto the Prinsesskade, with its Grand Café floating in the canal. He marched ahead with his head down, hoping he wouldn't pass anyone on the way.

When he turned right at the narrow Caeciliastraat, his shoulders relaxed. He hadn't noticed how tense they had been. Warm pain from his taut muscles radiated down his spine.

He went left into the Lange Lijsbethsteeg. At the end of it was Museum De Lakenhal, like an indomitable fortress complete with a moat and a bridge in front of it.

He went over the slender footbridge and onto the Lange Scheistraat that ran in front of the museum. At the end of the street, he turned left onto the Langegracht, only stopping when he reached the demolition site at the back of the Lakenhal.

Daniël had invited him to come along for a guided tour here a fortnight ago. A planned extension of the Lakenhal had led to the removal of four of the nearby houses. An artist had been asked to 'do something' with the buildings before they were knocked down. The resulting project had been called '*Verwoest Huis Leiden*' or 'Damaged House Leiden'.

The tour had been conducted by the artist herself. She saw it as a requiem for the demolished buildings, and a celebration of a new beginning. She had talked about death and new starts, terms that were usually reserved for sentient creatures, but which in her opinion could also be used for inanimate things like buildings. They also had a 'life', with birth, growth and death, and in some cases, a new beginning.

She'd had floors lowered, set at an angle or dropped down vertically so that they became walls. Everything had been done with the material that was already present in the buildings themselves, nothing came from outside.

A sign on the door said: NO ENTRY. WORK IN PROGRESS.

Peter grabbed the handle and rammed his shoulder against the door. It cracked then gave way almost instantly. He went inside, closing the door behind him as quietly as he could.

It was quite dark inside, but his eyes soon adjusted to the gloom, and a little light came in through the windows from the streetlamps outside.

The building had been almost completely stripped bare. Tools were scattered about on the ground, and there was a big sledge-hammer leaning against a wall. A long workbench was strewn with leftover food and empty beer cans.

The artist had mentioned something during the tour . . . Peter racked his brains, examined the wall that formed the back of the Lakenhal, but couldn't find what he was looking for.

He went upstairs.

It took him just a few minutes to find it.

Red and white tape was strung about half a metre away from the wall, along its entire length.

He went back down to the lower room, picked up the sledge-hammer, and dragged it up the stairs. It looked like the hammer he'd found at Quintus, but much more impressive.

The artist had said that she had been given free rein to do whatever she wanted with this building and the houses next to it as long as she took the load-bearing walls into account. The wall he was standing in front of now had also been left untouched because its single layer of bricks connected directly with the Lakenhal.

Daniël had looked at Peter and joked, a little too loudly, that you could get into the museum for free if you knocked a hole in this wall. The artist had overheard him, but only smiled painfully, as though she instantly regretted mentioning it.

But it would be very convenient for me right now if Daniël had been right, Peter thought, as he swung the hammer back and brought it down on the wall with a mighty crack. A dull thud echoed through the room.

Whatever he had to do to find Judith, he would do it. He let the hammer fall over and over on the same spot. With each violent blow, he tried to smash away his fear.

The wall was indeed only the thickness of a single brick and it didn't take long for Peter to create a hole in it about the size of a football. A few more well-aimed blows easily made the hole bigger. He put the hammer down on a large sack of cement next to the wall, and got on his knees to remove some more bricks by hand. They came loose surprisingly easily.

In the dimly lit space behind the wall he could just make out some paintings hanging on the walls. The hole was about half a metre above the gallery floor.

Peter wiped the sweat from his forehead.

He was amazed by how easy it had been to get in. But then, the Kunsthal in Rotterdam had been broken into by burglars using nothing more than a ladder and a screwdriver . . .

It had been so simple. Reality was stranger than fiction sometimes.

Peter stuck his arms through the hole, and then his head, followed by the rest of his torso. With a bit of wriggling and worming, he managed to crawl all the way through.

He started to brush the dust and grit from his clothes. And then he froze. Deep furrows gathered on his brow like ripples of sand formed on a beach by a strong wind.

He looked up.

Bach's *Matthäus Passion* was being played quietly through the gallery's speakers. He would recognise that music anywhere. It was appropriate for the time of year, but in the middle of the night in a museum?

The effect was spooky.

Peter knew the lyrics to *Matthäus Passion* by heart. Not just because he had listened to it so often, but also because he had taken part in a few *Matthäus Passion from Scratch* concerts. He'd studied the piece for one day as part of an impromptu choir and performed it in the evening.

As he walked through the galleries looking for something that might help him, he listened to Jesus and Matthew's words at The Last Supper . . .

Jesus – Take, eat, this is my Body.

Evangelist – And he took the cup and, giving thanks, he gave it to them, saying:

Jesus – Drink, all of you, from this; this is my Blood of the New Testament, which hath been poured out here for many in remission of their sins. I say to you: I shall from this moment forth no more drink from this the fruit of the grapevine until the day when I shall drink it anew with you within my Father's kingdom.

It was like being in a dream, wandering past paintings in semi-darkness, accompanied by the timeless music of Bach. Despite the gravity of his situation, he found himself softly singing along with the lyrics.

It made him think of the enthralling scene from Werner Herzog's *Nosferatu*, with the unhinged German actor Klaus Kinski playing Dracula. In it, Dracula's beloved meanders over the Grote Markt in Delft to the hypnotic drone of a Georgian folk song. The market square is filled with doomed plague victims, abandoning themselves to an absurd last supper with music, dancing, wine and song. A *danse macabre*.

Peter reached the main hall in the middle of the museum, where one of the museum's highlights, *The Last Judgement* by Lucas van Leyden was displayed. It had originally hung near the baptismal font in the Pieterskerk, but here it had been hung from posts on a pedestal in the middle of the room so that visitors could walk all the way around it. It was one of the very few altar pieces which had survived the *Beeldenstorm*, the 'Iconoclastic Fury' of 1566.

Bach was still playing in the background.

Soprano Aria – I Will Submerge Myself In Thee

The atmosphere created by the music and the images he recalled from the film complemented the mood of the painting perfectly. Lucas van Leyden had painted a vivid representation of the Day of Judgement as it was described in the Book of Revelation. The large middle panel showed Christ, flanked by his Apostles on either side. From his throne above the clouds, he looked down and watched as angels selected the people, all of them naked, who had been judged righteous. They were separating the chaff from the grain. The scene was one described in Matthew 25, in which the good people, those who clothed the naked, fed the hungry and gave drink to the thirsty went to the left, at Jesus' right hand. They were eventually taken up to heaven where an eternal reward was waiting for them. Those who had not done the Six Good Works described in the Gospel of Saint Matthew were dragged by terrifying demons to the other side of the altarpiece on the right, where the eternal fires of hell were already blazing. They were doomed to an eternity of torment, weeping and gnashing of teeth.

Something on the floor caught Peter's eye. He switched on the flashlight on the phone and shone it at the ground. There was a dotted line running from where he was standing to the back of the altarpiece.

He crouched down to look at it more closely.

The thin trail was made of tiny drops of something red.

20

Saturday 21 March, 3:00am

Peter stared at the red line that ran under the painting. It was like something from a gruesome version of Hansel and Gretel.

This painting was about the theme of eternal life too, Peter thought. Life after death, reward, punishment . . .

He slowly took a few steps along the trail, being careful not to stand on any of the red drops, then he walked around the painting.

Saint Peter and Saint Paul were painted on the back of the triptych on the two wings. They were both depicted sitting barefoot on rocks, and behind them was same landscape of water and mountains. The panel on the right showed Saint Peter dressed in green with a large, white cloth draped over his left shoulder. The panel on the left showed Saint Paul, wearing blue and wrapped in a cloth of red. A sword lay at Paul's feet and in his left hand he held a bible that rested on his left knee. Saint Peter was pointing at Saint Paul, but looking away from him, while Saint Paul pointed at Saint Peter while looking towards him.

The trail stopped at the image of Paul.

'What's this supposed to mean?' Peter whispered softly to himself.

Something gold-coloured twinkled in the light from the phone, near where the trail stopped. Peter got down on his knees and held his nose above the floor, tentatively sniffing the red drops. They had the unmistakable metallic smell of blood.

Now he looked at the gold-coloured squiggles on the floor. Someone had written something there. When he shone the light on them from the side, they became clearer.

It looks like . . . honey, he thought with astonishment.

He moved closer, until his head hovered just a few centimetres above the floor.

He couldn't make much of the gold scribbles; they appeared to be meaningless symbols. He straightened up a little and then bent over them again, holding his head to the side. Now that the light shone on them from a different angle, he saw that the scribbles on the ground were numbers.

Very clear numbers.

Was he supposed to look for numbers? For a code?

He felt a tiny spark of hope, glad to finally have *something* he could work with.

Bach, he thought suddenly.

He was about to slap his hand down hard on the floor, but caught himself just in time and instead let it land gently.

41!

If they wanted him to look for numbers, one of them had to be 41.

Bach always hid numbers in his music; simply composing music wasn't interesting enough for him. He had set up certain conditions for himself, obstacles to make his work more challenging, and worked symbolic numbers into his compositions . . . The most well-known example of this was the number 41. In Bach's time, the alphabet consisted of 24 letters; I and J were not separate letters, and neither were U and V. When the numerical value of the letters J, S, B, A, C and H were added together, where J equalled 9 and S equalled 18 and so on, the result was 41.

Excited now, he took *The Hitchhiker's Guide to the Galaxy* out of his pocket and opened it at pages 42 and 43, where the quote from the Song of Songs had been hidden.

Then it came to him. 42. They meant the number 42.

In *The Hitchhiker's Guide* the answer was being sought to the Ultimate Question of Life, the Universe, and Everything. A super-computer was built to work out what it might be, and after seven and a half million years, it finally produced an answer: 42. The answer was useless to the characters in the book, but perhaps not to Peter.

He put the book back in his pocket.

Now he had 42 from *The Hitchhiker's Guide*, 41 from Bach . . . and from Niobe in the synagogue . . . that atomic number was also 41.

41, 41 and 42 . . . Whatever that was supposed to mean. The tiny spark of hope he'd had was extinguished just as quickly as it had been ignited, like a candle flame sputtering in the smallest of draughts.

He followed the numbers on the floor with his finger, reading them aloud like a small child still learning his letters.

6 . . . 10 . . . And something that looked like 17. Added together they made 33. Maybe it wasn't Bach's 41 after all.

Or was it a reference to scripture? Chapter 6, verses 10 to 17? But which book?

Then he noticed three other squiggles – they were barely perceptible which explained why he had missed them until now – in front of the others. They looked as though they had been scratched with something sharp like a nail. The first was clearly a capital letter E, but the other two were harder to make out. Were they letters or numbers? They looked like an ornate letter P and an H.

Eph . . .

The word 'Ephesians' instantly sprang to mind, the letter from Paul in the New Testament. It was the obvious answer, since he was standing, or rather kneeling, in front of a painting of Saint Paul.

Ephesians, chapter 6, verse 10 to 17. It was a good place to start.

He dipped the tip of his little finger into the letter E and held it up to his nose, then tasted it, softly smacking his lips.

It *was* honey.

Ephesians, Ephesians . . . That was . . . Wasn't that the passage about the struggle against dark powers?

He quickly took the iPhone out of his pocket and typed 'Ephesians 6:10–17' into Google. He opened the first link. He read the verses in a half-whisper like a pious man rattling off a familiar prayer.

> Finally, be strong in the Lord and in his mighty power. Put on the full armour of God, so that you can take your stand against the devil's schemes. For our struggle is not against flesh and blood, but against the rulers, against the authorities, against the powers of this dark world and against the spiritual forces of evil in the heavenly realms. Therefore, put on the full armour of God, so that when the day of evil comes, you may be able to stand your ground, and after you have done everything, to stand. Stand firm then, with the belt of truth buckled around your waist, with the breastplate of righteousness in place, and with your feet fitted with the readiness that comes from the gospel of peace. In addition to all this, take up the shield of faith, with which you can extinguish all the flaming arrows of the evil one. Take the helmet of salvation and the sword of the Spirit, which is the word of God.

It was a well-known scripture, popular with priests and vicars who used it to urge their flocks to lead active, militant Christian lives as God's soldiers.

Peter stood up. He stared at the painting of Saint Paul, at the sword by his feet . . .

And then he saw it, as clearly and sharply as someone who, after years of not knowing their vision was poor, puts on spectacles for the first time.

But he didn't get the chance to process what he had just seen. The music, which had been playing in the background since he'd arrived, stopped abruptly in the middle of a movement.

The silence was overwhelming.

Peter rushed back over to the place where he had crawled through the wall. He heard a door open in the distance, followed by footsteps on the wooden floor.

He crawled back through the hole. It was more difficult this time because it was half a metre above the ground and the floor in the gallery wasn't on the same level as the floor in the house on the other side. He was almost all the way through when he felt a hand grab his ankle.

'Stay where you are!' someone yelled from the gallery. He held onto Peter's leg with an iron grip and tried to pull him back into the museum.

Peter kicked his left leg. His heel slipped out of his shoe, but he kept kicking. He felt his foot hit something soft, heard someone swear, and the grip on his ankle loosened. He kicked again, and felt the kick land. This time the man let go of his ankle completely. Peter hauled himself through the hole.

When he looked back, he saw a man lying flat on his back on the gallery floor. He had a security firm logo on the sleeve of his jacket. The man tried to catch a glimpse of Peter through the hole.

'Don't you dare . . .' the man shouted, but the rest of his words were muffled by the huge sack of cement that Peter had pushed over to cover the hole.

He fumbled his shoe back on and flew down the stairs. The door was still ajar. He ran through it and out onto the street.

The stately De Valk Windmill was bathed in light. In front of it was the enormous building site for what would become an underground car park. Seven storeys deep, Peter thought. Would they stumble upon a tunnel there too?

Wanting to avoid the city's main streets, he went left onto the Tweede Binnenvestgracht and then crossed the Steenstraat. It was only when he reached the quiet shelter of the area around the National Museum of Ethnology that he felt able to relax slightly. He walked towards the Morspoort, the western city gate.

Honey, he thought, honey, blood, 41, 42 . . . Ephesians . . .

Although it was certainly bizarre, the trail of blood fit with everything else: Bach's music, the Last Supper, Jesus instructing his disciples to commemorate his death and the sacrifice of his blood and his body with a meal of bread and wine . . . But the honey seemed out of place.

What had he just seen? The huge significance of the realisation he'd had as he knelt before the painting of Saint Paul began to dawn on him now.

Saints were always depicted with their particular attributes or emblems, like Saint Peter and his keys, and Saint Paul and his sword . . .

Fay had mentioned it when she told him about the third grade of initiation, *miles*, the soldier. At the beginning of the initiation ceremony, the candidate was given a sword and a crown. He was supposed to accept the sword and refuse the crown.

For our struggle is not against flesh and blood, but against the rulers, against the authorities, against the powers of this dark world . . .

The painting showed Peter with the sword at his feet. As though he had just refused Mithras' crown.

21

It was only by concentrating very hard that Judith was able to recall fragments of what had happened. Her brain felt so cloudy. Little by little, she put the puzzle pieces together until the whole picture emerged.

After her lunch with Mark and Peter, she had gone back to her office to drop off her things. She had put her camera in her bag so that she could take some photos of the items the man wanted to show her.

It had looked like it would be a routine job, something she'd done many times before: listen to their story, then look at the objects – letters, clothing, or whatever – and photograph them. The man lived in the Mierennesthofje on the Hooglandsekerkgracht.

Judith had walked the short distance from the faculty to his address and rung the bell. The lock had buzzed and she'd pushed the outer door open into a narrow, poorly lit passageway. At the end of the passage, another door had opened. The sun had been shining so brightly behind the person standing in the doorway that she'd not been able to make them out at first.

At that point, she'd felt a vague, nagging pain in her gut. It had been a silent alarm, but she had ignored it.

'Hello,' she said. She stood with her back to the door. 'I have an appointment with Mr Strauss.'

'That's right,' the person at the end of the hall confirmed. He sounded like a young man. 'That's my father. He's inside, come in.' He stepped back and held the door open for her.

Judith put one hand on the door to hold it open and shook his hand with the other. He said his name so quickly that she didn't make out what it was.

The young man walked ahead of her into the courtyard. It was an oasis of tranquillity, just like her own Sionshofje. There were only five or six houses here. Unlike with the *hofje* where she lived, where you might bump into a tourist at any time of day, the Mierennesthofje was closed to the public.

The houses were arranged around a large, lawned garden with a tree at its centre. The garden was bordered on one side by a wall at least three metres high.

They walked to the end of the courtyard, to the smallest house of them all.

Judith hesitated for the briefest of moments at the door. At first, she only took one step inside, as though she was testing the water in a swimming pool to check that it wasn't too cold. But when she saw an old man sitting in a simple kitchen with a bronze menorah, some books that were obviously quite old, and a stack of letters in yellowed envelopes on the table in front of him, she began to relax.

'Come in, come in,' the man said cheerfully as he started to rise from his chair.

'Oh, no need to get up,' Judith said and walked over to shake his hand.

He looked like he was in his mid-sixties, with a full head of grey hair, a little on the portly side. He looked healthy, but the light grey circles beneath his eyes betrayed a lack of sleep.

He shuffled back and forth in his chair a few times and then said: 'I asked my son to come over. He's such a great help to me.'

'That's absolutely fine, of course,' Judith said.

Although he had introduced the man as his son, Judith couldn't see any family resemblance. The young man brought over three glasses of cola with ice and lemon and put them on the table. She found it odd to be offered cola instead of tea or a glass of water, but the ice tinkled invitingly.

The old man raised his glass as though making a toast, and the three of them took a few sips.

As she drank, Judith noticed how thirsty she was. She'd not had anything to drink at lunch, and before she knew it, her glass was empty.

'There's plenty more, if you'd like,' both father and son said at the same time. But she put her hand over the glass to decline the offer.

She wiped a few beads of sweat from her forehead, despite not actually feeling hot. Maybe it was something to do with there being three people in the stuffy little kitchen.

They chatted at length about the items on the table. The man told her a long story about his Jewish great aunt who had been in a concentration camp. He hadn't seen her very often when she had been alive, so he had been surprised to receive a letter from the executors of her will telling him that he had been made a beneficiary. It had been a modest inheritance, he told her without sounding at all disappointed.

Judith soon began to find it difficult to follow his story. She felt dizzy, as though she was drunk. *This is not good*, she thought, and although she very much wanted to go home, it seemed rude to leave so abruptly. So instead, she blinked hard a few times and tried to concentrate on the job at hand.

At first, the menorah and books didn't look especially interesting. They weren't the sort of thing that the museum would immediately clear out a cabinet for. The letters looked more promising, correspondence from his great aunt and her husband who had been in Westerbork, the man explained. While they were in the camp, they had written letters to their family in Voorschoten and Leiden.

'*War Letters*,' the son chipped in. 'We thought that would be a good title, if they were ever published.'

Judith blinked again. She felt so woozy now that she thought she might faint. 'Sorry, I . . .' she stammered.

The old man and his son looked at her attentively, as though patiently listening to small child trying to tell a jumbled story.

'I'm suddenly not feeling very well. Could we perhaps do this another . . .' Judith's body began to tingle. Her heart was beating faster and faster. She was taken aback by how calm the two men were when she was so visibly unwell.

Suddenly everything went black. She fell forwards. Someone caught her just before her head hit the table. She was unable to move but she was still strangely aware of her surroundings. She heard the men talking to each other but their voices were distorted, as though a DJ had added weird effects to the mix of sounds around her.

One of them grabbed Judith under her arms and shoved her chair backwards. The noise the chair legs made as they moved across the floor was ghastly, like nails being scraped down a blackboard. It roused her slightly, but her vision was still black.

The other man held her ankles. It felt like they were dragging her away. The floor grazed her back painfully, and as they took her down a small set of stairs, her buttocks banged hard against each step.

Not long after that, they put her down. The coolness of the ground was a relief as it spread along her body. But it didn't last long.

They put something in my drink, she thought. *They're going to rape me.* Her instinct was to lash out wildly with her legs and her arms, to kick them, hit them . . . but she was paralysed. It felt like a nightmare, trying to escape but not being able to move.

The bitter taste in her mouth had been masked temporarily by the slice of lemon, but now it was overpowering. Vomit rose in her throat, a foul slime that tasted of bile and made her feel even more nauseous than she had been before.

She was aware of them picking her up again and dragging her down another set of stairs, a longer one this time. She felt the temperature plummet and the air became chilled and damp. It smelled musty and stale here, like a poorly ventilated cellar. Her senses seemed to have become sharper; she could hear and smell better, but she still couldn't see at all and she felt horribly groggy.

She had no idea how long they had been carrying her around for now, but it felt like an eternity. It was like floating through an underworld towards her death, a near-death experience without the tunnel of light. Now and then she heard stones scraping or hinges creaking. These noises were always followed by a draught, as if two doors had been opened opposite each other.

Eventually she was lowered onto a mattress. It was so thin that she could feel the bed beneath it. The door closed. And then there was absolute silence.

This must be what it felt like to be buried: unable to move, unable to see and unable to hear anything. There was an intense odour of wet earth and clay. Her body felt like a strait jacket or a wet suit a few sizes too small, oppressive and constricting. She tried to scream but all that came out was a rattling gasp.

After a while, she gave in to her exhaustion and fell into a deep, heavy sleep.

But now she was awake again.

And she had a plan.

And behold, I saw the young man going forth to meet his fate, spurring his horse on, all the while dreaming his glorious dreams. Look! Here I come, leaping upon the mountains, bounding over the hills. Your love is like a gazelle or a young stag. Look! I stand by the wall, gazing in at the windows, looking through the lattice. I speak and say to you: 'Arise, my love, my fair one, and come away with me.'

And behold, a snake shoots across his path, the wiliest of all the wild animals. The horse takes fright, rears and throws its rider. It causes a fit, the holy sickness, the young man's body trembles and shakes. Foam appears on his lips. His companions rush over to him, hold his tongue to prevent him from choking. He screams, he groans. He screws up his eyes as though he is looking into a bright light that no one else can see. He mutters an answer to a question than no one else can hear. 'Who are you Lord?' he asks. And then: 'What should I do?' Only he hears the answer: 'From the very beginning I have been your Lord. But now get up and stand on your feet. I have appeared to you to appoint you as my servant. Because you will be a witness of what you have seen and what I will show you. I will protect you from your own people and from the Jews to whom I am sending you so that you may open their eyes and turn them from darkness to light, and from the power of Satan to God. So that they may receive forgiveness for their sins and eternal life among those who are sanctified by faith in me.'

And then the young man grows still. He opens his eyes, but sees nothing. He is no longer even able to ride his own horse, so he is lifted onto the horse of a companion who sits behind him and holds onto him. For three days he is blind, and neither drinks nor eats. And he says: 'The Lord has appeared to me.' And his companions rejoice with him, but they do not know of which Lord he speaks.

And then suddenly, behold, the scales fall away from his eyes. He gets up and eats. Then, alone on his couch, he opens the letter which has burned all this time next to his breast. He summons a companion to translate the Hebrew words, the message from the high priest to the leader of the Jews in Damascus. His companion hesitates, refuses to convey the words to him, Saul, but he compels him to do so. And the message says:

Keep this man in Damascus for a few months. Give him some sort of task to occupy him, it does not matter what. My daughter is about to marry the man to whom she has been promised since birth. Keep Saul away from us. He amuses my daughter and she finds his zeal for the law entertaining. How can he possibly think he could ever be a match for her, this unclean, Roman Greek with his deformed manhood? He has been useful and will continue to be so, but as a servant of the law, as part of the temple guards, not as a member of my family. Farewell, Caiaphas.

He is consumed with rage. His humiliation knows no bounds. He hides under his blanket, hot with hate and shame.

But accounts of the wedding still reach him, a celebration the likes of which has never been seen. With his darling as the radiant centrepiece, like the queen of Sheba, a Bathsheba, as a Delilah, as the whore of Babylon . . .

And he prays: forgive me my God, that I have strayed from the path. Humbly I come to you. Use me. And help me to spread your message. I will find a way. And help me to take revenge on him, the man who has humiliated me, he who has darkened the light on my path. And I will thwart him, his religion and his law. I will destroy them from within, like a worm eating a chair from the inside. From the outside it looks unblemished, but woe to him that takes his place upon it. He will crash to the earth and wallow in dust. And her also, I shall bring her down, that serpent, with her treacherous glances. From the outside she is pure, but inside she is rapacious and wicked. It is better for man not to touch a woman!

And he leaves immediately for Arabia, and from there he returns to Damascus. There he stays for three years, in silence, as befits the true Bridegroom. He takes his old name once more, the name given to him by his parents. Paul the humble, the small, the insignificant.

And he thinks: I am strong in my Lord and in the strength of his power. I put on the whole armour of my God, so that I may be able to take a stand against the wiles of the devil. For my struggle is not against enemies of blood and flesh, but against the rulers, against the authorities, the cosmic powers of this present darkness and against the spiritual forces of evil in the heavenly places. Therefore, I shall take up the whole armour of my God, so that I may be able to withstand on that evil day. I will stand firm, with the belt of truth around my waist, with the breastplate of righteousness in place, and on my feet, sandals of peace. And above all of these, I will take the shield of faith, with which I will be able to quench all the flaming arrows of evil. I take the helmet of salvation and the sword of the Spirit, which is the word of my God, Mithras.

I am a Soldier.

22

LEO

LION

Twenty-one years earlier, spring 1994

The priest was discharged from the hospital the next day. After his sight had returned and nothing unusual had been revealed by further tests, there was no reason to keep him there.

He quickly resumed his work. The vivid memories of the vision he'd had in Archeon remained with him. He was reminded of it many times a day, sometimes unexpectedly, but he often directed his thoughts towards it himself.

He had put his activities with the Knights of Christ on the back burner for now, excusing himself with the need to avoid too much excitement. His fellow knights had been understanding. However, their protests against heretics continued unabated under the guidance of a young man who had recently converted to Catholicism and whose zeal was even greater than that of all the others combined.

He hadn't seen Ane since he had visited him in hospital. But he had started to look more deeply into the phenomenon of epilepsy and its association with mystical experiences. He wasn't sure why he hadn't done so before. Apart from a few medical leaflets and the instructions that came with his medicines, he had read almost nothing about it. It was simply a part of his life and whether he had more knowledge about it or less, that would never change.

However, now he was reading about the temporal lobe, an area of the brain which had not been the focus of much research until the mid-1950s. When this lobe was stimulated during brain surgery, patients reported experiencing a 'cosmic consciousness', a spiritual presence or other bizarre phenomena. Another area of the temporal lobe was associated with out of body experiences.

In the 1980s, the neuroscientist Michael Persinger developed the god helmet, a sort of motorcycle helmet that stimulated the temporal lobe to induce the same experiences.

The priest found it all very interesting, but this new scientific knowledge didn't detract from the reality of his own experiences. Even if the source of his vision had been his temporal lobe, couldn't it still be possible that he had communicated with another being? That this was the way in which man *could* contact other beings, like a precisely tuned radio receiving the signals from a radio station?

He enjoyed thinking about it. From time to time, he found himself overcome by those same feelings of peace and tranquillity again, of being accepted with all his faults, without judgement. He occasionally felt the urge to contact Ane, but it hadn't yet felt like the right time.

Ane's words had stayed with him. 'You can still be a priest, the Father you are now,' he had said, 'but with a different purpose.'

Ane had also suggested that the daily rituals he performed for his parishioners wouldn't change much at all. The format would remain the same but the substance would change. It was an intriguing idea, Tiny thought.

The moment of insight came one Sunday morning in the middle of a mass that was no different from the hundreds of other masses he had conducted before it.

When it was time for the Eucharist, the communion bread was brought to the altar first. The priest prayed:

'Blessed are you, Lord, God of all creation. Through your goodness we have this bread to offer, which earth has given and human hands have made. It will become for us the bread of life.'

Then the wine and water were brought to the altar. The priest said:

'By the mystery of this water and wine may we come to share in the divinity of Christ, who humbled himself to share in our humanity.'

He offered the chalice to God with the words:

'Blessed are you, Lord, God of all creation. Through your goodness we have this wine to offer, fruit of the vine and work of human hands. It will become our spiritual drink.'

The priest bowed his head and continued:

'With humble spirit and contrite heart may we be accepted by you, O Lord, and may our sacrifice in your sight this day be pleasing to you, Lord God.'

After washing his hands he prayed:

'Lord, wash me of my iniquity and cleanse me of my sins.'

And he ended with:

> 'Pray, my brothers and sisters, that our sacrifice may be acceptable to God, the almighty Father. May the Lord accept the sacrifice at your hands for the praise and glory of his name, for our good, and the good of all his church.'

After the Prayer over the Offerings and the Eucharistic Prayer – a 'call and response' prayer with the whole congregation – he extended his hands over the bread and wine and beseeched the Holy Spirit to change them into the body and blood of Christ.

> 'Lord, you are holy indeed, the fountain of all holiness. Let your Spirit come upon these gifts to make them holy, so that they may become for us the body and blood of our Lord, Jesus Christ.'

Now he recited the Words of Institution, echoing the words of Jesus at the Last Supper. He had said these words countless times before, but he still took a reassuring glance at the book that an altar boy held up in front of him.

That was the moment in which everything fell into place. It came not as a flash of insight, but as a very calm and suddenly perfect understanding of the actual meaning of the text.

> 'Take this, all of you, and eat it.
> This is my body which will be given up for you.
> Take this, all of you, and drink from it.
> This is the cup of my blood,
> the blood of the new and everlasting covenant.
> It will be shed for you and for all so that sins may be forgiven.

Do this in memory of me.'

He found it difficult to conceal his emotions. He was almost on autopilot when he invited his flock to join him in the Memorial Acclamation:

'Let us proclaim the mystery of faith.'

The congregation answered:

'When we eat this bread and drink this cup, we proclaim your death, Lord Jesus, until you come in glory.'

Finally he prayed:

'Look with favour on your Church's offering, and see the Victim whose death has reconciled us to yourself. Grant that we, who are nourished by his body and blood, may be filled with his Holy Spirit, and become one body, one spirit in Christ.'

The impact that this new awareness had on him was so great that it was only by exerting enormous willpower that he was able to finish conducting the service. He was grateful for the unchanging structure of the Catholic mass. His years of experience and familiarity with the fixed order of its elements had enabled him to perform the rituals and recite the prayers almost unconsciously.

After the prayers for intercession, the Lord's Prayer, and the Sign of Peace, it was finally time to break the bread. For a brief moment, he saw in his mind's eye that clear, blinding light again. This time he was able to look directly into it, without even having to blink. The feelings of love and acceptance that he'd had at Archeon flooded over him again.

'Lamb of God, you take away the sins of the world, have
     mercy on us.
Lamb of God, you take away the sins of the world, have
     mercy on us.
Lamb of God, you take away the sins of the world, grant
     us peace.'

The priest spoke these words with such intensity that some parishioners looked at each other and smiled in surprise. He looked as
though he might burst into tears at any moment. One or two
members of the congregation held their breath. But for the priest,
it was as though the words on his lips were new, as if this was
the first time in his life that he had said them, the first time he
had truly understood what they meant.

He raised the bread, holding it up to the bright light that still
blazed in his mind.

'Lord, I am not worthy to receive you, but only say the word
and I shall be healed.'

The light slowly faded but the fire within him burned as never
before.

Before he asked the congregation to come forward for Holy
Communion, he delivered the traditional warning.

'For as often as you eat this bread and drink the cup, you
proclaim the Lord's death until he comes. Whoever, therefore, eats the bread or drinks the cup of the Lord in an
unworthy manner will be guilty of profaning the body and
blood of the Lord. Let a man examine himself, and so eat
of the bread and drink of the cup. For anyone who eats
and drinks without discerning the body eats and drinks
judgement upon himself.'

174

The people came forward. For the next few minutes, the only sounds in the church were the muted music of the organ, shuffling feet, the odd cough.

The priest raised the host before each communicant and said:

'The body of Christ.'

The communicant followed this with an amen. Most of the faithful chose to rest their left hand gently on their right hand and receive the host into the left palm before bringing it to their mouths. A few of the older parishioners put out their tongue for the priest to carefully place the host upon it.

When everyone had taken their turn, the priest cleaned the paten and chalice. A few minutes of sacred silence followed, and after the concluding rite to which his flock responded with an amen, the Eucharist – literally 'thanksgiving' – was concluded. He blessed those present with a final sign of the cross.

'May almighty God bless you, the Father, and the Son, and the Holy Spirit.'

'Amen,' the congregation said in unison.

'Go in peace.'

'Thanks be to God.'

The priest stepped down from the altar and left the church to go into the sacristy. He was helped out of his vestments by a server, who arranged them neatly on a hanger. Usually after mass he stood at the door, chatting with worshippers and shaking their hands as they left, but today he feigned a headache and sent everyone away.

The light had revealed itself to him again, so brightly that everything and everyone around him had become invisible. Once again, he'd had the feeling that someone had been there, even though he hadn't seen them.

His throat felt dry, as if he'd just trekked through a barren desert. He poured a glass of water and drank it thirstily. Then he sat down and quietly recited the words that were at the heart of his faith. They seemed to have taken on a new meaning now.

'Take this, all of you, and eat it.
This is my body which will be given up for you.
Take this, all of you, and drink from it.
This is the cup of my blood,
the blood of the new and everlasting covenant.
It will be shed for you and for all so that sins may be
    forgiven.
Do this in memory of me.'

Eating Christ's body and drinking his blood in order to become one with him . . .

He stared at the crucifix on the wall, a particularly fine image of Jesus on the cross carved from a single piece of wood. It hung above the prie-dieu on which he usually knelt to pray before and after mass.

'Lamb of God who takes away the sin of the world.'

Just as he stood up, there was a knock at the door. He looked at it with irritation as it opened before he'd said, 'Come in.'

One of his parishioners stuck his head around the corner. 'There's someone here who would like to speak to you.'

'I . . .' he faltered. 'Can't they make an appointment?'

'We've already asked him to, but he's refusing to leave. He's being quite insistent I'm afraid.'

The priest sighed.

'All right, let him come in, but tell him that I can't give him much time at the moment.'

Somewhat annoyed, he stood in the middle of the sacristy to wait for the unknown visitor whose need to speak to him was so urgent that it couldn't wait. He folded his arms.

The door opened again. He was astounded when he realised that the visitor was Ane.

Ane closed the door quietly and came over to him with a broad smile on his face and his hand outstretched. 'Tiny,' he said warmly, taking the priest's hand and placing his other hand on top of it.

The priest mirrored the gesture by laying his other hand on top of Ane's.

'I was at mass today,' Ane told him. 'Actually, I've come to a few. I think it really started today, didn't it?'

'Did you see it too?' Tiny asked.

'Yes, I saw it,' Ane affirmed. 'He who does not eat of my flesh and drink of my blood, so that he remains in me and I in him, shall not know salvation.'

Tiny looked at him blankly, not understanding what he meant.

'That will come later. Right now it's like you're looking through a foggy mirror, but later, you'll see it for yourself.'

'See what for myself?'

'Come,' Ane said. 'They're waiting for us.'

Tiny hesitated for a second but then took his coat from the hook on the wall. 'We'll go out through the back door,' he said. 'It's quicker.'

He looked at the crucifix again and bowed his head, as if he was asking for both permission and forgiveness for what he was about to do.

The door that usually shut behind him with a quick click now closed with a soft groan, as though even the unoiled hinges were protesting his departure.

23

Had Paul been initiated into the cult of Mithras? Peter was stunned. That would be an earth-shattering discovery! If it was true, then much of Paul's known biography would make sense: leaving his home as a Raven to become a tent-maker in Jerusalem ... then the journey to Damascus followed by years of silence and withdrawal from public life as a Bridegroom ... then back to Jerusalem, full of belligerence and seeking out confrontation, speaking the language of war and wearing military clothing. The Soldier ...

And then there were those cryptic words in ... something about being taken up to heaven ... How did that go again, he wondered.

He took out the phone and typed in 'Paul third heaven'. The first hit was exactly what he was looking for. Although he doesn't mention his own name, Paul is clearly writing about himself in the Second Letter to the Corinthians, chapter 12, verse 2 to 4:

I know a person in Christ who fourteen years ago was caught up to the third heaven – whether in the body or out of the body I do not know; God knows. And I know that such a person – whether in the body or out of the body I do not know; God knows – was caught up into Paradise and heard things that are not to be told, that no mortal is permitted to repeat.

The third heaven, fourteen years ago . . . precisely the length of time that Paul stayed in Damascus. His words were similar to the mystical language of an initiate. ' . . . and heard things that are not to be told, that no mortal is permitted to repeat'. The initiate saw and heard things which he was forbidden to share with the outside world.

Peter entered a new search term: 'lion Mithras fourth grade'.

He frantically clicked link after link but they only led to general descriptions of Mithraism.

The Lion was under the protection of the planet Jupiter. The hands and tongues of the initiates were anointed with honey to keep their hands pure from evil deeds, and their tongues pure from evil words. It is possible that they also underwent a sort of baptism of fire. This may have been done by having flaming torches passed over their bodies, or by leaping over a fire. Fire was believed to have a purifying effect. Afterwards, initiates were considered to be made anew. They had now been promoted to another level in the religion's hierarchy, one which connected them to the sun, and thus also to Mithras, who was increasingly seen as the sun god, the *sol invictus*, the invincible sun.

That explained the honey, at least, Peter thought with satisfaction.

Honey, honey . . .

He tried a new Google search: 'Honey Leiden'. His screen filled with advertising, links to a review of the annual *Leidse Bijenmarkt*, the Leiden Bee Market, a shop selling beekeeping supplies . . .

And then he saw it: Hortus, the University of Leiden's botanical garden, home to the only beehives within the boundaries of the city's canals.

Not knowing what else to do, he decided to go there.

A short while later he reached the Morspoort. The street was quiet. He walked over the drawbridge next to the De Put windmill and into the Weddesteeg, past the house where Rembrandt was born. He dashed over the Noordeinde, then turned right at the Oude Varkenmarkt. He paused briefly at the Sebastiaansdoelen and looked up. He must have gone through this city gate hundreds of times, but this was the first time he had really looked at what was depicted above it. It's so easy to become blind to your surroundings in a city you know well.

Above the gate's arch was a statue of a knight wearing a helmet, sitting astride a horse and fighting a dragon. The creature lay half-dead beneath the horse and was making a last attempt to rise up and avoid the fatal thrust of the knight's spear. Saint George and the dragon . . .

Peter continued to the very end of the canal, but found that the wall around this side of the Hortus was much higher than he remembered. And it was smooth, with no protruding bricks that he could use to help him climb over it.

He scanned the street for something that he could lean up against the wall to help him. But he was afraid that it would make too much noise, and besides, he couldn't see anything that would be useful.

Then he saw the one-man canoe lying against the wall of one of the houses. He couldn't help smiling. This part of the canal connected to the Hortus via a short, vaulted tunnel.

He picked up the featherlight canoe and put it in the water. It wobbled precariously, but stabilised as soon as he sat down in it.

He gently pushed himself away from the canal wall with the paddle and with a few smooth strokes of the blades, he slowly moved through the water.

He paddled to the end of the tunnel that ran beneath the thick walls of the botanical garden, then he moored the canoe. The boat rocked heavily, which made it difficult to get out again.

The Hortus was his favourite place for a lunchtime walk or just to get some fresh air. Sometimes he'd chat with the beekeepers, both named Fred, one of whom was descended from the author of the first Dutch book about beekeeping. It was wonderful to see how an enthusiasm for something could sometimes be passed on to the next generation.

He started to walk down the path that ran along the side of the canal. The Hortus was bathed in the light of a full moon that cast long shadows of his body on the ground. He reached the side of a large building that backed onto the Nonnensteeg. There were a few wicker hives here, but no sign of the bees. He pressed his ear against one of them but it was silent. No buzzing, no vibration, nothing.

He warily tilted the hive up.

Empty.

He inspected the other hives in the same way, first checking each one to make sure there were no bees inside. He had hoped that something might have been hidden inside one of them, but he found nothing.

There was one more place he could look.

He followed the path that ran alongside the water of the Vijfde Binnenvestgracht and past the systematic garden where the plants were grouped into families.

Peter knew that there was another row of apiaries behind the building that housed the garden's offices and equipment store.

He walked around to the back of the building, but before he even reached the hives, he noticed something unusual. Two tiny glass dishes, like the ones found on hotel breakfast buffets, had been placed between two of the apiaries.

He picked them up. One of them contained butter, and the

other was full of honey. He held the little cup of honey up in the moonlight but he couldn't see anything unusual.

Butter and honey . . . he tried to find a link. What did they have to do with each other? Most of the clues so far had come from the bible.

'Land of milk and honey,' he murmured to himself. That was how the Promised Land was always described in the Old Testament. Then there was Samson, he thought to himself enthusiastically. It felt like he was getting somewhere now. As a young man, Samson had fallen in love with a woman and decided to make her his wife. Some time later, on his way to the wedding, he saw a dead lion. He discovered that a swarm of bees had nested in the lion's carcass and made honey. He took out handfuls of honey with his bare hands, and gave some to his parents who were travelling with him.

Lion and honey . . . but what about the butter?

He mulled it over as he walked back to the garden's main path.

As he went around the corner, he saw someone coming towards him. Peter instinctively made himself smaller. He tensed, ready to run, but instead of running, he stared at the person who was walking calmly in his direction.

At first, the figure was half hidden in the shadows of the trees, but when he was just a few metres away, Peter realised who it was.

24

When Judith looked up she saw that the ceiling was made of iron bars, like a cattle grid.

Gingerly, she bent over. The throbbing in her head intensified. She picked the candle up in both hands, then slowly stood up, a little at a time. She watched the flickering flame intently, terrified that it would go out. She held the candle out with her arms extended, like a priestess making an offer to her god in exchange for a miraculous escape from captivity.

Wooden planks had been laid over the bars above her, covering them completely.

Judith put the candle on the ground, very carefully, and pushed it against the cell wall. She dragged the mattress and blanket from the bed, a rickety wooden construction that had been carelessly put together.

If she leaned the bed, or the thing that was supposed to be a bed, at an angle against the wall, she could use it as a ladder to climb up and escape.

The bed wasn't heavy, but she was so exhausted that it took an enormous amount of effort to turn it onto its side. She bent

183

over, resting her hands on the long side of the frame for support, and tried to get her breath back. Her chest heaved violently, as though she'd just done a hundred-metre dash.

She was overcome by a feeling of such awful desolation that she dropped to her knees and began to cry uncontrollably. She slumped sideways, her entire body shaking. When she had calmed down slightly, a few minutes later, she stayed there, curled up on the ground like a foetus.

'Mark,' she whispered. 'Mark.' She rocked from side to side.

A little while later, she crawled over to the middle of the cell on her hands and knees.

Her head was still pounding. It felt like she was standing next to a piledriver.

The candle still cast its light evenly over the room. Next to it was a jug of water and a tin mug. It looked like something you'd take on a camping trip. But Judith didn't even try pouring the water into the mug. Instead, she held the jug to her lips and took big, greedy gulps as the lukewarm water ran down her chin and into her neck.

There was still a bitter taste in her mouth.

She dragged the bed around until the part that passed for a headboard faced the wall. Then she crouched on the floor at the other end and tried to push the bed up with her back. With her knees bent and the bed base resting on her shoulders, she slowly stood up, inch by inch, until she was completely upright. When she had found her balance, she took small steps backwards. The bed angled upwards, like a drawbridge being pulled up.

Now the bed was about a metre away from the wall. She turned around and pushed it away from her with both hands, so that it came to rest against the wall at an angle. It created a steep, broad ladder. She bent down to pull the footboard closer to her.

Her blouse was soaked with sweat now. She felt like she might faint at any moment, but she didn't want to stop.

She put her foot on the first slat on the bed base. She gripped the sides of the frame with her hands and took her other foot off the floor to see if the bed was sturdy enough to climb. The wood bent slightly but seemed to be able to hold her weight. She brought her other foot up so that both feet were standing on the same plank and pressed her body against the slats.

'And . . . that's . . . how I . . . climb . . . upwards.' She shivered as she sang the words of the popular Dutch children's song.

When she had climbed a third of the way, she reached up to see if she could touch the bars. She could. They felt cold and wet.

She climbed up another two rungs. Now she was able to grasp a metal bar with one hand and push at a plank with the other. The plank moved, but only a fraction, and her hope began to fade when no light came through the small gap she had made. The space above her looked even darker than the cell.

She climbed one rung higher so that she could use more force to push on one of the iron bars, but it was obvious that she wouldn't be able to get it loose. She grabbed onto the bar with her other hand, hoping that if she used two hands, she might be able to make it move.

She felt the wood under her feet start to bow. She carefully slid her feet across the slat to distribute her weight more evenly.

But the slat collapsed with a loud crack. Miraculously, despite landing on the next slat down, she was able to keep her balance. Then she heard a scraping noise coming from below her and felt the bed gradually slide away from the wall. She tried to hold onto it with one foot to stop it falling, but it was hopeless. The bed crashed to the floor.

Now Judith was dangling from the metal grate like an upside-down bat. She looked down to work out where the best place to land would be, then used the last of her strength to shove one of the bars along the grate so that it was positioned over the mattress instead of the wooden wreck below her.

Just as she was about to let go, she heard fumbling at the door, a bolt being drawn back. A moment later, the door opened.

A man appeared in the doorway holding a flaming torch. His face was hidden behind a balaclava.

He nervously entered the cell with small, shuffling steps. He swept his torch in a wild, wide arc around him. Only then did he look up and see Judith, who used his moment of confusion to drop back to the ground.

If her plan had been to elegantly spring back onto her feet like a cat and then overpower her captor, she failed completely.

She landed on the edge of the mattress, fell on her side and slammed into the wall. A searing pain shot through her ankle. She had lost the element of surprise now, but she wasn't about to give up. She jumped back up again, but too fast and had to hold onto the wall to stay upright.

The man observed all this in silence.

'Why am I here?' she whispered, without meeting his gaze.

She hobbled towards him, but he pointed the flaming torch at her, as though warding off a wild animal.

'Why am I here?' she said again, louder this time.

The guard cocked his head to the side as if he was considering whether he should reply.

'What do you want from me?' When she took another step closer to him, she felt the heat from the torch and realised how cold she was.

'Can you tell me why I'm here?' she asked again in a friendlier tone, hoping he might soften and give her an answer.

'I'm very confused, you can understand that, can't you?' she continued, speaking calmly as if this was a perfectly reasonable conversation with a normal person.

The man looked directly at her. 'I can't tell you anything,' he said. 'Sorry.'

He sounded sincere.

Was this the younger man that she'd met with the old man earlier? His voice sounded familiar.

'I don't know who you are or what you're doing. Why am I here? Why me?'

He didn't answer, but he looked like he might be wavering.

Judith broke down and began to cry again. 'Please,' she sobbed, 'let me go. Did I do something wrong? What did I do to you?'

'It's not about . . .' the man began. 'It's not really about you . . . It's about . . .'

'It's about what? Who?' Judith shouted with renewed energy.

'It's not about you,' he said again.

Judith sighed miserably.

He took a mobile phone out of his pocket. The modern gadget looked entirely out of place here. He aimed it at her, obviously about to take a photo.

'Help me!' Judith screamed as the flash went off.

The man tapped at the phone's screen. 'When I get back upstairs, the phone will send the ph—'

Before he could finish his sentence, he looked around, as though he had heard something.

In the doorway, Judith saw a hand holding a large piece of wood. It came down with enormous force on the guard's head. The guard dropped the phone and the torch as his hands flew to his head. As he whimpered and held his head with both hands, his invisible attacker hit him again. He crumpled to the floor like a marionette with severed strings.

The attacker picked up the phone and the torch. He shielded his eyes with his hand as though he was looking into the sun, so that only the bottom half of his face was visible.

Someone else must have been waiting behind him, because the unconscious man's body was dragged away from the door.

Judith nervously walked up to the doorway, ready to fall into the arms of her anonymous rescuer, whoever it was. But before she could take a step outside her cell, she was roughly shoved backwards.

'You're not going anywhere,' the man with the torch said firmly.

'But . . . you can't just leave me here,' she cried. 'Please, I won't tell anyone . . .'

He slammed the door shut.

Judith rammed her fists into the cold metal. It didn't budge. She pressed her ear to it.

She heard nothing. She stood in the middle of the cell and tried to focus on any sounds that might come from beyond its walls. But then she realised that the only sound she could hear was coming from *inside* it.

She could hear water dripping. She looked up at where the noise seemed to be coming from. High on the wall, in the corner by the door, was a pipe that opened into the cell. She had assumed that it was for ventilation, but now she saw with dread that it was the source of the drip.

The drip became a trickle. Then it stopped. As if someone had realised that they'd left a tap on and turned it off again. Judith heard scrabbling noises above her head, and then there was silence. She noticed she had been holding her breath and let it out again, but as she did, a powerful jet of water burst out of the pipe and into the cell.

Judith dove to the floor to grab the candle, rescuing it just in time. Water gushed from the pipe and poured into the middle of the cell. Filthy globs of foam floated on its surface. The puddle that had gathered around the drain in the middle of the room rapidly grew bigger and deeper. She knelt on the floor, holding the candle up away from the water, and tried to prise the metal drain cover loose. But it was shut tight.

Her voice caught in her throat as she began to scream.

25

'Raven?' Peter said, initially stunned, but then he launched himself at Raven. 'Raven!' he said again, beside himself with rage now. He slammed his palms into Raven's chest and pushed him backwards.

Raven didn't defend himself, but only stepped backwards to regain his balance.

'Where's Judith?' Peter yelled, raining flecks of spit onto Raven's jacket. Peter clutched his lapels and pulled him towards him. Raven appeared unmoved. 'Where is Judith? This is insane!' He let go of Raven but stayed threateningly close to him. 'You haven't hurt her, have you?'

'We've been watching you for a long time, Peter,' Raven said, seemingly oblivious to Peter's rage. 'I've already told you that you've been chosen. Or at least, that's what the people above me say. They've put a lot of faith and trust in you.' He put his right hand on Peter's left arm to reassure him.

Peter grabbed Raven's hand and twisted his arm, forcing him to turn around until he stood with his back to Peter, making them look like two male dancers performing a violent *pas de deux*.

The iPhone fell out of Peter's pocket in the tussle. He pushed Raven's arm upwards, and the young man arched his spine and threw back his head to lessen the pain. 'For the last time, *where* is Judith?' He pushed Raven's arm higher.

The young man could only squeal pathetically now. 'It's not . . .' he said, struggling to get the words out. 'I'm just passing the message on. Honestly. I don't know what you're talking about. I know who Judith is, but I don't know *where* she is.' He panted. 'Will you please let go, I'm telling you the truth.'

Peter loosened his grip.

Raven sighed with relief. 'I really don't know . . .' he said.

Realising that he wasn't getting anywhere, Peter let go of him completely.

Raven turned around, his face contorted with pain. He rubbed his arm and rolled his head from side to side. 'Look,' he said, almost apologetically. 'I'm only passing on the message they gave me. I don't know anything more than what I've told you, on my honour.'

'What the hell is going on here? Why do I have to do this?'

'She's . . . It's about you, that's all I know. They say "The hour has come." The eclipse yesterday . . .'

Just then the iPhone rattled on the ground. Peter automatically ducked down to see what the message was.

It was another photograph. It took what felt like an eternity for the whole image to load.

Judith looked desperate. She was staring straight into the camera. Her mouth was wide open, screaming for help. It made Peter think of Janet Leigh on the poster for *Psycho*.

'Look!' Peter screamed at Raven, shoving the phone in his face. But the image had already disappeared before Raven could see it.

'Can't you just take me to where she is?' he asked, quietly now, hoping that he might soften him up by appearing to be calm and reasonable. But Raven stayed silent. 'And what's all this with the phone?'

190

A smug smile spread across Raven's face. 'They see everything you do, Peter,' he said.

'And what about the police? At the synagogue?'

'They wanted to put pressure on you, so they sent the police to see how you'd get out of it. So far you've not disappointed us,' Raven said.

'Not disappointed you?' Peter said fiercely. 'What sort of nonsense is this? I've had enough. You go to your bosses and tell them that I'm not doing this any more. I'm not the "chosen one" or whatever they want to call it. I give up. You let Judith go and then—'

Suddenly Raven's eyes grew wide. 'Look out! Behind you!' he said.

Peter laughed and shook his head. 'I've heard that one before! That trick only works once, you know,' he said. But as he spoke, he heard the scrunch of feet on gravel behind him. Before he could turn around, someone grabbed his arms. The phone fell on the ground again. '*Now* what?' he yelled.

This had clearly taken Raven by surprise too. He opened his mouth, but instead of words, what came from his lips was a barely audible groan. He tried desperately to reach his arms around to his back, but failed. He fell to his knees, like an amateur actor performing a dramatic death scene. Then the rest of his body followed until he was lying at Peter's feet.

With absolute horror, Peter saw an arrow sticking out of Raven's back. Before he could think about where it had come from, the man behind him squeezed Peter's arms together until, just like Raven, he had to arch his back to try to stop the searing pain in his shoulder blades.

A figure loomed out of the darkness. He was carrying a bow in his hand, complete with an arrow, although he held it pointed towards the ground. He stood at a distance so that his face remained hidden.

Peter bowed his head in defeat. He closed his eyes, waiting for the moment that the arrow would hit his chest.

'As soon as you're out of the way . . .' The voice behind him was a staccato hiss and every word sounded like a spit pip. ' . . . the Father will come to his senses.'

'The *Father*? But . . . I didn't *ask* for any of this,' Peter said through gritted teeth. 'Let me go. And let Judith go!'

They stood at an impasse, their bodies almost tangled up in each other.

'I'll go home right now if you want,' Peter forced out. 'I don't want any of this. All I want is for Judith . . .' He tried to look behind him to see his assailant's face, but he couldn't. What he did make out was the man nodding to the archer who was still hidden in the shadows about twenty metres away. This time he aimed his arrow at Peter.

He won't shoot, Peter thought. That's cra— Within a fraction of a second, the archer had pulled back his arm and drawn the bow. Right before the arrow left the string, Peter used all his strength to buck forwards so that the man behind him was somersaulted across his back like an acrobat. A split second after the stunned assailant had landed in front of him, Peter heard a dry thunk as the arrow pierced the man's body. A sickening scream left the throat of the man Peter had used as a human shield.

Peter let him fall. He caught a glimpse of the phone still lying on the ground, but left it where it was. Then he ran, zigzagging through the garden as he'd seen people in films do to avoid enemy gunfire.

He sprinted towards the fence that formed a border between the Hortus and the grounds of the Observatory next to it. An arrow whooshed past his ear, missing him by a hair's breadth before coming to a trembling standstill in a tree.

He looked back nervously, but there was no one there.

The two-metre-high fence closed off this part of the botanical garden. He put his foot on a horizontal rail and pulled himself up as fast as he could. Once he was at the top of the fence, he leaned forward until he was almost horizontal and swung his legs over the railings. Their spiky tips jabbed into his stomach and chest.

He cleared the fence and jumped down, but his coat snagged on one of the sharp spikes at the top, leaving him dangling in mid-air. He reached up to tug at his coat with both hands, acutely aware that he was now an easy target for the archer. The problem resolved itself when the weight of his body tore the coat free and he dropped to the ground.

Peter sprang to his feet and ran away from the fence, half crouching, until he reached the porch of the Observatory buildings. He sheltered there for a minute or so, drenched in sweat and gasping for breath.

What had just happened?

He took deep breaths in and out.

With no idea what his next step should be, he closed his eyes and leaned against the window in the porch. The glass felt cool against the back of his head. He thought he heard a twig snap in the bushes behind him. He opened his eyes wide and held his breath, but when he heard nothing else in the seconds that followed, he breathed out again.

A loud bang came from the other side of the window behind him. Someone was knocking on the glass.

Peter filled his lungs with a huge, ragged breath and turned around. All he could see at first was his own frightened face mirrored in the window, but his reflection quickly changed into the face of a young man, not much more than a boy. The boy, who looked almost as terrified as Peter, stared at him questioningly. He was moving his lips, but because Peter couldn't hear him, he wasn't sure at first if he was speaking or dumbly opening and closing his mouth.

Peter read his lips. 'What are you doing here?' he appeared to be asking. Good question, Peter thought. He knocked on the window and pointed to the door.

The boy hesitated briefly, then reached for the door handle and opened the door slightly.

'What are you doing here?' he asked, audibly this time.

'Can I come in and explain? It's a long story but you might be able to help me.'

The boy screwed up his eyes as though it might help him to see Peter better, and then he nodded.

'Okay.'

The second the door opened, Peter heard something that sounded like tensed elastic being released. Instinctively he fell to the floor, and a fraction of a second later, an arrow ricocheted off the door while the boy was still holding it open.

Peter crawled inside on his hands and knees. 'Shut it! Shut it!' he screamed.

The boy took fright and closed the door before Peter was completely inside, jamming his ankle against the doorframe. 'Ow!' Peter cried, more from shock than pain.

The boy, who was now crouching on the floor, opened the door slightly.

Peter pulled his foot inside and the door closed with a reassuring click behind them.

Somewhere in the building, an alarm was blaring shrilly.

The boy sped down the hall. Peter saw him tap a code into a box on the wall next to a door and the noise was immediately silenced.

His rescuer indicated that he should follow him. Peter took another look behind him. He thought he saw a shadow in the bushes outside, but couldn't be sure if it was real or just his imagination getting the better of him. He knew the archer would be forming a plan to get inside the building. And Peter couldn't stay in here forever. The archer would be waiting for him when he came out.

'We're going upstairs,' the young man whispered, a little unnecessarily, Peter thought.

He passed a vending machine in the corridor that was empty except for a single king-size Mars bar, and he realised he was hungry. According to the clock in the hall, it was a little after five, which meant he had been awake for more than twenty-four hours now, with nothing to eat since the two cereal bars he'd wolfed down in the morning.

'We ought to call the police really,' the boy said from half way up the stairs.

'No,' Peter said emphatically. 'No police.'

The boy turned to face Peter and held out his hand.

'I'm Sebastiaan, by the way. And I can well imagine you'd rather I didn't call the police, Peter.'

26

'How do you know my name?' Peter asked suspiciously.

'You're a famous Leidener, aren't you?' Sebastiaan asked. 'I've got your book about Leiden at home. It was a graduation present.'

Peter relaxed a little and followed Sebastiaan up the staircase. 'So why are you here at night?' he asked. 'The Observatory isn't permanently manned, is it?'

'No, no, there wouldn't be anyone here, normally. You were just lucky.'

'What should we do about the man outside?'

'We'll hear him if he tries to get in. The whole building is alarmed, as you just heard. If he opens a door or breaks a window, we'll know straight away.'

Peter wasn't entirely convinced. 'But why are you here, then?'

'It was a bit of a special day today because of the equinox. We were open to the public, lots of families here with their children ... I'm studying astronomy and I volunteer here, deal with enquiries, run the beginners' astronomy courses. They return the favour by letting me stay the night sometimes so I can do some stargazing. Strictly speaking, it's not allowed, but . . .'

Peter nodded, but his thoughts had already drifted else-where. He had to get away from here as soon as possible. But there was an anonymous madman waiting for him outside with a bow and arrow, and he had already tried to shoot him with it. There were only two ways out: back over the fence into the Hortus, or via the main entrance on the Kaiserstrat. Both options were equally unappealing with a modern-day William Tell lurking in the bushes. 'Do you have a computer I could use? I need to look something up, if that's all right with you.'

'There's a computer in my room, but don't you think you should tell me why that man is after you, first?'

'It's—'

'A long story I suppose?'

'It is a long story,' Peter laughed dolefully. 'Where's your room?

They had reached the first floor now, a long corridor with rows of doors on either side. One of them was open. Peter followed Sebastiaan into a dark room illuminated only by the glow of a computer screen. He saw with relief that the blinds at the windows were closed.

Sebastiaan pointed to the chair at the desk and Peter sat down.

'It's so quiet here at night. I can look up at the sky with the telescope, or work on my dissertation. I get more done here than I do in a normal day in the university library. But . . .'

Peter had opened a browser and typed in 'butter honey'. The search results were all recipes, even one for honey butter. Puddings with honey and butter, spare ribs with honey and butter . . .

'Are you going to tell me or not?' Sebastiaan asked, sounding impatient.

Peter swivelled the chair around to face him. 'Of course, sorry. It's . . . I'm not entirely sure what's going on myself. The short version is that my friend has been kidnapped. I don't know why, but it looks like whoever did it has left clues that will lead me to her. At least, I'm assuming that's the idea, anyway. So that's the situation. I was in the Hortus because I thought there might be another clue there. And I did find something, but then that madman turned up with the bow and arrow . . . Someone caught me, but I managed to put him between me and an arrow. And then I ran away, climbed over the fence, but he followed me here, as you saw for yourself. He's probably in the bushes, waiting for me to come out.'

'And you want to avoid the police because of Van Tiegem.'

'Van Tiegem?'

'Your name and your photo are on nu.nl. It says that Van Tiegem disappeared and the police are looking for you because you were the last person to see him alive.'

'I had nothing to do with . . .' Peter said falteringly. He turned back around to face the computer screen. 'Well, not in the way you think, anyway,' he said gruffly. He wanted to try another search term, but was aware that he owed the young man a better explanation.

'There's a tunnel near the Burcht,' he told him without turning back around. 'They found it yesterday when the mayor was helping to install the first underground waste container at the city library. Or at least, that's what he was supposed to be doing. It all went wrong. The digger sank into the hole they'd dug for the container, then it turned out that there was a tunnel under it that nobody knew about. I went into the tunnel with Van Tiegem afterwards and I lost him. That's all there is to it. I went back, went to get help, but . . .'

'But?'

'It's a long story, all right? I don't know where he is, but now my priority is finding my friend Judith. I have no idea what to make of it all.' He went back to the web search.

He added the word 'bible' to 'butter honey' and hit enter.

The first ten results all pointed to a scripture from Isaiah, chapter seven, verse 15:

Butter and honey shall he eat, that he may know to refuse the evil, and to choose the good.

He scanned the other verses around it and easily recognised them: the prophecy made by Isaiah that Christians would later interpret as the proclamation of Jesus' coming birth.

Therefore the Lord himself shall give you a sign. Behold a virgin shall conceive, and bear a son, and his name shall be called Emmanuel. He shall eat butter and honey, that he may know to refuse the evil, and to choose the good. For before the child know to refuse the evil, and to choose the good, the land which thou abhorrest shall be forsaken of the face of her two kings.

Peter clicked on one of the other search results and read:

At no point in the New Testament is Jesus ever called Emmanuel. The belief that Isaiah's prophecy predicts the birth of Jesus is further called into question by the existence of a frequently cited translation error: Isaiah's reference to a 'young woman', *ha'almah*. If Isaiah had specifically meant to refer to a virgin, he would have used the word *betulah*. The word *ha'almah* has been erroneously translated with the Greek word *parthenos*, meaning 'virgin', and this error lies at the foundation of the cult of the Virgin Mary. However, the most important mistake in the Christian interpretation of this text is that Isaiah made the prophecy to King Ahaz on the eve of the destruction of his kingdom by his enemies, Rezin, the king of Syria, and Pekah, the king of Israel. The prophet Isaiah calmed the king's fears by reminding him that his wife was pregnant and would soon bear him a son who would be called Emmanuel, which means 'God is with us in our battle'. Ahaz was reassured, the child was born,

and the king won the war against Rezin and Pekah. Given
the situation, it is highly unlikely the king would have been
reassured by Isaiah's promise of the birth of a child that
would not take place for another seven hundred years.

What was he supposed to do with this? Did they want to tell him
something about Jesus? This was another text with a reference
to good and evil, darkness and light, and the endless battle
between them. Or was it about the verse number 15?

He typed in 'Bach numbers' and pressed enter.

He didn't need to click on the links in the search results. The
snippets of text under each link mentioned it again and again:
J.S. Bach and his numerological equivalent, 41.

What did he have so far? The numbers 41 and 42 from *The
Hitchhiker's Guide* and J.S. Bach, possibly another 41 from Niobe,
and now perhaps 15, the verse number from Isaiah. He couldn't
make any sense out of it. Might it be part of a code to unlock
the room where Judith was being held captive?

'And?' Sebastiaan asked from behind him, jolting Peter from
his thoughts.

'I found little dishes of butter and honey in the Hortus, next
to the beehives . . . I think they're a reference to a bible verse,
but I can't work out what I'm supposed to do with it. I had hoped
I'd find a new clue to tell me where to go next.'

'You know, it's a bit odd if you ask me,' Sebastiaan said. 'And
if you really are innocent, why can't you just go to the police?
We can get them to catch that nutter outside, and you can report
an attempted murder. The police can help you find your friend,
can't they?'

'No, no, they said . . . They made it very clear that I wasn't to
involve the police, and I don't want to do anything to make them
angry, or angrier than they are already, or than some of them
seem to be. They might do something to Judith.'

'But it doesn't make sense, does it? On the one hand, they're giving you clues to find your friend, and on the other, they're trying to kill you.'

Peter gave it some thought, but he didn't understand this part of the puzzle either. Unless it really was part of an initiation . . .

He typed in a new search term: 'Mithras grades'.

Less than a second later, he had more than 50,000 hits. He took a chance on the first link on the list. He scanned the text; his eyes flitted back and forth across the screen.

Saint Jerome described Mithraism's seven grades of initiation in ascending order of status. The first is Raven, *corax* in Latin . . . its symbol is the *caduceus*, the magical staff of Hermes or Mercury . . .

Corax, the raven, Quintus, Hugin and Munin . . . the second grade of initiation was the bridegroom, the *nymphus*. He'd found that clue in the synagogue under the chuppah.

The bridegroom was also called *cryphius*, 'the hidden one', cryptic, occult. The initiate was bound to Mithras in a mystical marriage. The symbols of this grade were the torch, the lamp and the crown. Connected to the sun . . . the torch is the wedding torch and the lamp represents the new light that enters the adherent's life when he forms an unbreakable bond with the sun god. It is probable that during the initiation of the *nymphus*, the Mithraeum, the Mithras temple, was flooded with bright light. Before the ceremony, the initiate withdrew from the outside world for a period of time, and took a vow of silence. This enabled them to become open to inspiration from the cosmos . . .

Something began to flicker in his subconscious, like the flame of a cigarette lighter that repeatedly flares up and then dies half second after it's been lit.

After the bridegroom came the third grade, the soldier, *miles*.

Those who had completed their period of silence returned to the outside world, but with a new status and purpose. The initiate was a warrior now, a fighter, connected to the planet earth . . . He was not fighting external enemies, but waging a spiritual war against his inner desires, not against flesh and blood but against the dark forces within himself.

Peter closed his eyes for a moment to focus his concentration and then he continued.

The god Mithras is a *deus invictus*, an invincible god. The follower joins his god's army. Having being initiated and taken the *sacramentum* or military oath, he is now a foot soldier in the service of Mithras. The sign of Mithras is made on his forehead. He is offered a crown and a sword, but the soldier is required to humbly refuse the crown, and recite the words: 'My only crown is Mithras. My crown rests with my god.' Images of the initiated *miles* show a sword lying at his feet.

'Paul!' Peter cried, like a father angrily scolding his child. I knew it, he thought. It had seemed like a crazy thought experiment at first, but now he was absolutely convinced. Everything was falling into place. In Van Leyden's *The Last Judgement*, Paul was also portrayed with a sword . . .

Full of enthusiasm, he turned around to tell Sebastiaan, but the doorway was empty. He went back to the screen and read about the next initiation grade, Lion, *Leo*, connected to the planet Jupiter.

To the ancient Persians, the lion represented the sun itself, *helios*. In this phase, the initiate was connected to higher

> powers. The tongue and hands were smeared with honey
> so that they would be as pure as the sun in word and deed.
> Novices also underwent purification via a baptism of fire,
> after which they became new men.

Peter looked behind him again but Sebastiaan still hadn't come
back. Should he look for him? Not just yet, not when he felt like
he was getting somewhere.

Searching with the words 'bible lion' produced webpages about
the lion as a metaphorical threat to the descendants of Esau and
Jacob, the Edomites and Israelites: 'I will come like a lion from
the thickets of the Jordan, leaping on the sheep in the pasture. I
will chase Edom from its land . . .'

He tried to settle his growing unease with the thought that
Sebastiaan had merely left him alone because he was so engrossed
in his research. But he didn't like the way he had gone without
saying anything.

The fifth degree of initiation was the Persian, *perses*.

Little was known about Paul's activities and whereabouts
during the fourteen years that followed his stay in Jerusalem.
Most Christians believe that he began travelling as a missionary
at this point, but there was no evidence for it in the bible. If you
read the scriptures carefully, you'd discover that he disappeared
for fourteen years. Paul's 'lost weekend' . . .

> The Persian is the divine reaper. He harvests the corn that
> springs from the blood and spinal fluid of the slaughtered
> bull. The Persian is a faithful follower of his god, protected
> by the planet Mars, no longer the child of his father and
> mother, no longer belonging to this village or that . . .

'I have become a Jew to the Jews, a Greek to the Greeks . . .'
wrote Paul, the chameleon, no longer belonging to this village
or that . . .

The Persian has grown, gained strength and wisdom, defeated his egoism. He has become one with all people. Who is his mother? Who are his brothers? All those who act in accordance with God's will are his brother, his sister, his mother.

The Persian, connected to the planet Mars . . . he remembered the solitary Mars bar in the snack machine . . . There were plenty of hits in Google for 'Apostle Paul reaping' . . .

And let us not grow weary in well-doing, for in due season we shall reap, if we do not lose heart.

The same went for 'Apostle Paul sowing'.

He who supplies seed to the sower and bread for food will supply and multiply your resources and increase the harvest of your righteousness.

But how would all this help him? What was the next step supposed to be? The sixth grade was the Sun-Runner, *heliodromus*, or messenger of the sun, the seventh was the Father, *pater* . . .

Before he could get any further, his train of thought was interrupted by the shriek of an ear-piercing alarm.

The sudden noise made him jump so violently that he was launched a few centimetres out of the chair.

He heard footsteps in the corridor, quickly coming nearer.

'Peter, Peter!' Sebastiaan shouted. 'You need to go! He's inside!'

Peter froze for a second and then sprang into action.

'Where should we go?' he hissed when he reached Sebastiaan in the hall.

'I don't know where he got in . . .' he replied, running to the stairs with Peter at his heels. 'Downstairs somewhere . . . If we go upstairs we'll be further away from him. Come on!'

As suddenly as the alarm had started, it stopped. The sudden silence rang in Peter's ears.

'That's strange,' Sebastiaan said. 'You can only do that if you have the code . . .'

Without making a sound, they crept up the stairs.

A light went on at the bottom of the stairwell. Whoever was trying to get to him, they were making no effort to conceal their presence.

The stairs took them to a corridor that was identical to the one they had just left.

'Now what?' Peter said hopelessly.

'I think,' Sebastiaan said, 'I think that coming upstairs might have been a bad idea.'

27

'What do you mean, coming upstairs might have been a bad idea?'

'We have, erm . . . we have a problem. It's being fixed on Monday. So stupid of me.'

'What problem?'

'There's a fire escape . . . We can get outside, but the door at the bottom of the fire escape doesn't open. The lock's broken. So we'd be locked in. Which wouldn't be ideal.' The tension in Sebastiaan's voice rose as he spoke. He turned around and walked back towards the staircase. 'There's no way out,' he said, before he ran down the stairs.

Peter decided to follow him, and watched as Sebastiaan disappeared around a corner at the bottom of the stairs.

Then he heard a scream so terrible that it hardly seemed human. It sounded like a wounded animal. Peter ran down the stairs, not giving a thought to the possible danger. When he reached the small landing half way down, he looked down the stairwell and saw Sebastiaan lying on the floor. Only his legs were visible. He was completely still.

In the corridor, a shadow loomed on the wall, slowly growing bigger. Peter prepared himself for a confrontation.

Far sooner than he had expected, the archer appeared at the bottom of the staircase. He stared directly at Peter, his face twisted into a taunting grin as he aimed his bow and arrow upwards. Without a moment's hesitation, Peter leapt down the rest of the stairs. Before his feet hit the floor, his fist landed on the archer's jaw with such force that the man fell backwards, slamming his head into the wall. He reeled drunkenly, giving Peter the chance to snatch his bow and fling it away from them. He broke the arrow in two.

He grabbed the man's coat and lifted him away from the wall. 'What are you doing?' Peter yelled. 'Who are you?'

A trickle of blood came from the man's nose. His eyes widened, then his head lolled to the side and his knees collapsed under him.

Peter, who was still holding onto the archer's coat, was dragged downwards as the archer fell. He let go of him before he hit the floor. He turned back to Sebastiaan who was lying motionless on his side next to the stairs. His right hand was gripping his left shoulder where an arrow was lodged in his flesh. His eyes were screwed tight shut. He looked as though he was trying to stay perfectly still because even the slightest movement would be agony.

Peter knelt down and gently put his hand on Sebastiaan's back. 'Can you stand up?'

Sebastiaan nodded weakly.

'Come on, get up. We'll go downstairs and I'll call for an ambulance.'

Sebastiaan nodded again, more obviously this time.

He rolled over very carefully until he was lying on his back. Peter crouched behind him and helped him to his feet.

Sebastiaan started to cry. 'It hurts so much,' he said, struggling to get the words out.

'I know, but we have to leave now. We'll call for an ambulance and they'll be here in a few minutes. You'll be okay . . .' Peter used one arm to hold the young man up as they haltingly descended the stairs.

'Shouldn't we tie him up or something?' Sebastiaan asked, groaning.

'He won't be able to do much for a while. I'll make the phone call, then we'll go outside and wait for the ambulance. We'll ask for the police too, okay? They can take him away.'

'But what about you?'

'I'll run as soon as I see the blue lights.'

'Where are you going to go?'

It was a good question. Coming to the Observatory hadn't produced any new clues. The Persian was the next step, but where should he look?

When they finally reached the ground floor, they went into the first room on the corridor. Peter put Sebastiaan down and went over to use the phone on the desk. He dialled 0 and then 112. After about ten seconds which felt like an aeon, a woman's voice came on the line and asked if he needed the police, fire service or an ambulance.

'Ambulance!' he shouted into the receiver.

'What's the address?'

'Kaiserstaat, Leiden, near the entrance to the Observatory.'

There was a short pause. 'The ambulance is on its way,' the operator said. 'Stay on the line.'

Peter considered hanging up. But at the very least, he wanted to describe Sebastiaan's injuries, so he did as she asked.

'Can you tell me what happened?' the woman asked after a short pause.

'Someone was shot with an arrow. In his shoulder.'

The operator was silent for a second or two. This clearly wasn't a scenario she had roleplayed on her training course. 'An . . . arrow?' she repeated dubiously.

'Yes, an arrow. They need to hurry.'

'And your name is . . .'

He hesitated.

'Could I have your name please?' she said again, more insistently.

Peter hung up, throwing the receiver down again and went back over to Sebastiaan. 'We're going outside. The ambulance is on its way.'

They walked to the front door with Sebastiaan stumbling next to Peter. When Peter opened the door, the alarm went off again, but he ignored it and closed the door behind them. They hobbled together down the long path that led to the main street.

'How are you doing?' Peter asked Sebastiaan with a sideways glance. But he could already see the answer on the young man's face.

Sebastiaan grimaced and shook his head.

'We're almost there, just a bit further . . .'

'What . . .' Sebastiaan stammered with obvious difficulty. 'What do they want from you? Who . . . are they?'

'I don't know. There are people . . . I don't know.'

They reached the end of the path and stood still until Peter saw an ambulance approaching on their right, coming out of the Witte Singel with its blue lights flashing. 'I have to leave you now. I'm sorry.'

Sebastiaan seemed not to be able to hear him. He fell, first onto his knees, and then onto his side, with his hand still holding the shoulder where the arrow was sticking out.

Peter crouched beside him and nervously looked to his right. The ambulance had turned the corner onto the Kaiserstraat now, and was crawling towards them as its crew looked for their patient. 'I really have to go. I'm sorry. The ambulance is already here.'

The ambulance was just twenty or thirty metres away from them. Peter stood up, ready to run in the opposite direction. He was stopped in his tracks by two police officers who had been observing the scene from a few metres' distance. They each took one of Peter's arms and clamped him so tightly between them that he gave up any attempt to escape. Now he saw the police car, parked diagonally across the street with its headlights dimmed, barely fifty metres away. He had been so focused on the ambulance that he hadn't heard the police car coming.

The ambulance had stopped next to Sebastiaan. A man and a woman jumped out. One of them attended to Sebastiaan, while the other opened the back doors and took out the stretcher.

'So what happened here?' one of the policemen asked Peter, without looking at him. He stared agog at the pavement where Sebastiaan lay groaning.

'Aren't you . . .' the other officer began.

'Peter de Haan, yes,' Peter finished the sentence for him.

'We've been looking for you all night, you arsehole,' the man said, bringing his face close up to Peter's. He nodded at his colleague who twisted Peter's arm behind his back.

Knowing that there was no use trying to resist, Peter voluntarily held his other arm out behind him.

The first officer removed a pair of handcuffs from his belt.

Peter felt the cold metal of the cuffs wrap around one wrist, then the other.

The other officer went over to talk to the paramedics who were tending to Sebastiaan.

'I haven't . . . I didn't have anything to do with this. I really don't have time for this,' Peter protested weakly. 'The man who shot him with the arrow is inside,' he added. 'I'd come to see Sebastiaan, the boy lying over there. Some idiot or other broke in and starting shooting arrows at us. I don't know why. I knocked him out. He's lying at the bottom of the stairs.'

The police officer immediately took out his radio and contacted the control room to ask for backup.

'And in the Hortus . . .' Peter said. 'He shot two more people with arrows in the Hortus. But I think they're dead.'

The officer looked at him aghast, then spoke into his radio again.

Sebastiaan cried out in pain as the ambulance crew gently manoeuvred him onto the stretcher and fastened him in with two wide straps. The collapsible frame and wheels unfolded below him as they lifted the stretcher up. They wheeled him over to the ambulance. The male paramedic stayed in the back with Sebastiaan. His female colleague shut the door behind them and raised her hand before getting into the driver's seat. Only now did she turn off the flashing blue lights. Then she turned the van around in the road and drove away.

The police officer walked back over to Peter and his colleague. 'Why don't you put him in the car,' he said, 'and I'll wait here.'

His colleague nodded. 'Right then, Mr De Haan,' he said, 'I'm arresting you on suspicion of the murder of Professor Van—'

'Murder?' Peter exclaimed. He tried to turn around, but the police officer roughly pushed him back.

'Professor Van Tiegem,' he continued. 'You have the right to remain silent.'

'Murder? What do you mean? Arnold disapp—'

'They've found him now, floating in the canal. Dead.'

'But . . .' Peter bowed his head. *Murdered*, he thought, horrified. *What's happening? Judith!* Panic got the better of him. *Surely they won't . . . not her too . . .*

'So, you can come with me and explain what happened in that tunnel,' the officer said as he manhandled him towards the car. 'And why that poor man had to die.'

'It was nothing to do with me. And I don't know what happened down there.'

The policeman didn't react.

'My friend, Judith Cherev, she's gone missing . . .' Peter decided to tell the police everything. 'I don't have much time left to find her. You have to help me!'

The police officer seemed unmoved. 'You can tell me all about it down at the station,' he said in the same calm, professional tone that he usually used to respond to the weak alibis that suspects came up with to prove their innocence.

'For God's sake!' Peter exploded. 'You don't understand!' He made a half-hearted attempt to wrestle free, knowing it was useless when his hands were behind his back.

The officer opened the back door of the police car and pushed him in, putting a hand over his head so that he wouldn't bump it.

He loosened one of the handcuffs. Surprised, Peter put both of his hands on his lap and felt a brief glimmer of hope, but then the policeman fastened the open handcuff to the grille that separated the back of the car from the seats in the front.

Peter stared dejectedly ahead, his arm held out in front of him, fingers laced through the wire mesh, like a monkey in a zoo.

The policeman slammed the door shut. Almost instinctively, Peter launched himself at the other door, but of course, it didn't open. And even if he had been able to open it, there was nowhere for him to go. The officer got in and started the engine. He drove slowly back to the other police officer who was still waiting where they'd left him. He got out of the car and joined his colleague.

Not long afterwards, another police car arrived and two more officers got out of it. Almost simultaneously, a Volkswagen van with a local security firm's logo on its side drove into the street. Two young men in uniform jumped out.

Peter watched as the policemen conferred with each other then, as if on command, drew their guns from their holsters and started moving towards the Observatory.

The officer who had arrested Peter came back to the car, got in, and started the engine again. He looked at Peter in the rear-view mirror. 'I'm going to take you to the station first. Then you can make a statement.'

'Listen, someone's playing games with me. I don't know who, but my friend, Judith Cherev, has been kidnapped. They gave me twenty-four hours to find her. I only have eight left.'

The officer turned on the radio.

They drove along the Witte Singel, passing the LAK building and the faculty. A short while later, they reached the Beestenmarkt and then drove past the De Valk windmill. The car slowed down and turned right for the entrance to the police station. They stopped and waited as the car park's automatic gate slowly slid open.

As the driver parked the car, two other police officers came out of the station.

The driver got out of the car and opened the back door. He leaned over with his knee on the back seat, removed the handcuff from the grille, and clicked it onto his own wrist.

'Is that really necessary?' Peter asked with a tired sigh.

The two other officers stood watching in silence.

'Hey, Mani,' one of them said. 'I thought you weren't working tonight?'

'I wasn't,' his colleague said, smiling, 'but I couldn't sleep, so I was listening to the scanner. I heard so much weird stuff going on that I had to come and see it for myself. Looks like it was a good job I did. We've got a lot of cars out tonight.'

Mani had a distinctly Middle Eastern appearance, jet black hair and light brown skin. Despite the early hour, he appeared to be friendly and upbeat, like a man who had found a source of inner peace.

They went into the station through the back door. When they got to the desk, Peter's handcuffs were removed at last. A female police officer took his details and cheerfully typed them into the computer.

'You'll be interviewed shortly,' she said to Peter, in a tone so animated she sounded like she was doing him a favour.

'I haven't got any bloody time for this!' Peter shouted, angry now. 'Judith is gone . . .' He slammed his fists down on the counter.

Before he knew it, two police officers had grabbed him by his arms and pushed him away.

I have to get out of here, Peter thought. He struggled to break free, but the two policemen carried on down the corridor, unfazed, until they reached the door to what looked like a cell.

'I can take it from here, I think,' Mani said. 'Isn't that right, Mr De Haan?'

Peter nodded dejectedly.

The other officer nodded and walked back along the corridor.

'You can take your belt off. And give me your shoelaces.'

Peter handed his belt over; there were no laces on his loafers. 'How long before I can talk to someone?'

Mani looked at his watch. Peter looked at it too and noticed the unusual numbers on its face.

The officer gave Peter an amused look. This clearly wasn't the first time someone had been surprised by his watch.

'Those are Arabic numbers,' he volunteered. 'I'm from Iran, originally. This was my dad's watch.'

Peter stepped into the tiny cell. 'Iran?' he asked.

'Yes, Iran. Although we prefer to use the old name for Iran, Persia.' Mani said, smiling at the puzzled look on Peter's face.

He began to close the cell door, but before it closed completely, he said, 'I am a Persian.'

28

Peter sat on the bed in his cell. It was more of a hard, plastic bench than a bed. Other than the bench, the room was completely empty. Totally scrote-proof, they called it.

There was a small, blue book next to him on the bench. He instantly recognised it as the Gideon bible that was often found in hotel room nightstands. He was surprised that the Gideons left bibles in police stations too. Or maybe it had been put there by a pious policeman. Someone locked in here for hours wouldn't just have plenty of time to think, they would probably have reached a point in their lives where they were susceptible to a bit of evangelism.

Next to the bible was a Mars bar. That was . . . a bit of a coincidence, Peter thought. Just then, he remembered what he'd read earlier about the Persian. 'No longer the child of his father and mother, no longer belonging to this village or that . . . The Persian is protected by the planet Mars.'

He picked up the Mars bar and examined it thoroughly, but there didn't seem to be anything unusual about it. So he ripped off the wrapper and took two big, hungry bites.

He picked up the bible and opened it. The famous words from the sixteenth verse of the third chapter of The Book of John were printed on the first page:

For God so loved the world that he gave his one and only Son, that whoever believes in him shall not perish but have eternal life.'

He quickly leafed through it. Then, holding the little book in his left hand, he thumbed the rest of the pages with his right hand. He didn't see any notes, or underlined scriptures. He put the bible down again, disappointed. Then he saw a thin ribbon marker tucked between two pages at the back of the book.

Nothing that had happened so far today had been a coincidence. This had to mean something.

He opened the bible at the page marked by the ribbon. It was Paul's second letter to the Christian community in the Greek city of Corinth, the last part of chapter 7 and the start of chapter 8.

He scanned chapter 7, in which Paul wrote about joy after sorrow. He had spoken to the community reproachfully in an earlier letter, but it seemed that they had now taken heed of his words and improved their lives.

No, no . . . This doesn't mean anything, Peter thought gloomily. *Maybe I'm reading too much into everything, like what the policeman said when he closed the cell door: I am a Persian.*

This was almost impossible, wasn't it? How far did this go? Who else was involved? The policeman, Mani, wasn't supposed to be working tonight. Was that allowed? Might someone higher up have told Mani to come to work to keep an eye on Peter? Or maybe he wasn't involved at all and his words had only seemed significant because Peter's brain was desperately trying to connect all the dots?

Who was behind this? What was the point of it all? And Judith . . . Oh God, Judith . . .

Peter got up and banged madly on the cell door with the flat of his hand. 'Hey!' he shouted. His voice echoed in the small space. 'Hey! I need to speak to someone. I'll tell you everything. We have to find Judith.'

There was no response.

High on the wall in the corner of his cell, he saw a tiny camera. He stood in front of it and jumped up and down, waving his arms around as though he was a desert island castaway waving at a ship in the distance.

The hatch in the door opened and Mani's face appeared.

'You need to be patient for a while,' he said affably but firmly. 'There's a bit of a commotion going on in town, as I'm sure you know.'

Peter rushed over to the hatch. Mani took a step backwards, even though Peter couldn't do much to him with the heavy cell door between them.

'What do you know about this, Mani? Why did you say you were a Persian?'

The officer looked at him bemusedly. Either he was a brilliant actor, or he really didn't know what Peter was hinting at.

'Because I *am* a Persian of course. Or Iranian. You were looking at my watch, so I explained it.'

'No, no,' Peter whispered. 'You know perfectly well what I mean. The Persian is the fifth grade of initiation . . . Mithras? Come on! There's a reason you told me you're from Iran, from Persia.'

'Should I have told you I come from Morocco?' Mani asked derisively. 'I told you because it's the land of my cradle days, as you Dutch say.'

'That Mars bar, did you put it there? And why is there a bible in here? Do you know where Judith is?' Peter narrowed his eyes and watched Mani's face closely, but he gave nothing away.

'I can go and get you some water,' Mani said.

Peter gave up and nodded. 'Yes, okay,' he said. The Mars bar had made him thirsty.

Mani shut the hatch, then quickly came back with a little plastic beaker of water. Peter reached for the beaker, but Mani held onto it. Peter thought he was taunting him, but then the man's face transformed, as though a cloud had come over it.

'We left one at the Observatory for you, but you missed it. So we had to improvise . . .'

'What do you mean "left one at the Observatory"?'

'The next person who buys a Mars bar from the machine there is in for a surprise.'

'But—'

Mani let go of the beaker so unexpectedly that it almost fell on the floor. Instinctively, Peter grabbed it with his other hand. As he did, Mani slammed the hatch closed.

Peter gulped the water then went back to the bench. He sat down and opened the little bible again, this time at chapters 8 and 9. His eyes flew over the text, then stopped at a sentence that he recognised as one of the hits from his web search at the Observatory. 2 Corinthians, chapter 9, verse 6: 'Remember this: whoever sows sparingly will also reap sparingly, and whoever sows generously will also reap generously.' The Persian was the reaper; he gathered the harvest of the seeds that had been sown and grown with so much care.

Both chapters were about the collection Paul had promised to organise at the famous meeting of the Apostles in Jerusalem. In these verses, the Apostles were agreeing that Peter and his associates would focus their ministry on the 'circumcised ones', the Jews, and Paul and Barnabas would concentrate on the 'uncircumcised ones', the Gentiles. Paul pledged to collect money for the Jerusalem Christians.

Peter recalled that this supposed fundraising was a conundrum that bible scholars had been scratching their heads over for centuries. Why was Paul collecting money from Christians in the

Roman Empire for Christians in Jerusalem when he didn't want to go to Jerusalem himself? And hadn't Paul said again and again that people should be responsible for their own upkeep? He emphasised repeatedly that he worked to earn his own daily bread. If people were unwilling to work, then they should suffer the consequences. Yet we were to believe that after many, many years, he returned to Jerusalem with this money? Had he wanted to buy the goodwill of the Christians in Jerusalem? Had he wanted to show that he was trustworthy, that he was committed to their cause? Whatever his intentions, he hadn't been welcomed back with open arms like a prodigal son. In fact, before he knew it, he'd found himself in conflict with everything and everyone. An angry mob of Jews dragged him from the temple and he only escaped being killed by surrendering to the Romans, who then arrested him. He was detained at a Roman base in Caesarea for two years, and in that time, no one came to help him, not even his Christian brothers, nor anyone from the church in Jerusalem. And the money he had collected was never seen again.

Most of chapter 10 was about Paul's opinion of himself and his own selflessness. An odd thing to pat yourself on the back for, Peter thought. Paul was using the language of a soldier again.

> For though we walk in the flesh, we are not waging war according to the flesh. For the weapons of our warfare are not of the flesh but have divine power to destroy strongholds.

But chapters 8 and 9, Peter concluded, were nothing more than begging letters playing on the Corinthians' sense of guilt. 'Hadn't the Christians in Macedonia, who are much poorer than you,' he urged them, 'given beyond their means? And they gave entirely of their own accord, but you I have to ask! Jesus became poor, so that by his poverty you might become rich. How can you refuse to follow the example of our Lord? By doing so, you will not only disappoint me, but also God . . .' And so he went on, on the one hand telling them 'this is not a command' and 'you should only do it if you want to' but on the other hand . . .

It was all about collecting donations, which of course, was also like reaping in a way. But what did it have to do with his next step? Clearly, they wanted him to go to a place where money was donated, but that happened in every church.

Peter closed the bible and put it down again. He regretted eating the Mars bar now. It had made him thirsty and he had no water left.

He lay down on his side, keeping his feet on the floor. Despite being utterly exhausted, he wanted to make sure he stayed awake.

But less than a minute later, he was fast asleep.

THE FOURTH VISION

And behold, I saw a man with hair like the mane of a lion. The Father anoints his hands with honey to keep them pure from every evil, from every crime and contamination. He anoints his tongue with honey to keep it pure from every sin. A burning torch is passed over his naked body. The flames lick at his skin, the smell of singed hair fills the temple. And so they make him clean, and so he becomes a new man.

And behold, he has returned to Jerusalem, a man in the prime of his life. He stays with Simon Peter because he wants to build on the foundations of his community. He sees none of the Apostles, except James, the Lord's brother. He tells them that he is joining them, will be one of them. People say of him: 'This man who used to persecute us now proclaims the faith that he once tried to eradicate.' They give praise to God for him.

And he stays there for two weeks, in Peter's house. He does not see the high priest, he does not see her, but he will destroy them. He will make Peter's church stronger; his shall be greater, and the Pharisees will be diminished, that brood of vipers. Like whitewashed tombs they are, that look beautiful on the outside, while within they are full of dead men's bones and uncleanness. They are full of hypocrisy and iniquity. They exalt themselves and will be humbled, but he humbles himself and will be exalted.

He is ready for battle. He has spent three years working on his plan, three long years. He will be an Apostle for the Apostles. His Lord will become *their* Lord, his message *their* message, and they will never be aware of it. He will go like a sheep in the midst of wolves. He must be as wily as a serpent and look as innocent as a dove. But he conceals his plans from Peter, he conceals his plans from James. They will bring him in like a gift, as the Trojans brought the wooden horse through their gates, jubilant at their victory. In brotherhood they will break bread together, in unity they will pray to the Lord.

And he goes back to Cicilia, back to Tarsus, like a bird returning to its nest. But the raven has become a lion, and every bit as strong. He captures his prey, this son, and returns to his den. He will rest only when he has devoured his prey and drunk its blood.

And behold, he travels for fourteen years, through Syria, Cicilia, Asia Minor and Hellas. He lives in Roma, he is indefatigable, writing letters and founding congregations. Five times he is punished by the Jews with forty lashes less one, three times he is beaten with rods, once he is stoned. He is shipwrecked three times. He is adrift on the sea for a night and a day. He travels constantly, in danger from rivers, from robbers, from his own people, from strangers, danger in the city, danger in the wilderness, danger at sea. In toil and hardship, through many a sleepless night, in hunger and thirst, often without food, cold and exposed. In Damascus, the governor under King Aretas closes the city in order to seize him, but he is lowered in a basket through a window in the wall, and escapes his clutches.

And so he proclaims his message. He breaks the bread, the

body of his Lord Mithras, and drinks the wine, the blood without which there can be no redemption. He teaches them: 'He who does not eat of my flesh and drink of my blood, so that he remains in me and I in him, shall not know salvation.' The people hear his message. They already know the stories; this is old wine in a new wineskin. They receive the message with joy. And he thinks: Like a lion I will attack Ephraim and like a young lion I will turn against the House of Judah; I myself will rend them, I will carry them off, beyond hope of rescue.

I am a Lion.

29

PERSES

PERSIAN

Twenty-one years ago, spring 1994

The new knowledge that Ane gave him was like drops of spring rain on dry desert soil. Tiny drank it in thirstily.

They met regularly, in secret. Both men felt as though they were balancing on a tightrope. To the best of his ability, Tiny continued to carry out his daily activities as the shepherd of his flock. He was forced to keep his new knowledge to himself. But it felt like a new world had opened up to him, as though the scales really had fallen from his eyes. He began to see his old knowledge, everything he had learned as a theology student, in an entirely new light when he spoke to Ane. He could continue to celebrate Holy Communion, the breaking of bread and drinking of wine, as he had always done. Nothing would change for the faithful, who looked up with him as he broke the large communal wafer and raised his arms to lift the chalice. The mystery of the mystical union with Christ remained exactly the same for them. But for him, everything had changed.

At first, Ane and Tiny concentrated on the stories he already knew. He revealed things that Tiny hadn't been told at his seminary. That the Israelites' stories weren't set down in writing until after their years in captivity in Babylon. That those written stories had been strongly influenced by the mythologies and traditions of other civilisations. The story of the Flood and Noah's Ark had been lifted directly from the Sumerian Epic of Gilgamesh. Long before Moses was born, Sargon of Akkad was cast adrift on the waves of the Euphrates in a basket sealed with pitch. That the Jews took Persian stories and ideas with them after their Babylonian exile, stories about the battle between light and darkness, heaven and hell, the advent of a saviour, that time had a beginning and that there would also be an end time when everyone would be judged . . . They worked all of these details into their stories. Just one generation later, they no longer knew which stories were true and which stories had been borrowed.

Ane pointed out the many anachronisms in the stories. That the camels in the story of Joseph being sold into slavery by his brothers were probably common in that area at the time the story was written down, but not likely to have been there at the time it supposedly took place. That excavations had revealed that the great city of Jericho, whose walls were said to have fallen when the Israelites walked around them seven times, was at that time still a collection of mud huts. That the 'mighty' Jerusalem was little more than an overgrown village. That the legendary Saul, David and Solomon were composites of many other people. That even after a century of digging, not so much as a golden thimble from Solomon's fabled riches had been found. That the bible should primarily be seen as a sort of title deed that the Israelites used to justify their claim to the Promised Land. 'This land is ours,' the Israelites said, 'because it was the land of our fathers and it was promised to us by God. Here, you can read it for yourself in this book. We have written it all down with great accuracy.'

That the Israelites had worshipped multiple gods, including the storm-god Yahweh and his wife Asherah. You could even read this in the bible, as in Psalms 82, verse 1: 'God has taken his place in the divine council; in the midst of the gods he holds judgement.' And that when you knew this, Yahweh's obsession with forbidding the worship of other gods made more sense; he was jealous . . . The second commandment said: 'You shall have no other gods before me.' That in the Hebrew version of the creation story, the word *elohim* was used, the undeniably plural form of the word *eloi*, 'gods'.

That the seventh-century authors of the Old Testament had tried to create an epic past, full of legendary heroes who were no more historically accurate than the tales of Virgil. An Italian wouldn't point to *The Aeneid*'s stories about the foundation of Rome to prove that Italians had a right to that particular piece of land. The bible's authors wanted their scriptures to unite their community with a shared history, determine their shared norms and values in comparison to those of the other tribes around them. Once you were aware of these things, your view of the bible was changed forever. It was impossible to unlearn what you had learned; to make what was known unknown.

The focus of Ane's stories began to move towards the character Jesus. He told Tiny that the so-called virgin birth was based on a mistranslation of the prophet Isaiah's words about a 'young woman' who would fall pregnant. And that in his Gospel, Matthew blatantly said that the story he was telling was very different to the one most people knew. He even introduced the *magi*. It was usually translated as 'wise men', but the men who came to the stable were no more or less than *mages*, Zoroastrian priests. The bible doesn't say how many there were; the belief that there were three was based on the number of gifts they brought with them. Later, the anonymous wise men would be portrayed as having three different skin colours, to show that the saviour had come to save every race. Their three ages reflected the three phases of human life. Centuries later, they were given names and their characters were constructed from earlier stories. Twenty-year-old Balthazar from Asia brought myrrh, as in Psalm 45, a wedding song celebrating the king's marriage. Verse 8 says: 'Your robes are all fragrant with myrrh and aloes and cassia. From ivory palaces, stringed instruments make you glad.' Forty-year-old Melchior from Europe brought gold, which was taken straight from Psalm 72: 'Long may he live, may gold of Sheba be given to him!' And finally, there was sixty-year-old Caspar who brought frankincense, a detail that was added to the story because of Isaiah 60, verse 6: 'All those from Sheba shall come. They shall bring gold and frankincense.' Gold symbolised Jesus' kingship, frankincense his priesthood, and myrrh his death.

That these wise men, who were actually astrologers, appeared at precisely the same moment that the Age of Aries ended and the Age of Pisces began. That this would go on to have great significance in Jesus' ministry, seen in the *icthus*, and in his words to Simon Peter and Andrew: 'I will make you fishers of men' . . . And that a new age was approaching, the Age of Aquarius, a time of great change.

And that for almost every story in the New Testament, you could find an equivalent in stories from other Middle Eastern countries, often many centuries older than the stories about Jesus. Stories about shepherds coming to worship a child, wise men seeing him and recognising him as the long-awaited saviour, about an angry king hunting the child down and trying to kill him, and the child escaping this fate because his parents were warned about the danger in a dream – and why did they not warn other parents so that they could escape too? – and about the child showing unusual wisdom from an early age. As the Book of Ecclesiastes said before Jesus was even born: 'there is nothing new under the sun'.

Tiny learned about all of these things for the first time. He wrote it all down, filling notebook after notebook.

From the priest's notes

Osiris and Isis — Osiris was the son of the earth god, Geb, and the sky goddess Nut. A huge festival took place in the spring when the dead god Osiris was buried. The 'body' that was laid in his tomb was a clay figure filled with silt from the Nile and grain. This effigy was made wet, causing the grain to germinate. A day of deep mourning followed the funeral, but on the third day, the priests announced that the tomb was empty and that Osiris had risen from the dead. The priest proclaimed: 'I have come forth out of the primeval waters . . . I have been made completely pure. I have taken off my garments and I have been anointed . . .' His sarcophagus bore the words: 'Whether I live or die, I am Osiris. I enter in and reappear through you.'

The other Osiris story was about his jealous brother, Set. He tricked Osiris into getting inside a chest which he then locked and threw into the Nile. But the chest was found by Isis, Osiris' wife. Set flew into a rage and hacked Osiris into fourteen pieces which he scattered throughout the land. Isis gathered the pieces — traces of this story are found in the tradition of hunting for Easter eggs in spring — and put his body back together. Although his penis was the one part of Osiris' body which she couldn't find, Isis was still able to get pregnant by him and bear him a son. This son was the god Horus, who was born twice. Once during the winter solstice in December, and again during the vernal equinox in the spring. Isis was also known as Stella Maris or 'Star of the Sea'. Images of her with Horus on her knee would later become the inspiration for images of Mary and her son Jesus.

Cybele and Attis – The Megalensia was a Roman festival celebrated in the spring, starting around 200 BC, connected to the Phrygian mother goddess Cybele and her consort Attis, who was both her son and her lover. At the beginning of spring on March 20th, a pine tree was felled to represent the death of Attis. It was brought into Cybele's temple, wrapped like a body in a linen shroud, in effigy of the young god at his death. The next day was a day of abstinence and mourning. The believers fasted all day and wept ceaselessly, lamenting the death of their beloved god. Many scourged themselves or cut their bodies until the blood streamed from their wounds. In the night that followed this day of bitter grief, the followers were considered to be reunited with the goddess, just like Attis, and their euphoria knew no bounds. The priests entered Attis' makeshift burial tomb, the priests would light a lamp and call out to the followers who were gathered outside: 'He lives!' Delirious with joy, they repeated the priests' words: 'He is truly risen! He lives!' Attis symbolised the grain kernel, dead and invisible under the dark earth, which then sprouts again, bringing forth new life. During the celebration, lambs and bulls were also sacrificed and the followers of Cybele would purify themselves by bathing in the blood, the blood of their god.

Dionysus – Dionysus was the son of Zeus and Semele, the daughter of Cadmus, King of Thebes. Semele was burned alive when Hera, Zeus' wife, disguised herself as an old crone and persuaded Semele to reveal the identity of the lover who visited her at night. Zeus saved their unborn child, Dionysus, by sewing him into his thigh. A few months later, he was born for the second time. Dionysus was the god of fertility; his power made nature flourish again every spring. In the springtime, people grieved for the grapevines that had withered in the winter and which looked as though they would never bear fruit again. The death of nature presented man with a mirror image of his own inevitable end. In some areas of ancient Greece, women went up into the mountains at night, half-naked and mad with grief at the death of Dionysus. They ripped apart wild animals with their bare hands, ate the meat raw and drank the blood in the hope that these frenzied rituals would bring their dead god back to life and unify them with him. The next morning, they went to the temple, carrying the seedlings of plants that they had found on the mountains, proof that their god had come back to life. They celebrated his resurrection exuberantly, with an abundance of wine, his gift to them. Indeed, his first miracle had been to turn water into wine. He was hailed as the Good Shepherd, and was also known as 'the true vine'.

Heracles – Every spring in the city of Tarsus, a figure representing the god Heracles was ritually burned on a pyre. The devotees knew that he hadn't actually died, but that he would be taken up to heaven. Because he had to descend into Hades before he could ascend to heaven, he was considered to be a divine saviour. In Euripides' play Alcestis, Heracles rescues Alcestis, the wife of his friend Admetus, from Hades and reunites her with her husband.

The essence of this myth was a combination of the most primitive hope – the hope of immortality and reunion with loved ones in the hereafter – and the most primitive of all fears – the fear of death.

Adonis – The Phoenician Adonis was revered in the Middle East, but the centre of his cult was . . . Bethlehem. His followers gathered every year in a cave to mourn his death and to rejoice at his resurrection three days later. He was the son of a goddess and after his birth he was placed in a wooden chest and given to Ereshkigal, goddess of the underworld, for safekeeping. He was so beautiful that Ereshkigal did not want to let him go. But she had no choice and was forced to part with him. Adonis was raised as a shepherd boy and was an avid hunter. During a hunt for wild boar he was hit by an arrow and impaled on a tree. His lover Inanna – a young incarnation of his mother! – refused to accept his death and went down to the underworld to bring him back. She reached a compromise with her sister Ereshkigal: Adonis would spend half of every year with Inanna, but he had to return to the underworld to spend the other half with Ereshkigal. He was worshipped as the god of the grain that dies under the millstone so that it can be baked into bread. In Bethlehem – which literally means 'the house of bread' – he was worshipped as the god of bread.

The mysteries were about chthonic gods, gods who were associated with the earth or its underworld. The earth was a fertile womb that brought forth food and took care of us as a mother takes care of her children. But she was also an open grave who always took back what she had given.

The mysteries were based on a symbolic act, a 'mystery play' portraying the death and resurrection of the deity. The initiate who was permitted to witness this was imbued with some of the power of the resurrection and would themselves be reborn after death. Like Persephone, the daughter of Demeter, the Greek goddess of agriculture, who spent six months of the year in the underworld . . . The natural world mourned with her mother who was so grief-stricken that she neglected to take care of nature. But when Persephone returned in the spring, nature joyously thrived once more. In the same way, believers would also be given new life; they would be 'reborn'.

Tiny wrote all these stories down.

The common thread was that the gods, whichever name they were given, conquered death and bestowed eternal life on their devotees. The god's suffering and death mirrored the suffering of all people; everyone recognised their own life's path in his story, but also what came after it: the divine promise that death was not the end.

Tiny learned that every mystery religion had elements that were known to everyone: the concepts and rituals of repentance, belief, baptism, communion, the laying on of hands, resurrection and final judgement were openly available to the uninitiated, the 'psychici'. The deeper meaning of the stories was meant only for initiated, the 'pneumatici'. Now, for the first time, he understood Jesus' words in Matthew 13, verses 10 and 11:

> Then the disciples came and said to him, 'Why do you speak to them in parables?' He answered them, 'To you it has been given to know the secrets of the kingdom of heaven, but to them it has not been given.'

And then, Ane told him about Mithras.

30

Tiny was woken by someone pounding on the door. Although it wasn't his usual habit, he had spent the night here. The outside world knew this house as the place where he studied, but it had been the society's operational base for centuries. It had been given to him soon after he had succeeded Ane as leader. He wanted to be here rather than in his house in the Leiden suburbs so that he could keep a closer eye on things as they developed.

At first, he thought that the banging was part of his restless dreams, but he realised that the noise was coming from the real world. He glanced at his phone to check the time. Half past seven.

He switched the light on and off three times to let whoever was outside know that he had heard them, a signal that the organisation had established over time. A small number of people in the group had a copy of the key to the courtyard door.

He pulled on his dressing gown and went into the kitchen, where a Soldier, a man in his late twenties, was waiting for him after letting himself in.

There were three glasses on the counter, each with a half-moon of lemon at the bottom, two still half-full of cola. They'd had to

232

carefully research the amount of GHB it would take to knock someone out without killing them. They'd used an estimated body weight to find the right dose, which had worked perfectly in the end. They had been able to mask the drug's bitter taste with cola and lemon.

'What's so urgent?' Tiny said calmly.

'There's been a rebellion,' the young man said nervously. 'What we know so far is that there are six men who are refusing to go ahead with your plan and are actively trying to stop you.'

Six men out of eighteen, Tiny thought. Typical . . . 'The dragon's tail swept down a third of the stars of heaven,' he murmured, 'and cast them to the earth . . . And the great dragon was thrown down to the earth . . .'

The young man gave him a puzzled look.

'Who are they? Are you sure?' Tiny asked him.

'Two Soldiers, two Lions, a Persian and . . .' The young man was clearly reluctant to reveal the identity of the sixth.

'And who?'

'The Sun-Runner, Father. I'm sorry.'

Tiny needed to sit down. The Sun-Runner, his intended successor . . . Had he really been so wrong about these men? Or had he simply asked them to do something they weren't ready for yet?

'Mani wasn't one of them?'

'No, not Mani. You know how loyal he is. He even went to the police station when he heard that Peter de Haan had been arrested.'

'Arrested?' Tiny said, horrified. 'And how do you know all this?'

'After you left the meeting yesterday, we stayed behind. There was quite a heated discussion . . . most of the group was in favour of your plan, but the six men I just told you about, they got up and walked out. I don't know what they're going to do exactly, but . . .'

'But what?'

'I understand from Mani that there was a confrontation with De Haan in the Hortus.'

'The Hortus?' Tiny repeated pensively. 'Then he'd made very good progress. I'd sent Raven there . . .'

'According to Mani, someone was there shooting with a bow and arrow. Peter de Haan apparently told the police that there were two victims. We don't know who they are yet, but we're afraid that Raven was one of them. We've not heard from him since then. De Haan managed to escape. He hid in the Observatory, but they got inside there too. A member of staff was taken to hospital with an arrow in his shoulder. And De Haan was arrested.'

'What else?'

'Arnold van Tiegem is dead.'

'*What?*'

'After the tunnel collapsed—'

'Yes, but that was the plan . . .'

'After the tunnel collapsed, Peter de Haan and Arnold van Tiegem went to have a look inside it. The rebels had two Soldiers down there waiting for them. Van Tiegem was the only one who went far enough into the tunnel. They knocked him out, and then they dumped him in the canal. He drowned.'

'And how do you know all this?' the priest asked, with a trace of scepticism in his voice.

'I talked to Mani.'

'But . . .'

'They were trying to get Mani to join them, so they told him everything. They pretty much poured a whole bottle of Beaujolais Nouveau into Van Tiegem.'

' Beaujolais Nou . . . why, in heaven's name?'

'Young wine . . . they stuffed a note into his mouth. It said "New wine in an old skin."'

Tiny knew how significant these words were. In a discussion with John the Baptist's disciples, Jesus told a parable about not putting new wine into old wineskins. The brittle leather bags would tear, the wine would be spilled and both wine and wine-skin would be lost. But if the new wine was put into soft, new skins, then both would be saved. Metaphorically, it meant that you shouldn't preach new ideas in an environment that was unable to make effective use of them.

In the case of Mithras, Ane had turned the parable around: old wine in a new skin. In other words: the old stories of Mithras recast as new stories of Jesus. You were using new ways to present something that everyone was already familiar with, but essentially, nothing had changed.

'Why did they do that?'

'Maybe it was meant to be a red herring. Like that note, they'll drive themselves mad trying to work out what that means. They stuck the empty wine bottle in the waistband of his trousers.'

Tiny sighed deeply. 'And the phone? You'd put an app on it, hadn't you?'

'Yes, Cerberus . . .'

Cerberus was an app that allowed you to remotely control your mobile phone. It could read contacts, track its location, turn on the microphone, record videos and take photos.

Tiny smiled at the name that had been chosen for this anti-theft app. Cerberus, or *Kerberos*, the monstrous hound of Greek mythology with three heads, a serpent for a tail, and the heads of countless snakes on his back. He guarded the underworld, making sure that the dead could not leave and the living could not enter.

'The phone went quiet for a long time at the Hortus. It's at the police station on the Langegracht now. They must have found it when they were looking for the bodies. We could see that it got there *after* De Haan arrived. He must have thrown it away or lost it. It means we can't follow De Haan now, in any case.'

'The camera?'

'It looks like the camera on the phone is broken, probably got damaged somehow. We're just getting a black screen.'

'Hmm.'

'What do we do now?'

'Go to our house on the Rapenburg? We can discuss it there.'

Tiny dashed upstairs to his bedroom, taking the stairs two at a time. He quickly put on his trousers and shirt, and pulled a warm jumper over the top.

When he got back downstairs, they both went down to the basement where they pushed aside a cupboard. They rolled away the rug that it had been standing on. Tiny used a long, iron crowbar to loosen a large flagstone. They pushed the stone aside to reveal a wooden hatch with a rusty metal ring.

Tiny found two flashlights and gave one to his helper. He opened the hatch and they descended into the darkness together.

They walked along the tunnel in silence until they came to a blank, stone wall. Tiny deftly pushed some of the stones inwards, and pulled others forwards. Then, with palms flat on the wall, the two men moved the wall aside. It scraped over the tiled floor, creating an opening just big enough for them to pass through.

They walked on.

'Father,' the young man said hesitantly, 'what if De Haan fails?'

'Listen,' Tiny said, 'if he's unsuccessful, it's a sign that the hour has not yet come. That I was wrong after all. It's simple: if we are striving to do the work of man, it will come to nothing. But if we are doing the work of the Lord, their opposition will achieve nothing, and they may even find that they are in opposition with him. Whichever it is, there's . . .' The priest stopped and turned around. 'There's no way back now. The die has been cast.'

After opening two more walls to clear their way, they arrived in a part of the tunnel that was different to the one they had just walked down. The ceiling was much lower and they had to stoop to avoid banging their heads. The tiled floor was replaced by a layer of sand on top of compacted soil and clay. Somewhere, water was dripping and puddles had gathered here and there on the ground. The passageway was much narrower here and the two men had to hold their arms out straight in front of them so that they wouldn't get stuck. The walls and ceiling were braced with wooden beams, a construction that looked makeshift and slipshod in sharp contrast to the well-made tunnels that had led them here. This space had not been part of the original design.

The tunnel branched off in different directions at regular intervals, but Tiny strode though it, confidently finding his way in the labyrinth. Whenever he came down here, he was filled with enormous pride in this underground city of theirs that the people above them knew nothing about. He was part of an ancient tradition, the latest in a long line of wise men who had passed their secrets down through the generations. It was a proud heritage.

Tiny and the Soldier slowed their pace when the way ahead of them changed again and resembled the tunnel where they had first entered the labyrinth: a higher, vaulted ceiling and a tiled floor. They stopped at a stone staircase.

The Soldier waited while Tiny climbed the stairs and rapped out a sequence of knocks on a wooden hatch above him.

The sounds of shuffling and banging came from behind the hatch before it opened.

They blinked in the light that suddenly illuminated their underworld.

'Hello Father.' The man in the room greeted Tiny with reverence.

'Hello Daniël.'

31

Peter was woken from a dreamless sleep by someone shaking him vigorously. He drowsily opened his eyes and found himself looking directly at Mani, whose face hovered alarmingly close to his own.

'Come on,' Mani whispered, quietly but urgently. 'We have to—'

Peter shot upright. 'What?' he said sleepily. 'I need to . . . What time is it? I don't have time for this. I can explain it all later.' He rubbed his eyes with his fingertips, massaging his eyelids in circles. 'So you *did* know what I was talking about,' he said. 'Do you know where Ju—'

'It's eight o'clock,' Mani said, cutting him off. He was still whispering but he sounded determined. 'Come on, we need to get a move on. I'm going to help you get out of here, but please, you have to do exactly what I say. In a moment, we're going to leave this cell together. As soon as we reach the desk, break free and run. Go out through the back door, the one you came in through. Here's your wallet.'

'And then? Where do I go then?' Peter asked, putting the wallet in his trouser pocket.

238

'There's a fence between the car park and the back gardens of the houses on the Oude Singel. Climb over it and try to go—'

They heard a voice. 'Hey, Mani, what's taking so long?' There was another officer standing in the doorway. 'Get a move on, they're waiting for you.'

'I was just telling him his rights. We're coming now.'

Peter stood up and put his arms behind his back.

'No need for that,' Mani said affably. 'It's only a short walk.' He allowed Peter to walk ahead of him and asked his colleague to close the cell door behind them.

Peter frowned and tried to look behind him, but Mani pushed him forwards. Peter didn't think his plan had a chance of working. He also didn't completely understand why Mani was helping him, but it seemed important to him that Peter completed his quest. It was worth a try. The worst that could happen would be that he'd fail and they'd arrest him again.

As they approached the desk, Peter saw the door to the car park on his left. The only other person in the hall was a female police officer, who looked at him curiously and gave him a friendly smile.

'Now,' Mani whispered, almost inaudibly, behind him.

Peter froze. Then he launched himself backwards, ramming his whole body into Mani. Mani crashed to the floor immediately, knocking over the female officer behind him as he fell.

She got back up again. 'Hey!' she shouted indignantly.

Peter ran to the door, flung it open and went outside, squinting in the bright morning sun. He sprinted to the back of the car park and found that, just as Mani had said, it was surrounded by a high fence. He heard the door open again behind him. Someone shouted at him to stand still. Without looking back, he jumped onto the bonnet of a parked car, then scrambled onto its roof. He gripped the top of the fence with both hands and launched himself over it. It was just like leaping over the vaulting horse at school, except that his landing was two metres lower and much harder. He was grateful for the bushes in the garden that broke his fall. Without thinking, he ran over the lawn to the back door of a house where a man, woman and two children were sitting in the kitchen eating breakfast. The children were dressed in football kits, ready to go to a match.

Four startled faces looked up when Peter opened the door. By the time the man had got to his feet, Peter had already reached the other side of the room.

'Sorry, so sorry,' he said as he ran into the hall. There was a bunch of keys hanging in the front door. In one fluid movement, he took them out, opened the door and closed it behind him. Then he locked it to make it more difficult for them to follow him. He threw the keys into a flower pot next to the front door.

He turned left and shot over the Janvossenbrug and onto the Vollersgracht. When he reached the end of the street, he slowed his pace to a walk. A running man was likely to draw too much attention. But he was also aware that the police would come out in full force to find him now.

He feverishly tried to think of what he should do next. He was three steps away from finding Judith: the Persian, the Sun-Runner and the Father . . . And he had just under six hours left.

'Collection, collection,' he said to himself.

The first thing he thought of was a church. It was obvious, yes. But which one? Leiden was full of churches: the Marenkerk, the Coelikerk, the Hooglandse Kerk, the Waalse Kerk, the Lutherse Kerk, there were two Pieterskerks, and that was just in the town centre.

Everything came back to Paul . . . Saint Paul.

The Pieterskerk, he thought suddenly. It had to be! Although everyone knew that the church was named for Saint Peter, few people knew that it was also dedicated to Saint Paul. Its full name should really have been the Pieter en Pauluskerk.

He had to keep moving. He decided to stick to the narrowest

alleys and took a zigzagging route to the Pieterskerk, with his head down, eyes to the ground.

When he arrived, he found the side door open. Inside, the church was bustling with people unpacking boxes of books onto trestle tables for what looked like a book fair.

He started to walk over to the other side of the nave where a large, antique wooden chest had stood for many years as the church's permanent collection box. The money inside it was no longer used for religious purposes – the church had been deconsecrated in 1975 – but for the maintenance of the church itself.

There was a man standing next to the collection box. Peter wasn't sure who he was or what he was doing there, so he changed direction in a way that he hoped would look casual to anyone who might see him.

He tried to conceal himself behind the copper bars of the colossal choir screen, the oldest in the Netherlands. A pointless exercise, since the wide gaps between the bars made it useless as a hiding place.

Above the screen's gates, a wooden panel in the form of two tablets proclaimed the Ten Commandments. On the reverse, there was a quotation from the eleventh chapter of Paul's first letter to the Corinthians about the institution of the Lord's Supper. That man was everywhere once you were aware of him, Peter thought with wonder. He was ashamed to admit that he'd not noticed these words before, even though he had walked past them dozens of times.

As always, it struck him as odd that so few believers were concerned by the absurdity of the request made by a Jewish rabbi that they should drink his blood to remember him after his death. There was no greater blasphemy, no greater violation of the kosher laws and their prohibition of the consumption of blood. And that was apart from the fact that Yahweh would forgive those who repented anyway, without first having to sacrifice his own son for them. Forgive us our trespasses as we forgive those who have trespassed against us – there was no sacrifice necessary. Child sacrifice . . . According to the Old Testament, there was no greater abomination in the eyes of the Lord.

Peter looked over at the collection box again. The man was gone. Without pausing to reflect on whether that was good news or bad, he decided to walk over to the chest. He answered the 'good mornings' of the booksellers with a nod, and hoped they'd assume he was one of them.

On top of the large wooden box was a slot surrounded by a frame of ironwork. Apart from a sheet of A4 describing how the money inside it would be used, Peter couldn't see anything that might help him.

He looked behind the chest and crouched down to see if there was anything near it on the floor, but there was nothing there.

Surely it won't be inside it, he thought, with a rising sense of hopelessness.

He looked closely at the A4 information sign in its hard, plastic cover.

The Persian . . . he thought. *The Persian is the reaper . . . Just like taking up a collection is a sort of reaping. Paul announced that he was going to take up a collection. Perhaps he did it to ingratiate himself with the Christian community in Jerusalem . . .*

Peter was aware that it would be dangerous to stand still for too long. But if there wasn't a clue here, where else could it be?

He read the sign again, hoping that a clue would jump out at him that he had missed the first few times he'd read it. Then he noticed something sticking out of the back of the plastic cover. At first it looked like part of the same sheet of A4 that the information sign was printed on, but when he turned it around, he saw that a small piece of paper had been tucked inside the cover. Using the nails on his thumb and middle finger like tweezers, he gently tugged at the paper until it came out.

It was a thin strip of paper. On it, was a single line of text.

32

The cave echoed with the sounds of frightened bleating. The lamb had been given sour wine mixed with myrrh and hyssop to calm it, but it still pulled at the rope that tied its leg to an iron ring on the wall. The terrified animal's bound leg hung almost horizontally in the air as it struggled in vain to escape.

The Father laid his hand on the lamb's head. He spoke softly to it and tickled it behind its ear, like a cat. This appeared to calm it. It pressed its small body against the Father's legs and took little bites of the fresh hay that had been put down for it.

They usually came together once a month, around the sixteenth day when the half-moon was waxing. There were also holy days, when despite being deep under the ground, they felt the power of the cosmos in every fibre of their bodies.

On March 21, they celebrated the summer solstice, the glorious moment when Mithras, their saviour, the lord of light, was once more triumphant in his cosmic battle against the darkness. But on this day, they also remembered the sacrifice of the bull made by their god long ago.

On September 21, they celebrated the Ascension of their Lord, who left this earthly sphere and would one day return.

They also came together on the day of the winter solstice, December 21. The days had grown shorter after June 21, and the darkness seemed to have the upper hand, but on this day the Lord proved once again that he was worthy of his name, *sol invictus*, the invincible sun.

And on December 25th, they celebrated his birth. Born of a virgin, in a cave, on the day that a star appeared in the heavens to show his birthplace to the wise men who came to honour him with gifts, and to the shepherds, who watched over their flocks in the fields. Together, they celebrated the arrival of the new light of the world.

But this day was special for many reasons. As they secretly gathered in the place where the loving, warming rays of their Lord would never reach, a miracle took place above them that had confused and even frightened people centuries ago. On this day, the sun would briefly disappear behind the moon, a sign from the heavens. This particular solar eclipse was especially meaningful, especially powerful, because it took place on the day before the spring solstice, a day that was already charged with energy.

Since that very first moment, since the first conversations with Ane after his epileptic fit at Archeon, Tiny had felt compelled to share the knowledge that had been revealed to him. After a time, the breaking of bread and the sharing of wine had taken on a new meaning, different to the one he had been taught at the seminary. It had lost some of its uniqueness, but gained something universal, a message that would be relevant to all of humanity. The good news had endured for centuries, existed for thousands and thousands of years in different forms, but the story itself had never changed. The message was the same: there is life after this life if you break free from the chains of your carnal desires that shackle you to an earthly existence. Eat the bread, drink the wine, participate in the irrepressible force that life is, the life that renews itself again, year after year. Choose the right side in the battle of light against darkness, be a soldier and fight.

The mystery of Mithras embodied everything that Tiny had ever believed in: the fight against inner demons, the scourge of the flesh, the light in the darkness . . . More so than Christianity. Over the course of history, Christianity had become detached from its original meaning, from its original substance. It was no longer connected to nature's powers of renewal. It had fallen prey to academics who wrote countless volumes about how this word should be interpreted, or the true meaning of that passage, or what the source of this Hebrew word was, or how often that Greek word had been used and in which contexts and by whom . . . People had started to take the stories literally. The literalists had eventually won, and with that, all the vitality of the faith had vanished.

On that day, Tiny would finally set in motion the plans he had begun so many years ago. What he had started in secret had gradually involved more and more people, and now, they were about to come out into the open, into the full glare of the public spotlight. There had been opposition of course, and now it was clear that not everyone had submitted to his will, but a father naturally sees more than his children see, knows best what is good for them. Ultimately, he had the blessing of the *pater patrum*, the father of fathers, the head of all the temples in the Lowlands.

He'd had the perfect man in mind almost from the very beginning. He would be their spokesman, their intermediary. This was a man who had shown that he was open to a view of the world that was different to the one most people had accepted until now. He was exactly what was needed to bring the message of Mithras to a wide audience, a born teacher . . .

This was also the day that Raven would finally join their ranks and serve in the army of the Lord.

* * *

The lamb was lying calmly at the Father's feet now, a perfect pastoral image.

The Father looked around the temple. It had originally been created from a natural subterranean cave, then extended by human hands. The temple faced the east, where their Lord rose every morning. The location was perfect, not least because it was next to a river which could provide fresh water for their rituals.

There were eighteen men in this group, and he was the nineteenth. It went without saying that every single one of them, every rank and every grade, would be present on a day like today. It was pleasing to see how some of them lost themselves in their roles. Some flapped their wings like birds and imitated the caw of the raven. Others roared like lions . . .

The pit at the back of the temple had been filled with water. A man lay on the floor, his hands bound with bird entrails. He was thrown into the pit, disappeared under the water, then resurfaced, coughing and gasping for breath, his hands stretched above his head. Then the Liberator came to cut the entrails with a sword and free his brother from his animal bonds. Two men lifted him out of the pit and he stood at its edge, dripping and shivering like a half-drowned cat.

Someone pulled down on a large, wooden handle, halting the flow of water. Someone else pulled another smaller handle to open the drain at the bottom of the pit. A vortex swirled in the water as it flowed away. The pit had to be empty for the offering they were about to make.

The grate was moved back over the pit and secured.

The hubbub in the temple died away and the men took their places on the large, stone benches that ran the length of both walls. Each was about twenty metres long and ten metres wide and padded with cushions.

The central aisle between these benches was decorated with seven simple black and white mosaics depicting the seven grades of initiation. This was the *via salutis*, the path of salvation that all believers were required to follow in order to be given redemption. An eighth mosaic depicted a vase surrounded by twigs full of buds, the promise of a new life.

The mosaics formed a sort of ladder, along which the soul descended at birth. The soul received a quality from each of the seven planets as it descended, which it then redeposited on the return journey after death.

The vaulted ceiling was decorated with stars, symbolising the heavens. In earlier times, their critics had been amused by this: how can you worship a god of light in a place of darkness?

They began their simple meal of bread and wine. The lowest ranks, the Ravens and Bridegrooms, served those who ranked above them. The bread stilled their hunger and the wine quenched their thirst, but it was also food for the soul, giving them spiritual strength and new life.

The Father and the Sun-Runner sat on two thrones at one end of the room. In an alcove behind them, a magnificent relief had been carved out of the living rock, just as the god himself had been. According to another legend, he had been born from a rock, created like the spark that comes from two stones when they are struck together, a light emerging from darkness.

They refreshed the colours of the relief every year with natural pigments, making it look as though it had been created only the day before.

The sculptor had excelled himself. His depiction of Mithras was superb. The young god, agile and strong as Heracles, was depicted forcing the huge, lumbering bull to the ground with one knee and pulling its head up by the horns. The god was both executioner and executed, the slaughterer and the sacrifice. He gave his own body in return for humanity's salvation. Mithras struck the beast in the heart with a dagger. The blood that flowed from the wound was transformed into ears of corn, the life-giving grain that would feed mankind. A dog and a snake reached up their heads to drink the blood from the wound. By licking at the blood, they hoped to absorb some of its invigorative power. A scorpion was carved next to the bull's testicles, gripping the genitals with its pincers, a symbol of man's struggle against his base desires.

The god wore a soft, red cap with the top pulled forward, a *mitra*. It would evolve into the mitre worn by Catholic bishops who would be oblivious to its pagan origin.

Behind Mithras was the Raven, bringing a message from the god Sol.

A torchbearer stood on either side of the scene, one with his torch raised, and the other with his torch lowered, emphasising the rising and setting arcs of Sol and Luna, the rising and falling of light, and also the arc of life and death. One torchbearer, Cautes, depicted the position of the sun in the morning, the rising sun. The other, Cautopates, depicted the position of the sun in the evening, the fading sunlight. Just like Jesus who was flanked at his crucifixion by a criminal and a penitent thief, evil and good, darkness and light.

Two braziers blazed in front of the alcove.

The Father broke the silence and spoke:

As the god kills the bull, I also kill my own passions.

Then he broke the bread across the cross-shaped indentation in the middle that symbolised the four winds and the four elements. He said:

Blessed are you, Lord, God of all creation. Through your goodness we have this bread to offer, which earth has given and human hands have made. It will become for us the bread of life.

He blessed the chalice of wine with the words:

Blessed are you, Lord, God of all creation. Through your goodness we have this wine to offer, fruit of the vine and work of human hands. It will become our source of eternal life.

He placed the bread and wine on the small altar in front of him.

Take this, all of you, and eat it.
This is my body which will be given up for you.
Take this, all of you, and drink from it.
This is the cup of my blood,
the blood of the new and everlasting covenant.
It will be shed for you and for all mankind.
He who does not eat of my flesh and drink of my blood, so that he remains in me and I in him, shall not know salvation.

The members solemnly repeated this last sentence, as one voice, one body.

The Father continued:

And so our saviour and saint, our Lord Mithras, blessed be his name, has offered his body, a beneficial and creative act. Through his sacrifice, he has given us new life, like the grain of wheat that dies in darkness after it has been entrusted to the bosom of Mother Earth then rises once more into the light and bears fruit. So is one grain multiplied one hundredfold, another sixtyfold, and another but thirtyfold and yet it still bears fruit. So our Lord gives us life again and again. We must use the talents the Lord has given us. We are not worthy to receive him, but he speaks and we shall be healed.

Before the bread was passed around so that each member could break off a piece, he looked around the room then spoke the words of warning that they all knew so well.

Whoever, therefore, eats the bread or drinks the cup of the Lord in an unworthy manner will be guilty of profaning the body and blood of the Lord. Let a man examine himself, and so eat of the bread and drink of the cup. For anyone who eats and drinks without discerning the body eats and drinks judgement upon himself.

They ate the bread in silence, taking turns to drink wine from the chalice as it was passed around.

Then the Father stood up.

Eighteen pairs of eyes looked at him expectantly.

'Gentlemen,' he began, casting a critical eye over the men in front of him. He rested his gaze on each individual member in turn, as though assessing their devotion, nodded and then said: '*Hora est.*'

33

Peter read the text on the thin strip of paper.

There is a time to sow and a time to reap.

Was it a reference to a time? The '*hora est*'? The words were reminiscent of the famous chapter in Ecclesiastes that was often used at funerals.

There is a time to be born, and a time to die . . . a time to plant, and a time to pluck up what is planted.

Or was this about a specific date? Because up until now, they've seemed to want me to look for numbers, Peter wondered. 41, 41, 42, 15 . . . What was next? It looked like a completely random list of numbers. He hoped it wasn't some sort of complicated mathematical code, because he practically needed a calculator just to count his fingers.

When did Paul go to take up his collection? When was he in Jerusalem? There is a time to reap . . . A time, that had to point to a date.

He nervously scanned the church. Nobody seemed to have

noticed that he was hovering by the collection box. He needed a computer, but where would he find one?

He remembered that a café had opened here last year on the side of the church that was on the Kloksteeg. He'd had coffee there a few times. A pleasant, quiet spot where you could read the newspaper in peace. And there was a door that connected it to the church.

He hurried towards the corridor that led to the café, staying close to the wall. As he got closer, he could see that the office, where the doorman usually sat, was completely deserted. Inside, on the desk, a computer displayed the Pieterskerk homepage. Reassuring sounds of classical music and a hissing espresso machine drifted in from the café.

Peter knew that he was taking a huge risk, sitting at the desk inside this oversized aquarium, but he was running out of time. He walked down the corridor, and took another quick, cursory look around him, then went into the office.

He sat at the computer and quickly typed 'Apostle Paul collection' into the search bar. A second later, he had millions of results. He scanned the snippets of text under the links, but they were mostly bible commentaries and calls to support Israel. He added 'date' to the search terms which produced slightly fewer results. Wikipedia was the first hit as usual, but a few lines below that was a sentence that immediately caught his attention: 'In AD 58, Paul went to Israel to give the money he had collected on his travels to the community in Jerusalem.'

Peter hesitated. Was this the number he was looking for? A time to reap . . . He opened Wikipedia.nl and typed '58' into the search box. It led to a list of events that had taken place in AD 58, and there, near the bottom, was Paul's collection.

Palestine
The Apostle Paul returns to Jerusalem with the money he has collected. However, he is accused of treachery and is arrested and imprisoned in Caesarea.

If this was what he was looking for, then his clues so far were 42, 41, 41 and 58. He still couldn't make any sense of them, but now an idea was taking shape at the back of his mind. The answer was there, not quite within reach yet. Just like when the students in their association jackets had eventually led him to the ravens in the Quintus boardroom.

Suddenly, the café's sliding door shot open, and a young man in a waiter's apron appeared. He came to a halt and gawped at Peter in surprise.

The glass walls of the office muffled the waiter's voice, but Peter didn't need to be a lipreader to see that his mouth was forming the words, 'What are you doing in there?'

Peter waved, as though he was greeting a colleague for the first time that day. He immediately got up and left the office to head towards the café, but the man blocked the doorway.

'Might I ask what you were doing in there?' he asked, trying to sound authoritative but without much success.

'Sorry,' Peter said, 'I know this looks odd, but the battery on my phone is dead, and I really needed to look something up. I haven't taken anything.' He put his hands in the air to prove it.

The waiter didn't move.

Peter put his hand on the man's arm, and tried politely to move him aside. 'Come on, don't be silly,' he said, using the same tone he took with unruly students. 'My phone's dead, I had to look something up. It's no big deal. I really do need to get a move on now, so would you please just let me through?'

This time the waiter allowed Peter to pass. 'Okay then,' he said, and then, trying to sound firm, he added: 'But don't do this again, all right?'

Peter nodded and meekly bowed his head. He walked through the café, and heaved a huge sigh of relief when he made it outside. He left the Kloksteeg and disappeared into the narrow alley of the Lombardpoort, went through Gekroonde Liefdepoort's little garden and came out among the tall, tightly packed houses and flats of the Langebrug. Then he turned right, towards the backs of the shops on the Breestraat. He still had no idea what to do next.

When he saw Kapper Eric, the barbershop, it suddenly struck him that a haircut and a shave might make him less recognisable. Eric's was famous for its stained-glass windows and vintage interior. Taking a seat in one of his old barber's chairs was like travelling back in time to the 1950s.

Apart from one gentleman who was already having his hair cut, Peter was the only customer. He hung his coat on the hat stand next to a trench coat and a baseball cap.

'And what'll it be, sir?' the barber asked. His own hair was so perfectly styled that he could have been a catalogue model.

'I think I'd like to go short for a change,' Peter said. 'Close-cropped, let's say number one.'

The barber looked at him in the mirror with amusement. 'And what has brought you to this, might I say, rather radical decision, sir?' he asked, running his fingers almost tenderly through Peter's hair. 'Such a fine head of hair at your age . . . It would almost be a travesty.'

'It's . . . well, I've given it a lot of thought,' Peter said. He hadn't expected any resistance. 'It's a long story, but I've reached a new phase in my life. A fresh start, you could say. I don't want to give you my whole life story, but—'

'You should hear some of the secrets people tell me while they're sitting in that chair. You could make a whole TV series out of them.'

'Cut!' Peter joked.

'Yes, that would be a good name for it. But anyway . . . A new spring, a new hairstyle,' the barber said, relenting.

'And a shave please.' As far as Peter knew, this was the only place in Leiden where you could get a shave.

'As you wish.'

The barber helped Peter into a cape, draped a long, white cloth around his neck, then clicked an attachment onto some hair clippers. 'This is a centimetre,' he said, 'and I won't go any shorter. Any less than that and you'd be practically bald.'

Peter nodded.

Ten minutes later, he was finished.

'It's not really much of a challenge, this sort of hairstyle,' the man said, sounding disappointed. 'But I can at least take pride in being able to give you a good shave. It's a disappearing art.' He wet Peter's face and neck, and then covered them with a soapy lather.

Peter closed his eyes and enjoyed the warm water and the way the barber's fingers gently massaged his skin.

He worked silently, taking more time than he had for the haircut.

Peter had been so caught up in looking for Judith that he hadn't had a chance to stop and think about how insane this whole thing was. He had been chosen, Raven had said. But who had chosen him? On what basis? And why did they have to kidnap Judith because of it? Was it some sort of initiation? You surely couldn't initiate someone against their will. And why were there also people trying to *murder* him? But he couldn't go back now. He had to try to find Judith as soon as possible.

What was his next step supposed to be? According to the web search he'd done at the Observatory, the next clue would have something to do with the Sun-Runner. After that came the Father. But where would he find a Sun-Runner?

The Sun-Runner was also called Heliodromus or Heliodromos, which, based on the small amount of Greek he knew, could mean 'path of the sun' . . . At high school, he'd made a solar motion demonstrator on an astronomy course. The little paper gadget modelled the sun's path across the sky, demonstrating how it changed according to the location and time of year. The path the sun took across the sky was actually dependent on your position as well as the season.

Sun-Runner, Heliodromus, path of the sun . . .

The most obvious place to look would be the Boerhaavemuseum, the Dutch National Museum for the History of Science and Medicine. It held a vast collection of objects from the history of science, including Willem Blaeu's giant quadrant, Antoni van Leeuwenhoek's famous microscopes, and Christiaan Huygens' pendulum clocks. It also housed scale models of the solar system. And solar motion demonstrators.

Peter looked in the mirror. His exhaustion was written all over his face. The wrinkles on his forehead looked deeper than ever.

Freshly shorn and shaved, he hardly resembled the man who had walked into the barbershop just twenty minutes earlier. He was finished even sooner than the customer who was already being served when he arrived. He gave the barber a satisfied smile as he brushed the tiny hairs from his neck and unfastened the cape.

He paid with cash. The barber said goodbye, then grabbed a broom to sweep up the hair on the floor.

Peter reached for his coat on the hat stand, then stopped. He looked around. The barber was concentrating on sweeping the floor. His colleague was still cutting the hair of the customer who had arrived before him. In one fluid movement, Peter swept both the trench coat and the baseball cap off the hat stand and made his way outside with them.

As he walked down the alley, he put on the long coat, jammed the cap down low over his eyes, and kept his head down. His disguise was so good that he felt brave enough to head towards the busy Breestraat. All Clark Kent had needed to do to hide his identity from Lois Lane was put on a pair of glasses. Compared to that, this was a complete metamorphosis.

He walked along the Breestraat, staying close to the shop fronts, until he arrived at the town hall half way down the street. Then he crossed over to the V&D department store and the building site that was part of the Aalmarkt redevelopment project. He turned right into the Vrouwensteeg, and went over the canal at the end of it via the Kippenbrug. He passed the organic greengrocer's where he bought a seasonal vegetable box every week, then went across the Haarlemmerstraat to the Vrouwenkerksteeg where the Kijkhuis cinema stood.

This route brought him close to the courtyard where Judith and Mark lived. He had come full circle, in a way. Did this mean he was on the right track?

He had thought from the very beginning that the solution to this puzzle would magically appear when he had found all the clues. But now that all he had was a growing string of meaningless numbers, he wasn't sure of that any more. What would he do if his next clue was another number? Or a seventh number after that? He wasn't a genius like Robert Langdon, who could instantly recognise the Fibonacci sequence in a seemingly random set of numbers, or crack a secret code that was known only to medieval philosophers. If the next clue wasn't something obvious, he had no idea how he was supposed to solve the puzzle. And what would happen then?

And what the hell had happened to Arnold? Who was behind that? He was amazed he hadn't given any thought to the poor man until now, when he was the reason Peter had been arrested. He had never liked Arnold. Not so much because he was given the professorship that Peter had felt was his, but because he simply wasn't the right man for the job. His interest in the subject left much to be desired, and he was far too busy with himself and his network.

Peter's thoughts had been so focused on Judith that he'd had no time to worry about Arnold. When would this end, he asked himself miserably. He desperately wanted to find Judith safe . . . The close friendship they had formed over the last twenty years was one of the most precious and valuable things in his life. He had often fantasised about what it would be like to spend his life with her, but he knew these were just daydreams. She was so happy with Mark, and he was the right age for her, not twenty years too old, like Peter.

When he reached the door of the Boerhaavemuseum, he pushed down on the handle and leaned into it with his shoulder. Standing here out on the busy street left him exposed. He needed to get inside as soon as possible. But the door didn't budge.

The museum was still closed.

34

A day earlier, Friday 20 March, 10:15am

'At two o'clock this afternoon,' the Father said, 'the light of the outside world will penetrate our world. Today, for the first time in more than twenty centuries, what was invisible will be made visible. We will reveal ourselves. The world will know that we are here.'

Most of those present voiced their approval. But some of the men stayed silent. They stared straight ahead, avoiding the Father's eyes.

'After his initiation, Raven will wait in the place that our Lion Daniël has prepared for us. The lightest of touches will be all that is needed to cause the ceiling – or the bottom of the pit to them – to collapse.'

He looked around the room again.

'I expect Raven to be discovered at three o'clock. The ninth hour. And then, in more than one respect, we will be taking a leap in the dark.'

The room was not only silent now, everyone in it was perfectly still, as though they were performing a tableau vivant.

A Soldier raised his hand. The Father gave him permission to speak. 'With the greatest respect, *Pater*, and I know I've asked this before, but how do you see our future after this? How will we recruit new members? Now we observe people for a year before inviting them to join . . . Will people soon be able to just fill in an application form on the internet?' He asked the question in a mocking tone.

'Listen, listen . . . This is all new, and I understand that you need time to get used to it. Our group will stay just as it is. It may mean that we will have to meet somewhere else, or we might be able to continue to hold our services here. But our meetings will continue to be private. Nothing will change about the way we recruit new members. The only change will be that the world will know we exist. We can tell people what we stand for, up to a point, without giving away our secrets. Think of the Freemasons. Everyone knows about them, but you can't just become one of them.'

The Father paused. 'The important thing . . . The most important thing is that people will see that *our* beliefs lie at the heart of many of the ideas in other religions and belief systems. People will be amazed when they discover the origins of their own faiths. You should see it as an opportunity to introduce our ideas to a wider audience.'

He took a sip of wine, swilled it around in his mouth, then spat it on the ground. 'Finally, after two thousand years, we will be able to give Paul, our Paul, the prominence that is rightfully his. Our theological genius, who has been venerated for the wrong reasons . . . He poured the old wine of Mithras into the new skin of Christianity. He ensured its survival through the centuries, like an animal that remains hidden because of its camouflage, or the chameleon that adapts its colour to its surroundings. Our titan of Tarsus . . .'

'What about your own congregation?' someone else protested.

'Yes, that's very . . . well, it will be difficult. I . . . We'll see what happens. But . . . our ideas will appeal to many people. Doesn't everyone give in to temptation sometimes? Don't most people have the feeling that the mind is willing but the flesh is weak? The soul is bound by the flesh, and it is kept there by every bad choice we make, but we . . . We have found the means of escape. We can control those base desires. What a message that is! And the world is ready to hear it. Our story may be centuries old, but our message is as new as it was when it was first proclaimed.'

As he spoke, the Father's normal voice transformed into the one he usually used to deliver his sermons. Even the men who had just spoken their objections listened as though entranced.

'The rituals will not be spoken of. Knowing our secrets would be more than some people could cope with.'

Tiny took a piece of bread and held it up for them all to see. Then he did the same with the chalice. 'People will see that the bread, the body, and the wine, the blood, are universal . . . That they are not exclusive to this religion or that, but relevant to everyone, regardless of where they were born, or the faith they were raised in. When our Paul wrote in his second letter to the Corinthians that he was cunning, that he "got the better of you by guile", it was with good reason. If he hadn't—'

'That's enough!' one of the Lions shouted, leaping to his feet. 'How much longer do we have to listen to this? We've been in the shadows for centuries. That's why we've endured. I see no good reason for us to—'

'Silence!' the Father shouted with such ferocity that the man who had dared to criticise him dropped dumbly back onto his seat. 'Do not speak about things of which you have no under-standing. Put your trust in those above you. There have been signs, and I do not need to repeat them, there have been clear, unmistakable signs. That is why . . .'

Tiny slammed his palm down so hard on the altar that the chalice of wine almost fell over. 'That is why I have decided, as your leader . . . as your *Father* . . .' He said the word with great tenderness. ' . . . to take us into a new era. I have chosen a man who will bring our message to the world, if he succeeds in the task I have set him. I have been watching him for many years . . . He *knows* things, as does the woman who is also part of this plan. If he completes his quest, then I will know that the signs have not deceived me. He will be the face of our organisation.'

He looked at the Sun-Runner who was sitting next to him. 'I still intend for you to take over from me. You mustn't concern yourself about that. But this Peter is a gifted speaker and he has a brilliant mind. He has already—'

'But what if he fails?' someone asked.

'Then nothing will have been lost. Then we retreat back into the shadows, and I will step down. The Sun-Runner will take my place, and you will find a new place to meet. But it will not come to that, I give you my word.'

The room was quiet.

Another man got to his feet, a Soldier. 'The, um . . . new members,' he began hesitantly, 'will they have to follow all of our rules?'

'Brothers,' the Father said, full of fire, 'I believe that in the early days our Lord chose me from among you to spread the good news and bring people to him. Our Lord, who knows the human heart, will show his trust in them by giving them his strength, just as he did to us. And in cleansing their hearts by faith, he will make no distinction between them and us. So why are you putting God to the test by wishing to burden these new people with a yoke which neither our ancestors nor we have been able to bear? On the contrary, I believe that we will be saved through the grace of our Lord, just as they will be.'

At that, they were all silent.

Jakob, a Bridegroom, spoke up. He said: 'Brothers, listen to me. The Father has told us how our Lord himself has devised a plan to form a group from the unbelievers that will honour his name. It echoes the words which have been passed down to us: "After this I will return and I will rebuild my house which has fallen; from its ruins I will rebuild it. I will set it up, so that all other peoples may seek the Lord – even all the unbelievers over whom my name has been called. So says the Lord, who has been making these things known from long ago." In my opinion, we shouldn't overburden those who are newly converted. But we should let them know that they should abstain from what is strictly forbidden: lewdness and fornication, theft, malice and lies, and eating meat that has blood in it.'

Murmurs of consent filled the room, although there was also quiet tutting from those who disagreed. The Father looked approvingly at Jakob.

'Good,' the Father said, 'then we'll move on to the reason we have gathered today. And whatever happens tomorrow, we will meet again tomorrow evening.' He stood up, untied the lamb, and led it to the pit.

The wooden planks were removed again. Raven disappeared into a passage at the rear of the temple, led by the Sun-Runner. In a corridor at the bottom of a flight of stairs, a door stood open.

The Sun-Runner ushered him through it. Raven stood in the middle of the room and the door was closed behind him.

Light from above made its way into the cell. He had been here before. A few months earlier when he was proving his worthiness, they had locked him in this room in total darkness, without telling him when he would be freed.

Or if he would be freed.

Afterwards he had found out that they had left him there for three days and three nights. He had been tormented by a thirst so terrible that he had tried to drink his own urine. But it was no easy task to catch your own piss in your hands in pitch darkness. Despite almost vomiting – it was the idea of it more than the taste – he had been able to moisten his mouth and throat. Later his thirst had made him so desperate that he had tried again. The acrid stink of ammonia that rose from the pathetic puddle he'd caught turned his stomach so much that he threw it away, flapping his fingers in disgust. But the smell stayed on his hands.

When they had eventually come to free him, he was almost convinced that he had passed over into the land of the dead. The light from their torches looked like the light at the end of the tunnel that people described after near-death experiences.

The word 'thirst' wasn't anywhere near adequate to describe how much he had longed for water. They had found him hallucinating, completely disoriented, and unable to stand without help. But he was a true soldier of Mithras and he had not given up.

Now he was here again, ready to become a member of the brotherhood.

The Father had positioned himself in the middle of the grate above the pit in which Raven stood. The lamb lay on its side at his feet.

A Lion handed him a knife. The flickering torchlight glinted on the blade.

The Father raised his arm above his head.

'You have saved us by the shedding of the eternal blood!' he cried.

Raven looked up. 'You have saved us by the shedding of the eternal blood!' he echoed.

The Father expertly drew the knife across the lamb's neck, slicing its artery with a single cut. A few seconds later, it was limp and still.

Warm blood gushed from its neck in a pulsating stream, falling like a consecrating rain into the pit below. Clothed only in a loincloth, Raven smeared the life-giving blood into his body. He tipped his head back and opened his mouth wide to take in as much blood as he could. As spatters of blood sprayed from his lips, he uttered the hopeful formula that had been incanted by thousands before him. 'His blood be on us and on our children!'

With one voice, the men above him repeated the wish that others might be cleansed by the blood of their Lord. 'His blood be on us and on our children!'

When the lamb had been drained of blood, Raven stood still like a bloody pillar and softly murmured a prayer.

The others sat on the benches with their eyes closed, bowed their heads and held up their hands, palms facing upwards, each lost in his own thoughts.

After a time, the Father got to his feet. He turned to face them, raised his arms in a gesture of benediction and said, 'Go in peace.'

'Peace be with you,' the men mumbled.

'The peace of our Lord be with you always.'

'And with your spirit.'

'*Et lux in tenebris lucet.*' And the light shines in the darkness.

'Amen.'

Tiny Strauss left the temple, leaving behind him a thin trail of the blood that still dripped from his fingers.

35

Judith stood on top of what was left of her bed. She knew she was only delaying the inevitable, but did it anyway. She had put the mattress and the blanket on top of it to make a little mound, like an island in a swollen river.

The water was rising, very slowly but undeniably. It flowed steadily out of the pipe in a smooth arc, splashing into the murky green puddle on the floor, throwing up foam and little bubbles.

Judith pressed her back against the wall behind her, desperately trying to get as far away from the water as she could. But it was hopeless. It was already sloshing over the top of her little hill.

She held the candle close to her chest, cupping her hand around it to protect the wildly flickering flame.

She gathered her courage with a deep breath and stepped into the water. It was already up to her knees and so cold that her arms were covered in goosebumps. She waded to the door and although her fists already ached from banging on it, she rammed them into it again.

What else could she do?

She went back to the iron ring in the wall. The candle was too wide to fit into it, but she dripped candle wax around it as best

266

she could and then forced the bottom of the candle into the ring. When she was confident that it wouldn't fall out, she let go.

She went back to the bed and threw the blanket and the mattress into the water. The mattress floated like an airbed, giving her a tiny glimmer of hope. If the water kept coming in, she might be able to float on it and buy herself a little more time.

She took hold of the bed so that she could push it into the corner of the cell, next to the pipe that was still spewing out water. Then, like a karateka gathering strength for a kick with a loud 'kiai!', she screamed at the top of her lungs and lifted it up.

She slipped, flew backwards, and landed on her back under the water. The bed landed on top of her. A moment later, she lifted her head above the surface, coughing and spitting out the water that had ended up in her mouth. It tasted of canal water. She recognised the taste from childhood summers when she and the other children in her neighbourhood jumped from the canal bridges into the murky *grachten* below them.

After a lot of pushing and shoving, she was able to manoeuvre the wreck of the bed into the corner of the cell and lean it against the wall at an angle. She took off her blouse and shivered. Climbing up the bed was much more difficult this time. It threatened to topple over if she didn't stay exactly in the middle of it.

Eventually, she managed to get as close to the pipe as she possibly could. She started to stuff the sleeve of her blouse into the narrow opening, using two hands to force it in against the water that kept pushing the fabric back out. As the opening narrowed, the water pressure increased and spouted into the room with even more force. Judith's fingers were stiff with cold and cramp, but when she had finally stuffed most of the sleeve into the pipe, the stream of water gradually slowed to a thin trickle that seeped through the soaked blouse.

Judith breathed a sigh of relief and climbed down again.

Without her weight to hold it against the wall, the improvised ladder slid back down again.

She gingerly lowered herself onto the mattress to see if it would hold her weight but it was soon obvious that she was too heavy for the flimsy thing. She sank to the bottom of the water, and the two ends of the mattress stuck up out of it like a letter V.

She stood up again, wrapped her arms around her upper body, which was naked now except for her bra, and fixed her eyes on the blouse in the pipe, as though she might keep it in place just by staring at it.

The water level in the cell was no longer rising. But the pressure building behind the blouse soon became too much for the wall to bear. A wet patch had begun to form around the edges of the pipe where it emerged from the wall. It didn't take long for the loamy clay to start coming away. Chunks of it splashed down, like slabs of ice falling from a melting glacier.

She was struck by the ridiculous thought that she mustn't cry because her tears would only make the water rise faster. And then, like a breaking dam, the wall burst open and the water flooded into the cell with even more force than it had before.

She stood in the middle of the cell. How long would it take for this space to fill up completely? The water flowed so powerfully that the water level must be rising. But when she looked at the wall, there was no evidence of it getting higher. Even so, if someone didn't come to help her soon, at some point she would be pushed up to the grate above her head and drown.

She covered her ears with her hands to protect herself from the sounds of her own screaming.

THE FIFTH VISION

And behold, I saw the man . . . forty-eight years old, no longer the child of his father and mother, no longer belonging to this village or that, but become one with all the people. Who is his mother? Who are his brothers? All those who act in accordance with the will of his Father, the lord of light, are his brother, his sister, his mother.

And his mission is successful. He has already made many disciples for the way. His story has become their story, the bread of his Lord is the bread of their Lord, the blood of his Lord is the blood of their Lord. In one fell swoop, his message has created division among the Jews, incited the anger of the high priest, and grown his followers to a number that already surpasses that of Jesus' early disciples.

And behold, some men come down to Judea from Antioch, saying that the brethren must have themselves circumcised as Moses commanded them. Paul and his brother Barnabas are consumed by rage. The pain he feels when urinating is a constant reminder of his humiliation, the mutilation of his manhood. His attack is aimed at the heart of this covenant. No one should have to suffer as he has.

And they decide to go to Jerusalem.

After fourteen years, he returns. They go to Phoenicia and Samaria to tell them about the conversion of the Gentiles, bringing great joy to all the believers. In Jerusalem, they are welcomed by the Apostles, the elders, and the rest of the community. Paul and Barnabas declare all that God has brought about through them. But some believers who belong to the sect of the Pharisees insist on the laws of their forefathers: the non-Jewish believers must also be circumcised and keep the law of Moses.

And Peter is compelled by the Spirit and gets up and says: 'God has made no distinction between them and us because he has cleansed their hearts by faith. Why are you putting God to the test by putting a yoke upon the neck of the disciples which neither our ancestors nor we have been able to bear?' At this, all those assembled are silent, and they listen to Barnabas and Paul who tell them of all the signs and wonders God has done through them among the Gentiles.

And hark, James gets up and says: 'God has formed a plan to take from among the Gentiles a people that will honour his name. Therefore I have reached the decision that we should not trouble those Gentiles who are turning to God, but we should write to them to tell them that they should abstain from things that are polluted by idols, and from fornication and from meat which still contains blood, and from blood itself.'

And Paul and Barnabas go back to Antioch with a letter from the Apostles and the elders. Their mission is to preach the Gospel to the Gentiles, while Peter and his followers will preach to the Jews. They take with them a letter containing the decision that no greater burden will be placed on the Gentiles than that which is strictly necessary: 'Abstain from meat that has been sacrificed to idols, from blood, and from meat which still contains blood, and from unchastity. If you keep yourself from these, you will be doing what is good.'

And hark, they read the letter to them in Antioch and the community rejoices at its encouraging words. Paul and Barnabas remain in Antioch teaching and preaching the message from Paul's true Lord.

And Paul sends his followers out as lambs in the midst of wolves. They take no purse with them, no bag, and no sandals, and he forbids them to greet anyone they meet on the road. Whatever house they enter, they must first say: 'Peace to this house!' Then they remain in that house, eating and drinking what they are provided, for the labourer deserves to be paid.

And Paul thinks: I will reap the harvest that comes from the blood of my Lord. The harvest is plentiful, but the labourers are few. He asks the Lord of the harvest to send out labourers to gather it in.

I am the divine reaper.

I am a Persian.

36

HELIODROMUS

SUN-RUNNER

Twenty-one years ago, spring 1994

After his eighth fit, the visions stopped.

He'd had the first vision after falling from his bike at Archeon. It had taken him completely by surprise. Seven more had followed. Much like dreams, he had never been able to tell how long they lasted. Time seemed not to exist when the visions came, as though the voice was speaking to him from another dimension.

By the second or third time, he had learned to recognise the signs that told him that he was about to have another vision. Always in the evening and always when he was alone, in bed. Shortly before they started, he'd feel tingling in his hands and on the top of his head, and oddly, on the soles of his feet. His breathing would slow down and he'd feel as though he was slipping away. The sounds around him disappeared, like swimming below the surface of a perfectly calm sea.

Then the light would appear, shining with an incredible brightness. The voice that spoke from it was neither male nor female. Tiny would lie as still as possible, afraid that the slightest movement would break the spell. Almost as unexpectedly as the voice had begun to speak, it would stop again.

When the visions stopped, the priest did all he could to make them return. He lay on his back in bed, closed his eyes, and focused on breathing in and out. Sometimes, his fingers would begin to tingle and he would wait expectantly for something to happen. But he would wake the next morning without having heard the voice.

The voice had told him a story, a story in seven parts, about the secret history of the Apostle Paul, full of insights into his life and work. They shone a brand new light on the story he knew, the story the world knew. How Paul's thirst for revenge had led him to create a literary Trojan horse that had penetrated right to the heart of the Jewish community.

Tiny had written the visions down and shown them to no one but Ane. Ane said that the visions were absolute proof that the Lord intended Tiny to be his successor. Tiny progressed with astonishing speed, working his way through all the grades while still performing his daily duties as priest and shepherd of his flock.

The sixth stage, that of the Sun-Runner, was the last grade before he took over as leader of the group and became the Father. It was ironic that he would keep the title with which most of his parishioners already addressed him.

To become a Sun-Runner, you had to separate yourself from your own people, your own background. You had to imagine yourself as being at one with the cosmos to which you were inextricably connected, and unwaveringly self-aware and self-assured, like a Buddhist monk, unaffected by the worries of everyday life. By doing so, you would become as steadfast as the sun in the sky. The sun never worried about whether it would shine or not. It just did.

During his initiation, he had been made to lie in a stone sarcophagus, like someone waiting to be buried, until he saw a blinding light. The light had been so intense that he had been unable to see, but two other members had helped him out of his temporary coffin. A flaming torch was pressed into his hand and he was crowned with a wreath of golden leaves, like a halo.

During this stage, he dedicated many of his sermons to preaching about the hundreds of references to light in the bible. About the people who roamed in the darkness and saw a dazzling light, about how God turned darkness into light, and rough places into level ground, about how those who walked in darkness and no longer saw the light could always trust in the name of the Lord. The metaphors were obvious of course; man had always been fighting a battle against darkness. Our fear of the dark was primitive, a fear that had never completely left us. Fear of unknown things lurking in the shadows that could reach out and grab you if you weren't careful. His homilies about light always resonated with the people in the pews. Everyone had wrestled with darkness at some point in their lives.

And of course, he preached about Jesus himself, particularly the Gospel According to John, full of metaphors about light and darkness. How light had come into the world, but people loved darkness rather than the light because their deeds were evil. And Jesus, who said of himself: 'I am the light of the world; he who follows me will not walk in darkness, but will have the light of life.'

That was how he had stumbled on the Ebionites, considered by many to be the earliest Christians, perhaps even the only real Christians. They still existed, albeit as a tiny group in the Middle East, but they had endured.

He had read about them as a student, but had always seen them as more of a curiosity than anything else, something that had unexpectedly, perhaps even unintentionally, survived the storms of time. They were a little like the coelacanth, a fish that

273

was thought to have been extinct for sixty-five million years but, to the amazement of evolutionary biologists, a live specimen had turned up in a trawler's net in 1938.

The Ebionites were Jews who had always followed Jesus. Not Messianic Jews, and so not so-called Jewish Christians, but Jewish in the same way that Jesus' first followers and disciples were: they were circumcised, followed the dietary laws, upheld the rules set down in the Torah and so on. They called themselves 'the poor ones' – *ebionim* – after 'the poor in spirit' who would inherit the kingdom of heaven. They were Jewish in every respect, and regarded Jesus as their guide and teacher, but also as the biological son of Mary and Joseph. They were said to have their own version of the Gospel of Matthew which left out the story of the virgin birth.

According to the Ebionites, when Jesus was baptised by John, God 'chose' him, so to speak, by virtue of him being the most righteous person on earth. He was the very first person to follow God's law absolutely. Because of this perfect obedience to the law, he was justified and named Christ, the Anointed.

According to the Ebionites, Jesus' followers did not worship him, nor did they see him as their saviour. Jesus' brother James continued the Christian movement after his death, but in the eyes of the Ebionites it was hijacked by Paul, the Jew who suddenly became a 'Christian'. They called him a false teacher. The Dutch language version of the Ebionite Manifesto states:

> We declare that Paul of Tarsus should be considered a false teacher, who opposes circumcision, the mark of Covenant, and opposes G'd's Torah, and in so doing has strayed from the Way taught by Yeshua, the anointed son of Miryam and Yosef.

They write:

We expose your Apostle as false; your testament as false; your society as false; your church, its rulers, your governments as false. Our allegiance and hope is to the G'd of Israel alone.

They had their own gospel, the Gospel of the Ebionites, of which only a few fragments were still known to exist. Ironically, it was only because the early Fathers of the Church quoted so extensively from their gospel in order to refute it that anything had survived at all. The information that formed the basis for the Ebionites' two-thousand-year-old claim that Paul was a heretic could be found in this gospel. They were right, Tiny thought, but they had no idea in which respect they were right.

In his work *Panarion*, the Medicine Chest, better known as *Adversus Haereses* or 'Against Heresy', the Church Father Epiphanius of Salamis described no less than eighty heretic groups. The entire thirtieth chapter was devoted to attacking the Ebionites in a wide variety of ways.

When Tiny read sections 8 and 9 of paragraph 16 in this chapter, his eyes were truly opened.

16:8 Nor are they [the Ebionites] ashamed to accuse Paul here with certain fabrications of their false Apostles' villainy and imposture. They say that he was Tarsean – which he admits himself and does not deny. And they suppose that he was of Greek parentage, taking the occasion for this from the (same) passage because of his frank statement, 'I am a man of Tarsus, a citizen of no mean city.'

The next paragraph was even more significant:

16:9 They then claim that he was Greek and the son of a Greek mother and Greek father, but that he had gone up to Jerusalem, stayed there for a while, desired to marry a daughter of the high priest, and had therefore became a proselyte and been circumcised. But since he still could not marry that sort of girl he became angry and wrote against circumcision, and against the Sabbath and the legislation.

The Ebionites said that Paul had converted not just once, but twice. He had first converted to Judaism in the hope that he might marry the high priest's daughter. He changed his Roman name, Paulus, to the Jewish name Saulus or Saul. When he converted for the second time, to Christianity, it was from a desire for revenge because they had rejected him. From that moment on, he was known as Paul again. His parents may well have been Greek, but they had acquired Roman citizenship in Tarsus, probably for a considerable amount of money. When Paul was about to be flogged without trial after his arrest in AD 58, he could rightly ask the centurion: 'Is it legal for you to flog a Roman citizen who is uncondemned?' When the centurion heard this, he went to the tribune to tell them that they were dealing with a Roman citizen. The centurion said: 'What are you about to do? This man is a Roman citizen.' The tribune went up to Paul and asked him: 'Tell me, are you a Roman citizen?' And Paul answered: 'Yes.' The tribune said: ' It cost me a large sum of money to get my citizenship.' To which Paul replied: 'But I was born a citizen.'

Although the Ebionites had been right about Paul's double conversion, they hadn't known about the brilliant way in which he had avenged himself.

Paul had reconverted to Mithraism, the religion of his ancestors, but he had disguised himself as a Christian to take revenge on the high priest and his daughter, and thereby on all Jews. By inserting the well-known story of Mithras into Christianity, he was able to expand the new Christian religion, and diminish the Jews.

'I got the better of you by guile,' he had written. But nobody had ever realised the extent of his cunning, or the genius of the scheme with which he had exacted his revenge.

Until now.

37

Peter leaned against the wall of the Boerhaavemuseum and tried to look nonchalant but he couldn't help peeking inside every few seconds to see if someone was coming to open the door.

The sound of a key finally being turned in a lock felt like a release, as though he was a prisoner being taken out for his daily hour on the yard.

He entered the museum's spacious lobby. He hung his coat on the coat rack but kept the cap on. The employee who had opened the door was already sitting at the till. The lobby was otherwise empty.

He had a *Museumkaart*, an subscription card that gave him entry to all the state museums in the Netherlands, but he bought a ticket anyway, and avoided making eye contact with the receptionist.

Peter pushed open the glass doors that led to the gift shop and the café, went past the anatomical theatre and took the stairs to a hall that housed a display of medical instruments. Then he went into the hall on the right, which contained the museum's stunning collection of planetaria. He examined the magnificent Leidsche Sphaera planetarium, with its planets that hung fixed in their orbits around the sun, but saw nothing that might be a clue to his next move. He stared at the sun, the planet that protected the Sun-Runner, but there was nothing unusual about that either.

The museum had other solar system models which were smaller but their construction was every bit as ingenious as the two-and-a-half-metre-tall Leidsche Sphaera. He examined those too, and again, found nothing. What had he expected? A note taped to the sun with a new number on it?

At a loss, he wandered through the room, hoping he might stumble upon something he had missed earlier. He paused to look at an old bible in a glass case, surprised to see it here. Weren't the bible and science supposed to be at odds with each other? Then again, the very first scientists had seen it as their duty to use scientific research to support God's revealed truths in the bible. If the facts didn't agree with God's word, then the scientist had surely made a mistake and ought to re-examine his evidence. Like Galileo Galilei, who claimed that the earth revolved around the sun rather than the other way around. The church pointed out that in the bible, God clearly answered Joshua's prayer for the sun to stand still so that he could have a few more hours of daylight, and that therefore, Galileo must be wrong.

When he thought about it, Peter realised that it wasn't so odd to see a copy of the *Statenbijbel* here. It was the first official Dutch-language version of the bible, translated directly from the original Hebrew, Aramaic and Greek. The information label next to it said that it had been commissioned by the Synod of Utrecht in 1618. Eight years later, a group of translators in Leiden had begun the enormous task and completed it almost twenty years later in 1635. After it had been approved by the

States General, it went into print. The City of Leiden paid 2500 guilders for the rights to print the text in Leiden, an immense sum in those days. Half a million copies were printed over the next twenty years. One of those copies was now on display here behind thick glass, open at one of the Psalms. At first, Peter thought that this particular chapter had been selected for practical reasons because the Psalms were in the middle of the bible. But when he looked more closely, he saw that it had been chosen for a deeper reason, one which was relevant to this room, and relevant to a museum dedicated to the history of science.

The bible was open at Psalm 19. The title read: 'God's Glory Revealed in Creation and the Law'. In other words: by studying God's work, his creation, you could draw closer to God and develop a deeper understanding of him.

Peter read the first verses.

Psalm 19 God's Glory Revealed in Creation and the Law

[1] To the Overseer, a Psalm of David.
[2] The heavens are recounting the honour of God, and the work of His hands, the expanse is declaring.
[3] Day to day uttereth speech and night to night sheweth knowledge.
[4] There is no speech and there are no words, their voice has not been heard.
[5a] Into all the earth their line hath gone forth, and to the end of the world their sayings.[1]

This translation still played a central role in church services in the Netherlands, yet you almost needed a dictionary to be able to understand it.

[5b] For the sun he placed a tent in them.
[6] And he, as a bridegroom, goeth out from his covering; he rejoiceth as a mighty one, to run the path.
[7] From the end of the heavens is his going out, and his revolution is unto their ends, and nothing is hid from his heat.[2]

At that point, Peter realised he was looking in the wrong place.

38

As a student, Daniël had often attended the services held by the Leidse Studenten Ekklesia, an ecumenical church for students in Leiden. The services were held in the Hooglandse Kerk every Sunday morning at half past eleven, a fairly reasonable time for students, although they attracted people from all walks of life. People in his social circle had often given him pitying looks when he confessed – because that's how it felt – that he went to these services.

He had been raised as a Catholic, but like many teenagers, he had almost completely lost interest in his parents' faith by the time he was fifteen or so. However, he hadn't lost interest in religion. He enjoyed the RE lessons at his Catholic high school much more than the other pupils.

He borrowed books from the library about spiritual subjects like chakras, channelling and auras, with titles such as *The Seth Material, The Aquarian Conspiracy* or *The Dancing Wu Li Masters*. He read Carlos Castaneda, Baghwan and Sai Baba, core titles in the New Age movement that had become fairly mainstream by then. He was impressed by *The Empty Mirror* by Janwillem van de Wetering, an account of the many months the author had spent in a Japanese Zen monastery, and its sequel, *A Glimpse of Nothingness*, both books that Daniël devoured.

He would sit in his little attic room and open his atlas to the maps of Nepal and Tibet and dream of distant travel to remote monasteries with ascetic monks in orange robes, living on a strict diet of water, vegetables, rice, and yak butter.

He made a short-lived attempt at meditation, complete with burning joss sticks, which his parents weren't particularly thrilled by.

The exotic nature of these eastern religions and philosophies which had made them so attractive to him was ultimately also what repelled him. They were too strange, too foreign. It made his study of them feel like an empty theoretical exercise rather than a meaningful part of his life.

He left his eastern phase behind him when he went to study archaeology in Leiden, but he was still vaguely interested in religion. As the cliché goes, the criminal always returns to the scene of his crime, and so Daniël eventually began to attend church services again. In the beginning, it was because he'd been invited by a girl he liked. But the second time they'd gone to church together she'd brought her boyfriend along and held his hand throughout the entire service, even during the prayers. However, Daniël had found the services pleasantly relaxed and welcoming, and so he carried on going to them. The sermons often had a philanthropical theme, and the various pastors, both men and women, gently encouraged the congregation to turn their faith into deeds. Sometimes they sang psalms, but usually, the hymns were modern songs by the poet and theologian Huub Osterhuis, or catchy sing-alongs from the Taizé repertoire. He could still remember the words to his favourite song, based on the words of Saint Teresa of Avila.

Let nothing disturb you,
Let nothing frighten you,

All things pass away:
God never changes.
Patience obtains all things.
He who has God
Finds he lacks nothing;
God alone suffices.[3]

But just as the philosophies of the east had failed to stick, he found that the ecumenical, neither-fish-nor-fowl Ekklesia services were ultimately too informal to become a permanent part of his life .

So, after many churchless years in which his empty Sundays lacked focus and purpose, he went back to the bosom of the mother church.

The church he returned to was the Coelikerk in the middle of the Haarlemmerstaat, a house of God built in the neoclassical style. He had always found it a beautiful building, but his main reason for choosing it, at least initially, was its location within walking distance of his student digs. To a large extent, the liturgy was fixed of course, and very little had changed since his youth. It gave him the warm feeling of being part of an ancient tradition, with its 'call and response' prayers, the way the liturgical colours changed according to the season of the church year, the candles, and the familiar smell of incense rising from the silver censer as the altar boy swung it back and forth.

He could have found all of this at another church, but the priest, Tiny Strauss, quickly became his reason for staying. Tiny's short sermons had an intensity that Daniël had never witnessed from other Catholic ministers. He celebrated communion by breaking the enormous host – the same size and shape as a small frisbee – blessing the wine, and reciting the standard formulas with such passion that an observer might think that the priest was doing all of these things for either the first or last time in his life, and that for him, the host truly was transformed into the body of Christ, and the chalice truly was filled to the brim with the precious blood of the Lamb of God who took away the sins of the world.

And it was at the Coelikerk that Daniël met Mani.

He had assumed that Mani was an asylum seeker at first, someone who had converted from Islam to Catholicism. Or a Christian who had fled a Middle-Eastern country torn apart by war and bigotry.

He turned out to be neither.

Mani belonged to the Parsis, an Iranian-Indian religious group descended from the Zoroastrians in the former Sasanian Empire of Persia, currently Iran. From the third century to the seventh, the main religion in this region was Parsism.

Mani had been in need 'spiritual food', as he called it, and the Coelikerk suited his needs. He recognised a lot of his own religion in the services, although Daniël didn't realise just how similar they really were until later.

By chance – or at least, Daniël had assumed for a long time that it had been by chance until Mani eventually told him otherwise – Mani and Daniël found themselves sitting next to each other on a pew one day. They got on well, despite Mani being ten years older than Daniël. He was progressing in his career and had a family, while Daniël was wrestling with his thesis, which ironically, considering the grand dreams of his youth, was about the archaeology of the Lowlands. They had shared interests in religious ideas, literature and music, but also in football and certain TV programmes.

Daniël soon started looking for Mani in the crowd of faces every Sunday morning. He usually found him quickly; his dark skin and black hair stood out in the sea of grey. They often went for coffee together at Annie's Verjaardag or on the bridge next to Café van Engelen. Sometimes they took a walk around town or the Hortus.

His wife and children never joined them, but Daniël met them when Mani invited him to his home for Nowruz, the Iranian New Year celebration with Zoroastrian roots that dated back to a time long before Islam's arrival in Iran.

Mani had explained that he and his family believed that the *haft sin*, literally 'the seven S's, should be present in every home for the new year. They carefully set a table with seven symbolic things that began with the Persian letter 's'. There was wheat for rebirth, a pudding for abundance, dried fruit for love, garlic for healing, apples for health and beauty, sumac berries for the colour of sunrise, and finally, vinegar for a long life and patience. And they kept up a cherished tradition of growing seven different plants or seeds to symbolise the fact that a new life cycle had begun.

On the *haft sin* table, there were also coins for wealth and good luck, eggs for fertility, and an orange floating in a dish of water to represent earth floating in space. A goldfish in a bowl symbolised life, and a double-sided mirror reflected the light from burning candles, one for each child in the family, one for each new life . . .

Mani had told him about Zoroastrianism, the religion founded by the prophet Zarathustra in Ancient Persia somewhere around the sixth century BC. Its central ideas were about the eternal battle between good and evil, light and darkness, god and devil . . . You could be on the side of the good god, the creator Ahura-Mazda, or his wicked adversary, Ahriman, the destructive spirit who sought to drive a wedge between god and man out of spite. The good god had other gods around him, like Mitra, whose name meant 'agreement', 'alliance', or sometimes: 'testament'. There were also gods with names like Varuna, Agni and Indra which would later appear in Hinduism. Zarathustra was murdered in the fire-temple at Bakh and his last words, spoken to his killer, were: 'May Ahura-Mazda forgive you, as I do now.'

It was believed that a saviour, a *Saoshyant*, would appear at the end of time, a messiah who would destroy all evil. After the final battle, Mitra would be one of the three judges to separate those who had done good from those who had done evil, so that their souls could be judged. By doing good deeds, speaking good words and thinking good thoughts, everyone could play their part in the battle, everyone could be a soldier in the good god's army. The good god was symbolised by an eternal flame which the priests kept burning in the temples. These were the very same priests or *magoi* in the Gospel of Matthew, who came from the east to witness the birth of Jesus that had been predicted by Zarathustra, and who honoured him with gifts of gold, frankincense and myrrh.

As Daniël later realised, he was slowly but surely being drawn towards the inner circle. Until one day, after mass, the priest invited him and Mani for coffee in the sacristy.

It was then that he became properly acquainted with Tiny Strauss on a personal level. He spent an increasing amount of time with him, usually together with Mani. Daniël was honoured to be invited to his study house in the Mierennesthofje where they had long discussions about religious and philosophical matters. Tiny and Mani always listened attentively to what he had to say in a way that he was sure no one had ever listened to him before, except perhaps his Dutch teacher, during oral exams in high school.

After a year or two, when he had gained their trust, he was finally introduced to 'the group'. It began with veiled remarks that hinted at a sort of society, a men's club that met regularly. The comments gradually became more overt until the day came that he was told that they were part of an ancient fellowship and that the members had agreed to recommend that he become one of them.

At Tiny's house, he was blindfolded and his head was covered with a black hood so that he was unable to see anything at all. Tiny and Mani took hold of his hands and he followed where they led him, shuffling uncertainly like a little old man.

They went down some stairs and into the basement. He had seen it many times on his way into the house, but never been in it. To his surprise, they didn't stop here, but carried on, descending again via a long staircase. The temperature plunged as they went lower, and the air grew damper.

They walked a long way, or so it felt to Daniël, and every so often, Tiny and Mani stopped and let go of his hands. Then he heard stone scraping over stone, hinges squealing, and the men's breaths becoming laboured.

Eventually, they came to a set of stairs that was too narrow for the three of them to go up at once. Only Mani held onto him here, with his soft, well-cared-for hands, like a father about to take a shy child into a room full of grown-ups.

They walked up the stairs and he tripped over the top step, not realising it was the last one. Then the hood was removed, followed by the blindfold. But he didn't screw up his eyes against a bright light as he had expected to. It was almost dark.

He was in a long room, a cave, and in front of him, twenty men sat opposite each other on long benches. Warm light came from four small torches and two braziers that burned in front of an impressive, coloured relief of the god Mithras. Many of their conversations had been about Mithras lately and he recognised the god immediately.

Each of the members stood up in turn to shake his hand and welcome him, the aspiring member, ready to take his first step on the ladder of the *via salutis*.

Now, many years later, Daniël stood in the house on the Rapenburg where one of the seven entrances to their underground world was hidden. He had progressed to the grade of Lion.

His position in the city council's archaeology department had allowed him to play a crucial role in the execution of the Father's plan. He had been able to weaken the bottom of the hole where the first waste container was to be placed in such a way that it would be certain to collapse as soon as the digger touched it. He hadn't intended for the whole machine to tip over into the hole of course, but there had been surprisingly little fuss made about it afterwards.

A section of the covered-over Roomgracht lay beneath the house they were in now. The canal had led from the Rapenburg canal to the Doelengracht. Centuries earlier, it had been the site of a large nunnery. The Roomgracht had separated the lay sisters' areas of the nunnery from that of the cloistered nuns. After the Reformation, the nunnery's buildings had gradually made way for houses, and this house had belonged to the society from the very beginning. When it was built, somewhere between 1630 and 1635, the Roomgracht was covered over and the society connected the resulting tunnel to the system of passageways underneath the house.

Daniël had come to the Rapenburg house along with many of the society's other members, except for the six who had fallen away. Five, now, because one of them had been accidentally shot by his co-conspirator in the Hortus. Daniël could see Augustinus, his old student association, through the living room window.

They had all been sitting here for a while now, not knowing what to do. The Father was still absolutely committed to carrying out the plan, despite it not having gone as expected the day before.

A certain hardness seemed to have come over him, a bitter sort of doggedness that they hadn't seen in him before.

For many years, the Father had nurtured a deep desire to bring them out into the open so that they no longer had to meet in secret. He wanted the truth to be brought to light. Why allow all those people to walk in darkness, he often asked himself out loud. No one, after lighting a lamp, puts it away in a cupboard. No, they put it on a lampstand, so that it can do what it was made for and spread its light to all in the house.

Hadn't yesterday's eclipse been a clear sign that they were acting with the approval of the Lord, the sun, himself? A solar eclipse on the very day they had begun to come out of the shadows. It was as if the universe was conspiring to make everything happen just as Tiny wanted.

Mani had given a brief account of what had happened at the police station and ended his report with an urgent question. 'Wouldn't it be wiser to end Peter de Haan's mission? Now that the defectors are trying to scupper our plans?'

Tiny shook his head resolutely.

'The die is cast,' he said, 'as I've already told you. There is absolutely no way back now.'

'Where is Judith, actually?' Daniël wanted to know.

'That's not relevant. Only I, Raven and . . .' Tiny said, then sighed. 'Only Jakob and I know that.'

'She's not in the temple, is she?' Mani said in alarm. Allowing the uninitiated into the temple, the holy of holies, was unforgivable in his eyes.

'No, not in the temple,' Tiny said reassuringly.

'Where's Jakob?'

'He should have been back by . . . I sent him out last night to take a photograph of Judith and send it to Peter de Haan. But as Peter no longer has the phone, I'm not sure he's seen it. I've not heard from Jakob since.'

Nobody spoke.

'Gentlemen, might I suggest,' Tiny said at last, breaking the silence, 'that you simply stay here? I'm going to leave for a while to take care of some business, shall we say.'

He finished speaking and stood up. The men followed his example. He raised his arms in the air, as though he was standing on the altar of the Coelikerk on a Sunday, offering his congregation the sign of peace. But instead he said: 'He is light and in him there is no darkness at all.'

'Light shines out of darkness,' they responded, 'and has shone in our hearts to give the light of the knowledge of his glory as it shines in his face.'

'But Father,' Daniël said, although it felt like the wrong moment to say something, like an author scribbling an extra sentence onto the end of a chapter. 'His twenty-four hours will be up at two o'clock. If Peter fails . . . Do you intend to just let Judith go from wherever she is, shake her hand and wish her well? And then say to Peter: "Ah well, you did your best. You didn't make it, but no hard feelings"?'

An unintended sharpness had crept into his words.

Tiny came over and stood in front of him, much closer than he was comfortable with. For the first time in all the years Daniël had known him, he could see a side of the priest that he would rather had been kept hidden. Now there was no sign of the usual friendliness, wisdom or life experience in the priest's eyes. Instead, he saw something outright diabolical, a look that suggested not the *beginnings* of madness but full-blown insanity.

Tiny leaned forward until his forehead was lightly touching Daniël's. Through clenched teeth he snarled: 'Then their light . . .' he almost spat the words out, ' . . . will be extinguished.'

39

Peter went back through the museum, retracing the steps he had taken on the way in. To a certain extent, the Boerhaavemuseum had been a long shot, but despite that, it given him an idea about where to go next. Even so, he felt a little stupid for not having come up with the idea sooner.

The lobby was still hushed and empty. He greeted the receptionist with a polite grunt as he made his way to the coat rack. He put on the coat and cap and made a firm resolution that when this was all over, he would put them in a plastic bag, go back to the barber's and hang them on the door.

A moment or two later, he was outside again. He turned right and passed the back of Judith's house. He glanced through the window, half expecting to see her working at her table, just as he had done so many times before. Peter desperately wished that everything would go back to normal.

He went to the Turfmarkt via the Caeciliastraat, then crossed the street diagonally to go towards the Nieuwe Beestenmarkt. He passed the halal butcher and greengrocer's which was busy and bustling, as usual.

He knew that this wide street made him very visible and that he ought to be careful, but he could already see his target in the distance. The huge sundial outside the De Valk windmill. On its semi-circle of cobbles, slightly raised from the street, white cobbles formed Roman numerals around the outside to mark the hours. The cobbles sloped down to the middle of the semi-circle, where a metal pole, at least five metres long, emerged from the ground with its sharp tip pointing at the sky.

Peter crossed the road and stood on the edge of the sundial. According to the pole's shadow, it was about quarter to ten, but the real time was forty-five minutes later. Someone had once told him why it wasn't accurate, but he had forgotten the finer details of their explanation.

He walked around the perimeter, not sure what he was looking for. There was a little sign with information about the sundial. He read it carefully.

The Sundial at the De Valk Windmill

History
The sundial was created in 1983 when the route of the city's ring road was modified. It is based on a design by traffic engineer Cees van Groeningen, made in close consultation with the staff of Leiden University and the Leiden Observatory.

What is a sundial?
A sundial is an instrument that tells the time by using the position of the sun. The oldest known sundial dates from approximately 1500 BC and was found in Egypt.

How does a sundial work?
The earth rotates on its axis. Because of this, the shadow cast by an object will constantly change its position. In the Northern

Hemisphere, when a shadow points north, it is exactly noon. The sun is in the south and stands at its highest point, precisely above the meridian. It is then twelve o'clock local solar time. Using this information, the dial can then be divided into sections and hour lines can be marked out to show the time according to the different positions of the shadow.

Despite knowing it was pointless, Peter looked behind the information board, but there was no note hidden there.

The Sun-Runner, the Sun-Runner . . .

After that came the Father . . . Where was he supposed to look for that?

A builder emerged from a cabin behind the fence next to the sundial. The Lammermarkt square was completely hidden by security fencing covered in plastic banners. Behind them, an enormous hole in the ground had been created by the excavation works for what was to be the biggest car park in Leiden, and the deepest in the whole of the Netherlands.

'I'd take a good look at the time while you still can, because you won't be able to for much longer,' the builder said.

'How come?'

'We're demolishing it next week. Or "dismantling" as they prefer to call it.'

'Oh, that's a shame,' Peter said with genuine disappointment. 'But it will be put back, won't it?'

'More than likely. But don't quote me on that. I can ask for you if you want. There's someone here who knows a lot more about it than I do.'

'Erm . . . okay. Yes, please,' Peter said, hoping that talking to someone who knew a lot about sundials would provide some inspiration.

The builder went into the cabin and soon came back with a young woman who bounded energetically towards Peter. She looked well put together: her long hair was neatly styled, and she was wearing trendy glasses. All in all she looked rather out of place in this environment.

'Good afternoon,' the woman said. 'My colleague said you had a question about the sundial.'

'It's . . .' Peter realised that he didn't know what he wanted to ask her. 'I understand that it's going to be removed?'

'That's right. It'll be removed next week. And it isn't coming back, sadly. There won't be anywhere to put it when the car park is built.'

'That's a shame. I've always liked it, although it's actually rather useless, isn't it? I always forget why it doesn't tell the right time.'

The woman's eyes lit up. 'Oh, but I can explain that! It's not that complicated really. Hang on a second and I'll come around to you.'

She walked around the cabin and went towards the building site entrance. Seconds later, she reappeared and walked over to Peter with an outstretched hand. She was beaming, like a teacher who has just found out that one of her students is actually interested in her subject.

'I'm Anouschka, Anouschka Jongsten. Lovely to meet you.'

'Peter de . . . Peter de Vries. Likewise.'

'It's like this,' Anouschka began. 'A sundial, as you might expect from the name, tells the solar time. That's actually the true, local time, separate from whatever our modern technology tells us it is. You could say that noon is when the sun is at its highest point in the sky. In the Netherlands, the official time is always ahead of solar time. And today, March twenty-first, is a bit of a special day because day and night are exactly the same length. In perfect balance, you might say.'

Peter nodded.

'Six months from now, there'll be another perfectly balanced day, and then the big drama of light and darkness starts all over again.'

'What do you mean by that?' Peter asked, his interest instantly piqued by the words 'drama of light and darkness'.

The woman smiled at him in the way that people sometimes do when they are genuinely pleased that they know more about a subject than the person they are speaking to. 'Whole mythologies have been built around that, haven't they?' Anouschka said, 'Maybe even whole religions. The battle between darkness and light? From what I can see, they're all based on a simple natural phenomenon, namely that the days grow longer and then they grow shorter again.'

Peter stared at her, but she seemed not to notice. Was he becoming cynical or was it actually a bit too much of a coincidence that she had started talking quite specifically about a battle between light and darkness?

'But,' she continued enthusiastically as she walked over the spot on the ground where the sundial's shadow ended, 'you wanted to know why the time we see here is different to the time on your watch? Look, the shadow is pointing to about ten o'clock. That's the real local time. But your watch says it's quarter to eleven. That's because our official local time is based on the solar time at fifteen degrees longitude east.'

The hairs on the back of Peter's neck stood up, almost as if his body had picked up some sort of signal before his brain did.

'For every degree of longitude you go west, the official time is four minutes ahead of the local solar time,' Anouschka said. 'Plus, the earth's axis is at an angle and it moves around the sun in an elliptical orbit. The difference between the two times builds up over the year, and that means that we need something called the Equation of Time. That changes from day to day. In the spring and summer, it's somewhere between plus six minutes and minus six minutes, and in the autumn and winter, it's between plus fourteen minutes and minus sixteen minutes. And then on top of that, although this doesn't apply right now, six more minutes are added in the summertime, but that doesn't start until the third of April.'

'So right now . . .'

'Right now . . . Leiden is at about 4.5 degrees longitude east. That's 10.5 degrees further west than the fifteenth eastern degree of longitude. So, on our watches it's 10.5 times 4, making 42 minutes ahead of the true local time. And then we add 7.5 minutes for the Equation of Time, and 42 plus 7.5 is 49.5 minutes. And that . . .' She made a triumphant flourish with her arms. ' . . . is exactly the time that my watch says it is now.'

Peter politely looked at her watch and then nodded, sticking out his bottom lip to show that he was impressed.

But what was it about what she'd just told him that had made the hairs on the back of his neck stand up? He was still trying to work it out as he held out his hand. 'Thanks. I'm impressed that you could explain that off the top of your head without any preparation.'

Anouschka tried to smile modestly but she couldn't hide the fact that she was quite proud of herself. 'It was a pleasure,' she said, shaking his hand.

Anouschka walked away. But a thought popped into Peter's head, like Lieutenant Columbo who always had one more question for his chief suspect, just when they thought their interrogation was over and they had got away with the crime. 'That pole!' he shouted after her.

She turned around. 'Officially you're supposed to call that "pole" a gnomon or a style, you know, but I'll let you off. What about it?'

'Why is it at an angle?'

'Ah, there's a very simple explanation for that,' she replied. She walked back over Peter. 'The gnomon needs to be parallel with the earth's axis. For us, that means an angle of 52 degrees, because we're at 52 degrees latitude north. The gnomon's tip has to point to the north, to the North Pole in fact. That's why it's also sometimes called a "polar style".'

She took a compass from her trouser pocket, the sort of cheap-looking thing you might win at a funfair.

'Look,' she said, holding the compass out on her palm so that Peter could see it. 'The needle points north . . . So the sea is over there . . .' She pointed with her hand. ' . . . and well . . . I'm sure you don't need an explanation.' She gave the compass to Peter. 'Here, you can have it.'

'Have it? Are you sure?'

'Oh yes, it's fine. We've got a whole box of them in the office. It's just one of those silly little promo things.'

Peter turned it over. The name of the construction company that was building the car park was printed on the back. 'That's great, thanks!' he said.

He said goodbye, somewhat distractedly and Anouschka went back to the cabin. Peter stared at the face of the compass, like an archaeologist trying to work out exactly what he's just dug up.

Longitude east, Latitude north . . .

Of course! It was blindingly obvious now. The numbers he had found could be co-ordinates. Longitudes and latitudes . . .

But his excitement at this discovery soon faded. Because all he had was the sequence 42, 41, 41, 15, 58 . . . Was that 42 degrees – he assumed that was the northern latitude – and then 41 minutes and 41 seconds? And then f15 degrees east with 58 minutes and then another missing number for the seconds?

But if Leiden was at 52 degrees north, then 42 degrees would be somewhere in Southern Europe . . . Spain, Italy or Greece. But they didn't expect him to find all the clues and then still have enough time left to get on a plane, did they?

42 for *The Hitchhiker's Guide*, 41 for Niobe, 41 for Bach . . .

He started walking. He was starting to feel nervous about standing in one place for so long. He put the compass in his trouser pocket.

He left the Binnenvestgracht and crossed the Steenstraat. To avoid the busy streets, he went into the National Museum of Ethnology's tranquil grounds. He walked past the office buildings where the museum's staff worked during the week and headed for the museum entrance, but instead of going inside, he sat on a wall to organise his thoughts.

He must be missing something. In theory, it wasn't such a crazy idea that the numbers pointed to a location.

'Niobe, Niobe, Niobe,' he mumbled to himself. 'Nb, Nb, Nb.'

Peter could have kicked himself. He *had* been right after all. It was nothing to do with an atomic number. 'NB' also meant *noorderbreedte*, the Dutch word for north latitude or 'degrees north'. But then wouldn't he still need a clue with 'OL' for *oosterlengte* or east longitude?

But even then . . . in Southern Europe?

A computer, he thought, *but where am I going to find one this time?*

He stared blankly ahead. Then he saw two people coming out of the museum.

The museum's study hall of course, it was open to the public. He had spent a couple of weeks there as a student, working on a paper about Mayan temples in Guatemala.

He went up the stairs to the entrance and when he got inside, he bought a ticket, paying in cash again. He went straight to the library and sat down at the first free computer he saw.

The cursor blinked invitingly, waiting for a search term that would no doubt produce hundreds of thousands of results within half a second.

If I combine the first three, Peter thought, *then I get 42 NB 41. But that's not enough. So, what if this is supposed to be 42 41 NB and then 15 58 OL? Although, strictly speaking, I haven't found an OL yet. Then again, our official time is synchronised with the solar time at 15 degrees eastern longitude, so . . .*

He typed the co-ordinates into Google using Dutch notation, 42° 41' NB 15° 58' OL, and hit enter. The first page was mostly made up of links to Dutch websites about listed buildings. There were plenty of co-ordinates in the snippets under the links, but they didn't look useful. He scrolled through the results and saw pages with climate data, travel journals written by someone on a boat, astronomical data. He clicked the 'x' in the top right corner of the screen in frustration, and the web browser disappeared. Then he saw the Google Earth icon on the computer's desktop.

He clicked on it and typed in the co-ordinates again. Nothing happened.

'English, of course, English,' he hissed softly through clenched teeth.

He looked up the English words for *noorderbreedte* . . . north latitude. NL then? Oosterlengte . . . east latitude. EL?

42° 41' NL 15° 58' EL.

When he had entered the co-ordinates, he hovered his finger nervously over the enter key. He held his breath and pressed it.

ENTER.

Nothing happened.

Damn.

He tried again, but removed the spaces this time.

42°41'NL 15°58'EL.

Nothing again.

Then with spaces after all the numbers.

42° 41' NL 15° 58' EL.

Nada.

Now he removed all the spaces.

42°41'NL15°58'EL.

Zilch.

He removed both of the Ls and put a space in the middle.

42°41'N 15°58'E.

He hammered the enter key with his index finger, like someone trying to make a point in a debate.

Bingo.

The globe on the screen began to spin. The broad yellow lines that marked out the borders between the countries were moving towards Southern Europe, just as Peter had guessed. It slowed down when it reached Italy, and then, to Peter's immense disappointment, came to a standstill in the middle of the Adriatic Sea, half way between the coasts of Italy and Croatia.

Was Judith on a ship? If that was true, this had been an impossible task right from the start. Rage and panic welled inside him, making his throat feel as though it was being squeezed shut.

I must have made a mistake, he thought. *This can't be right. Judith, Judith, Judith . . . where are you?*

How many combinations of those numbers were there? Four times three times two times one . . . twenty-four possible co-ordinates.

He decided to start with the number 42, since that was the first number he'd found.

42°41'N 15°58'E – middle of the Adriatic Sea
42°58'N 41°15'E – the Black Sea in Georgia
42°15'N 58°41'E – somewhere in the middle of Turkmenistan
42°41'N 58°15'E – desert to the south of the Aral Sea in Uzbekistan
42°58'N 15°41'E – the Adriatic Sea again
42°15'N 41°58'E – Georgia, inland this time

With a doggedness born from despair, he kept going, starting each set of co-ordinates with the number 41 this time. Although he was starting to lose hope that this would get him anywhere, he typed in 41°42'N 15°58'E.

The globe started to turn again. It was heading towards Italy. The rotating image came to a standstill on what looked like a winding mountain road. Peter zoomed out until he saw the name of the mountain: Monte Sant'Angelo. The bright blue water of the Adriatic Sea appeared on the screen again. The co-ordinates pointed to a little town on the west coast, right on what was called the 'spur' of the Italian boot, the little jut of land above the heel.

He knew that place! The recognition filled him with excitement. Many years ago, he had travelled across Italy on his way to Bari to catch the ferry to Patras on the Peloponnese, a peninsula on the Greek coast. He had spent two days in Monte Sant'Angelo, staying as he always did, in the cheapest, most out of the way hotel he could find.

Something told him he was on the right track now. Monte Sant'Angelo was one of the most important pilgrimage sites in Europe because the archangel Michael was believed to have appeared there a number of times in the fifth century. An impressive church had been built on the site in his honour, the San Michele. But even more significant than that was the place that Michael had appeared: on top of a cave where, for centuries, another important place of worship had stood.

The temple of Mithras.

40

Monte Sant'Angelo . . . Peter couldn't imagine that after making him search the length and breadth of Leiden, they now wanted him to look for Judith in . . . Italy? This had to be about something else. He was convinced that he was on the right track, especially since there was an important Mithraeum there. But what did they want him to do?

He typed 'Monte Sant'Angelo' into Google, but the results were mostly from Italian websites, so he clicked on 'pages written in Dutch'. Wikipedia was at the top of the list as usual, but there were also links to travel blogs.

He visited site after site, reading frantically, looking for something that he might be able to use.

Monte Sant'Angelo
The Monte Sant'Angelo or mountain of the holy angel, has been steeped in mysticism since the beginning of time. Archaeological excavations have produced evidence of religious activity taking place here as long ago as the Stone Age.

In the month of May in 490, a local nobleman entered

a cave on the mountain and saw a bull inside. Shocked to find the animal lying there, he shot an arrow at it. The arrow miraculously bounced off the bull's skin and wounded the nobleman instead.

Lorenzo Maiorana, the Bishop of Siponto, was informed of the miracle, and shortly afterwards, the archangel Michael appeared to him. Michael told the bishop that he himself, disguised as the bull in the cave, had wounded the nobleman. Michael told Lorenzo Maiorana that the cave was to become a sacred place of worship. There would be no more shedding of bulls' blood. The bishop immediately understood that the archangel was speaking of the blood of the bulls that had been sacrificed there to the god Mithras. There had once been a Mithraeum in the cave, a temple to the ancient cult of the sun god Mithras.

After 490, the archangel appeared twice more to the Bishop of Siponto. The third and final time was during the consecration of the cave. Just as the bishop was about to pronounce his blessing, Michael appeared and told him that no blessing was necessary: he had already consecrated the cave himself. A procession made its way up to the cave to see the miracle that had taken place: the believers discovered that an altar had appeared, and beside it was the footprint of the archangel, embedded in the rock.

This wasn't what Peter had been looking for, and yet, at the back of his mind there was a loud, insistent voice telling him he was missing something.

He scanned the search results. Every few seconds he stumbled on something that made him think he was closer to finding the solution and a glimmer of hope ignited inside him. It reminded him of playing 'hot and cold' as a child, when his friends would hide an object and shout 'warm, warm, warm' as he got closer to finding it.

I'm nearly there, I'm nearly there . . . he thought, but as quickly as the hope had ignited, it faded again when he found himself at another dead end.

He knew that he didn't have time to read all of these webpages, but what else could he do? If he got up and walked away from this computer now, he would still have no idea where to go next.

Everything kept coming back to the battle between light and darkness. He read about the four archangels – Michael, Gabriel, Raphael and Uriel – who fought against darkness and against the fallen angels who were spurred on by their leader Lucifer, which meant 'Lightbearer'. He had once been one of God's most high-ranking angels, before he lost the battle against his own inner darkness . . .

Peter went back to the sites about Monte Sant'Angelo.

The Route of the Angel

The road that leads from Mont Saint-Michel – the shrine to the archangel Michael in Normandy – to the cave in Puglia, was called the Route of the Angel. Before long, the route had become an important strategic connection between the Channel in Normandy in the west, and the Adriatic Sea in the south. It partly overlapped with the Via Francigena, an even older pilgrimage route that stretched from Canterbury to Rome.

Over time, a small village grew around the cave on Monte Sant-Angelo. The large number of pilgrims who flocked to the site at the beginning of the second millennium made the construction of inns and other dwellings increasingly necessary. A small local economy began to develop, fuelled by the visiting pilgrims, which eventually led to the creation of a permanently inhabited town. Monte Sant'Angelo was added to Unesco's list of World Heritage Sites in 2011.

The cave, the cave . . . There had to be something there that would help him.

The Cave

A growing number of pilgrims and devoted believers visited the cave, including the Byzantine emperor Constantine II, Holy Roman Emperor Henry II, and a significant number of popes and famous monks. Some of them claimed to have seen the archangel themselves. In the year 867, a monk by the name of Bernard the Wise travelled to the holy cave from Northern France. His own monastery, Mont Saint-Michel, was built on a peninsula where a bull had been seen in a cave by a bishop. From this moment on, inspired by the remarkable similarities between the two sites, many pilgrims from the north carried on to Monte Sant'Angelo after visiting Mont Saint-Michel.

And now the cave itself . . .

The entrance consists of a double arcade with a statue of Saint Michael displayed prominently above. To the right of the entrance is the sanctuary's bell tower. The tower's shape recalls the towers at Castel del Monte (which appears on the Italian 1 eurocent coin). The 86-step staircase leads down to the cave below and ends in a nave containing a number of tombs. Once inside the cave itself, the altar comes into view, dominated by a statue of the archangel as warrior. A passage leads to the Cappella dell'Altissimo at the rear, which features a larger, baroque altar. This is the place where the bull once lay, but now the angel stands watch here, guarding the gate of heaven.

Peter clicked on one of the photos on the site, the double arcade that led to the cave. He read the Latin text that was chiselled into the stone. This couldn't be real . . .

Terribilis est locus iste . . .

The first part of the text meant: 'This is a fearsome place.' But it was the second half of the sentence that jumped out at Peter:

Hic domus dei est et porta coeli.

'Here is the house of God and the gate of heaven.'

The seventh grade was the Father, *pater*, just like . . .

He shoved his chair back wildly, sending it toppling to the floor, to the irritation of some of the other museum visitors who gave him annoyed looks. He picked up the chair and leaned on the back of it with both hands to regain control of his breathing. This was it! He knew where he had to go.

He managed to walk calmly through the museum, but once he was outside, he picked up his pace and ran.

Porta Coeli.

The Coelikerk.

41

'*Hic domus dei est et porta coeli, hic domus dei est et porta coeli, hic domus dei est et porta coeli.*' Peter whispered the words over and over as he left the museum grounds and headed towards the Morspoort.

Here is the house of God and the gate of heaven.

These words, carved into the stone above the entrance to the Mithras temple in Monte Sant'Angelo centuries ago, were the very same words written above the imposing columns on the front of the Hartebrugkerk on the Haarlemmerstraat. That was why everyone called it the 'Coelikerk'. Many people weren't even aware of its official name. And even Hartebrugkerk wasn't its real name. Officially, it was called *Onze Lieve Vrouwe Onbevlekt Ontvangen* or the Church of Our Lady of the Immaculate Conception, in honour of Mary who was born free from all personal sin and preserved from the stain of original sin on her soul.

But would they have dared? Dared to openly choose this, of all texts, as the motto for the church? Had no one ever made this connection before?

Above the gilded letters, painted in the centre of the triangular tympanum, there was even an all-seeing eye. To the layman, this was a Christian symbol of God's omniscience, but it was in fact the eye of Horus. God sees everything, a sort of Big Brother before the concept even existed, making sure that people behaved themselves even when they thought no one was looking. Hadn't that been a concept in the famous story about the French philosopher Voltaire? He himself criticised those who had faith in an all-knowing God, but as the story went, after dinner one evening, he was lingering at the table with friends, discussing whether God was real or not. When the servants came in to clear the table, he asked his friends to pause the conversation until they were gone. 'Because,' he said furtively, 'if they hear that God does not exist, how am I to stop the footmen from stealing my silverware?'

However, the all-seeing eye is originally Egyptian, a representation of the eye of Horus, the sun god.

It would be so obvious to anyone who took the time to look into it. But Peter was still shocked by this blatant statement, out in the open where the public walked past it, day in, day out. He was on his way to 'the Father', the *pater* . . . The priest in a Catholic church was a father too, after all, so he knew that this was where he was supposed to go. But he didn't know what, or who he would find inside the church.

When he got to the Morspoort, he forced himself to slow down to avoid attracting attention. He walked through the gate's archway. As he began to catch his breath, a small door flew open in a building on his right. Before he realised what was happening, someone had pulled him inside with considerable force, dragging him through the door like a rag doll. He was too taken by surprise to offer any resistance. Whoever it was stumbled backwards into the narrow hallway and crashed into the steep staircase behind him, as though he hadn't expected it to be so easy.

Peter landed on top of him and drew back his fist to retaliate, but with an agility that caught him off guard, the man manoeuvred himself out from underneath him. The man stood up and left Peter lying on the floor. Without taking his eyes off Peter, he pushed the door shut with his heel.

Only then did Peter see who he was dealing with.

'Da . . .' The shock closed Peter's throat before he could say the rest of the name.

'Daniël, yes,' the man said, finishing the name for him.

Peter lay on the floor, stunned, not knowing what to expect. 'But what . . . what are you *doing*?'

'I'm involved in it too.'

Peter stared at Daniël, at the face he knew so well. The city's archaeologist, the man whose hand he had shaken only yesterday to wish him luck at the start of his big project in town.

'Listen,' Daniël said. 'We don't have—'

'I don't have time for this, Daniël. Where's Judith?' Peter shouted as he tried to get up.

Daniël pushed him back down with such authority that Peter fell backwards, slamming his back into the stairs. 'We don't have much time, I know,' Daniël said. 'But you need to know who you're up against. Then you might have a better idea of what you're about to get into.'

'How did you know I was here?'

'I knew you'd find your way to the sundial, the sixth clue . . . I saw you there, talking to that woman. Then I followed you to the museum, and waited outside until you came back out. And then you started running towards me . . .'

'And you just happened to have the key to—'

'This building is ours, Peter. It has been for centuries. It was ours before there was even a wooden church here. We're small, always have been. At least, in terms of how many of us there are. But we're powerful. We're everywhere. We have people in high places, men with money and influence . . . And for a group of our size, we own much more than you'd expect: mansions on the canals, houses near the Burcht and the Pieterskerk, houses in *hofjes*, housing associations . . .'

'Just tell me what it is you want to tell me,' Peter snarled at him through clenched teeth.

'I work for the Father,' Daniël said. 'He's chosen you to . . . The Father thinks that the hour has come for us to go public, to share our group's knowledge with the wider world. Christianity as we know it . . . so much has been covered up, as I'm sure you know, there's so much more going on under the surface than people think. The real story of Christianity is the one our group has been passing down for centuries.' The words tumbled out of him as though he was trying to tell two or three stories at once. 'But in those days, after that suffering, the sun will be darkened, and the moon will not give its light,' he said suddenly.

Peter recognised the words, a verse from the Gospel of Mark, the speech that Jesus had given to his disciples on the evening before the Feast of Pesach or Passover, the day of his arrest.

'The Father has been planning this for a long time. When he saw that there would be a solar eclipse in 2015, and then another one on the twentieth of March, the day before the equinox, he took it as a sign from God. "Then he will send out the angels, and gather his elect from the four winds, from the ends of the earth to the ends of heaven," as Mark's Gospel says. Nobody knows the day or the hour that the moment will come, only the Father . . . He's been able to convince me that he's right, and I think that the world ought to know about us. We don't need to hold big services in public, but we should pass on some of our knowledge. It doesn't mean the end of Christianity as we know it: it's more of an enhancement of it. When you know how old the story is, about God's son dying and being resurrected in the spring, when you know it has a profound truth at its heart . . . then you appreciate other beliefs even more because everyone is telling the same story. It doesn't change anything about the story that people have always been told. That's why our Father still celebrates the Eucharist with his congregation, breaking the bread and sharing the wine. You could say that Paul repackaged our story as Christianity. The meal of bread and wine, the life-giving sacrifice, death and resurrection, being cleansed by the blood of the lamb, a reward in the hereafter, being reunited with loved ones, the battle between darkness and light . . . It's the Mithras story, all of it. And I agree with the Father that it's time to return our Lord to his rightful place.'

'But . . .' Peter said, wanting to end the conversation and find Judith.

'But . . . some of our members are opposed to the plan and yesterday they started actively working against us. They're doing everything they can to derail it . . . You saw what happened to Raven for yourself. But now that you've made it this far it looks like the Father was right after all.'

'About?'

'That you really are the chosen one, the intermediary, the one who will tell—'

'An intermediary . . . A messenger, like Raven? Are you finished talking now?' Peter was ready to explode with impatience. 'I need to keep going. You said I'd made it this far. So do you know if I'm supposed to go to the Coelikerk next? Is that where they've got Judith?'

'I don't know. It sounds . . . logical. You've made it through six stages and the ladder ends with the Father. But the point is, the Father is the only one who knows everything. Raven knew, apparently, but he's gone now. And Jakob, but—'

'So why did you bring me here?'

'Because I was starting to have doubts. I needed to see you for myself. And the Father was threatening to . . . You know, I can help you.'

'I just want *one* thing: to find Judith. I'm not interested in anything else,' Peter said. He stood up and took a step closer to Daniël, so that their bodies were almost touching. 'If you would just get out of my way,' he hissed, 'then I can go to the church.'

Daniël shook his head and gestured at something behind Peter, almost invitingly, like a waiter showing a diner to a table.

Peter turned around and saw a small, wooden door in the wall. It was barely more than a hatch.

'We can go through here,' Daniël said.

He twisted the iron ring that served as a doorknob and opened the little door. A blast of cold air hit their faces, bringing with it the odours of mould and wet earth.

As though he was trying to suggest that Peter had a choice, Daniël stepped into the darkness first, crouching down to avoid hitting his head on the lintel.

'But small is the gate and narrow the road that leads to life,' Daniël said, his voice echoing down the tunnel, 'and only a few find it.'

Peter hesitated. If he turned around now, he could easily go back through the door, out onto the street and walk to the church himself. On the other hand, that would mean going over the busy Blauwpoortsbrug and making his way through the even busier Haarlemmerstraat.

It sounded like Daniël was opening another hatch. Peter could hear metal on wood. Then the dark space was illuminated by the bright light of a burning torch.

Peter stuck his head through the hatch and saw Daniël disappearing through a hole in the ground. Only the top half of his body was visible. He held the torch up and pointed it at Peter.

Peter went all the way through the opening and closed the door as well as he could behind him.

They went down a winding staircase until they reached a tunnel about five metres lower. It looked identical to the one they had discovered under the library the day before.

So it is a labyrinth, Peter thought.

'This way,' Daniël said simply, as if he hadn't even considered that Peter wouldn't follow him. 'This will take us to exactly where you want to be.'

'*Teribilis est locus iste . . .*' Peter recited.

Without looking back, Daniël replied, with a hint of amusement in his voice: '*Et porta coeli.*'

42

The water was now so deep that Judith could no longer stand up in it. She paddled desperately, treading water to keep her head above the surface. Every so often, she tried to lift her body high enough out of the water to grab onto the grate above her head, like a water polo player aiming at a goal. But it remained just out of reach. She had hoped that hanging onto the metal bars would be less exhausting than constantly treading water.

This can't be how I die, she thought. *Imprisoned for reasons I can't even begin to fathom and about to drown if someone doesn't come and rescue me soon.*

Sobbing, she began to pray, an old psalm that welled up inside her.

'Save me, O God,' she sang softly. 'For the waters have come up to my neck. I sink in the miry depths, where there is no foothold. I have come into the deep waters. The floods engulf me now.'

She found that singing was strangely comforting. A sort of peace came over her, as though she was ready to accept her inevitable end.

'Rescue me from the mire, do not let me sink. Deliver me from those who hate me, from the deep waters. Do not let the flood-waters engulf me or the depths swallow me up or the pit close its mouth over me.'

But the peace it gave her was brief. Before she was able to sing the last words, her voice cracked and broke.

With each passing minute, the bars above her head grew closer and closer.

THE SIXTH VISION

And behold, I saw the man. He travels tirelessly along the ways of the Lord, collecting money as he has promised. As steadfast as the sun that makes its way through the sky, he goes from village to village, from town to town. For the path of the righteous is like the light of dawn, which shines brighter and brighter until full day. And he is protected by Venus, the morning star, surrounded by love . . .

He could have been wealthy, and yet he stays poor for his converts so that by his poverty they might become rich. The believers in Macedonia give more than they can spare, because one who gives freely will grow all the richer and one who with-holds will only suffer want. A generous person will be enriched, and one who gives water will get water. One who gives must give generously from the heart. And in Corinth too, each one gives as he has made up his mind to, not reluctantly or under compul-sion, for God loves a cheerful giver. They are truly the children of their Father in heaven.

He tells them about Isaiah and how he prophesied that the treasures of the sea would be brought to Zion, how the riches of the nations would be brought to the Lord.

And behold, he travels back to Jerusalem. People warn him

not to go further, but onwards he goes, like a river flowing unstoppably to the sea. The prophet Agabus binds his own hands and feet with Paul's belt: 'This is the way the Jews in Jerusalem will bind the man who owns this belt and will hand him over to the Gentiles,' he says. But Paul answers that he is willing to be captured, willing to die for the name of his Lord. But they do not know of which Lord he truly speaks.

In Jerusalem, the eternal city, he meets with James and all the elders. They give praise and glory to God when they hear of the work Paul has done in his ministry among the Gentiles. But they are also concerned that thousands of Jews no longer obey the laws of Moses, they do not circumcise their children, and they have abandoned the dietary laws. Paul is overjoyed because they have no idea whose message they have really accepted, or that an even greater conflict hangs over their heads.

And behold, for their sakes, he goes to the temple with four other men to be purified. After seven days, the Jews seize him, Jews from Asia. For the first time, he is afraid. They cry: 'Fellow Israelites, help! This is the man who is teaching everyone everywhere against our people, our law, and our temple; more than that, he has actually brought Greeks into the temple and he has defiled this holy place.' Not long before this, they had seen him in the city with Trophimus the Ephesian, and they supposed that Paul had brought this Gentile into the temple, a serious offence. The city is in uproar. The people rush together and drag Paul out of the temple. The doors are shut and they try to kill him, as they once killed Stephen when they laid their cloaks at this very man's feet.

But behold, his fellow countrymen come to help him. When the Jews see the Roman soldiers approaching, they stop beating him. The tribune arrests him and orders him to be bound with two chains. Then they take him to the barracks, safe from the angry mob.

Paul knows that his mission is complete, that he has achieved his goal. Just before he is taken inside, he gives another speech about his life, about his conversion on the road to Damascus, a story he has told so often that he has even started to believe it himself. His words are like oil to a flame. 'Away with this man!' the people cry. 'Such a man has no right to live!'

And behold, the tribune orders that he be flogged during his interrogation to find out the reason for this outcry against him. Then Paul knows that it is time to remove his mask. No longer must he keep his true self hidden. 'I am a Roman, just like all of you,' he says. 'You are forbidden to flog a Roman citizen, especially without trial. I was born a Roman citizen.' This strikes fear into their hearts and they do not hurt a hair on his head.

Forty Jews swear they will touch neither food nor drink until they have murdered Paul. Paul's nephew warns the Romans about the plot, but no one comes to raise his spirits, not one of his brothers, not one of his sisters. He is alone. He is taken to Caesarea, accompanied by two hundred soldiers, seventy horsemen, and two hundred spearmen. Their compatriot will be safe, far from the murderous hands of the Jews.

And hark, the high priest Ananias comes down with some elders and Tertullus, a lawyer, to present their case against Paul to the governor. 'We find this man to be a pest who has incited rebellion among Jews all over the world.'

For two years, Paul remains in Caesarea. He needs only to give the money he has collected to Felix the governor and he will be a free man. But Paul is stubborn and refuses. Felix is succeeded by Porcius Festus. The old accusations resurface and then, *then* Paul finally appeals to the emperor. 'You have appealed to the emperor; to the emperor you will go,' Festus says.

And behold, King Agrippa comes to listen to Paul, and Paul tells his story again, now with even more conviction than before.

Agrippa and Porcius Festus withdraw to discuss the case. 'This man has done nothing to deserve death or imprisonment,' they say. And Agrippa says to Festus: 'This man could have been set free if he had not appealed to the emperor.' Now they must send him to Rome.

Everything is going according to plan. Paul gives thanks to his Lord that he has spared him, that he has given him the wisdom he needed and put the right words in his mouth to fool them all. The followers of the Way will spread the word of his Lord Mithras, hidden behind the mask of Christianity.

And Paul knows: I am free.

Just as nothing can stop the sun from making its way through the sky, nothing can stop me on my path.

I am a Sun-Runner.

43

PATER

FATHER

Twenty-one years ago, spring 1994

But, Tiny realised, not even the Ebionites knew just how well he had fooled them all. Not to this day . . .

From Tiny Strauss' notebook
Paul left Tarsus, the centre of the Mithras cult, and went to Jerusalem as a Raven. Initiated into the first grade, his new status as messenger meant that he had to leave home.

Paul was a tent-maker by profession, and so he was able to support himself. He went to live with the Father, the leader of the Mithraists in Jerusalem, so that he could study with him and prepare himself for the second grade of initiation, the Bridegroom.

In those days, the temple, like most non-Jewish temples, was in fact an enormous abattoir, an open-air butcher's shop where many people bought their meat. Animals were sacrificed there on an industrial scale. Sometimes the carcasses were burned, but usually the animals were cut up after their sacrificial deaths and sold. This was an important source of income for the priests, who were more or less ordained butchers in divine service. During Pesach, an estimated 250,000 animals were slaughtered on behalf of the hundreds of thousands of pilgrims who visited the eternal city to celebrate the holiday.

A permanent stench of blood, decay and death hung over the city. Stinking, black clouds rose from the perpetually burning fires in the crematoria where the animals were burned. All of that combined with the heat of the Middle East, the flies, the rats, the maggots . . .

The sacrificial animals were ritually slaughtered by means of a single cut with a sharp knife across the carotid artery after a short prayer by a priest. When it was done correctly, the animal immediately lost consciousness and bled out. Rivers of blood flowed from the temple, drained away by two underground channels.

Paul lived and worked in Jerusalem and was a familiar face in the temple. It had a never-ending supply of hides from the countless animals that were killed there, and he bought them in bulk for his tent-making business. And it was there that his eye was caught one day by the high priest's beautiful daughter. Love can strike like a lightning bolt . . . Gone was his desire to follow the path of Mithras, gone was his ability to focus on the next stage.

He still wanted to be a Bridegroom, but with her, under the chuppah, breaking a glass under his foot to show the fragility of happiness.

He became a Jew and had himself circumcised. And speaking of blood . . . when the mohel was circumcising him, his hand slipped, either from clumsiness or because someone bumped into him, who can say, but it must have been a bloodbath. Perhaps the tip of the glans was sliced off. It's possible. Those knives were razor sharp. He bled like a stuck pig, like a sacrificial animal bleeding dry on the temple steps. Urinating was painful for the rest of his life afterwards, a frequent, daily, burning hell. He could forget about herds of goats descending from the hills of Gilead, he would never even see her breasts like fawns let alone touch them, he would never find out if her lips really tasted of honey. He had been in love, and like all those who are in love – some things never change – he'd thought that the world was his for the taking, that the object of his love looked at him in the same way he looked at her. But nothing could have been further from the truth. She wanted nothing to do with him. Paul was fairly unattractive, perhaps bow-legged . . . And she a Jewish beauty, in the flower of her youth, promised at birth to a man chosen by her father so that two families could be united forever.

She toyed with him; in his feverish fantasies, one smile that revealed teeth as white as sheep coming up from washing was her consent. But she laughed at him behind his back, made fun of him with her friends, amused them greatly with her imitations of the fawning, love-sick looks he gave her as he haggled with her father over the price of hides, the way he stuttered when he saw her, the handful of Hebrew words he knew . . .

He was a tent-maker, up to his elbows in bloody, stinking hides all day. There was no dirtier job possible to a Jew. It was like a Hindu body burner from the lowest caste setting his heart on a brahmin's daughter . . .

To win her heart – and that of her father of course – he abandoned his trade and joined the temple guards. He was more fanatical than all the others put together.

It's quite possible that he was present when Jesus was arrested, that he was one of the officers armed with sticks who arrested him in the Garden of Gethsemane. What is certain is that he was there when Stephen, the first of Jesus' followers to be martyred, was stoned. This is where he makes his first appearance in the bible as Saul instead of Paul. Everyone laid their cloaks at his feet because they would get in the way when they were throwing rocks at Stephen.

He was sent to Damascus to take a letter to the high priest there.

Saul thought he was being asked to complete an important task, or even a test that would prove him worthy to his future father-in-law, like Heracles performing twelve labours for Eurystheus, King of Mycenae. He would have dragged King Minos' bull from Crete to the mainland with his bare hands if the high priest had asked him to . . .

On the way to Damascus, he dreamed of a wedding the likes of which had not been seen in generations, the wedding night, the cool evening breeze blowing through the windows carrying delightful perfumes, the glasses of wine on the table, the little bunch of grapes that she would teasingly feed him, an erotic promise of what was to come, the moonlight on her perfect body, the body he would soon make love to . . . Sometimes these thoughts made his member so stiff that sitting on a saddle was almost impossible and he was barely able to ride his horse. He would take her in his arms, he would be tender, and she full of passion . . . they would melt into each other, become one body. They would both be naked and unashamed of their nakedness with each other.

But on the way, Paul had one of the epileptic fits that had plagued him since childhood. He fell from his horse and had a renewed encounter with his Lord, Mithras, to whom he had made a solemn promise when he became a Raven, when the blood of the bull had rained down on him and he had washed himself clean in the life-giving essence of his sacrifice.

He went blind and his eyes stayed closed for three days, but everything was clearer to him than ever before. Saul knew that he had strayed from the true path, that he had allowed himself to be blinded by love, or lust, the desire that shackles the soul to the body, nails the body to the cross . . . Paul was torn.

On his sickbed, he had someone read him the letter that the high priest has asked him to deliver. His future father-in-law, the man he longed to address as abba, *father . . . The only purpose of this entire mission had been to keep him out of Jerusalem during a wedding the likes of which had not been seen in generations, a* wedding between his beloved and her unworthy bridegroom, the son of the high priest's influential friend. The rage, the humiliation . . . he had allowed himself to be carried away by the serpent's treacherous glances. It was Eve all over again.

And he swore he would take revenge, not just on her, not just on the high priest and his brood of vipers, no, he wanted to bring down all Jews, erode Judaism from the inside so that it would collapse. Like a giant with feet of clay, he would pour water over those Jewish paws until they could no longer bear the weight above them.

He was ashamed because he knew that he had strayed from the true path, that he had betrayed his Lord for a worldly woman.

He rose up with renewed energy, stronger, more determined than ever. He would be a Bridegroom, yes, but not hers – it was better for a man to be alone. For three years he prepared himself, for three years he hid away with his old brothers, who had brotherhoods everywhere. They welcomed the prodigal son back with open arms.

He revealed his plan to them, his way of introducing their Lord to the many people and places where his name was not yet known. Some of them were opposed to it and thought that its success would be at the cost of their religion, their privacy, the secrets meant only for the initiated . . . But he was able to convince them. Most people, he explained, wouldn't even be aware that they were worshipping Mithras. The story of their god, their Mithras, who sacrificed his blood and his body so that they could have a life in the hereafter, an eternal life in which they would be reunited with the loved ones who had passed away before them . . . That would be the story that people would believe in and tell each other, perhaps even for hundreds of years after Saul and his followers had died. But at the same time, the story also contained a deeper layer, one which would only be revealed to the initiated. Something would remain of the mystery that could only be fully understood after initiation. The majority of people would actually stay on the outside, on the periphery, and be content with a literal interpretation of the stories, believing that these formed the core of their faith.

After three years of preparation, Paul re-emerged in Jerusalem as a Soldier, ready to undertake the most dangerous task of his life, perhaps even the most brilliant operation in the history of mankind. He visited Peter, and Jesus' brother James, and stayed with them for two weeks. He convinced them that he had become a sincere follower of Jesus. He had changed his name back to Paul so that he could assimilate with the Roman world and rid himself of his association with Judaism.

He may have gone back to the temple to catch one more glimpse of the high priest's daughter, that veritable daughter of Eve, perhaps watching her from behind a pillar as she walked with her husband and firstborn child.

For fourteen years, he travelled tirelessly, telling the story of his Lord Mithras, but now disguised and with a new name: Jesus the Christ, old wine in a new skin. After all, Jesus' sacrifice also resulted in new life, which is, in effect, the perpetual rhythm of the seasons. And by eating his flesh and drinking his blood, people could also become one with him and gain eternal life.

He railed against the laws that no longer applied after the death and resurrection of Jesus. There was no more need for the scourge of circumcision. There was no more need to burden people with a yoke that he was hardly able to bear himself. The people should be allowed to eat and drink whatever they wanted . . . He announced the good news in the synagogues. To his great joy, he irritated the local Jewish communities and was able to draw people away from them. The first to join him were the women, who were already confined to marginal roles, followed by their husbands and children, the slaves, the outcasts.

And he saw that he was successful, and that his message was popular.

His story about a God who personally cared about you, looked after you, the sacrifice that had been made for you so that you were free to come to God, the promise of the hereafter . . . The meal of bread and wine to remember the sacrifice made by Mithras, by

Jesus, that allowed you to become one with him. Those were ideas that non-Jews already knew very well, a familiar story, old wine in a new skin.

As the movement grew and grew, the threat it posed to Judaism in Jerusalem became greater and greater. He cleverly laid the blame for the crucifixion of their Lord and saviour at the Jews' feet, an outstanding accomplishment, since everyone knew that only the Romans carried out crucifixions. The Jews were allowed to sentence and execute their own people. If, as is described in the Gospels, the Jews had found Jesus guilty of blasphemy, then they could simply have stoned him themselves without the involvement of the Romans, as they had done with Stephen. The Romans didn't consider blasphemy against the Jewish god Yahweh to be a crime at all. What did they care if the Jews bickered among themselves? The point was that Jesus had committed an entirely different crime, something that the Romans considered to be a very good reason for crucifixion: overturning the tables in the temple courts. It was Pesach, and hundreds of thousands of Jewish pilgrims from all over the Roman Empire had come to Jerusalem to celebrate. The city was bursting with people, it was a powder keg and the Romans were very wary of anyone who might light the fuse. An uprising against Roman authority could have happened at any time, which made the atmosphere very tense. When Jesus and his disciples caused a riot in the busy temple courts, the Romans sought to nip it in the bud immediately. That proved to be fatal to Jesus. And that was the reason that he ended up on the cross – because of the Romans, not the Jews!

Paul created a whole new structure on the foundations of his own old religion, his own Mithraism, and created a labyrinth in which everyone would eventually become lost. Although he had barely any interest at all in the earthly life of Jesus, he came up with an entirely new interpretation of what Jesus had said. He took the movement started by Peter, James and all the other men and women who had heard Jesus speak in person, and made it part of his own story.

He was a Sun-Runner now. He wrote letters and travelled far and wide. He followed the path of the sun and left behind all the worldly bonds that had fettered him so that he could unwaveringly follow his own path.

Paul felt fulfilled. He was drawing closer to his goal: discord within the original community. The very first people to follow Jesus, those who had continued to go to the temple as Jews, now became the apostates . . .

After fourteen years, he went back to Jerusalem for the great Apostolic Council. They agreed that he and his helpers would focus on preaching to the Gentiles, exactly what Paul wanted. It would open up a world to him that was infinitely larger than the limited confines of Palestine. He sensed the end of the eternal city was approaching, a consequence of the increasing unrest and the Romans' brutal oppression. He set off on another journey, but he would return one last time with the money he had collected in the Christian diaspora as a sign of goodwill . . . And that was where he appears to have miscalculated. No one wanted to accept the money. He was arrested and his end appeared to be drawing near.

But they hadn't reckoned on his ability to take control of a seemingly lost situation and turn it around. Paul was a pre-modern Houdini. Paul, the escape artist.

44

'So you're one of those notorious "secret societies"?' Peter asked, making the quotation marks audible in his voice.

'Yes,' Daniël replied simply, 'but we're not out for world domination, and we're not the ones who were really behind 9/11, no illuminati nonsense. We were secret, as you put it, but we prefer to say "hidden", separate from the world. Not because we're doing anything dark or sinister, quite the opposite in fact. It's because our light would be more than most people could cope with.'

'And then your leader thought: enough of this secrecy, let's open the windows, let the air in? Something like that?' The smoke from the torch made Peter's nose itch.

'No,' Daniël said, 'or, actually yes. Yes, he wants openness. The world should know we exist. We have nothing to hide. But no, not everyone will be able to just become a member. Or at least, that's not the intention. You'd still need to be invited to join and you'd still be forbidden to tell anyone about what you'd seen and heard. But the story should be available to everyone. Many people actually know it already, but they're specialists.'

The tunnel branched out ahead of them. They went left, and

then almost immediately turned right. Peter knew he needed to stay close to Daniël if he didn't want to get lost in this subterranean world.

'But the deeper story . . .' Daniël continued casually. He appeared to know the tunnels like the back of his hand. ' . . . the layer underneath, *that* will be kept for an inner circle, only those who've been initiated. It's high time that people knew – and not just religious people, but everyone who says that our society is Judeo-Christian – that the things they believe in are stories, not literal events. People beat each other's brains out over these stories when their original authors never meant them to be taken literally.'

'And I suppose your version is secretly the true version? But then you're doing exactly the same thing, aren't you?'

'I thought you'd say that.' Daniël looked over his shoulder, laughing bitterly. 'But our story is at least closer to the original source. In many respects, the Lord that we worship is no different from the Lord of the Jews or the Christians, but we admit that our stories should be read as allegories. And that's why many people will find us more appealing, and why many people will want to join us.'

Peter had no idea which part of the city they were walking under. They weren't taking a straight route to the church, that much was clear.

A whole system of tunnels . . . Yesterday he hadn't known it existed until the mayor and the digger had disappeared into the pit and Peter had found the young man covered in blood in the space below it.

'But why was Raven covered in blood? It couldn't have come from being hit on the head with those bricks. I mean, he was *completely* covered in blood.'

'Have you heard of the *taurobolium*?'

'Bull sacrifice.'

'Bull sacrifice, exactly. Or rams or sheep, if the person making the offering wasn't rich enough. The person being initiated stands in a pit with a grate over his head. Above him, the sacrificial animal's throat is cut and the blood runs through the grate and onto the person below. He smears it into his body, washes himself with the blood. And he opens his mouth to try to drink some of it. The blood cleanses you of everything you've ever done wrong so you can start again with a clean slate. It guarantees you a life in the hereafter, reunion with your loved ones.'

'And Raven . . .'

'Raven was going through his initiation. We can't just smuggle a bull into the temple, so we always use a lamb. We can get it inside quite easily in a big wooden crate.'

'But Daniël . . . I would never have thought that you . . .'

Daniël turned around. With the zeal of a street evangelist, he said: 'If you only knew, Peter, what it's like to know the truth, to be free. I hope you find out one day.' He turned around again. 'We're almost there, by the way.'

'And you do this in your temple, your Mithraeum? Where is it?' Peter asked, continuing the conversation he had just interrupted.

'Maybe you'll get to see for yourself. The Catholic church always built its churches on sites that were already sacred to the local population to make the shift to Christianity easier. People could carry on performing their own rituals, just as they always had, but with a Christian slant.'

'And my role?' Peter asked.

'The Father has been watching you for years. It's . . .' But the rest of his words went unspoken when a figure appeared from around a corner.

'Dr De Haan, I presume . . .' The speaker was standing menacingly in the middle of the passage in front of them, a torch in his hand.

Two more men stepped out of the shadows behind them.

They were trapped.

45

'You bastard!' Peter shouted.

Daniël opened his eyes wide and started to say something but before he got the chance, Peter gave him a vicious shove. Daniël stumbled forwards into the startled assailant in front of him, dropping his torch as they both fell to the floor. As his assailant fell, his torch was pressed into his body, setting his clothes alight. He tried to get up, but slipped and fell down again.

Peter made use of the distraction to grab the torch from the floor and quickly slip past Daniël and the man in flames on the floor. He stopped a little way down the passageway. The tunnel was flooded with light now. The man had struggled to his feet and stood in the middle of the tunnel, like a flaming human torch, desperately trying to take off his clothes. The last thing Peter saw before he ran away was that the man had fallen down again and was rolling around on the ground.

Daniël, that traitor . . . he thought, incensed. *If only I'd stayed above the ground.*

The sound of the man's screams faded as Peter ran around

the corner. A long passageway stretched out in front of him. He had no idea which way to go, but he kept running.

He soon heard footsteps behind him. Someone was following him. The light from the torch made him easy to follow, but without it, he would get nowhere. The footsteps came closer. Whoever was following him had the advantage of speed because Peter had to slow his pace to stop the torch being blown out. The flames trailed behind the torch, sometimes even appearing to separate from it.

He knew it was hopeless. The footsteps were right behind him now.

Just as he was about to turn around and lash out, someone grabbed his lower legs. The torch flew from his hand, but somehow, it stayed alight.

He tried to kick himself free, but the man had his legs in a vice-like grip.

He managed to twist his body so that he was almost lying on his side, and then lift his torso up from the ground as though he was doing sit-ups. His pursuer, a small, bald, heavy-set man, was clearly at a disadvantage now with both of his hands wrapped around Peter's legs. He tried to free one of his arms, but failed.

Peter had never fought anyone in his life, not as a boy and not as a man. He hadn't ever dared to get into a fight and he'd rarely been in a situation where he'd needed to. On a couple of occasions at school, he'd patiently lain on the school playground and waited for the teacher on duty to come and free him from whichever child had him in a headlock. Their schoolmates had booed in disappointment when his attacker had eventually let him go.

But now he felt an enormous, primal strength gathering inside him, driven by rage, like lava spouting from a volcano. He drew back his fist and landed a punch on the nose of the human bear trap at his feet. He heard the bone crack – a horrible, dry sound. Blood spurted out of the man's nose, exactly as he'd seen it happen in films. The man shrieked and held his hands over his face, but

Peter punched him again, hard on his left ear this time. Then he kicked the man away from him until he lay groaning on the floor. Blood oozed between his fingers.

Peter stood up, picked up the torch and began to walk, without any thought at all to his opponent's fate. His right hand was covered in blood. He wiped it on his trousers, but blood stayed smeared on his skin.

The tunnel split again, and he randomly chose to go left. *Where do I go, where do I go*, he thought. *And which direction am I even going in to start with?*

After about fifty paces, he remembered the compass in his trouser pocket.

He stood still and listened to make sure no one was coming. All he could hear was the gentle sound of water flowing beneath his feet. Then he took out the compass and held it up to the torch flame so he could see it more clearly. The passage ahead of him appeared to go south. *We can't have walked further than the Coelikerk*, he thought, *otherwise we'd have reached it already.* The church must be to the east.

He had no idea if he was right. Maybe they had taken a circuitous route and gone straight past the church. This was probably a shot in the dark.

He walked further down the passageway. After a few dozen metres, it split in two again. He chose the path that looked like it had the most easterly direction, towards where he thought the church would be. He took a few more turns left and right, until he felt sure that he was gradually heading east.

He heard voices up ahead. He instinctively put the torch behind his back to shade some of its light, then took a few steps towards the noise. There was a T-junction ahead of him. Two male voices were talking in the passage on the left.

' . . . then?'

'We'll see when we get there.' The speaker was clearly having trouble hiding his annoyance about something. 'Listen to me,' he went on, 'I didn't come up with this plan overnight. I've been working on it for years . . . given it a great deal of thought. And I haven't done anything in secret, I haven't gone behind your backs. I've been open and honest about everything.'

There was no reply from the other man.

'Not in the beginning, that's true, but I don't have to. I'm your leader, I'm your *Father*.'

Peter was so keen to see the man who called himself Father that he had to suppress the urge to go around the corner. But he wanted to hear what they were talking about first.

'Ane put his trust in me, I don't need to explain any of that to you. The sun disappearing, right before the equinox . . . All the signs indicate that I'm right. This morning, they started to investigate the tunnel where they found Raven. They'll bring excavators, drills, they'll use force to break down the walls, and they'll use scanners to find the tunnels . . .'

'We can still call it all off,' the other man argued. 'And then they'll just always wonder what the labyrinth under their city was all about. They might never even discover the temple.'

'But I *want* them to discover us! Can't you get that into your head? Are you *deaf*?'

The second man didn't respond.

'Come on,' said the man who called himself Father. 'We need to be at the church before Peter gets there.'

'And if he doesn't make it?'

Peter didn't hear a reply.

But just as Peter was about to go around the corner to let them know he was there, the Father spoke: 'I've already said this to Daniël too: if he doesn't make it, then we've failed. We'll abandon the plan and the two of them will disappear. He'll get Judith when he's on the altar in the church and not one step, not one second sooner.'

It began to grow darker, a sign that the light source was moving further away from Peter.

Peter followed the two men, being careful to stay out of sight. His own torch was almost burnt out now, but he kept it behind his back.

He trod so softly that he felt like he was floating above the ground. With each step, he let his foot hover in the air for a moment, like a lion stalking its prey, or Saint Peter walking on water.

He peered around the corner and watched one of them put a torch into a ring on the wall and then extinguish it with a quick blast of breath. As soon as the flame went out, he heard a door or a hatch being opened. In the faint light, he could see the first steps of a stone staircase. Footsteps echoed through the tunnel as someone went up the stairs.

Now, at last, he could bring the torch out from behind his back. He shuffled across the passage until he could touch the wall with his left hand. After ten or fifteen metres, he reached the alcove where the staircase began.

As he put his foot on the first step, he felt her behind him, Judith. The feeling was as unexpected as it was familiar. He was afraid that if he turned around to look, she would disappear again, back down into the deep darkness. If he didn't look back, he could take her with him, up into the light, where the first rays of spring sunshine were bringing new life to the earth.

But the urge was too strong. He turned around. Of course there was no one there, and as soon as he looked back, those feelings of warmth and affection were gone, like a duvet being yanked away on a cold winter morning.

He stood there for a while, staring into the darkness. He felt a cold draught whip past his legs, a phantom gliding past him.

He was about to turn back around and go up the stairs when he heard a sudden noise come from somewhere nearby.

More footsteps.

Slowly but surely, the contours of a body came into view, like a corpse rising from the bottom of a lake and breaking the water's surface.

46

Clouds of ancient dust filled the tunnel where two workmen had succeeded in creating the first hole in the wall. The two men, the three police officers and Janna Frederiks wore protective masks so that they wouldn't breathe in the grit and dust.

Despite the strangeness of the situation, Janna found herself being carried away by the excitement of it all. The rumours that they'd always dismissed as urban legends had suddenly become fact. A labyrinth of tunnels under the city could be turned into a huge tourist attraction. Just imagine, she thought, they would be able to give guided tours of this hidden world, just like the ones in Rome, Paris and London. And what sort of archaeological treasures might they find? What if there were people buried down here too, from centuries ago? The catacombs of Leiden . . . What an amazing story that would be!

Her excitement at the possibilities made her disappointment all the greater when she saw the amount of force that was being used to break open the first wall. She understood why this investigation, a murder investigation in fact, was the police team's main priority, but the destruction of these ancient walls was like

334

a dagger in her archaeologist's heart. There was bound to be a clever mechanism built into the wall that would make it open, but they had probably destroyed it forever now.

How far did this system of tunnels go? Did the passages stretch all the way beyond the boundary of city's canals? Were the Pieterskerk, the Hooglandse Kerk and who knows which other churches all connected below the ground? How old were these tunnels? Had they been built during the Spanish Siege of Leiden?

She was already mapping out a walking tour in her head, with fun activities for children – you couldn't avoid those these days – and she would have a role in the spotlight of course, as one of the people who had discovered the tunnels. But an interactive treasure hunt with an app would be tricky when there was no network coverage down here . . .

Janna was jarred out of her daydreams by the unexpected thud of a large chunk of stone. The hole had been made big enough to walk through.

She was overcome by a hot feeling of shame for having allowed herself to be carried away by fantasies about the tourism opportunities in the tunnels, as though nobody had died because of them.

The dust began to settle, like sand sinking to the bottom of shallow water after a storm, and the workmen stepped back from the hole. They all took off their masks. In contrast to their grey hair and dusty clothes, their faces looked freshly washed.

'Right then, you can go in if you like,' one of them said with a heavy Leiden accent.

Janna and the police officers switched on their flashlights. They had the honour of being the first to see what was behind the wall. Like an Egyptologist entering a burial chamber that had been sealed for twenty centuries, Janna gingerly stepped over the threshold of rubble and through the hole. To her surprise, she found herself in another passage, just as well-constructed as the one behind her.

The three police officers followed her, going on tiptoe, just as she had done, as though they expected to fall through a booby trap and be skewered on rows of long, sharp spikes. No one had really believed that this system of passageways was likely to exist. So how far-fetched was it to imagine that its makers had created a security system or set traps, like a gigantic ball of rock that would come rolling towards intruders when they passed a certain point?

The passage stretched out in front of them, but they stopped at a large alcove. There was a set of steps that led upwards and then appeared to stop after about five metres.

One of the police officers took a few tentative steps up the stairs. Moments later, he triumphantly reported that he had a weak signal on his mobile phone.

'I'll see if my satnav works,' he said, 'then we can get a rough idea of where we are.'

It took a few moments for the navigation app to start up, but then a little blue dot appeared on the screen that showed them which part of the city was above them.

'We're at the back of the Hooglandse Kerk now, somewhere near the Hooglandsekerkgracht . . .'

The others looked up in suspense, waiting for a more precise location.

'Here, I've got it,' the officer said, enlarging the map with his fingertips.

'We're under the Mierennesthofje,' he said, pointing at the mobile phone in his hand. 'If two of you go up there now, we can see if you can locate us. I'll stand at the top of the steps and bang on the ceiling or we can shout. You might be able to hear us. There's something here that looks like it might open.'

'I suppose we can give it a go,' one of his colleagues said, 'but I don't know if the sound will carry that far. The stones above us look quite thick to me.'

'You two stay here,' the oldest officer said. 'I'll go. You can come with me, Miss Frederiks.'

It was an order, not an invitation.

Janna and the police officer walked back to the entrance.

'Did you know Mr Van Tiegem well?' he asked.

'We bumped into each other quite regularly. Professionally, not socially,' Janna replied, not sure if he was asking out of interest, or if it was a clever interrogation tactic.

The officer shook his head.

'Why do you ask?'

'It's . . .' he said hesitantly, and looked behind him to make sure they were alone. 'He turned out to have a blood alcohol content of nearly 0.8 percent. A normal person would be pretty much dead at that level.'

'He could take his drink, yes . . . But should you be telling me this sort of thing?' Janna asked.

'Yes . . . you're right. I . . . Forget I said anything.'

They climbed back up to street level via the rope ladder.

Another police officer helped them out of the pit. 'What's the situation down there?' he asked.

'We've knocked one of the walls through,' his colleague said. 'The tunnel continues behind it. The others are waiting near a staircase now. We're going to walk round to the Mierennesthofje, behind the Hooglandse Kerk. It looks like that staircase leads up to the courtyard, or to a house in the courtyard.'

'Excellent. I'll pass that on.'

Janna and the police officer walked past the Hooglandse Kerk onto the Hooglandsekerkgracht, a street that had once been a canal. They crossed the street towards the Mierennesthofje's courtyard.

'Forget what I just told you,' the officer said.

'Don't worry about it,' Janna reassured him.

By now they had reached the door that led into the *hofje*, where five doorbells were arranged one on top of the other. Janna pressed them all.

They heard a voice through the intercom. It was difficult to understand, as though the person speaking was deliberately crumpling an empty crisp packet next to the microphone.

The officer gently pushed her aside and shouted, 'POLICE!' at the intercom.

Janna couldn't help laughing at his behaviour. It was so unexpectedly bossy that she was sure he was trying to demonstrate that he was assertive and professional after all.

They heard a buzzer as the door unlocked, then they pushed it open. The door at the other end of the narrow passageway opened before they reached it. An elderly lady appeared in the doorframe, then stepped back to let Janna and the police officer into the courtyard.

Janna noticed how calm and peaceful it was here, away from the busy streets. It was like stepping out of a concert hall during a performance and closing the soundproofed doors behind her.

'You gave me a fright,' the lady said, timidly.

The officer introduced himself with his surname. Janna used her first name.

A plaque on the wall bore the name of the housing association: DIOGENES. Janna smiled at the irony of a housing association being named after a philosopher who, according to legend, slept in a barrel.

'It's a bit of a strange story, madam, but . . .' the officer began. 'Did you hear about the incident in town yesterday? The mayor was trapped inside a digger. It fell into a pit when they were installing an underground waste container.'

'Yes, I read about that, yes.'

'Well now it turns out that there's a tunnel, right under where he fell in. We came across a stone staircase in that tunnel just now, and we have reason to believe that it leads to somewhere here in the Mierennesthhofje.'

The three of them looked around as though they half expected to see a sign saying TUNNEL ENTRANCE somewhere, but all they could see was a rather untidy garden with a large lawn, dominated by an enormous oak tree.

'And now you want to look round my house?' the lady said in a voice that sounded faintly upper-class and a little amused. She had recovered from her initial shock remarkably quickly, but she also didn't seem at all surprised by the news that a tunnel ran under her house. Maybe she was too old to be surprised by anything any more, Janna thought.

'That's right,' the man said. 'Our colleagues are somewhere under here right now and we'd like to know exactly where. If we can find out which house the tunnel entrance is in, then we might find someone who knew about it already.'

'Come in then,' she said invitingly. 'But surely I'd know if there was a door to a secret tunnel in my kitchen, wouldn't I?'

They went inside. The house had looked tiny from the outside, but inside it was surprisingly spacious.

'The basement is down there on the left,' the woman said. 'I don't use it much. It's too cold and damp. It's more of a larder and storage area really. Mind your head.'

They went down a small flight of stairs, but realised straight away that this wasn't the place they were looking for. The floor was made of smooth, evenly poured cement, with no irregularities that stood out as being unusual.

'Who else lives in the *hofje*?' the officer called up to the woman in the kitchen.

They both walked back upstairs to the kitchen.

'There's an older lady next door. She's been here for thirty-five, forty years. Nobody really lives in the house next to hers. It's a local priest's retreat house. He goes there to study. Opposite here . . .'

The lady babbled on, as though they were tenants who had just moved in and she was telling them all about their new neighbours. Janna interrupted her before she could ask if they wanted to stay for a cup of coffee. 'I don't suppose you have keys to the other houses?' she asked.

'No, sorry,' she answered. 'But the housing association will have them. They need to be able to get into all the houses in case there's an emergency, if there's a gas leak, or something like that, or a problem with the water . . . But there won't be anyone there today of course.'

'Do you have much contact with the other residents?' the officer wanted to know.

'I wouldn't say we were in and out of each other's houses, but we say hello. The priest, Tiny Strauss, I don't speak to him much. He's an extraordinarily friendly man, he really is, I must admit, and that's speaking as a Protestant.'

Janna and the officer laughed along politely with her.

'Unusual name for a man, Tiny,' the officer remarked.

'A little unusual, yes, but there are a few of them you know,' the lady said. 'Tiny Kox from the Socialist Party, and Tiny Muskens who used to be the Bishop of Breda . . . Mr Strauss just comes here to get away from it all. It's a busy life, being a priest, you see. He's usually on his own, but I have noticed rather a lot more people coming and going over the last day or so. There was a man there just half an hour ago that I've never seen before. But he left again after about ten minutes.'

The officer raised an eyebrow.

'Shall we look at his house first, then?' Janna suggested.

They walked along the path to the priest's house and the policeman rang the bell, but it made no sound. He peered through the window, and knocked on it a few times, but there was no answer.

'Now what?' Janna asked.

The officer sighed and took out his mobile phone. 'I'll call the station, get a search warrant,' he said, walking away from her.

He came back a minute later. 'We've got permission. It's an emergency after all. The public prosecutor—'

'Doesn't he need to be here for that?'

'She doesn't need to be here, no. It's a woman,' he said. 'Sexist,' he added. Janna couldn't tell if he was joking or not. He took the baton from his belt. 'Step back, please.'

He turned his own face to the side, and then used the thick end of the baton to aim a couple of quick, heavy blows on the small window next to the front door. He tapped the remaining shards of glass from the frame and stuck his arm through it. He groped around for the door handle, a bulbous knob that made a dry click when he turned it.

He opened the door excruciatingly slowly, like a father entering the room where his children are sleeping and trying not to wake them up.

'There's one question that I've always wanted to ask a priest,' he said.

Janna found it an odd moment to say such a thing.

'That Jesus of his, why did he only heal someone here and there, raise a couple of people from the dead, or make the odd lame person walk again? Isn't that all small potatoes for someone like him? Why didn't he do something on a bigger scale?' The officer looked at her seriously, as though he expected her to have an answer. 'Why not just feed everyone who was starving, or give water to everyone who was thirsty? Why not make all the blind people see, and the lame people walk? It's like Superman having all those superpowers and only ever going after the muggers in Metropolis.'

Inside, there were three tall glasses on the kitchen counter, each with a half-moon of lemon left in the bottom, and two still half-filled with cola.

The old lady had surreptitiously followed them. She took a seat at the kitchen table.

Just as they had done in the first house, Janna and the police officer went down into the basement. Sunlight shone in through the high windows that ran along the length of the wall

They heard muffled knocking somewhere in the distance, like the sound of piles being driven into soft earth.

The two of them stood still, like hunters afraid they might step on a dry twig and frighten off their prey.

341

The ceiling was slightly too low for Janna and she was forced to stoop over.

They heard the knocking again, but it was difficult to tell exactly where it was coming from. Maybe the others weren't standing below this house, but in the house next door. Or even under another building next to the *hofje*.

The officer jumped up and down a few times. The reply came back immediately, one knock for each jump.

There was a large cupboard in the corner of the basement. Underneath it was a plain-looking rug.

Without saying a word, they both began to push the cupboard across the flagstone floor, dragging the rug with it.

When they stood back, they saw a large flagstone in the corner of the stone floor where the cupboard had been. It very clearly had no mortar around its edges.

The officer looked around the room and spotted a crowbar leaning against the wall. The flattened end was rough and worn and grey with dust.

He picked up the crowbar and tapped the stone with it. The reply that came back this time was a muffled cheer.

He sprang into action, jamming the end of the crowbar into the gap around the stone.

Lifting the stone up was more difficult than it looked, but after some prying and pushing, he succeeded in working it loose. The officers in the tunnel helped to lift it by pushing upwards with their shoulders.

The men standing at the bottom of the staircase in the tunnel screwed their eyes up against the sunlight.

'There's no one else in the house,' the officer said from the top of the stairs, 'but we know who it belongs to, and that's a good start. Would you happen to know where Mr Strauss might be right now?' he asked the old lady.

She thought about it. 'I think he might be in the church? The Hartebrugkerk is open on Saturdays.'

342

'She means the Coelikerk,' the officer said to his colleagues as they came up the stairs into the basement.

Janna turned around and started to walk to the courtyard door, but before she reached the end of the path, she was stopped in the garden by three police officers.

47

It was Daniël.

'If you come just *one* step closer, I'll set you alight,' Peter said, waving the flame at Daniël to show he meant it. In the fast fading light of the torch he could see that Daniël's clothes were burned and singed from the tussle earlier.

'I'm here to help you!' Daniël hissed. 'I was every bit as surprised as you back there! They weren't on our side. They *aren't* on our side . . .'

Peter aimed the torch at the ground, but he was still on his guard.

'You have to trust me . . . We don't have much more time and we really need to go back to the surface now.'

Peter was hesitant, but he knew there was very little time left.

'Come on, Peter, you know me. Let's go up now, I'm worried . . .'

They both stood where they were, at an impasse.

Peter lifted the torch a little higher, bringing it closer to Daniël. The muscles on Daniël's face twitched spasmodically, as though he had a nervous tic.

Daniël shrank backwards.

The torch flame grew weaker still.

Peter gripped Daniël's arm. It felt hard and tense, like a sturdy oak branch. 'Where's the third man?' he asked.

'He stayed with the one who was on fire. I just ran. I don't think he could have survived that, anyway. What about the one who went after you?'

'I knocked him down and left him bleeding.'

'Then there are two left.'

'What do you mean?'

'One was killed at the Hortus, and there were three here, so that means there are two left. I don't know where they are, but there were six in total. They might have convinced more men to join them.'

Peter sighed deeply. 'Okay,' he said. Daniël's arm relaxed beneath Peter's fingers, like a vacuum pack of coffee softening when it's snipped open. He let go of him. 'What are we going to do?'

'These stairs lead to the sacristy,' Daniël said. 'I'm impressed that you managed to find this entrance, by the way.' He tried to pass Peter on the stairs, but Peter blocked his way.

'Here,' Peter said, 'hold this.' He gave Daniël the torch. It gave off so little light now that he could hardly see Daniël's face at all.

Daniël took the torch from him. The other men had left their torch in a ring on the wall. He lit it with the weak flame from the torch in his hand, flooding the passageway with light.

Peter slowly walked up the stairs. There was a hatch at the top. He tilted his head and pressed his ear against the wood to listen for noises above him. When he was sure he couldn't hear anything, he gradually pushed the hatch upwards until he had cracked it open by a centimetre or two. He didn't dare to open it any further.

'What are you doing? We can't stay here,' Daniël said. He stood next to Peter and opened the hatch, still very cautiously, but much wider than Peter had dared to. Daniël peered warily over the edge

345

of the opening in the flagstone floor above them. 'There's nobody here,' he whispered. 'Come on.' Without making a sound, he opened the hatch door all the way and hauled himself through it.

Peter followed him, glad to be out of the dank, musty air in the tunnel.

There were two slabs of stone stacked one on top of the other, close to the hole in the floor that they had just climbed out of. The room they had emerged into was sparsely furnished, with just a table, a chair, and wheeled clothing rail with long robes hanging from it.

This room looked deserted, but they could hear loud men's voices coming from somewhere else in the building.

Peter crouched down and began to creep into the Coelikerk on his hands and feet. When he looked behind him, he saw that Daniël was following his example. They hid behind a bench near the altar.

Peter peeked around the corner. He saw an old, rather heavy-set man standing in the aisle, absolutely still, like a statue waiting to be mounted on its plinth.

Peter craned his neck further, like a turtle poking its head out of its shell. Then he saw why the man wasn't moving. Someone was aiming a bow and arrow directly at him. Peter couldn't make out if it was the same archer he had encountered in the Hortus. Whoever it was had company. Someone was guarding the church entrance.

There was another man sitting in one of the pews. His hands were in the air and he was staring miserably ahead.

'This is where it ends for you, Father,' the archer said. 'You've exposed us, the worst sin you could commit . . .'

The archer gradually drew the bowstring back. 'You've failed,' he said. 'It's all been for nothing. And where's your so-called chosen one? Well? He was supposed to find his way here within twenty-four hours.'

'There's still time,' the heavy-set man said calmly, as though the bow and the arrow weren't even there.

Peter slowly stood up and emerged from his hiding place.

Daniël grabbed him by his coat, but Peter pulled himself loose. Furious, but filled with energy and the hope that he would soon see Judith again, he walked straight towards the men in the aisle, waving his arms, like a castaway trying to attract the attention of a passing ship.

'Here I am!' he shouted.

48

The heavy-set man looked at Peter with an expression of great joy, like a father watching his son score the winning goal in a football match. With his full head of grey hair, he looked like an orchestra conductor, a man of a certain age who had lived a good life.

Peter did not return his look with the same joy. 'Are you the Father?' he shouted angrily as he approached him. When he got closer, he saw that the man had big, dark blue circles under his eyes.

'I am . . . the Father, yes,' the man replied. He appeared to be genuinely surprised by Peter's anger.

'Where's Judith?' Peter snarled through clenched teeth.

'Judith?' the man repeated. 'She's . . . we'll go to her shortly. But . . . But you have nothing to worry about. You did it, my boy! It is *finished*!' He walked towards Peter with open arms, as though he had completely forgotten that there was someone aiming an arrow at him. 'I'm Tiny . . . Tiny Strauss. I'm the priest here at—'

'Hey!' the archer shouted furiously, trying to bring his target back to reality.

'*Where* is Judith?' Peter asked again.

It wasn't the priest who answered him this time, but the archer. 'You could say Judith's sins are being washed away right now.'

'How do you know where she—' the Father said, turning to stare at the man with the bow and arrow.

'I want to see Judith! Now!' Peter interrupted him.

'Don't worry,' the Father said in a soothing tone, as if he was speaking to his beloved congregation from the pulpit. 'But first we need to deal with this, er . . . situation.'

'How *could* you?' the other man shrieked at him. 'And now you want to give this important role to someone we don't even know? I would drag you outside and stone you in front of the whole world if I could.'

'Listen to me,' Tiny said, his voice suddenly severe and full of authority, like a teacher who has finally had enough of a pupil's antics. 'I am, and will remain the Father of this group, and that means of you too. I've seen signs, and the hour has come . . . I've explained it to all of you.'

For a moment, the man appeared to be willing to listen. He slowly lowered the bow, whether in capitulation or because his arm was growing tired, Peter couldn't tell.

'Not everyone will be able to become a member,' the priest continued, 'that will always be special, reserved only for those who can pass our tests. But we're going to educate people. We'll give them the true story, give them light in the darkness that they're all stumbling around in.' He straightened his back, thrust his chin forward, and took a few steps towards the rebels. 'Very little will change for most of them,' he went on. 'It's old wine in a new skin, remember? Perhaps a few people will leave, but it won't make any difference to the faith itself. Something can still be true even if it never actually happened, can't it?'

Meanwhile, the church door opened and Peter heard the man who was standing guard say in a surprisingly friendly tone: 'I'm afraid we're closed for a private service. But do come back later.'

The door closed again and the man resumed his position.

'We don't need to burden the newcomers with the same regime as us,' Tiny said, 'when we ourselves sometimes find it difficult to follow.'

The archer looked as though he was considering everything the priest was saying.

'You're the Sun-Runner . . .' the priest said sounding disappointed. 'I had expected you to show more insight.'

'Why him?' the man asked, nodding his head at Peter.

'For now we see through a glass, darkly . . .' Tiny began.

'*Stop* that! Why him?' he asked, aiming his bow and arrow at Tiny again.

'Trust me,' Tiny said simply. 'He's shown himself to be worthy, he's *proved* himself. He's exactly the face we need to show to the outside world, a perfect spokesman. I've been following him for many years. He—'

'Erm . . . excuse me, but do I get a say in this?' Peter asked indignantly. 'I've had more than enough of your theatrics. You can argue about all your own nonsense later, but now you're going to take me to Judith.'

The archer glanced sideways at the man still guarding the church door like a nightclub doorman, face blank and arms folded across his chest. He aimed his bow higher and bent his head back slightly, as if he was asking his accomplice's opinion on what he should do.

Tiny took a few more steps towards the archer, who responded by moving backwards to maintain the distance between them.

'"The sun shall be turned to darkness,"' Tiny began. His voiced echoed through the cavernous space. It was the voice of an experienced preacher, accustomed to making his voice carry to the pews at the back of his church. '"The sun shall be turned to darkness and the moon to blood, before the coming of the Lord's great and glorious day . . ."' That prophecy, that's about us in the here and now, Sun-Runner. The sun was turned to darkness yesterday, wasn't it? Then doesn't that mean that the hour has come?'

'*Your* hour has come!' the man cried.

The church door opened again. The doorman was about to give the visitors his line, but the door was flung open with tremendous force and the man who was supposed to be keeping intruders out fell to the floor.

Three armed policemen stormed into the church, and when they saw the archer, they expertly removed their guns from their holsters as they ran. Janna Frederiks followed in their wake.

Alarmed by the noise and anxious to see what was happening, Daniël leapt out from his hiding place.

One officer held the doorman at gunpoint as he lay helpless on the ground. The other two aimed their pistols at the archer. 'Drop your weapon! Now!' one of them screamed at him.

The archer didn't move.

'Put your weapon down on the ground! Slowly!'

Apparently unfazed, the man looked away as the police officer aimed his gun at him with his arm outstretched. He started to lower his bow and arrow to the floor. Defeat and resignation were written on his face, like a sportsman who knows that his team has lost the match before the final whistle has even blown.

'Throw your weapon on the ground,' the armed officer commanded again. 'Now!'

'Okay,' the archer said.

The officers visibly relaxed their shoulders by a few centimetres. Peter and Tiny put down their hands.

But a fraction of a second later, the archer had raised his bow again. '*Hora est!*' he screamed, his face warped with rage.

The officer widened his stance, bent his knees slightly and closed one eye.

The bowstring was drawn as taut as it would go. Just before the arrow left it, there was a dry bang, like a firecracker being set off.

351

The archer recoiled, jumping back awkwardly and hurling his bow in the air as though it had burned his hands. He fell to the ground with a heavy thud.

At almost exactly the same time, the priest sank to his knees, clawing at his throat with his hands.

Peter could see the bloody arrowhead sticking out of his neck.

Tiny keeled forward, gurgled, and then fell on his side. A pool of blood began to form under his neck and spread across the floor. He lay there, his eyes still open, his tongue protruding from his mouth, like an unceremoniously slaughtered animal.

Within two strides, Peter was at his side. Seemingly oblivious to the fact that the man had just been fatally wounded, he knelt down, brought his face close to the Father's cheek and screamed desperately in the man's ear: 'Where is Judith?'

The priest's eyes were wide open, glassy and blank like the eyes of a dead deer on the side of a motorway.

Peter realised that the man wasn't going to utter any famous last words and got to his feet.

'Come here!' Daniël called to him. 'Come on!'

'Stay where you are!' a police officer shouted. 'Call for backup!' he shouted to his colleagues at the door.

Peter wanted to go over to Daniël, but didn't dare.

The officer who had shot the archer shouted, 'Everyone get over here! Hands behind your heads!'

Peter laced his fingers behind his head.

'You as well!' the officer shouted at Daniël, who immediately complied.

Daniël jerked his head to beckon Peter over again.

Peter stared at him for a moment and then gave him an almost invisible nod before starting to count, mouthing the words silently.

One . . . Two . . . Three.

When he got to three, he sprinted to the altar.

'Hey!' the officer shouted, sounding shocked.

Daniël and Peter ran back to the sacristy.

They heard the policeman yelling behind them and fast footsteps coming closer. When they got to the sacristy, Peter grabbed the clothing rail and dragged it behind them. Daniël had already disappeared through the hatch and into the tunnel. Peter followed, pulling the rail behind him. It clattered down the stairs and then became lodged in the narrow space so that no one else would be able to get through.

They heard the footsteps come to a halt above their heads. Someone began yanking at the rail, but it didn't budge at all.

Meanwhile, Daniël had grabbed the torch from the ring on the wall. It was still burning.

He walked down the tunnel, in the opposite direction to the way they had come.

'Do you know where Judith is?' Peter asked him.

Daniël turned around. 'I don't know for certain but I have a good idea where she might be. I'm almost sure she'll be there.'

'And where is that?'

'I think the plan was for you to go to the temple with the Father.'

'So where's the temple?'

'Where it's been for two thousand years,' Daniël said. 'Under the Burcht.'

49

'Under the Burcht?' Peter exclaimed. 'But it can't be! That castle wasn't built until the ninth century!'

'So? Why do you think they chose to build it there? Our beliefs came over with the Romans. They'd already built a temple, on that spot, under the ground.'

The tunnel they were walking through seemed to come to a dead end. Daniël put his torch in an iron ring then expertly pressed and pulled some of the bricks in the wall. He pushed on the left-hand side of the wall and slowly but surely, it started to revolve.

Peter looked at him in amazement. 'This is . . .' Before he could say more, Daniël motioned him to hurry through.

When they had both walked through the gap, Daniël pushed it back into place. 'If anyone comes after us, they won't be able to get past that.' He picked his torch up again and walked in front of Peter. 'Have you ever heard of ley lines?' he said as he walked briskly through the tunnel.

'Ley lines?' Peter replied. 'I don't think this is the right moment for—'

'I'm telling you so that you'll understand. Ley lines are paths of energy that form a network across the entire globe. Temples were almost always built on the paths of ley lines. The most powerful places are where two lines cross and their energy is literally combined. The Christians didn't build their churches on top of pagan temples for nothing. The pagans already knew those sites were full of energy.'

'And the Burcht . . .' Peter said.

'And the Burcht was built at the point where two ley lines cross. One of them comes from direction of Hooglandse Kerk, and the other from the Pieterskerk. Where do you think our city's name comes from?'

Peter thought back to his conversation with Mark a day earlier and Mr Goekoop of Zierikzee's theory about the Burcht.

'We're under the Oude Rijn,' Daniël explained. 'And there are two ways to get to the temple from here. There's a hidden entrance in the tunnel you found yesterday – and there's this one.' He showed Peter a large key. 'You get a key when you reach the fourth grade,' he said in answer to the unasked question. He turned the key in the lock, then laboriously pushed the heavy door open onto yet another tunnel.

Peter was astonished to see long niches in the walls of this new tunnel, each covered with a marble slab. There were names engraved on the cover slabs, just like the ones he had seen in the catacombs in Rome. However, in Rome, the marble niches were left open after being destroyed by grave robbers and the bodies they'd once contained had turned to dust long ago.

But here, right by the entrance, was a marble cover that looked new, as though it had only recently been installed.

Pater
Ane Nias
1930–2010

Someone had been buried here only five years ago! Nias . . . A Greek name?

As he rushed through the narrow tunnel, he passed slabs with dates that went back many years, all with the same format: *Pater*, name, year.

Whether it was real or imagined Peter wasn't sure, but the smell of death and decay seemed to be all around him.

Daniël turned to look at him. 'Ane was the last one to be buried here. Tiny Strauss is his successor.'

'Tiny Strauss? The man who . . .'

'He's our Father now. He's also the priest in the Coelikerk.'

'So how do you become the Father? Can anyone do it?'

'No, not just anyone. Not everyone makes it as far as the black belt in karate, do they? And if the group gets too big, it splits up.'

'So that means . . .'

'There are dozens of groups in the Netherlands . . . And hundreds in Europe!'

Frescoes had been painted on the walls between the niches, and also on the ceiling. Some of them looked so bright and fresh they could have been painted the day before, but others had faded long ago and were so vague that it was difficult to make out what they portrayed.

There were starry skies, suns, moons, bulls and Mithras, but also images of God as a shepherd with a lost sheep on his shoulders. There were paintings of a young man surrounded by lions that nuzzled him like overgrown house cats. Daniel in the lions' den . . .

A staircase at the end of the tunnel led downwards.

'We're almost there,' Daniël said, as though this was a guided tour and he was trying to build the excitement for the highlight of the trip.

The staircase brought them into a small room where Peter noticed a knife and a chalice among the objects on a stone table. Robes were hung on the wall. They walked through this room

356

and into another much larger space. Its mysteries were still hidden in the flickering shadows cast by the torchlight.

Daniël walked around the room, lighting the torches on the wall with the flame from his own.

Peter's jaw literally dropped in amazement, as though he was miming the word in a game of charades.

This was a Mithraeum, exactly like the ones he had seen in images on the computer in the Ethnology Museum, but real and completely intact, painted in bright colours, as though a museum had gone to great effort and expense to give visitors a vivid experience of the past. It was all here: the ceiling covered in stars, the two long benches for the worshippers to recline on, the mosaic of the seven grades on the floor, a statue of Mithras conquering the bull, with a fresco of the same scene painted on the wall behind it.

'But she's not here,' he said disappointedly.

'No, I don't think she's here,' Daniël said.

He walked down to the furthest end of the temple, where wooden planks formed a square on the floor.

As Peter got closer to it, he noticed the sound of flowing water.

Daniël gave Peter a confused look. 'We shouldn't be hearing water. Not now,' he said. He started to lift up the planks.

Peter hurried over to help him.

Removing the wooden boards revealed a metal grate, and below that, swirling, foaming water.

'This isn't—' Daniël said.

Then suddenly – a horror film director could not have timed it more perfectly – Judith's deathly white face rose up out of the water, gasping for breath. Her head hit the iron bars with a loud thud. The water was just a couple of centimetres below the metal grate now.

Judith's eyes were wild with fear. She pressed her face as close to the bars as she could in a desperate attempt to fill her lungs with air.

357

The men leapt off the grate.

Peter screamed her name and began to frantically tug at the bars, but they didn't move a millimetre.

Daniël ran over to where the splintered remains of two wooden rods stuck out of the wall. 'Damn!' he cried. 'These are supposed to turn the water on and off. And open the drain. They've been broken!'

What sort of monster would do something like this, Peter wondered. *Deliberately let someone drown . . .* 'Do something!' he screamed.

'There's a door! There's a door!' Daniël yelled back. He took a torch from the wall and ran down a staircase next to the water-filled pit.

'We're coming!' Peter screamed, fighting back tears. But Judith had already disappeared back under the water.

He followed Daniël down the stairs into another passageway and found him trying with all his might to lift the latch that was holding a door closed.

'There's too much pressure behind it!' Daniël yelled.

Peter grabbed the torch from the ring on the wall where Daniël had left it. He banged the end of it into the latch arm until it started to move. The torch flames licked at his skin and he smelled the acrid odour of burning hair.

After a few well-aimed blows, the latch was almost entirely out of the hook. Peter hit it once more and it came loose.

The door flew open with such force that it knocked Daniël backwards onto the ground.

Peter managed to step aside fast enough to avoid the door, but the water surged through the opening so powerfully that he was knocked over too. He struggled to hold the torch above his head and out of the reaches of the raging water.

Like a birth in reverse, Judith's legs emerged through the door first, followed by the rest of her body. The water dragged her a few metres down the tunnel, and then she stopped and lay like driftwood left on a beach by the ebbing tide.

The heavy deluge was over now, but they could still hear water pouring into the cell.

Judith lay on her stomach, white as a sheet, with her arms stretched out in front of her.

Peter rolled her on her side and shook her hard. 'Judith!' he shouted, 'Judith!'

Daniël scrambled to his feet.

'She's not breathing,' Peter said desperately. 'She's not breathing.'

'Mouth-to-mouth!' Daniël cried. 'Put her on her back, tilt her head back, hold her nose and breathe into her mouth.'

Peter passed the torch to Daniël and began to breathe into Judith's mouth, but nothing happened. He did it again. And again. Then Judith's body convulsed, and he looked at Daniël hopefully.

'Keep going!' Daniël shouted.

After a few more breaths, Judith's head jerked upwards. She spluttered and coughed out a wave of murky brown water. And then another. Judith breathed deeply, in and out, like a baby taking its first breaths. And then she began to cry.

Peter took her in his arms and cried along with her, rocking her gently and whispering, 'Judith, Judith.'

She looked up at him for a moment and smiled weakly. Then she closed her eyes again.

'Some maniac opened the valves,' Daniël said. 'The Sun-Runner. It must have been him. The Father would *never* have intended this to happen!'

'We need to get out of here,' Peter said.

'This way,' Daniël said. 'It's the shortest route.'

Daniël helped them both up. Judith tottered like a new-born calf still trying to find its balance. The two men held her steady. Her vulnerability seemed all the greater because she was wearing only a skirt and bra. Peter could see goosebumps on her skin.

Daniël let go of Judith and started to walk down the passageway in front of them. He came to a stop at a blank wall. He took a few more hesitant steps and then stopped again.

With his arm still wrapped around Judith, who leaned heavily against him, Peter tried to see why Daniël had stopped.

A dark form lay on the ground next to the wall. At first Peter thought it was a pile of clothing, but when he looked more closely, he saw legs, arms and a head. It was clearly a man. He was groaning.

The water was just a couple of centimetres deep here. It lapped up against the man's side, making him look like a shipwreck survivor washed up on a distant shore.

'Jakob?' Peter heard Daniël's shocked voice say.

Perhaps roused by the chill of the cold water seeping into his clothes, the man, who was apparently called Jakob, slowly began to stir. There was a large, black balaclava lying next to him.

Daniël helped the man to sit up. He had a sizeable wound on the side of his head. His hair was matted with congealed blood.

'I'm . . .' he tried to speak. 'They . . . I was knocked out.'

Daniël looked up at Peter, but Peter didn't dare to let go of Judith. Eventually, Daniël managed to help Jakob to his feet himself. He leaned him against the wall, and only let go when he was sure that he wouldn't fall down again.

'Where did that . . . where did that water come from?' Jakob asked. 'It was dry when I . . .'

The stink of stagnant canal water hung in the air.

Daniël expertly pressed and pulled the bricks in the wall, then pushed it open.

The simple brilliance of it impressed Peter all over again.

When they had gone through the opening in the wall, they could see light in the distance. They were almost back at the hole in the tunnel under the Nieuwstraat. Peter recognised it from the bricks that he and Daniël had stacked into piles the day before when they were rescuing Raven.

A journey of a thousand miles ends with a single step, he thought.

They slowly made their way along the tunnel behind Daniël. Jakob was a strong man and able to walk unaided, although he still needed to steady himself on the wall now and then.

Every few metres, Judith stopped and rested her head on Peter's shoulder. She didn't open her eyes.

Daniël reached the opening first. The rope ladder was still there. He extinguished the torch so that he had both hands free to climb up.

'Hello!' he cried, looking up through the hole. 'Is anyone there?'

Within seconds, the faces of two policemen appeared above them and looked down into the tunnel, their eyes wide with disbelief.

'It's us,' Daniël said, climbing up to the surface, rung by rung. 'We found Judith Cherev. And Peter de Haan too. He's still down here but he'll be out shortly. And there's someone else.'

Peter took off his coat and put it around Judith's shoulders. Together with Jakob, who looked terrible but otherwise seemed to be completely recovered, he helped Judith up the ladder.

He sighed with relief as he watched her climb up to the blue sky and the fresh air that she had so desperately been gasping for just minutes earlier. Although her feet missed the rungs a few times on the way up, she eventually made it out onto the street.

Jakob followed her, so that now only Peter was left in the tunnel.

Jakob knelt at the side of the pit and held out his hand to help Peter up. But before Peter could grab hold of it, the rope ladder came loose and tumbled towards him. He had to jump aside to avoid it hitting his head.

Except for the brief sleep he'd had at the police station, Peter had been awake for almost thirty-two hours now. Strangely, although he felt exhausted, hungry, and thirsty, he was surprised to find that he also felt relieved and proud that he had been able to rescue Judith, as a novice, an initiate who had successfully completed his quest.

From out of the darkness in the tunnel Peter heard a voice, so clear that he almost believed that the speaker was standing right next to him. 'Know that I am with you and will keep you safe wherever you go.' He peered into the distance but there was no one there. Then he looked up, but saw no one above him either. He shook his head and blinked. His tiredness must have been getting the better of him.

But then he heard the voice again. 'I will give you bread to eat and clothes to wear. You will come home safe to your loved ones, and I, the Lord, will be your God.'

He was suddenly overcome by a powerful feeling of peace and tranquillity.

He looked up.

Jakob's face appeared over the edge of the hole. He lowered a length of red and white police tape towards him. 'Tie the ladder to this and I'll pull it up!' he shouted.

Peter did as he said and, a few seconds later, the ladder was lifted upwards. The police tape stretched and strained perilously, but it didn't snap.

When Jakob had securely fastened the ladder to the pavement with the steel pins, he let it fall back down again.

Now Peter was able to climb the ladder that connected him to the sky above him and the ground below his feet.

Half way up the ladder, he paused.

Hanging there between heaven and earth, he felt like a bird hovering in the air.

And the thought revealed itself to him:

I am a Raven.

THE SEVENTH VISION

And behold, I saw the man in his cell. He knows that his mission has been successful. The Jews are fighting amongst themselves. The followers of the Way are increasing in number. Nobody obeys the laws or has themselves circumcised. They eat what they want, which angers the Jews and angers the people who knew Jesus.

For two years, he writes letters, dictates so many versions of the story of his life to his secretary that he no longer knows which parts of it truly happened and which did not.

What is the truth?

He was called Paul, then Saul . . . allowed his manhood to be mutilated for a woman, that serpent. And now he bears the name that his parents gave him once more.

And as Paul, he travels to Rome. He writes the report of the journey before he leaves, a journey full of ordeals. He writes of a shipwreck and of floating on the waves clinging to the wreckage of the ravaged ship. He tells of a winter spent on an island, of raging storms at sea, of hunger and thirst – a story worthy of Odysseus.

And he goes to Rome. After a journey of no more than a week or two, without so much as a ripple on the azure waves of the Mediterranean, he arrives in Ostia.

In Rome, he speaks to the Jewish community. Here too, he succeeds in confusing the hearts and minds of many, and here too, he drives a wedge between them.

Father is set against son, son against father, mother against daughter and daughter against mother, the mother-in-law against daughter-in-law and daughter-in-law against mother-in-law.

And hark, he challenges them and says: 'The Holy Spirit was entirely justified in saying to your ancestors through the mouth of the prophet Isaiah: "Go to this people and say: *You will indeed listen, but never understand, and you will indeed look, but never perceive.* For this people's heart has grown dull, and their ears are hard of hearing, and they have shut their eyes, so that they might not look with their eyes, nor listen with their ears, nor understand with their hearts. Because otherwise they would repent and I would heal them." Let it be known to you then, that

God has already sent this message of salvation to the Gentiles and they will listen.'

And behold, he stays in Rome for two years, in the house that he has rented himself, and welcomes all who come to see him, proclaiming the kingdom of God and teaching about his Lord with all boldness and without hindrance.

After two years, he has been forgotten by everyone. No judge bothers him, no court case hinders him on his path. His accusers did not ever come to Rome.

The Jews' only fight is with the Roman rulers in Israel. They are waiting for the Messiah who will one day come to free them from the uncircumcised heathens.

And behold, Paul bids a warm farewell to his brothers and sisters. He gives his final instructions and he travels to Hispania. The money he had collected is almost gone. He has only enough to pay for the crossing.

He is a *pater patrum* now, the father of fathers. He has shown others the way and wants nothing more for himself. 'Your will be done' is his motto.

He is *summus pontifex* now, the bishop, the *magus*. With the ring on his finger and the staff in his hand, he waves to his disciples on the quay, his children, for the last time.

And behold, he turns away from them so that they cannot see his face. He smiles, because he is cunning and he has got the better of them by guile.

He turns his face to the sky and lets himself be warmed by the rays of his Lord, the invincible sun.

He travels through Hispania, not as Paul, not as Saul, but as a man with no name. The journey is almost over, his task is almost finished.

And behold, he takes his seat in the stands to watch the games. He sets the earthenware jug of wine at his feet. He observes how the bull is slaughtered in the arena, how the offering is made anew. 'His blood be on us, and on our children,' he prays, in the hope that they will also taste the joy brought by the random sacrifice. Then he says: 'And you have also saved us by shedding the eternal blood.'

He catches one of the hunks of bread that has been thrown into the crowd. He tears off a piece and puts it in his mouth. 'Take this and eat; this is my body which is given for you,' he prays, chewing the bread contemplatively before swallowing it.

Then he picks up the jug from next to his feet and fills his mouth with wine. 'Drink, this is my blood poured out for many.'

He drinks until the jug is empty. 'He who does not eat of my flesh and drink of my blood, so that he remains in me and I in him, shall not know salvation.'

And behold, while the people climb onto the benches and wave white cloths, cheering for the bull killer, he gets up. He takes one last look behind him.

Consummatum est, he thinks, satisfied. It is finished.

I am the Father.

EPILOGUE

Friday 28 March 2015, 3:00pm

When a second attempt was made to install the underground waste container outside the public library, Mayor Freylink was once again invited to do the honours. Ever the good sport, he accepted. The hole he had made in the foundations during the first attempt had been closed up.

This time, the set-up was much simpler. The container dangled in the air from a steel cable, like a net full of fish above the deck of a ship. The *burgemeester* held a glass of champagne in his hand and when he was given a signal, he threw the golden liquid at the side of the container. The dozens of spectators who had turned up to watch applauded politely.

It took the police some time to reconstruct the events of the 20th and 21st of March.

They were unable to form a complete picture of what had happened, but it was clear that Judith had been kidnapped by Tiny Strauss and one or more accomplices. For reasons that were unclear to the police, Peter de Haan had been given the task of finding her within twenty-four hours. He had eventually succeeded, helped in the final hours by two members of Strauss' group, Daniël Veerman, the city archaeologist, and a man called Jakob. After the three of them had emerged from the tunnel, Jakob had apparently vanished from the face of the earth.

The archer had died after being hit by a police bullet. He turned out to have been the leader of a small group of men who had rebelled against their spiritual leader. Another rebel had met his end in the Hortus Botanical Garden when he was accidently shot with an arrow. Yet another was burned alive in one of the tunnels. The two men, who according to Peter's witness statement had been with this last victim, had not been found. Eventually, only two men were arrested: the man who had been with the priest in the Coelikerk, and the other man who had stood guard at the church door.

Both men were still in custody, one of them in connection with his possible involvement in Arnold van Tiegem's death. The role the second man had played was still being investigated. Neither could give the police any useful names. Everyone involved in the operation had used a pseudonym, much like members of the war-time resistance had taken a *nom de guerre* in case they were ever caught.

Daniël and Mani's friendship had apparently been the exception to this rule. Mani was given a disciplinary suspension pending an investigation into his role in Peter's escape from the police station. But no charges were pressed against either Daniël or Mani; the organisation they belonged to was not, after all, a criminal one.

The police were unsuccessful in tracing the other members of the brotherhood, which led to speculation in the local press about which prominent citizens of Leiden had been members, or still were.

Tiny Strauss had been killed instantly when an arrow gored his neck. His parishioners were shocked, both by his death and by the news that he had been the head of a secret society. Strangely, many of them seemed to be relatively unperturbed by this last

367

detail. Naturally they thought it odd, but he had been such a good Father to his congregation that most of his flock posthumously forgave him.

They had not, however, been told all the details of the case. Their benevolent view would surely have been changed by the image of their beloved priest standing over a pit to slit a lamb's throat. The archdiocese would not hear of a church funeral for him. In the eyes of the bishop, Strauss had been involved occult practices in the very bowels of the city that were so terrible they could not have withstood the light of day.

Raven's real name turned out to have been Frank Broele. He was a teacher of classical languages at a high school in Leiden who dressed as a Roman legionary and took part in historical re-enactments in his spare time.

The city council had immediately recognised the potential for a successful tourist attraction in the labyrinth of underground tunnels and started the process of mapping them out. The temple would become the breathtaking final stop on an exciting, archaeological guided tour below the city. After London, Paris and Rome, Leiden would have its own hidden world beneath its streets. The city's inhabitants had already dubbed it 'The Leiden Labyrinth'.

Peter opened the outer door of the Sionshofje and locked his bike in the broad passage. He walked across the lawn to Mark's little house and found the door ajar. He drummed on the window of the living room where Mark and Judith were sitting on the sofa together.

Judith greeted him with a warm smile as he walked in.

'Hi Peter,' she said and stood up to give him a hug.

Mark got up too. 'Can I get you a cup of tea? Or coffee?' he asked. Without waiting for a reply, he disappeared into the kitchen to put the kettle on.

Judith and Peter sat down on the sofa.

'How are you?' he asked. They had only seen each other twice since her rescue from the water-filled cell. Of course, he had visited her during her brief stay in hospital. She had been assessed to make sure she hadn't suffered any physical damage from her time in underground captivity.

'Oh, fine,' she replied. 'I'm just still a bit nervous about being at home on my own. The slightest noise makes me jump . . . or I convince myself that someone is looking through the window, watching me. That's why I spend a lot of time here at Mark's. Which isn't so bad, of course, but I do feel like I've lost some of my freedom.'

'That will probably get better with time, won't it?'

'Yes, probably. It's . . .' She paused to think of the right words.

They heard Mark in the kitchen, rattling teaspoons and putting tea glasses on the table. Even after all these years, Peter felt a pang of jealousy at moments like this when he saw the cosy domesticity that was absent from his own home.

'I don't know how to describe it.' Judith was trying to finish what she had started to tell him. 'That moment when I first saw you, I was still panicking, but then . . . When the water reached the metal bars, I actually became very calm. As though this was it, and the breath I had just taken was the last one I would ever take. I sank under the water again, everything went black, and then there was nothing, really. The next thing I was aware of was waking up in your arms . . .'

Mark came in carrying a tray filled with glasses and a steaming pot of tea.

'You're not trying to tell me you had a near-death experience, are you?' Peter asked.

'No, no, nothing like that. I didn't see a tunnel of light, or any dead relatives. But afterwards, I did have the feeling – and the feeling has only grown stronger since then – that I was living on borrowed time. Like I had been given a gift. I really do feel reborn. I want to focus on what's important from now on instead of getting caught up in details that don't really matter. I don't want to get angry any more, about the people or things that only give me negative energy . . . Does that make sense?'

Peter and Mark both nodded.

'And you? How are you doing?' Judith asked Peter.

'It's strange . . .' Peter said. 'I've heard about so many new things, gained so much new insight. It's going to take me a long time to put all the puzzle pieces together. And all that knowledge . . . I truly believe that knowledge can set you free . . . Maybe if you have a better grasp of the world around you, you dare to go through it more confidently, and you dare to let go, because you know that you'll always find your way back. A bit like walking around a town that you know well. You feel more confident about going down an unfamiliar side street there than in a town you don't know, where you wouldn't stray off the beaten path.'

'That's a nice analogy,' Mark said with an approving nod.

'So you feel free,' Judith concluded, smiling at him.

Peter nodded. 'As a bird.'

Acknowledgements

I thank André van Dokkum, who with his great knowledge of early Christianity helped me tremendously in developing the basic idea for this book. His chronological reconstruction of Paul's life and travels also came in handy.

I would like to thank Maarten Dessing for reading the original version of the manuscript, which at that time was at least sixty or seventy pages thicker. Because of his good analysis and the conversations about this I decided to change the initial chronology and get a lot of material out of it.

I would like to thank editor Lisanne Mathijssen for bringing me on board HarperCollins. Her meticulous reading of each version and detailed commentary has ensured that the book has gained a lot of speed.

The editors of the latest version by Lidia Dumas were extremely precise - it is almost unbelievable how many mistakes and mistakes I had overlooked.

I would also like to thank Heleen Buth and Jan-Joris Keijzer from HarperCollins for their trust in me. The moment I signed the contract with HarperCollins, in the autumn of 2015, the idea for this book existed only in my mind.

The mysterious E.B. from the Jewish community of Leiden gave me information about Jewish marriages and the choepa in Leiden.

Saskia Balmaekers from ciaotutti.nl was kind enough to allow me to quote extensively from her website where she writes about Monte Sant'Angelo.

I am grateful to Marlene Bolkestein for her extensive tour of the Mierennesthofje and for me borrowing her books about Leidse hofjes.

Classicus and colleague Frank Broeke took care of the Latin quotes. As a thank-he, as Raven in this book, he unfortunately quickly took the lead.

I would like to thank construction historian Michel van Dam of the BAAC for the tour of the building site of the Aalmarkt project, where no tunnels had been discovered until that moment.

I would like to thank Gerard Huissen for making his photographs of the mosaics in Ostia of the seven degrees of Mithras - and Jan Theo Bakker for his great help in my search for those photographs.

Ronald Kaptein gave me the permission to quote his article about the religious brain on skepsis.nl extensively.

Johan Lammers, the Chairman Association of A.L.S.V. Quintus, kindly gave me a tour of the building of the student association at the Boommarkt and told me a lot about Quintus.

Willy Leenders provided me with precise information about the functioning of a sundial, so that the information in that area was completely correct.

Sijbrand de Rooij, curator of the RMV, Leiden expert and city guide, has also designed a great city walk for this book.

Henk Schaap helped me by shedding light on the poem Na samém konci by J.H. Krchovský (`At the very end ... `).

Tanneke Schoonheim from the Historic Association of Leiden University helped me to find answers to questions about the most diverse subjects, such as facing bricks, sundials and muted canals.

I would like to thank Cees and Jenneke van Veelen for their hospitality because in the summer of 2016 I could stay for a week in their beautiful farm to write. The view from the showroom on the meadow was soothing and inspiring.

Cees Vergroen, the designer of the sundial at mill De Valk, has provided me with information about the realization of it.

From Jan Wieles and Piet de Baar I was allowed to copy texts from their booklet Gedemptegrachtenwandeling of the Gilde Leiden.

I thank Hamide Dogan for reading the different versions of the book with great care and attention. Her remarks were like Ariadne's thread with which I always found my way out of the labyrinth when I threatened to get lost - and that does not only apply to my book. Reading the manuscript together has given the term close reading a completely new content.

Dünya remains our radiant sun, to whom this book is dedicated.

Leiden, October 3, 2016

Consulted literature

ARMSTRONG, K. PAULUS _ Onze liefste vijand. Amsterdam, Hollands Diep, 2015.

ASLAN, R. DE ZELOOT _ Het leven van Jezus van Nazareth en de geboorte van een religie. Amsterdam, Uitgeverij Balans, 2014.

DOANE, T.W. _ Bible myths and their parallels in other religions. Kessinger Publishing's, Whitefish Montana, Reprint 1882.

DOHERTY, E. _ The Jesus Puzzle: Did Christianity start with a mythical Christ? Ottawa, Age of Reason Publications, 2005.

EHRMAN, B.D. _ How Jesus became God: The exaltation of a Jewish preacher from Galilee. New York, HarperOne, 2014.

FINKELSTEIN, I., N.A. SILBERMAN _ De Bijbel als mythe: Opgravingen vertellen een ander verhaal. Den Haag, Uitgeverij Synthese, 2006.

Freke, T., P. Gandy _The Jesus Mysteries: Was the "Original Jesus" a Pagan God? Three Rivers Press, New York, 2001.

HART, M. 't Wie God Verlaat Heeft Niets te Vrezen. De Schrift Betwist. Amsterdam, Arbeiderspers,1997.

HART, M. 't De Bril van God. De Schrift Betwist II. Amsterdam, Arbeiderspers, 2002.

KAAIJ, E. VAN DER _ De ongemakkelijke waarheid van het Christendom: De echte Jezus onthuld. Uitgeverij Boekscout.nl, 2015.

Kriwaczek, P. _ Op zoek naar Zarathoestra. Amsterdam/ Antwerpen, Uitgeverij Atlas, 2003.

Lapide, P, P. Stuhlmacher _ Paulus, rabbi en apostel: Een joods-christelijke dialoog. Kampen, Kok, 1981.

Lietaert Peerbolte, B.J. _ Paulus en de rest: Van Farizeeër tot profeet van Jezus. Zoetermeer, Meinema, 2010.

Meijer, F. _ Paulus: Een leven tussen Jeruzalem en Rome. Amsterdam, Singel Uitgeverijen, 2013.

Raymondt, S. _ Mythen en sagen van de Griekse wereld. Haarlem, Fibula-Van Dishoeck, 1982.

Riet, P. van 't De levensloop van Paulus: Wat zijn brieven ons vertellen en wat Lukas ons verhaald heeft. Zwolle, Folianti, 2012.

Sanders, E.P. _ Paulus. Kampen, Uitgeverij Kok, 2000.

Slavenburg, J. (red.) Het grote boek der Apokriefen: Geheime vroeg-christelijke teksten. Deventer, Uitgeverij Ankh-Hermes bv, 2009.

Sutherland, J.G. _ De Bijbel en de antieke mysteriën. Wassenaar, Servire, 1975.

Tierney, P. Goden, graven, mensenoffers: Onthutsende feiten over de dood als rituele handeling. Baarn, Trion, 1990.

Tresmont, C. _ Paulus. Utrecht/ Antwerpen, Pictura-Boeken, 1960.

Verhoeven, P. _ Jezus van Nazaret. Amsterdam, J.M. Meulenhoff bbv, 2008.

Vermaseren, M.J. _ Mithras: De geheimzinnige God. Amsterdam/ Brussel, Elsevier, 1959.

Voskuilen, Th. _ Alias Paulus: De Grondlegger van het Christendom als Geheim Agent van Rome. Veen, Bosch en Keuning Uitgevers N.V., Wommelgem, 2002.

Wieles, J, P. de Baar _ Gedemptegrachtenwandeling. Leiden: Het Waterambacht Leiden/ Historische Vereniging Oud Leiden, 2015.

Wilson, A.N. Paulus: De geest van de apostel. Amsterdam, Prometheus, 1997.

Websites (August 2016)

Wikipedia, search terms: archangels, Adonis, circumcision, Eucharist, Greek mythology, initiation, Isis, child sacrifices, Mithras, Monte Sant'Angelo, mystery cult, Mysteries, Niobe, sacrifice, Osiris, Paul, ritual meal, bullfighting.

ceisiwrserith.com/mith/whatismith.htm
http://ciaotutti.nl/reizen-door-italie/puglia/de-route-van-de-engel/
www.debijbel.nl
www.dereensteen.be/De-Mysterien-van-Mithras-een-
    tweeduizend-jaar-oud-geheim
ebionite.org/otherlang/nedertr.htm
www.grenswetenschap.nl/permalink.asp?i=880
www.heiligen-3s.nl/heiligen/08/14/08-14-1087-arnoldus.php
jewishencyclopedia.com/articles/13232-saul-of-tarsus
www.leidschdagblad.nl/regionaal/leidenenregio/article27359706.
    ece/Aanleg-vuilcontainers-legt-Leidse-historie-bloot-
    video?lref=R1
www.leylijnen.com/kerken.htm
www.masseiana.org/panarion_bk1.htm#30
www.nieuwwij.nl/opinie/de-terugkeer-van-het-alziend-oog/
paulproblem.faithweb.com/non_jewish_ideas_pharisee_how.htm
www.positiveatheism.org/hist/rmsbrg08.htm#EBIONITES
skepsis.nl/religieusbrein/
www.tertullian.org/rpearse/mithras/literary_sources.htm
nl.unawe.org/middelen/lesmateriaal/NL_Zonneloper/

YouTube (August 2016)

Christian dilemmas 1 - www.youtube.com/watch?v=i-lpjvexeuk
Christian dilemmas 2 - www.youtube.com/watch?v=AuJBmRr7sLs
Christian dilemmas 3 www.youtube.com/watch?v=Jo_6whlQllI
Christianity: Conversion from Egyption religion Isis, Amen-Ra,

Mithraism & Osiris - www.youtube.com/watch?v=tNca8e1Syd8

Constantine and Christianity - www.youtube.com/watch?v=c3RjtaU7zxs

The cult of Mithras - www.youtube.com/watch?v=AQWX689T-YY

The Forbidden Hebrew Bible's Buried Secrets Revealed.Biblical Archaeology - www.youtube.com/watch?v=tQBQ1wIsIdM

The hidden story of Jesus - www.youtube.com/watch?v=dcrygSAqfj4

Jesus vs Paul: True Christianity vs False Paulianity - https://www.youtube.com/watch?v=pRbuKDJhzU4

Mithras, Jesus and Paul - www.youtube.com/watch?v=efQZW3efP_E

Mithras: Lord of the cosmos - www.youtube.com/watch?v=GKUwA58t0BQ

Mysteries of the Bible: Paul the apostle - www.youtube.com/watch?v=-p2FVuefmcg

The mysteries of Mithras - www.youtube.com/watch?v=ySQmbn5eqEQ

The Origins of Christianity Mithras. The Persian Religion - www.youtube.com/watch?v=e6J8hPr58Qc

Paul and Jesus: James D.Tabor - www.youtube.com/watch?v=vqAiDOFQSJc

The Search for the Historical Paul: John Dominic Crossan - www.youtube.com/watch?v=txdUXCY0clU

Was Jesus Christ a Copy of Horus, Mithras, Dionysus, Krishna and other pagan gods? - www.youtube.com/watch?v=3xxiogSYQ2Q

What's wrong with the Apostle Paul? False Apostle? Destroyer of Christianity? - www.youtube.com/watch?v=3RfOHNIRh6A

Why Jesus didn't have to die to atone for sin (Jewish Voice Messianic Jews for Jesus Jonathan Bernis - www.youtube.com/watch?v=jB7EZ5fgr4I

Notes

1 In the translation of The Bible in plain language: 1 A song from David. For the song leader./ Heaven shows the power of God / 2 Heaven tells all people / how mighty God is./ High heaven shows everyone / what God has made: / sun, moon and stars ./ 3 Heaven tells it every day, / heaven says it every night, / in a language of its own./ 4 It is not an ordinary language, / no language with words./ It is a language without sound./ 5a Yet the message passes the whole earth, / it goes around the world.

2 5b God gave the sun a place in the heavens./ 6 Every morning the sun comes out bright./ Then he begins the road he goes every day./ 7 At one end of the sky the sun rises, / at the he ends up at the other end./ He gives heat to the whole earth.

3 Let Nothing Disturb You is based on a poem by Saint Teresa of Avila, the well-known Spanish mystica from the sixteenth century. The original text goes like this: "Nada te turbe, nada te espante,/ quien a dios tiene nada le falta/ Nada te turbe, nada te espante/ solo Dios basta."